Sandra Nichols
Found Dead

Sandra Nichols Found Dead

A Novel

GEORGE V. HIGGINS

A JOHN MACRAE BOOK

Henry Holt and Company

New York

Henry Holt and Company, Inc.
Publishers since 1866
115 West 18th Street
New York, New York 10011

Henry Holt® is a registered trademark of
Henry Holt and Company, Inc.

Library of Congress Cataloging-in-Publication Data

Higgins, George V.
    Sandra Nichols found dead: a novel/ George V. Higgins.—1st ed.
      p. cm.
    1. Lawyers—Massachusetts—Fiction.   I. Title.
  PS3558.I356S25 1996
  813'.54—dc20   95-31689
                                         CIP

ISBN 0-8050-3747-0

Henry Holt books are available for special
promotions and premiums. For details contact:
Director, Special Markets.

First Edition—1996

Designed by Paula R. Szafranski

Printed in the United States of America
All first editions are printed on acid-free paper. ∞

10 9 8 7 6 5 4 3 2 1

Sandra Nichols Found Dead

■ ■ ■ 1

To put the Wade/Nichols case in some kind of perspective: it may have been the toughest one I've ever handled in my professional life of more than thirty years, and it wasn't even criminal. I do criminal. My name is Jerry Kennedy and I don't take civil cases. This is widely known—I have made it so. I refer civil matters out to civil lawyers, who very kindly don't do criminal and therefore thoughtfully refer such nasty stuff to me. I am not myself uncivil, or try not to be, at least; I just prefer to play it smart, which means: do what I'm used to doing, and therefore know how to do well—well enough at a minimum to convince civilians watching that I do know what I'm doing. So far that's been good enough. That may be criminal, but it's not forbidden by law. So: why did I take the mixed-breed Wade/Nichols case, the hardest case I never tried? Which looked like it was civil but was really criminal? And, when you came right down to it, *de facto* made me into what I'd never been before in my whole life, a fucking *prosecutor*?

Henry Lawler made me do it.

"Now I'm not gonna sit here on my ass and try kid you," Henry said to me. "This one won't be easy, but I have to make you do it. Well, that isn't strictly right: what I really have to do is make *some-body* do it, and it could be anyone. With a law degree, that is, and a

1

bar membership. In the abstract, 's what I'm saying. But I'm not pick-ing *any*one; I'm picking you to do it. This thing has to be done right."

"Henry," I said, "we're classmates and old friends. Getting older by the day and still on this side of the grass, say amen and praise the Lord. Did I ever sit on your hat? Did I ever tell you to go *shit* in your hat, and then pull it down over your ears? Did I run over your dog or run off with your wife, or even go into your court and play little mind games with you there? I did not—I did none of those bad things. My record is clean and unblemished on that score, whatever else I may've done. I never go into no damned probate courts, no matter how much I like who is in them. Except when I'm getting divorced, which was just once, and much more than enough; I'm not gonna do that again."

"Yes you are," Henry said, secure in his sunlit and ocean-breezed chambers up there in Newburyport, out of my reach down in Boston, in that same infuriatingly unflappable calm he'd developed well before college and law school, long before I ever knew him. "Yes you are, too, and: no, you are not. There's no need for you to come here. There never will be a need, either, unless I miss my very good guess. My guess is that you'll be in federal court, trying a Wrongful Death action. I've already appointed you on the record.

"I have to do this to you. The monthly camera club dinner-meeting's tonight, and since I'm on the board I have to go to it." He was seeking commiseration for eagerly participating in an activity he would've paid money to do. The walls of Henry's office are adorned with a gallery of large black-and-white portraits, some of the most sensitive photographs I have ever seen. The display changes as he makes room for the new—he painstakingly prints them in his own darkroom—by giving the old to their subjects. Henry's a splendid photographer of people because he's a wonderfully sensitive man. That's why his friends cherish him so—which does not mean, as we've often had to reiterate, that we're therefore willing to pose for a day at his studio out by the sea, where the light colludes in his art.

"This means that I'm going to see Royce Whitlock tonight, and he'll ask me again if I've gotten someone to take care of the late San-dra Nichols's kids. Royce is nearly always present at the monthly din-ner meetings of the camera club. He's a very devoted member. He's that way about everything he does; he's also a very dedicated police officer, and when he can't close a case to his satisfaction, he keeps at it 'without day,' as we say, when 'forever' 's what we've got in mind. He's been hounding me about this case for almost a year, month after month after month. He'll continue to hound me 'til I do as what he wants, and I've had about all I can stand. So now I'm gonna do it to you. So tonight I can tell him: 'Yes I have, Royce. I've found you a prince among players, a champion lawyer-type person. He'll do your young orphaned charges proud. And he'll cost them an arm and a leg.' Looking out for your interests as well, you will note; I'll be careful to tell him that, too. *So:* your appointment's being typed up as we speak. I'll sign it before I go home. Play your cards right and make a nice fee, along with making some new friends for yourself among the state police, which isn't against your religion. The paper'll go out in tonight's mail to you—you should have it in hand by Christmas, easy. By Easter at the very latest. And do have a lovely Thanksgiving, in case I don't see you by then."

"*Hey,*" I said, "you can't do this to me. I don't know from Wrongful Death actions. What I know from is murder-one actions. Armed robbery and MV manslaughter. Tax evasion; embezzling; bribery and corruption. I don't know any damned civil stuff. Henry, you can't do this to me. I'll make a big fool of myself."

"Won't be the first time, you managed to improve on nature," he said. "And you won't unless you get silly for Lucy, in which case you're no friend of mine. But just between us, I could see how a man could do that."

"Who the fuck is 'Lucy'?" I said.

"One of your clients," he said. "One of your wards in the *Estate of Nichols, In Re Nichols*, as it's formally known. Maybe better aliased *Jarndyce v. Jarndyce*, all the trouble it's already caused. Docket number sixty-eight-thousand, six-ninety-five; ninety-four, dash, nine-eighty-one. We don't got a Durante 'million of 'em' yet, but we're certainly well on our way."

■　　■　　■　　**2**

Late that next afternoon, I found Det. Lt. Royce Whitlock of the state police where he usually went for lunch on his days off: downstairs in the basement of a thriving cement-block mini-mall in Lynnfield—convenience store selling milk, cigarettes, potato chips, and lottery scratch cards and keno tickets that kept a bunch of older guys in satin jackets rapt in front of a TV screen; two-chair barber shop; sewing supplies store; packy; and a take-out sandwich shop. He was in the gray-tweed movable-partioned cubicle provided for the recording secretary of the North Shore Camera Club. The club was reasonably prosperous and subscribed not only to *Outdoor & Travel Photographer*, *Photographic*, and *Popular Photography*, but also to *National Geographic*, *Sports Illustrated*, and several other nonspecific publications recommended by club members as regular sources of photographic inspiration.

I got to know Royce Whitlock very well in the course of handling the Wade/Nichols case, having, as Henry Lawler'd predicted, very little choice in the matter, once he'd drawn me to Royce's attention. "I do have to say," Henry told me, "he is an enveloping fellow. Can be a pain in the ass. A *considerable* pain in the ass."

I found Royce to be all that and more. He was as methodical as he was dogged. Every moment of every hour of every day of every week of every month of every year had to be marshaled, ranked and filed, to *count*. "No loose ends. No leaving loose ends on things. So nothing gets overlooked. That's how I spend all my time. Making sure nothing's untied." *All his time* meant: including lunch hours on his days off; Royce ate his homemade meatloaf or Spam sandwiches and drank his Coca-Cola from the can at the club in order to combine his two main personal interests in what he called his "pre-retirement years": studying photography, by reading the latest news published about it, and spending no money to do it. Photography itself was a dual-purpose pursuit. It was a pastime he passionately enjoyed, and he'd developed a lot of skill at it. If that by itself wasn't enough to make it justifiable to him (as it wouldn't've been; Royce had a strong puritanical mistrust of mere enjoyment and frivolous delights), its practice also improved his performance of official duties.

"Sometimes it makes the official photographers mad, they're at the scene and taking their pictures, and then after I've finished asking my questions and taking my notes, I take out my equipment and start taking pictures myself. The first time they think I don't trust them. But after a while, I convince them: 'No, no, that's not it; it isn't that. I know you know what you're doing. And when this comes up for trial if it ever does, your shots're the ones that'll be used. These I'm taking: they're just for my use. To help me make sure I really *see* everything, right now while I'm here: pay attention, and focus on things. So that then I'll remember, when the case comes up, what I saw and I thought it all meant. Making notes on film, okay? Think of it that way; in addition to the words I write down in my reports.' So, and generally then they believe me. And at the same time that I'm doing that, now, I'm also keeping my technique up to date, good and sharp for when I retire."

I've met several people like Royce in my checkered career. Generally they've seemed to me to have been rather frazzled and distracted folks, never fully occupied or absorbed by doing what they're doing, always in a state of preparation, perpetually checking off items on a list, getting ready to do something else; not living: preparing to live. I've always felt powerlessly sorry for them, wished that there were something somebody could do to help them get more enjoyment out of life. But you wouldn't try that with Royce; Royce wasn't a man to provoke that sort of meddlesome solicitude. He knew exactly what he wanted to do with his life, and that was just what he was doing. I kept my big mouth shut; I'm old enough now to do that.

Royce was no rookie, as you gather. He'd turned fifty-one that year. He'd served in Vietnam with the navy SEALs, underwater demolitions experts. He didn't talk much about that, which, I have found, generally indicates that the nontalker most likely quietly and efficiently killed a sizable number of people, while finding the work disagreeable. He did not discuss family matters outside the home—maybe he didn't inside the home, either, but I wouldn't know about that. He confined his personal workaday conversations to discussion of those two hobbies that he catered to at lunch on his days off: "Photography, and being cheap. Which is what enables me to save my dough for the other hobby that I plan to take up after I retire: travel. The trips I've always wanted to take, places where I've never been. Alaska and Kenya, and the Great Barrier Reef. Tuscany and Normandy. The Brazilian rain forest. No Southeast Asia, thank you; I've seen enough of that to last me a good long time, buncha little yellow guys in black pajamas, wearin' sandals they made outta tire carcasses, poppin' up all the time out of tunnels they dug in the ground right under my feet and trying to blow my ass off. Just because I was in their country, tryin' to send them to Buddha. People say they've forgiven us now, but I dunno, I'm not sure. I'm not goin' back to that place. Goin' other places, such as Ireland, where I've never even been, so nobody hates me there yet, and I can take pictures of them. Hard to take good pictures, concentrate and all on your composition and the lighting, so forth, when someone's tryin', shoot you. You see my point on that. But anyway: can't do all those things on just a pension alone. I'm gonna need some extra money. So until I get to retirement I'm not spending a dime I don't need to."

Whitlock's second wife, Agnes, two years older than he, was mindful that he'd been a wonderful stepfather to her two little boys "after their rat-bastard father disappeared and never even saw them, got in touch with them again. Can you beat that? Just *took off*, God only knows where he went to. And then they never heard from him again. Can you *imagine* a man doing that? What kind of a man would do that? Leave his wife, maybe, sure, I can understand that; maybe I did drive him nuts. But to just walk away from his own kids like that? What kind of a father does that? It isn't a natural thing. But he did it, the bastard, and I got to admit I dunno what would've happened to those two kids of mine, they'd've been left with just me. All this stuff you're hearing all the time now, about being a big brother, the ads they've got on TV? Every boy needs a big brother, someone to look up to so he'll see how he should grow up? I believe that. I believe that's very true. And . . . , what is it: 'Male role model.' And it's all kids who need that, not just the black kids, you know, like it sometimes seems like they're saying it is. Little white boys and girls, as far as that goes, they also need that force too, in their lives. That controlling force. So they'll learn what a man should be like and know how he should behave, conduct himself in this world. So they can conduct themselves in their lives later on, after they've gotten grown up.

"And see, that's what *they* had, my two did: they had Royce to look up to. If they hadn't've had that, I don't know what would've happened. Royce to look up to, you know? He was important to those boys, a very important thing in their lives. This state cop–stepfather that they had, that had his principles and you could see, he really stood for something: that they could look up to, and they did, they really did. And this was a man, had no experience. Never had kids of his own. But he never let that stop him, get in his way— nope, he was a champion dad. My God, but he was a prince. So, I'll forgive him a lot for that, for what he did for the boys. He can be tighter'n a Pullman window, but he *never* was cheap with the boys."

Agnes shared the first and the third of his passions (photography and planning for retirement), and therefore, sometimes with her teeth gritted, had managed to tolerate for more than twenty years the side effects upon her of his obsessive stinginess: looking the other way in fast-food restaurants as he swiped paper packets of sugar and plastic envelopes of ketchup, mustard, and relish out of the self-service canisters. Spending their vacations at home. Allowing him to cook his "special chicken," "special steak," and "special swordfish" on their gas grill (one of three thrillingly extravagant Christmas presents jointly given by the boys, fed up with the weekly sum-mer-Sunday, family-visit, backyard struggles to ignite bargain-grade charcoal briquettes; the other gifts were the aboveground, redwood-decked swimming pool and the thirty-six-inch TV on which they [Royce, I gather from Agnes, restlessly, concerned he was wasting his time] watched football and basketball games while the pool, covered frozen in the cold, piled up with wet leaves and snow) to celebrate her birthdays and their anniversaries at home "instead of going out and blowing all that dough in some damned expensive restaurant."

She knew she could always expect to get secondhand or discontin-ued camera equipment, and little else, for Christmas and on her birthdays, and she endured it. She did have to admit that he shopped wisely, "bottom feeding," as he called it, for both of them: barely used, top-grade items like her Nikon F, his underwater Nikonos, and the back-breakingly complete professional-grade Hasselblad kit—camera body; 35 millimeter, Polaroid, and 2¼ by 2¼ backs; four lenses rang-ing in focal length from fisheye–extreme wide angle to three hun-dred-millimeter telephoto; two strobe lights; a gold reflector and an umbrella; eye-level viewfinder; about a dozen filters: one-year-old equipment listed at retail at more than $13,000—that was his pride and joy.

He considered that he'd "stolen" it with his winning bid of $3,250, at an estate sale liquidating a veritable storehouse of adult toys accu-mulated by a rich young man who'd dabbled in most of the arts before dying of AIDS. The Nikons he had acquired by his usual method, scooping them up when they were traded by "goofy" enthusiasts who found it always necessary to have the newest model of anything. "So they wind up trading prime, cherry stuff every year. Because the cam-era companies know them, know they're out there, and're truly nuts, and as long as they keep making dinky little changes that won't mean a goddamned thing to the pictures that you'll get, but say they're bringing out new models, the suckers'll come running, every time, lin-ing up to buy. Hey, I'm not complaining. The manufacturers get their money and I get top equipment, cheap, before the guy who bought it even had it long enough to really learn to use it, even—much less wear it out."

He had two valuable Leicas, a IIIF and an M3. He had paid $350, market value—which they could not afford—for the IIIF at a camera store on Bromfield Street in Boston in 1972, when he had coveted it so long that the sight of one in mint condition was more than he could bear. The M3, in his possession since she could not remember when, he had purchased privately from a fellow North Shore member temporarily deranged by lust to possess the then-brand-new M6, carefully insisting upon giving the afflicted owner fifty dollars more on the snap-up than he could have gotten on a trade-in. That enabled Royce to stand firm two years later when the inevitable happened and the recovered sufferer, become remorseful, sought to get his M3 back, in his contrition offering twice what Royce'd paid him; with a clear conscience Whitlock had been able to turn him down. "If you can keep your head when all those about you are losing theirs, you can get some really good photographic equipment, cheap."

It was at his request that Agnes limited her choice of gifts for him to supplies of premium film—Kodak Lumiere; before that Fuji Velvia; he found the Velvia reds just a hair too hot—and darkroom supplies. He agreed the new automatic developing machines had made it so that any idiot who can push a button, if he knows which button to push, can do as good a job with color as anybody prolly needs—even if he does drool all over himself while he's doin' it. But I *enjoy* doing it the old way. I *like* doing it myself, and that way if it goes wrong, don't come out the way I want, well, I know who to blame, all right; I know who screwed up. Or if it does come out the way I want, but doin' it's made me see a better way, well then, I learned something, then, didn't I? Which I would not've learned if I'd paid someone else to have all the fun. And that's another thing I like, learning something new. Which I think is a good reason for doing anything that you don't have to do, and even for doing things that you *do* have to do."

But she still had her misgivings. More than once she had grimly confided to friends her fear that he "might be going to have a lot of trouble getting over being cheap—which is really his *main* hobby, you know, being tighter'n the childproof caps on aspirin bottles—when the day comes to cash in and take all those trips he's always saying're

9

the reason for it, and then the question's gonna have to be: 'Well, all well and good, but will he be able to do it?'

"And if he doesn't do it, like he's said so long we're going to; if after we've been through all of this, then we *don't* get to Glacier National Park and the Painted Desert; the Atlas Mountains in Morocco; Iceland; the west of Ireland; take those trips and all; if it's all been just talk to camouflage the miser's work, or he's dead from a stroke, or all crippled up, so he can't go no place anymore, any way, so the money just stays in the bank, well, I ask you: What am I going to do then? I won't have no choice, will I, now? If that's it then I'm going to have to kill him.

"Just take his damned gun and shoot him. It's just as simple as that. And I don't mind telling you: I worry about it; I worry about it a *lot*. Because the man's gettin' worse. I *see* it; I *know*: he wasn't anywhere *near* as bad as this, as bad as he is now about it, thank the dear Lord and His Blessed Mother, when we still had the boys at home with us. You know? They would've rebelled at him, is what they would've done. If he'd treated them the way he makes me treat him and so forth: no real Christmas presents or nothing, and on your birthday the real-big, *unusual* treat of havin' dinner right where you have it every other night, at *home*. But with them he was *generous*. Whatever they needed, he always got for them. And if they just *wanted* something, you know? If it was something that they didn't really *need*, or like that, but: they *wanted* it, you know? They just had to have it, the way all kids always are? Well, if it was reasonably *reasonable*, if he could do it for them without puttin' us all in the poorhouse, when then, that was what he did. But since they left home, well, he's gotten worse. The older he gets, the worse he gets."

For eighteen years the two of them had alternated two-year terms as recording secretary for the club. In exchange for diligently keeping the minutes of meetings, they got the cubicle and first crack at fresh, new magazines, some three hundred dollars' worth a year. "Before they get all rumpled," as Agnes put it. "I hate it when I just went to read a magazine the first time and it's been all wrinkled up. Like someone coughed on it, or blew their nose, or maybe sneezed and then it dried. Or had coffee spilled on it or something. I feel like I'm in a dentist's office that way, waiting to get a tooth filled and I know it's gonna hurt."

Late in the afternoon on the third Thursday of the previous October, Whitlock had resignedly responded to the call from the Andover Police to the Essex County District Attorney's Office in Salem. The call reported a designated wetland trespasser's near-hysterical conviction that the large green plastic bag she had stepped on (while illegally—though very tenderly—uprooting Boston ferns to border her rock garden shade-preferring flower beds at home) contained "a dead body."

The Andover policeman's tone of voice had conveyed his deep skepticism of the lady's claim. He had made it explicit: "It's prolly just a big bagga somebody's shit, somebody's trash, that somebody threw from a car inna middle of the goddamned night when there was no one else around so they didn't see him do it. Somebody's goddamned oily paint rags, or some other goddamned thing the fuckin' dump won't take—oh excuse me, beg your fuckin' *par*don: fuckin' sanitary *landfill*—maybe batteries or something. It's not *environmentally correct*. So as a result the guy got all pissed off and said to himself: 'Okay then, fuck it. I'm not gonna keep all that crap in my garage no longer; get spontaneous combustion and my fuckin' *house* burns down.' So what he does as a result, he goes and throws it inna swampland, and which of course all these whinin' yuppie assholes, it never occurs to them is exactly what will happen—in fact it's *guaranteed* to happen— if they start passin' all these asshole laws they're always passin', sayin' what we got to do, and what we'd better not if we know what's good for us. Oh no, they don't do *that*. They'd never do a thing like that, use their fuckin' *heads* and do some thinking for a change. Oh no, they don't do that—might *hurt* themselves or something, if they did a thing like that.

"But the book says we gotta call you when someone tells us there's a body, and we go by the book here. And so I'm callin' you, all right? Procedure. I apologize. Wastin' your time like this."

One of the things that I've had to learn and then relearn, time and again, is how people actually live out their lives. Very few of the people I have represented, been hired and paid good money by them to mind their business for them, and have therefore by necessity gotten to know pretty well; even fewer of the other people, honest, respectable citizens, that I've come to know real well not because they got arrested but because for one innocent reason or another they figured in my clients' cases—very few of either kind've lived the same way I do. They exhibit surprise when they learn—from things that I've let slip—that I don't live the way they do. Royce was genuinely surprised when I told him that no, as a matter of fact, the appearance he had noticed was not a bit deceiving: I really didn't have any other interest in my life, other than my legal work and the books I bought to read when I went home from it at night. He was skeptical when I claimed that that occupied my mind as much and pleasantly as his photography engaged his. It was as though he'd been a Trappist monk who'd discovered that for several years he'd been living in a cell adjoining a bloody damned atheist's. He'd never dreamed such people existed, that such outlandish things went on. He didn't know what to make of it. He was truly amazed. *"Nothin'?"* he said. "Nothin' like that at all? And you live by your-self, with no family at all? I don't see how you can get along like that. I really don't unnerstan' it. I would think a man would go nuts." I could see him resolving to watch me more closely from then on, in case I decided to do that, go nuts. He plainly hadn't seen any reason to think that I'd gone nuts before that, but from now on he'd be on the alert.

Anyway, because he had that consuming side interest, Whitlock had known that the Andover cop hadn't been wasting his time with the fern lady's report. He'd exhaled a long breath and said no, it was all right, and had gone outside to his car knowing in his heart that the fern lady was right: there was in fact a body in the bag. He knew this because the camera club held its monthly meetings on the third Thursday of each month (except July and August, when so many were away, leaving few to attend the informal summer meetings) and the rotating five-member Social Committee—headed that year by Roger Cole—"put on a feed," as they called it, after the business meeting. The feed had been a custom at the club since the first year of its founding in 1948. Those who had been members forty years and more regarded it with a fondness approaching reverence, deem-ing it the glue that had held the group together when so many other camera clubs had "just withered on the vine. They had no fellowship, you see. The darkroom and the slides, lectures, and equipment introductions; they just aren't enough. You have to socialize, so the members are your friends. That's the reason why this club's survived and become a tradition; why when the other clubs go under, their old members join up here and drive thirty miles to meetings; why North Shore's always had its pick of the best speakers and first look at new equipment: tradition's what it is, tradition. NSCC's got a *name*. We're a group of *friends*. Photography just happens to be something that we share."

Whitlock hated to miss the buffet, even though he often complained it was seldom particularly good. I went to one, as his guest, subject to that warning. The meal was self-served on cheap, thin-gauge paper plates that buckled, attacked with white plastic knives and forks, and generally cold except for one hot dish each month. The night I went it was a mucilaginous tuna-macaroni casserole that you could've used to set kitchen tile, if it hadn't had the soggy potato chips, grayish canned peas, and carrot chunks in it. But Royce told me that was just an unfortunate fluke: that night's hot-dish committeeperson was a woman under the delusion that she was a good cook, and she'd therefore prepared her own dish. Most of the committee members made no secret of their view that they had better things to do with their Thursdays and stoves that were too small to devote either the hours or appliances to making up a tub of stuff sufficient to feed forty, and therefore arrived for the meetings toting buckets of drive-through fried chicken and cartons of supermarket deli counter awful-greasy-awfuls to the meetings. Royce said the chow mein—for some unfathomable reason a popular choice, turning up three or four times a year; "My guess is it must be cheap"—was especially frightening. He told me he'd once called it "low moon tide in a very dirty harbor," thus deeply offending the woman who'd brought it. She said: "Well then next time, big mouth, bring a sandwich. And if there's anything else we're serving tonight that doesn't come up to your high standards, well then, you just take a nice big helping anyway, *and stick it up your ass*."

But he'd paid for the buffet, in advance. Tasty or not, the cost of the meal was included—no option to decline it, those who cherished it suspecting darkly and correctly that most of the newer members would exercise such an option, were there one—in the annual dues of $100 per person, $150 for family membership. By Whitlock's resentful calculation, half of those dues went for food. So that meant he and Agnes had already laid out somewhere in the neighborhood of six bucks for their dinners, as he'd reminded her each time that he complained about the food and she'd replied that he was not obliged to eat it.

"I *am* obliged to eat it," he said. "You bet your life I am. If I'm obliged to *pay* for it, then I'm obliged to *eat* it. I'm not gonna subsidize all those scrimy old bastards, cheaper even'n *I* am, not a goddamned chance. If people like us started skipping the meal, I know exactly what they would do: they'd claim they hadda charge more for it 'cause it costs more per serving to buy food in smaller quantities, and so they'd raise the price of the meal in the membership fee and start buying even *more* food every month. And then they'd split it up and take it home in paper bags, and live off of it for a week. Uh-uh, I'm not gonna make it *that* easy for 'em. I may die of food poisoning, I know, but that's a chance I'm willing to take. I intend to eat all of those meals that I paid for, if I possibly can."

It therefore stood to reason that any report of a dead body coming in on the third Thursday afternoon of any month—except July or August—would indeed prove to involve, as he said with bitterness: "A real-live, honest-to-God, *dead fuckin'* body. Which will keep me at the scene 'til after midnight, and make me miss my fuckin' dinner— that I already fuckin' *paid* for. And because when I get home Agnes will've eaten, and most likely gone to bed, I will have a choice between either grabbin' a big burger in a bag on the way home— which I will also have to pay for, meaning that I will've bought *two* dinners but I'm only eatin' one—*and* that'll be cold by the time I get it home where I can eat it; or having corn flakes for dinner. And I know why this is: it's because if it wasn't for my bad luck, I would have no luck at all."

"Well, that's a comfort," I said. "My own history reads a lot like that. That's what brings me here today, I guess: a long run of bad luck."

"You've been around some," Whitlock said, as though that had been a shrewd judgment. "I heard of you. You been around, and you look like you have. You got a few miles on you. You ever see one like this before, a case like this one before?"

That was easy. "No," I said. "I didn't want to see this one."

He nodded with the chill gratitude of the miserable for companionship and said: "Me either. This's a really tough one. Well, no help for it, I guess. Have to just make it up, as we go along, hope for the best and that's all."

■   ■   ■

N ow let me tell you what I base this all on," Whitlock said to
me. "I base this all principally upon my own investigations
and what they have turned up, and also upon what's been told
to me by some people I respect.

"Peter Wade's not a good man, not by any means. He's lazy and
he's oversexed. His family spoiled him, growing up, and he's pam-
pered himself ever since. He's forty-six years old. Never held a job, his
whole life. Never done a lick of work, at least I know about, not that
he's ever had to—and given how much I do know about him, lot
more'n I ever wanted, how he's spent his life, if he'd ever done a day's
work, believe me, my friend, I would know.

"He's like one of those people that you don't see so many of
around much anymore, you know? Useless people. Ornaments, but
Christmas's long ago over; tree's been taken down and gone to the
dump. This time it's not coming back. So they stay useless, the rest of
their lives, unless they get worse, and restless, so they do some actual
damage. Which appears to be what he did. They don't really go out of
their way to actually *bother* anyone, but they bother them just the
same. Just by the way they carry themselves, their whole attitude
thing, you know? They don't do *anything*, but just the same they're
annoying. One of them comes around where you can see him, he

really gets on your nerves. Like one of those big fat houseflies, kind with those shiny green wings? Makes a lot of softish noise, gets on your nerves, just having the bastard just buzzing around. Really pisses you off.

"Peter Wade's like that, once something's happened and he's gotten into your life. After that you're gonna sort of always be *aware* of him, always aware he's around. Like one of those ugly Civil War monuments, or a stone wall. Only his kind're more like the fly: he doesn't stay put. His kind doesn't stay in one place. They pop up, time to time, in various places, and even though they're always the same, for some reason you're always surprised. Not that you *should* be surprised; you should've known that they would. Like Joie Chitwood and His Hell-Drivers. You go to a fairgrounds in August, you should expect to find them there, putting on a big show. Because that's what it is that they do. Or used to do anyway—I don't know if they're still at it now. But *why* they do it—except for the money, which certainly is a good reason, or at least a good reason for them—why sane people pay them their *money* to do it: that is a quite different matter.

"Like when I was growing up: Channel swimmers. People who swam the English Channel. See who could do it the fastest. Trying to set records, you know? You'd see them in the Movietone News, when I was a little kid and I got fourteen cents together so I could go to the movies. Or my parents took me, see *Ben Hur* or *Spartacus. Samson and Delilah*—whoo-ee, Hedy Lamarr. Victor Mature was Samson— he had bigger tits'n she did, but I doubt he was as smart, even in real life. And after the cheap movie, before the feature one, they had the movie news. And there'd be this funny-looking woman, or a man with a little jockstrap kind of thing on, a bathing cap, always looking very awkward. And also like they're freezing their asses off, in black-and-white, on Dover Beach or someplace—I don't know where it was. Some kind of beach somewhere in England, or sometimes, I guess, in France. There was a woman named Gertrude Something-or-Other— Ederle? Looked like somebody's mother: she did it a lot. And then there was another one that did it absolutely naked, and there she was, a picture of her, getting ready to do it, right in front of you, and you *knew*, the guy'd just *told* you, she didn't have a suit on. Oh-boy, oh-boy . . . oh, *boy*, because you couldn't see a thing. Not even a nipple protrusion. She was all covered over with this black axle grease or something, black thick grease to keep her warm while she swam bare-ass to France. Bogus albino walrus with black fat on the outside: that was what she was. Eleanor Holm, I think her name was. Came back here and got married to some guy or other, run one of those fuckin' big-time nightclubs in New York. Former big speakeasy guy—now what the hell was *his* name? Now I'll be up all night, trying to remember that. And I remember thinking even then, even when I was a little kid, even if I couldn't see her nipples: "What the hell is this *for*? What the hell *good* is this? Why are they all doing this thing? Who *cares* who can swim the fastest? Just what the hell is this shit *for*, that they are all doing here? They want to get across the Channel—okay, isn't there a boat? And if there *is* a fuckin' boat, which I know damned well there is, 'cause she's got three or four with her, then why's she doing this?' And then the answer come to me: it was very simple. They were doing it, fighting all the tides and all the currents, all the waves and all the rain, and all the shit like that, because they wanted to see if they could do it, and make some money off it. And that was really all it was.

"That's the kind of guy Peter Wade is. He does things for no good reason. He's a disorderly person. I don't mean he's ever been arrested for disturbing the peace or anything, although I'm sure his money's gotten him out of more'n one, 'opportunity,' let's say, when he was completely eligible, yes, very eligible. 'Motor vehicle incident,' say, when he might've been arrested for drunk and disorderly as well as several other things. Such as maybe, well, not exactly now, bribing a police officer, but just making it perfectly clear, you know? That if he didn't take a bust for this, the cop wouldn't be disappointed he did him the favor, later on down the line. Not that I can prove something like that happened, because no, I can't. But Peter's the kind of guy who'd do it, if he thought it needed doing and he had a cop who'd do it. And he would've had one, too—that's the kind he would've had if he ever tried to do it. A cop who'd maybe hesitate and say: 'I really shouldn't do this,' and then go ahead and do it, do it anyway. Because Peter's good at that. One of the things he's very good at is sizing people up, judging human weakness. But anyway, no, I'm not saying that he did that, or that he makes affrays, or anything like that, gets in fights in bars. What I'm saying is that there isn't any kind of *shape* to his life, you know? There isn't any order in it, and it doesn't seem to bother him, way it'd bother you or me. He's not *about* anything.

"About the only constant in it is that when he sees something that he thinks could be useful to him, protect him while he goes careening around the world, completely out of control—in case he bangs into something, as he knows he's sure to do, he's done it so many times before—he grabs onto it and adds it to his inventory. Like a life preserver. Another-thing-that-might-come-in-handy-if-I-get-in-the-shit-again. Like his lawyer, Arthur Dean. The man is an absolute *shit* and Peter knows this. But shit or not, he looked like he might come in handy some day, and now that that day's here, and he has. Don't have to be smart, don't have to think, just like you don't have to work, if you're lucky, and rich. You don't have to think, and be smart, and right, if you're rich. All you have to do is buy lots of things, snap up every damned good one you see. And then, well just you wait: most of the things'll turn out to be worthless, but some of them will turn out to've been really great buys. And that's what his Arthur Dean toy is today, one that turned out to be a great buy.

"I don't like people like that," Whitlock said. "I don't like people like Peter Wade is. I got a prejudice against them. Wait 'til the Mass. Commission Against Discrimination finds out about that one, huh? I'll be up on charges, you bet. STATE POLICE DETECTIVE ADMITS PREJU-DICE AGAINST KILLERS. KILLER ACTIVISTS OUTRAGED.

"I don't give a shit. I admit it. They do, *they annoy me,* even *before* they bang their good wife on the head with a sock full of coins. Or sand, or something. Stuff her in a garbage bag and throw her away in a swamp. For absolutely no good fucking reason, except a great deal of money, money they wanted to keep. So to do that and get what else they wanted, her out of the way so they could have another new wife, they have her banged on the head. Divorce is such a *pain in the ass,* you know? And it also takes a lot of time and costs a lot of money. In this case, very expensive. So those were the reasons they did it. No other reason they did it at all, except that they wanted to do it, and therefore, that's what they did. Because it just fucking *suited* them? Is that it? That's a bad attitude for a man to have. He shouldn't take that attitude. He shouldn't *do* that evil sort of thing, and when he does, I resent it."

"Especially bad if you happen to be the good wife," I said, "that gets bopped on the head with the blunt object. That really could spoil the weekend." I've always tried to show a certain amount of compassion for the victim of violent crime, when I've been representing the guy who almost certainly did the foul deed, but I'm talking *about* him to a policeman. So this was nothing really new for me, except that all of it was: this time, thanks to Henry, I was representing not the probable perpetrator but three living victims of the foul deed (whom I hadn't met yet), talking to a cop seething with frustration that he didn't have the killer, and therefore who'd all but adopted those kids, become surrogate dad, determined to see justice done any way that he could, and Henry'd said I'd be that way. For once I couldn't even *seem* to be pretending, if I knew what was good for me.

"A sock filled with sand," Whitlock said, frowning. "Except if it wasn't a sock filled with sand. That's a small problem in this case, one of too many small problems, and they're all the big problem with it. The big problem's why you got pulled into this case by your ears, and the stuff in the sock, if it was a sock, is just one of those many small problems, because it's a sock we don't got."

He stood up behind the desk and began to pace in place, not quite the same way military units and marching bands stay in step while they're waiting for parades to start: left-right and left-right and left-right, but with the same idea: making no forward progress at all, just pretending to have something to do, not lifting either foot all the way off the floor. "There so *many* small problems in this damned thing no DA'll indict it for me. I can't say I really blame them. Lots of small problems like things we can't find. Too many things we don't know, and can't find out. I hear myself saying to Bob Farr in Essex, then to Phil up in Exeter County: 'Well, dammit all, man, then let's get an indictment. At least put some pressure on him, and on people who know and could tell. Maybe, who knows? Maybe we catch a break, and it happens then, *bang*, we got him. We *got* the son of a bitch. Goddamn, at least give it a try. We can't let this guy just go free, just get away with it here.' And they look at me and say: 'I'm hearing this? With my shell-pink ears? From Royce *Whitlock*, I'm hearing *this*? I should get a murder one indictment? In a case I know going in I can't prove? Royce, I hate to say this, but somebody's got to: You have to get out more, my friend. Take a vacation, go away somewhere, even someplace cheap, if it has to be that, big-fat-roaches-and-don't-drink-the-water. But you really need a good rest for yourself, you're talking this ragtime to me.'"

He shook his head sadly. "They're right, of course, and *they* know that. I know it, too. And so that was why I went to Henry. See if maybe he could think of something, something that'd at least protect these three kids of Sandra's . . ." He smiled. "See what's happened to me, this late stage in my life? I've gotten so I think I know her, or knew her—actually met her in life. Is this what they meant by 'obsession'?"

"I don't follow," I said.

"The medical examiner," Whitlock said. "She couldn't even catch a break from the medical examiner, after she was dead. The medical examiner was Doctor Armand Gilbert. You ever hear of him?"

I winced and said I had.

"Yeah," Whitlock said, drawing it out, "most people in our line of work have. 'Doctor Cuckoo,' as he's better known. Gilbert *said* that he *thought* it was sand. In the sock. That somebody hit her on the head with. At the inquest he said it, I mean. But he wasn't really sure, and anyway, everything he said, the way that he behaved, you could tell right he didn't really think it mattered much. As though he'd been saying: 'Gimme a break here. This was dead riffraff on my hands. Never mattered much alive; why should she matter dead?' "

"My god," I said. Old Armand does have a gaudy reputation; he's been known to nonchalant cases. He had a case once on the Cape when the killer chainsawed the victim in half, and split up the body between two different cranberry bogs in Wareham. It apparently affected his brain. He's been known to lapse back into his testimony in that case in several other cases since then, saying under oath that the bodies of people who died in bed in Weston had been cut in half and thrown into swamps in southeastern Massachusetts. "Did he really say *that*?"

"No, no," Royce said, "that was just how he acted. At least how I thought he was acting. Not that it matters that much, I suppose. Didn't seem to affect anybody else that way, but that's how I saw it, anyway. Jesus Christ. What a thing to have happen to you, huh? Coins or sand, doesn't matter. Either one: what a fuckin' thing to have *happen* to you. Here you are, you're mindin' your own business. Prolly feeling kind of good, even, you took the time to think about it. Winter's finally over. It's a nice day in springtime, nice May or June day in New England, and there you are: you're goin' down to this excellent school in this lovely old New England town, where *your* kids're going to school, like they've always been hoity and toity, and you've always been that way yourself. When you know and they know that that's all the good old *stuff*. You used to be lower'n *dogs*. If it wasn't for fuckin' and suckin', performin' various services there, for horny rich guys who like fun, you'd all be no better off today—and *that* makes it all even better. The lilacs're probably still all in bloom in all the dooryards again, and you're in your work clothes, your jeans and your Keds, to help out your kids, start bringing their stuff home from school for the summer; also talk some about the exams.

"You got no illusions. You know who you are. You know people can tell, when they look at you, you been rode hard and put away wet. But that's okay. You never pretended to be much. Your first husband ran off with a blond cosmetologist from Chicopee, that tramp, and then he leaves her for the redheaded, gum-chewin' beautician with these huge, enormous . . ."

"Hold on a sec, there," I said. "Who was this first husband I had that ran off? And how do you know that that's what he ran off with, the second time, 'a redheaded, gum-chewing beautician,' huh? How the hell do you know that?"

"I interviewed her," Whitlock said. "I tracked Sandra's first husband down, to interview him, and the tramp was home during it. During my interview with him. And that's what she was, what I said: a redheaded, gum-chewin' tramp, ten or fifteen pounds overweight, these days. Enormous setta jugs on her. Pretty flabby now, but when she was young and firm and all upright like that, she must've had 'em pantin' down the drugstore afternoons. She told me she was a beautician. I don't make this stuff up that I'm telling you, you know. And she told me she was from Chicopee. Just like Sandy's mother did. Sandra's mother told me the exact same thing. I'm not allowed to make things up. I'm not some fuckin' newspaperman, you know, makin' up stuff about total strangers, never did a thing to me.

"And then later on when you thought you had a good thing going with this with guy Hugh Cameron, used to own his own tractor rig, doing okay with it, too; but then he just took off on you, too. He did the same exact thing. Just vanished into the mist. But by God, you hung in there, three kids and all, the odds dead set against you. And whaddaya know, then your luck looks like it turned. Did a complete pirouette, a one-eighty, and now the whole world's bright and new. And then what happens to you? Somebody bangs you real hard on the head, and that's the end of you. You end up in a bag in the swamp.

"Sandra Nichols wasn't God's favorite child. Sandra Nichols had a very hard life. All I'm after here—along with revenge, of course, that; for a woman who can't get her own now—is finding some way that those kids she had come out of this with at least something they used to have. At least some of what she worked so damned hard to get for them, that in the end got her killed for it." He paused. "Can you think of anything that might do that? Anything that might help to do that?"

"There's one possibility comes to mind," I said. "I'm no expert at it. I'm making no guarantees, and I'll have to know a lot more'n I do now before I can really say: 'Okay then, we should do it; this is what we should do.' You understand what I'm saying here? I'm committing to no course of action just yet. All I'm saying is: I'll take a look."

He nodded. "Well," he said, "that sure isn't much. But it's more'n I had going in."

■   ■   ■   4

Let me try to put things in perspective here. I've been practicing law in Boston since I was sworn into membership in the
Massachusetts bar in the fall of 1964. I was married then to
the former Joan McManus—I called her "Mack" to avoid confusing
people who might otherwise have thought I was carrying on with Ted
Kennedy's then-wife—and we had a little girl named Heather. We
called her "Saigon" when she was little, because her conception made
me a daddy and daddies didn't get drafted, so before she was even
born I owed her—she had been my permit to stay home from the war
in Vietnam. She was also the reason why Mack had given up her job
(and the salary we'd lived on through law school) as manager of the
thirty-seven-member clerical staff—they typed up deeds and other
instruments in those precomputer days before the floppy disk made
many of them obsolete—in the Newton branch office of Coleman &
Guthrie, Inc. That was real responsibility for a woman in her mid-
twenties; the office was the New England regional clearing house for
what in those days was the second-largest residential real estate company in the country. Mack's future looked securely brilliant indeed.
So much so that when she married me and then got pregnant, we
thought she was more or less taking a breather before resuming her
climb. As things turned out, we were wrong.

I had just turned twenty-six when Heather first started kicking around. I had no secure professional prospects (meaning one of these three things: an office set aside, with a brand-new desk and chair waiting for me in it, in the family law firm; good enough—okay, top—grades in law school to have senior partners lined up beaming at the door of a major law firm to welcome me aboard; or a lock on a government patronage job). So since neither Mack nor I had any family reserves of money to call on, there was a certain urgency in the job-hunting process. I did the best I could, under the circumstances, and started out with a menial job in the small firm of Culp & Hurley in downtown Boston (the circumstances being that no one else offered me any job at all). The two partners openly fretted about adding to their overhead by hiring me, or anyone else, having no great profits to spare, but they really did need a sixty-dollar-a-week research-and-pleadings drone, and (after much thoughtful deliberation that Mack and I found absolutely agonizing) apparently decided that I was either the most deserving or else the most hangdog—and thus likeliest to be docile—of their four humble supplicants.

Still, I don't mean to seem ungrateful for that employment. Sure, every hour I worked in that office chafed me like a hair shirt, and I dreaded going to it every day. But I was also thankful to have been given a choice between pumping gas for the statutory minimum wage and making a bit more practicing the law I'd spent three years in school to learn. I really needed that job, and even thirty years later I still appreciate the fact that each of those two guys, neither of them getting rich either, agreed to reduce his take-home pay by half of the price of my keep. A daily barrel of laughs they were not. They were worried and harried, and testy sometimes, and at all times they made sure they got their full money's worth out of me. But they weren't just sloughing the toil off onto me, loafing on the fruits of my labors; they were also good, conscientious, hardworking men themselves, and I made sure they got full value, too. They were fair; I know if they'd suddenly gotten rich, I'd've become quite well-off too. And if I'd been able to see such a rainbow-happy future even faintly glimmering for me with their operation, even on a horizon very far away, I would've stuck it out.

The trouble was, I couldn't. A little more than a year of donkey work at Culp & Hurley was enough to convince me and Mack that it wasn't ever going to get any better. What they had laboriously built was a self-limiting, time-intensive, tedious, commercial practice that looked like the foundation of a thriving little business-litigation firm but amounted to a glorified bill-collection agency tarted up with law degrees. There's only so much of that dreary business around, and as all paltry treasures always are, it's the object of quietly desperate competition. Joe Culp and Victor Hurley, somewhat handicapped in the struggle by their scrupulous refusal to tell lies about their competitors, had cornered about all they were likely to get.

But it wouldn't've really mattered if the supply'd been infinite: if C&H had gotten three times more business, then they'd've had to bring in two more lawyers along with promoting me (I know they would've) as new partners, and hire at least two new pot-wallopers to replace me for the chores that I was doing. So while it looked like there might be a chance that their firm would grow, as a beagle pup may become a champion adult beagle hound, but not the horse that wins the Triple Crown, so I could see C&H becoming a lot bigger, but I could not see it ever going to make a partner in it rich.

Or provide any member of it with a great deal of fun, either. At least the fun I had in mind, the fun of trying big cases. The clients were small businessmen, almost all nice guys, on paper "executive officers," but in fact the boldest and most energetic kinfolk, sons and sons-in-law, of families owning closely-held corporations. Their wholesale building-supply outfits (plumbing fixtures and supplies; tile and linoleum; bricks and cement; lumber, siding, and roofing materials; paint; apartment-size appliances; wiring and lighting supplies; all of that sort of thing) were never going to become major players, certain to generate and able to pay high legal costs (in fact what was going to happen to them, though no one saw it coming then, was the steamroller advent of the national warehouse chains—the "category killers" Home Depot and Home Quarters—that would discount most of them right into history).

The people Culp & Hurley sued for their clients weren't huge industrial competitors who'd violated the Sherman Antitrust Act by restraining trade, stealing patented processes, or engaging in price fixing; they were independent contractors who'd bought "on tick"—credit—what they needed to do their jobs, and then screwed up by dipping into their own receivables accounts (carelessly mingling progress payments with profits actually earned on jobs completed, so they felt richer than they really were, spending next month's profits today). Then when the time came for them to write their own checks, to meet the accounts *payable* for those materials and supplies they'd needed to earn the progress payments, they didn't have the money handy and had to be sued before they'd pony up. Small beer, in other words.

Now here are some immutable words for every lawyer to live by: if your clients aren't rich when you get them, and they're never going to get rich after you've forged a bond with them; and the people whom you sue in their behalf not only aren't rich but are getting sued because they're at least temporarily insolvent; then no matter how good you are, or how hard you work for your clients, unless you're better at choosing stocks or picking horses, you're never going to have lots of dough either. So, while it was theoretically possible that Culp & Hurley might triple their business, without making any one person in it much richer, it didn't look to me then as though even that much was going to happen. As I saw it, the firm simply wasn't destined to grow to a size that would support a third (even a very junior) partnership for me, as well as a new Bob Cratchit to replace me. Later events proved my appraisal had been accurate. In 1987 Culp & Hurley, still a two-man operation, disappeared without a ripple into the maw of a "merger" with an interstate octopus firm out of New York ravening for Offices Damned Near Everywhere, and locally-licensed meek vassals to staff them. I doubt very much that my first and last two employers in the law had relished the sale of their independence and their hard-won practice to Monster, Behemoth & Giant, but when you're in your early fifties and you're stuck fast where you are, if someone offers you a premium price for signing over the modest thing you've got—along with, of course, your balls—you don't really have much choice. If I'd stayed with C&H I'd be a bitter man today. Now and then I get one right.

It all seemed to be fairly clear—scary, but still, pretty clear: I had to go out and try to run my own show, and if that meant I'd fall flat on my ass, well, at least I'd know then what my destiny was. Mack still admired me back then. She wanted me to be happy and successful, and not just because she wanted to be well-to-do. She hoped so devoutly that I wouldn't have to give up on the law, which I'd always wanted—she thought that I'd be gloomy ever after—that she began to believe that I'd succeed, and more than that, become rich and famous, "or reasonably solvent," as she put it, we being friends in those days (what we are today is two middle-aged people who with some regretful tenderness remember having been friends and even lovers, too, once upon a time, and act with respect for the memory), "and well-enough known, at least around town, so I can get a check cashed, and rich enough so it won't bounce."

I was more pessimistic, but I managed to be fairly cheerful, too: I figured I'd land on my ass and run out of borrowed money in about a year, then have to scramble for a steady, boring job if I intended to support my family. Not a thrilling prospect, but I was prepared to face it; many honorable men have had to do that, and done it without too much whining. At least I'd have the consolation of going into it without regret, knowing I'd taken my shot. Insurance claims adjusting's not exactly the gunfighter's glamorous trade, but out of it I could make a reasonably happy and secure wage earner's life for us, and I'd never have to look back afterwards.

Fourteen years later, considering that daunting beginning, things seemed to be going along pretty good. Not spectacularly, no, lest you think I'm boasting here, but still, not bad at all. From loyal classmates in law school who'd had the kind of professional prospects I lacked, I'd managed to cobble together enough referrals of scruffy small-time criminal cases—most of them involving acts really more shameful or disgraceful than criminal, involving, one way or the other, the excessive use of beverage alcohol, whether taken too generously before driving (no one being hurt as a result, and only my client's car damaged) or while engaging in heated (but unarmed) discussions with spouses at home or strangers in bars. But they were enough to get me regular appearances in the criminal courts, and that's how you get criminal business, and build up a nice little practice.

So, in 1979, fifteen years out of law school, we owned not only our first home, a four-bedroom garrison-colonial on Kevin Road in Braintree Highlands, Massachusetts ("Owner transferred, must sell now." "$26,500" had been first entered, then crossed out and "$22,750" put in its place—we got it for $21,500) but also a modest summer place on the Irish Riviera, down at Green Harbor, in Marshfield. Heather was going to Fontbonne Academy in Milton, aiming for Dartmouth

College (where in due course she'd get in, but not remain long enough to earn her degree). Mack was gingerly retesting the waters in the real estate game, but this time not seeking a staff job, no; this time she was looking to work where the money was made: as a regular agent (she'd taken the test and passed easily, because she'd taken it very seriously and she wasn't stupid at all).

Coleman & Guthrie's nearest outpost didn't want her. They claimed to have no openings and said they'd put her name first on their list, as an ex–C&G manager, to be called when the next slot opened up. During the next month they hired two other women, neither with any experience. Mack said it was because they'd been divorced and hadn't remarried. "Men always pretend they feel sorry for fresh divorcées." In a doleful voice: " 'She doesn't have a man to take care of her now. She needs the job more than you do.' When the real reason is they figure a horny divorcée's sure to be an easy lay, especially if it's pretty clear it's 'put out or lose the job.' "

But the shirttail operation that'd sold us our house, Southarbor Realty—consisting then of one part-time typist and two fast-talking young guys; one named Ace, one named Roy; working hard day and night to look grandly busy doing very little in a basement office; cream-colored cinder-block walls; neon turquoise indoor-outdoor carpeting; three veneer desks; four phones; bad Polaroid pictures of houses for sale Scotch taped in untidy clumps all over the walls; one flight down under the tobacco store at South Shore Plaza—took her on. Mostly because she said she'd start on spec, no draw, no dough until she sold something, but that wasn't the way that she told it: "They hired me even though I'm *not* divorced," she liked to say airily, then. "For a while I almost thought that you had to be, so many of the women in the business seem to be. But it turns out that's not a requirement. These guys know talent; they saw me and they gave me a job." Talent in the real estate game is the ability to make not-very-much seem to be quite-a-lot; I can respect that—it's often come in handy in my own trade, too.

Anyway, at the time we thought that divorce stuff was a little pleasant, harmless banter. Once again we were wrong. Later it turned out to be a nasty, harmful joke—on us. I was not one bit amused. It hit me very hard. I felt as though I'd been killed but sentenced to go on living anyway, not only summarily deprived of what'd been going to be the best part of living out my life but denied as well the quiet peace of being dead.

It's tough when you reach that point in your life where you start to find yourself making more entries in your diary of memory under *Departures*, people who've left your life too early, for one reason or another, than you're making under *Arrivals*, new people coming in (I suppose I could count my grandchildren in that column, but while we do have that legal relationship by blood, I've seen so little of them, way out there in Colorado, it doesn't really seem to me as though they're really in my life). The deaths—Bad-eye Mulvey, my trepid private eye; Welden Cooper, also now deceased, at the time of the divorce the best friend that I had—have been rough enough, but Mack's departure in that divorce was brutal.

It hit me hard and I took it hard, from the moment that it first began to dawn on me what was going on: Mack was having an affair at work, screwing Roy down at his beach house. That was the first of the three liaisons that I know about; there may have been others, more fleeting. Later, before the divorce became final, she equalized matters among the now-very-successful partners and took to fucking Ace in *her* new place, a condo overlooking the Cape Cod Canal. The last one I heard about was the guy she's now married to, Ben Suras, of Suras Continental, S.A. It apparently began soon after he'd commenced negotiations to buy out what was by then the twenty-three-office Southarbor operation for what for him was pocket change: slightly over nine million bucks. Felicitous timing on Mack's part, I must say. I don't know whether her talented personal corpus was inventoried among Southarbor assets involved in the transaction, like those of the ballplayers under contract on a pro team changing hands, or she cut her own separate deal as a free agent on the side. I don't know whether there was a prenuptial agreement, or what its terms were if there was. But I suspect this union will last: Mack is now at least pretty rich—Ace and Roy'd cut her in on a good profit-sharing chunk of stock when they took the partnership public in '88, so figure probably a million of those nine must've gone to her. Depending on what arrangements she's made since, she may be very rich indeed. And powerful as well, a condition that she coveted a lot more than she knew, or at least revealed to me. Mack's life has turned out well for her. She was more resilient than I'd been, able to catch her breath, regroup her forces, and go on to other things. Of course she'd been able to see long before I ever could the train that was coming, was able to make preparations. She was, after all, the reason it came. I was just the guy stalled on the track.

When Henry elbowed me into the Sandra Nichols case, I still hadn't recovered from the blow. I wasn't fully sure of why—half hoped, I guess, I was wrong—but I suspected I'd never get any better. I didn't think my nature would allow it. I was growing my own body armor, the way a lobster grows a new tough shell. All sorts of practical people told me, in the first season of my dismay at what I saw as Mack's mortal treachery, that love affairs happen all the time, and that they don't have to become terminal to the marriages involved unless the injured parties insist. I truthfully told them I agreed with that; I still agree with it today. The day I heard from Bad-eye what she'd been up to with Roy, I realized two things: I'd never be able to trust her again, and that meant our marriage was over. So: both criteria for termination had been met, satisfied in full: I was the injured party, and I insisted on termination. I'd do the same thing again, if God forbid I were to find myself in that situation again. That was why I was pretty sure I'd never get better: that I'd never be able to take the chance of leaving myself open to another shot like that (as I sometimes get one right, as I did when I left Culp & Hurley, so I sometimes get one completely wrong, and this turned out to be such an instance, but I'm getting ahead of myself here).

I realized at the time that my intransigent refusal to kiss and make up—assuming Mack wanted to do that, which I very much doubt that she did; she'd found she rather liked fucking around, after all those years of prim rectitude—was not considered the correct adult attitude. I know about half a dozen people who've serenely attended their ex-wives' or husbands' later weddings. I couldn't do that. If that is what constitutes mature behavior now, it's not the sort of thing I've ever thought I could manage. Mack knew it when she remarried. When she called me and told me it was going to happen, and that Heather, separated by then from nitwit Charlie, at last, would be coming back east to attend (your daughter as your ex-wife's matron of honor: somehow it seems as though there must be something wrong with that, but I can't quite put my finger on it), it was like hearing about an upcoming event I knew at once I had no wish to see, none at

all. So there was to be a new chapter in the continuing story of someone I'd known and thought well of, long ago, and unless I protected
myself from it, I'd be made sad all over again. All I said was that I
wished her the best. She said she knew that, and thanked me for it,
but had just thought she should let me know about it so I didn't
encounter Heather on Beacon Street some day and find out by surprise. I did appreciate that. There are not as many compensations as
I'd like in the gentling that age sometimes brings, but I must admit
there are some.

Now I *will* do some boasting. Pretty early during those fourteen
years on my own I learned to my satisfaction that I'm not a bad hand
at my chosen trade. People who can judge such skills came up and
told me so. They'd had a chance to see me at work in others' behalf,
and since the criminal sessions are almost always full, at least in the
mornings, there were quite a few of them. Some of them were people
whom I did not represent, but who'd become dissatisfied with the
lawyers that they had. A fairly sizable number were other solo practi-
tioners, occasionally asked to recommend a lawyer for a codefendant
in a multidefendant case. I in my turn took careful heed of the lessons
available from watching my elders at work. So in time I developed a
reputation, the best stock in the trial lawyer's trade, and that was what
brought me the legal business of Edmund M. Franklin, "Cadillac
Teddy," as he was known then, and as he's known to this day.

Teddy was thirty-two years old when I first formally represented
him, back in '79. For seventeen years the police of Massachusetts had
been convinced that he'd been stealing certain cars. Cadillac cars; and
they'd stopped him dozens of times, each time only to find him driving—cold sober, all papers in order—a perfectly legal Cadillac. This
cat-and-mousing led to a certain amount of frustration on their part,
as some of you may remember. A state trooper, Torbert Hudson, disappointed in his effort to bust Teddy for driving a hot Cad (the one he
was driving was legal), ate Teddy's temporary driver's license (he'd
lost his laminated one) and then lugged him for driving-no-license.
Between then and the time set down for trial, Trooper Hudson
stopped Teddy's wife's Cad and ate her registration, arresting Dotty
for driving without *that*, thus bringing about what I was told at the
time by a cop the most memorable afternoon he had spent in over
twenty years on duty in the Dedham jail. The development prompted

me to explore more deeply Trooper Hudson's employment record. He turned out to have a history of very strange decisions made at scenes of potential arrests. Both of the Franklin cases were dismissed in court, as was Trooper Hudson from the state police, and Teddy in effusions of gratitude thereafter did wonders for my legal practice, all but dragooning new clients to my office on the sixth floor at the Little Building, 80 Boylston at Tremont, at the southeast corner of Boston Common, across from the subway kiosk.

I no longer hang out there, to my regret. Emerson College in March of '94 bought the old twelve-story building for $5 million out from under me and all the other tenants, many of them also single-practitioners of one sort or another—a lot of dentists; an optometrist or two; a loan shark masquerading as a venture capitalist; surely at least one fence, disguised as an estate agent; maybe some doctors; a discreet large lay-off bookie, perhaps; a few lawyers, like me; some accountants? I'm not really sure; except for sharing elevator rides in cordial anonymity, we didn't socialize at all across professional lines—to convert into a dormitory. The place that I'm in now's much closer to court, and, I suppose, suits my status and dignity better: a sublet condo space of about seven hundred square feet on the fourth floor of 20 Beacon Street opposite the State House, just down from the corner of Park Street. Not as ornate—no rose marble walls and gray marble floors; gray pillars with gold capitals, like you'll find two or three of the new Tombs of the Pharaohs recently opened in the financial district—but quite elegant, really, all soft-gloss-paneled in honey-toned oak; thickly carpeted; hushed; nicely furnished. It murmurs of class, and good breeding, and voices not raised, and as unlikely as it seems, I'm told I look right at home in it, almost as though I belonged. Maybe so, but it's not to my genuine liking. Never having had much interest in status or dignity—none at all, in fact, during that seedy, shabby, down-at-the-heels period of about three years (it seemed like a decade) bracketing the divorce—I guess I resent the expense of maintaining those ephemera now, in the appropriate style. I do it, though, for the usual reason: spending that begrudged money brings in even more money, and in that hope those of us who still remember when we were chronically short of cash can tolerate some small discomfort.

Billy Ryan, the late former commissioner of the Massachusetts

Department of Public Works, was most reluctantly the initial source of funds first to restore and then improve my station in life. We had a lawyer-client relationship made in heaven, a glorious synergy. He paid me $100,000 to defend him against the contents of a thick indictment packed with allegations of bribery and corruption charging him with doing precisely what everyone in Massachusetts with normal hearing or basic reading skills knew that he'd been doing ever since the end of World War II. He did not give me all that money because he thought me a worker of miracles, or even a deserving fellow. He gave it to me because he was desperate for a lawyer and no one else still arguably in his right mind would take the case. I took it, hopeless of winning, because I was desperate, too: on my uppers, broke, after the divorce; depressed and drinking too much; and thanks to the whispering ministrations of my scalier, slithering competitors in the noble practice or criminal trial law, making things even worse than they were, my reputation was in the Deer Island sewage filter bed. I wasn't threatened with going to prison, but except for that small difference, I was as bad off as Billy. Unless I managed to do something for him, my life would be over with too. Devil take win or lose: I needed the fee, almost as much as a challenge to meet. I had no choice but to take him.

I won the impossible damned thing. Billy walked out of court a free man. I was able to do that because, praise the Lord, ours is a punctilious system. To put a guy in jail it's not enough for everyone to know that he's a crook; in order for that to be done, someone must first manage to prove it . . . beyond a reasonable doubt. I always pause before I utter that last clause, to assure it the great reverence it deserves as the last barrier between a civilized citizenry and a lynch mob. And also, of course, as the last forlorn hope of the fellow who either has to get a break or watch his life destroyed before his very eyes. The Commonwealth couldn't make that proof at Billy's trial, for one of two reasons: either because I was once more at the height of my powers, the top of my game, chain-lightning on cross, an evangelist on summation (as I was, and prefer to believe that's how I won), or else because my good friend and loyal client, Teddy Franklin, entirely without my knowledge (or, God save the mark, permission), had put the fix in. Not because he loved Billy, or even knew the old pirate; no, in order to make me look good. Or so Teddy led me to believe, four years after Billy's trial ended in the sweetest words defense lawyers ever hear: "We find the defendant not guilty, Your Honor"—but since then he's denied it, as he promised he would. The other parties to the dirty deed, if there one was done, are all dead. So to this day I'm not really sure which it was. All I can be sure of is that defending Billy Ryan was professionally the smartest thing I ever did. It made me something I had never really been, in my palmiest days before that: a brand name in the criminal defense bar. Brand names get the big money.

So now I do mostly white-collar crime, and most of my income's in corporate checks, partly for advising company officers how to prevent theft and embezzlement (Thou shalt not lead thy trusted officers into temptation) and partly for advising them how to avoid violations of punitive laws (self-dealing and insider trading; patronizing the Midnight Hazardous-Waste Dumping Service; looting the assets for the enrichment of the board of directors, to the damage of the investors) that could lead to much nastiness even after knuckles have been sharply rapped for criminal offenses (such as treble-damages shareholder lawsuits).

Granting that those clients and their concerns have far more cash to spend on lawyers, no small consideration to be sure, are they as much colorful fun as Teddy and all of his rogues were? No, they're not, not by a long shot. But Teddy and his fellow rogues aren't as much fun themselves anymore, either, after the passage of time. Teddy's forty-seven now and semiretired. He still spends about six months of the year here, in the house that he and Dotty have in Sharon, the rest in their condo in St. Thomas, overlooking the Caribbean, but he doesn't steal cars anymore. He's leading the quiet life now. "Hey, so I mellowed, all right? I'm playing the golf; catching the fish; no more tennis for now, not after the bypass, no tennis least 'nother a year. But what the hell, right? I play cards, go the track. Little Vegas, you know? Hop over the Caymans, little action; now and then I take a swim. It's not a bad life at all. I worked hard all my life, ever since I turn fifteen. I earned what I got, no one gave it to me. So did Dotty, she always worked too. So why shouldn't we both enjoy it, you know? She's takin' it easier, too—when I had my attack there, well, sure, it scared me, but her I think it scared even more. So she's also not floggin' the duck so hard anymore. Lettin' her sister-in-law do part of it, take some of the burden off of her, running those fuckin' salons—two of them've got three of them now. She's takin' it easier too. It's good. I like it like this. No cops watching me all the time, sittin' outside-ah my house, you know? Gettin' me so pissed off I belt one of them, and then what happens? *I'm* the one payin' the fine? When the fuckin' cop started the thing? Who needs that grief anymore? Not me, I'm too old. And what I got's not a bad life at all."

He can take this expansive view because when he was in "the secondhand Cadillac trade," as he likes to describe it these days, he "wasn't flashy. I didn't just throw it away, some young asshole just made his first score. Years ago, what I did, before I even knew you, the first thing I did, got myself a good broker, this guy I know down in Greenwich. Greenwich, Connecticut, right? Met him first as a customer, mine. He's dead now, prostate got him, and he didn't deserve that none, either. Stevie was always a very nice guy—bought quite a few Cads offa me. Cads for him, for his wife, and I think one or two for his girlfriends—'fore he got older, and nervous. So, this's when I first start gettin' some money, I take my problem to him. I say to him: 'Stevie, all right? You tell me now, you're the stockbroker here: What do I do about this? You're doin' all right here, I can see that, you got the dough to buy all of this iron off me; you must be doin' all right. And *I* am doin' all right. But this's just *now*, am I right? Some day we're both gonna be old. So, now you tell me: What do I do now, start plannin' for when I get old? How do I go about doin' this thing? Like I'd know what to do if I did. Like I say: I'm all right, I'm doin' all right, I got a few bucks to my name. But what happens, someday, if I got to stop workin'? What am I livin' on, then? All of this money, it's gonna run out, just sittin' 'round like it's been doin'. I'm beginnin' to think: "It doesn't make sense. It don't make any sense. You gotta do somethin' with this. Stevie would know what to do. He unnerstans all of this stuff." So, you wanna help me with this?'

" 'Sure I will,' Stevie says, 'I'm flattered you asked.' And he did that, he did that for me. He took my money, invested it, wisely, you know what I'm saying by that? He actually said that to me: 'I'll be sure to invest it wisely for you, so then what you'll be is a genuine wise guy, makin' real wise-guy investments,' he said. Got a big kick outta that— he thought that was a pretty good joke. And the way that he did it, he set it all up, I didn't do almost nothin'. And I got to say, it worked out real good. I could then pay my taxes and say if they asked me: 'Well, where did you get this? This money that you say you made?' I could then just say: 'First, you look at my job, and then you look here, where the rest of it came from, all right? All these wise investments I made, what I got from my job there, my job with the pool company.' "

Teddy was nominally employed as East Coast management representative for the Dolphin Pool Co. of Bakersfield, California. He had business cards—and very little else—to prove that. I believe there is, or used to be at one time, a company by that name at the address listed on his cards. But maybe there wasn't. I was careful never to probe too deeply. "So I get no shit from the damned IRS, like you hadda contend with there once, and it cost you an arm and a leg. No, I put my money away, nice and careful. And in that I was actually smart."

I have never inquired what investments he made. Only once did he confide in me. He told me he bought a lot of GM stock: "Hey, *I* know they make good cars. Who would know better'n I do? I got enough of the things." When it comes to talking about cars, especially Cadillacs, Teddy's command of the language slips a little: the verb *steal* disappears from his vocabulary. "One their divisions at least, and I also figure, long's I'm around, keepin' busy, doin' what I do, got customers calling, there'll always be someone needing new a one, take the place of the one that I took. So all by myself and the people I sell to, I can almost guarantee you there'll always be a good steady market in those things—as long's I still do what I do."

Teddy's got a lot of entertainer in him. He doesn't outright falsify things, but sometimes the urge to flesh out the details and add to the suspense seems to get the better of him. His claim about investing in GM may've been one of those occasions; I've never known whether I believed it. But one way or the other, it doesn't matter now: whatever it was that he put his money into in the stock market, it obviously turned out well for him. And so now that the Cadillacs are fitted with electronically coded locks and ignitions, "those trick gadgets I don't understand? Well, it doesn't matter: I'm pretty well fixed. Let the kids figure out how to pop them units. Me? I'm all set: I'm mostly retired. You did a great job for me, Counselor, back durin' my active days, there. Thanks to you I was never inside. But there's always a chance, there is always that chance, especially if you try to do something you don't really know how to do. Or you try to do what some ballplayers do, hang on long after you're finished. And then when you get caught doing something like that, something you don't know how to do, right? Then not even Jerry can save you. I kind of don't think I'm gonna put myself in that position—I'm way too old now to do time."

So that in a time-snapshot's about where I was when Henry Lawler attached me like a mechanical arm to do Royce Whitlock's bidding in what then a dead-end case. What I got filled two dark blue plastic milk crates: the stenographic record of the inconclusive inquest, *In re Nichols;* a thick sheaf of written reports and statements of interviews conducted by Royce; a thin envelope of scientific test results; three envelopes of photos that Royce copied for me. And a fat file of newsprint, of course. The papers'd treated first the disappearance of Sandra Nichols—all of the print media appeared to have settled fairly early on the decision to call her by her maiden name, inasmuch as she'd never changed it on her driver's license after any of her marriages, however many there had been—and then the subsequent discovery of her body, matter-of-factly, inside on the metro region pages. The importance of a disappearance/murder to the Boston *Commoner* varies inversely with the distance of the victim's residence (New Hampshire) and the place (Andover) where the body was found, from Boston. But the New Hampshire papers had played it big, top right on the front page. The Manchester *Union Leader* was on top of the collection with the banner headline: SANDRA NICHOLS FOUND DEAD. And the two-line streamer subhead, smaller type: BODY OF ENFIELD SOCIALITE MISSING FIVE MONTHS FOUND IN NEARBY BAY STATE. Wicked, left-wing Massachusetts. Of course she'd been murdered here; what else did she expect?

Altogether the package weighed a little over twenty pounds, but what it amounted to was very little. Later on under my aegis, after I too'd become intrigued, it turned into *Kyle et al v. Wade* (Lucille Kyle, at twenty being the eldest of Sandra Nichols's three children, was named first in the complaint), U.S.D.C., Mass., Civil Docket No. 94-879-F, fighting against the redoubtable Arthur Dean, the absolute shit Royce'd mentioned. And then that misbegotten vicious mongrel criminal matter, disguised as courtly civil case, threatened to grow up into one of the damnedest bloody alley fights I've ever had.

I guess I'm glad now that it came my way. Perhaps I'd been getting complacent. But then again, I hadn't noticed. I certainly hadn't been

by any means bored out of my wits in my newly peaceful and prosperous life, running a genteel and refined quasi-criminal practice out of a
Beacon Hill brick-front, for all the world a somewhat netherworldly
clone of my classmate Roger Kidd's elegantly soft-spoken trusts-and-
estates firm (now in deference to his senior eminence, not to mention
his economic importance to the firm: Kincaid, Bailey, Kincaid and
Kidd) just down the street on the other side, but I wasn't exactly
thrilled, either. What I'd been doing was having a very nice, quiet
time, making what was to me a good deal of money, seeking at my age
(fifty-six) mostly contentment, alone after work in the world. I guess
what I was was somewhat preoccupied, by what I can't be quite sure,
but whatever it was was enough. I hadn't been looking for change, or
excitement. So, had I been asked, I never would have volunteered to
get Royce off Henry's back. But since I hadn't been consulted, just
roughly shanghaied into the job, and had to go along with it. I gave too
little thought to where it might be leading and so I let it take me too
far, falling right in with their little folie à deux, making it into folie à
trois. I'd plan to be born into my next life with more sense, if it
weren't for the fact that then, I suspect, my new life wouldn't be very
much fun.

■   ■   ■   5

Among many significant events of the past quarter century that I and millions of other Bay State residents didn't notice at the time was the 1973 enactment of Chapter 229, Section 2, of the General Laws of Massachusetts. It took effect bright and early January 1, 1974. The reason that I didn't notice it was not because Mack and I'd gotten drunk the night before at the Kevin Road New-Year's-Eve-Bring-Your-Own-[Cheap] Booze Bash. We *had* done that, of course, it being more or less expected, a kind of tradition. All of us were young marrieds who could still drink quite a lot before falling down, having studied that real hard in college, and because most of us were strapped for cash, cheap booze was the best we could afford. Besides, if you got sporty, dug into the egg money and treated yourself to a jug of the good stuff, it'd be gone by the time you went back to the kitchen to make your second round. The motto was "You don't lose your license for *walking* under." The actual site shifted from house to house each year through the neighborhood, except for the Whipples'. They were very nice, unassertive, Seventh Day Adventists who firmly refused to allow liquor in their home, and given certain other regular features of the Bash, there was much to be said for their principled stand. Especially if your house had been the one where the Bash had been held that year, and you awoke to the aftermath on the morning of New Year's Day as head of the clean-up crew, bad hang-over no good excuse. Each year we participated at least one husband would get sloppy drunk and pass out, leaving his nearly as disoriented wife, forgetting everything but her discontents, free to go around get-ting even with him by grabbing other husbands' private parts, once or twice happening on a gentleman also judgmentally impaired by booze and sneaking upstairs with him, rumor had it to give him a blow job. But that sacrifice was [im]purely voluntary on her part, not required to earn the "that slut [fill in name]" title for that particular year. Responsibility for performance of the ritual appeared to have mysteri-ously fallen on just three of the eleven couples; only one of the pairs carried it out each year, but one of those pairs always did. As far as I know they all stayed married; Mack and I, and another cou-ple who joined happily in the equally traditional post–New Year's sanctimonious tsk-tsking of each given year's shameless pair, wound up divorced. Those whom the gods would destroy they first make righteous.

Anyway, the reason I didn't notice the passage of the statute was that I was practicing criminal defense, not civil, tort, law. So the pas-sage of the compensatory Wrongful Death Act, radically changing the centuries-old Common Law we'd inherited from England, had no application to, nor any bearing on, any of the cases in my office that year. A lawyer's not a person who knows the law; a lawyer is a person who's learned how to *find* the law that's needed in a given situation. And also how to *read* it, a correlative that some lawyers overlook, to the sorrow of their clients. But few of us employ that ability until we acquire a client whose case obliges us to do something more ambi-tious than merely keep up with small changes in the specialty familiar to us.

So I know a quite a bit more about the act now, since I had to work it up before I knew what I was doing *In re Sandra Nichols*. If I had not needed to do that, learn exactly what the legislation would enable me to do, and how the courts've interpreted its terms, a time consum-ing but essential chore, I would not have done it. You don't need to do it, in order to follow the case that came out of it, and so I'm not going to inflict very much of it on you.

The oversimplified gist of it is that until the new law was passed, it was a lot cheaper for a careless person to kill a useful citizen than it was to cripple him for life, so that he could no longer work. The old shorthand was that if you ran over a highly paid fellow, you should back up and run over him again, because he wouldn't be in pain or suffer so long and therefore his estate couldn't recover as much in damages. His executor could try to get something for what the poor devil's death really cost his family, but that was about the size of it; they had no real way to get even, such as by cleaning out the evildoer's bank account.

Under the new law, it's a quite different matter. If someone else negligently, willfully, wantonly, or recklessly causes the death of someone you're relied on for love, *or* companionship, *or* financial support, *or* good counsel, or a dry newspaper every morning, almost anything of real importance in the ordinary person's life, you can now sue the happy-go-lucky killer for a whole array of things, and make him wish sincerely not only that he never ran over your loved one but that he himself had never been born: "[T]he loss of reasonably-expected net income, services, protection, care, assistance, society, companionship, comfort, guidance, counsel and advice;" "the reasonable funeral and burial expenses" of your loved or trusted one; and (this is where the clouds parted and a bright light shone down on *In re Nichols*, beginning its gradual transformation into *Kyle et al v. Wade*) "punitive damages in the amount of *not less than five thousand dollars* [italics mine] in such case as the decedent's death was caused by the malicious, willful, wanton or reckless conduct of the defendant or by the gross negligence of the defendant. . . ."

I was reasonably sure that if I could prove somehow that Peter Wade'd bashed his wife's head in with a sock filled with sand, or if, as seemed more likely, he'd hired someone else to do it, almost any judge would find that constituted a malicious, willful, wanton, or reckless act, sufficient to force open the brassbound coffers of Peter Wade's great treasures and compel them to disgorge *a great deal more than five thousand dollars in damages*, in order to punish old Peter, to benefit the heirs of Sandra Nichols.

One more thing and the law lecture's over: If I brought this wrongful death action that Henry Lawler'd in mind, I wasn't going to have to prove *beyond a reasonable doubt* that Peter Wade'd deliberately had his wife's skull crushed, as a DA trying a murder charge would. It would be okay if by some miracle I did contrive to pull that off, but to win I wouldn't have to. I wasn't going to have to find enough evidence to prove the existence of the critical facts to *a moral certainty*—meaning somewhere in the neighborhood of, say, 96 to 97 percent certain, if you want to quantify it. Technically all I needed was enough evidence to make Peter's central part in Sandra's death 51 percent certain: likelier than not that he'd had a hand in it. But I planned to err as far as possible on the side of generosity. When I said that to Royce he looked dour and said: "Yeah, well, don't get your hopes up. I've been living with this thing for damned near a year now, and I can tell you: it's a slippery son of a bitch and it's a thin one. Squirms out of your hands just as soon as you start to think, well, you got it. You get enough evidence to hike the proof up to around fifty-five, fifty-six percent likely, you'll be doing damned well."

On the criminal side there are three things the prosecutor has to prove if the defendant wasn't caught *in* the act, *at* the act, standing in his own bedroom over the hideously mutilated naked body of his wife's lover, with a wild look in his eye and so much slickening blood on his hands he couldn't keep his grip on the maple handle of the hatchet, so that it fell to the floor: Motive. Means. Opportunity.

MOTIVE

Assuming the defendant wasn't *really* nuts—as opposed to retroactively nuts, which amounts to declaring "I must've been out of my mind, because if I wasn't they're gonna really hammer me for this"— and truly didn't know what he was doing, motive is a solid reason to commit the foul deed. Generally—in all the cases I've ever heard of, at least—it's one of five of the Seven Deadly Sins: pride, greed, lust, anger, or envy. Or a combination of two or more of them. I suppose you could argue that the cannibals surviving the Donner party'd killed their dinner partners out of gluttony, unless they then dined moderately on the flesh and dabbed delicately at their lips after ingesting each morsel, but I wouldn't try it, myself. And I can't really imagine how anyone could murder anyone out of sloth. *Let* 'em die, maybe, if they were helpless, out of sheer lazy refusal to attend to their vital needs, but that doesn't constitute murder.

In Peter Wade's case, where it seemed pretty clear what had gone on, but pretty damned hard to prove it, if there had been enough evidence to charge Peter with Sandra Nichols's murder, the prosecutor would probably've proceeded on a theory something like this mortal mixture:

Pride: Royce said Wade'd gone though his whole life acting as though he was above the law or any other silly, irrelevant rules and could do exactly as he chose, with impunity. "Your classic rich kid," Royce said with complete disapproval. "His wishes've always come first. The rest of us're only here in case he needs us, and if he doesn't we're to stay out of his sight and his way."

Lust: Royce believed that Peter'd gotten tired of Sandra, as he had of his previous wives, and found himself a new honey to take her place. "He'd found a new filly to move into that wife stall. Which meant of course that Sandra had to clear out of it, pronto. As she would've done, I'm sure, nice cooperative kid she'd always been, do anything a man asked—'Around-the-world; sixty-nine; hanging from the chandelier; three or four in a bed: anything you'd like to do, in your wildest dreams'—so long as he asked her politely. But Peter, of course, soon as he'd seen his lawyer, didn't *want* to ask, even rudely. Once Bowers reminded him what he'd signed, he didn't want the subject to come up, at all. The mere thought of it curdled his blood."

Anger: Royce's view was that when Peter'd realized what it would cost him to divorce Sandra, under the terms of their prenuptial agreement, he'd become quite upset. "He must've been fucking *enraged*. But not at himself, for insisting that his own family lawyer draw up the damned thing in the first place. Even though Bowers'd told him at the time: 'You really shouldn't do this; this's not a good idea,' or words to that effect, which Bowers swears he did. And then after he'd rejected Bowers's advice, did he get mad at *himself* for being fool enough to sign it? *Oh, no,* absolutely not. When something happens to Peter that he doesn't like, it's always somebody else's fault. Just a matter of figuring out whose. Well, in this case it had to be Sandra, she being the only other person involved in the thing at the time. So then, he'd be pissed off at Sandra: for being smart enough to look at his marital track record before he stumbled onto her, and see for herself how shittily he'd treated his first two wives. How cheap and mean he'd been, when he pensioned those two ladies off. And as a result get some protection for herself and her kids—whom Peter of course was claiming back then that he absolutely adored. So that when her turn'd

44

come to land on Peter's discard heap, she'd go to it a rich lady. At least by the Nichols family's terms, which'd up until then would've been something like 'I still got eight bucks in my pocket, and it's only a week more 'til payday.' In her case, post-Peter, she would've had a real bankroll, six zeroes after the three and the buck sign, somewhere in that prime neighborhood. Sandra was gonna be *rich*. And her kids'd be comfy as well. And all of that delightful stuff at dear Peter's *huge* expense."

Envy: "You could throw a little of that into the poisonous broth. He may've gotten tired of her, but she was still a damned-good-looking girl. She was still only in her mid-thirties, hard's that is to believe, you look at the history she had. But she'd made every minute count, excellent use of her time. She'd been a very busy lady, ever since she was quite young, and she'd learned how to do a lot of things that most men like to have women do to them. And how to do them very well, so that even though they might've had them done before, by other ladies, and later have them done again, also by other ladies, they'd remember her always, as among the very best. So here is Peter, kicking her back out into the world, not only still attractive, and nice—and skillful, can't leave that out: knowin' every nerve, the damned body— the stock in trade she'd always had, but now with her three kids all pretty much grown—not much distraction from them anymore; she could fuck all day long if she liked. Plus which, now she was gonna to be *rich*. Rich on money *his* family'd made. For him, as he saw it, not for some little tramp that he just happened to've married one time, but he's over that now, and now he wants her out."

Greed: Royce paused and licked his chops as any connoisseur would. "The nineteenth-century generations of these families that built up the great New England fortunes were a single-minded and cold-blooded bunch of buccaneers. I take nothing away from them. But they could take a philosophical attitude toward the occasional setback, you know? Around the turn of the century, when the uproar and commotion started about treatin' workmen and young women halfway decently, well, not to say they didn't fight it, fight it tooth and nail, but when they lost, not that they always did, by any means, they were good sports about it. Took their losses and shut up, and went home grinnin' at each other. There was more where that came from, and now they'go get that. They were a bunch of robber-dogs, but they were dogs robust enough to take their lickings and come back to fight another day.

"Their descendants in many ways're rather weak tea, at least compared to them. I know it's not a fair judgment, comparing now to then. There isn't any more, now, where they got their loot, not anymore. And so their descendants, like Peter Wade, as casual as they can afford to be about their lives from day to day, have to understand—he does—that if the principal gives out, the interest does, too.

"You trim three million dollars–plus off Peter's family trust, and you've trimmed a quarter-million or so every year thereafter off Peter's trust allowance. You won't've left him destitute, very far from that. He won't end up behind the counter, wearing a clean uniform, at your local Burger King, asking 'You want fries with that?' But he will notice it, for sure, he takes a hit like that—this year, next year, and in perpetuity. A quarter-million bucks a year out of Peter's trust fund checks, over twenty grand a month, is a concept Peter understands. It's also an idea that does not appeal to him. The prospect of that happening to him, that would have to make him think. Make him think about bad things that he would never, ever, do—unless he had to do them, to keep his reserves intact. And then he would do them.

"Talk about the rock and the hard place: he must've been be*side* himself. He's gotta get his brand on this new heifer, little charmer, otherwise she runs away. She was no mean hand herself at driving a bargain. But to do it, he's got to boot his good wife out the door. She's sure not leavin' on her own. And now it's dawned on him; he sees what happens then. With all of the advantages she's gonna take with her, how much trouble's she gonna have, finding a new man for herself, probably better'n he's ever been? Maybe even someone he knows himself, some pal of his, had his eye on her a long time, just waiting for Peter to find a new girl—knowing sooner or later he's bound to; that's something he's always been good at, and Peter's a creature of habit—and give him a chance to move in. And wouldn't *that* be just neat. Knowing what Sandy was doing on him, suckin' BBs through telephone cables, just like she used to do for poor Peter's peter. If he didn't actually *feel* envy yet, he could sure see it on the horizon.

"See, the temptation you have to avoid at all costs, when you're dealing with Sweet Peter Wade, is to start thinking that Peter, who's got *so* many bad qualities, is also stupid as well. You're wrong when you do that. It isn't so. Peter isn't a stupid man. He does things that look and are stupid, time and time again, but when he really needs to, wants to, he *can* tell a hawk from a handsaw. He doesn't do it very often, maybe, because he's got no need to or he's in a hurry and he just can't spare the time. But when he wants to, when it suits him, he can think ahead. He can do sequential reasoning, just like adults do. And sometimes he actually does it; he figures simple things out.

"Like that if he leaves a good thing unattended, somebody's liable to take it. And even thought he's all through using it, he still doesn't want that to happen. So when he gets tired of one of his toys, his cars or his boats or his houses, he doesn't usually let go of it, for somebody else to enjoy. He's the original dog in the manger. He just puts it away, what he's through with. Keeps all his old toys around, perfectly useless to him, but where he can still keep an eye on them. Make sure no one else's playing with them, having more fun than he used to have, making him wish he had them back.

"Until Sandra came along he'd only done that with his material *things*, never tried it out on one of his women. But as a man grows older, he becomes more so, set in his ways even more. I think what Peter thought was, oh, maybe not real thoroughly, but still, I think he thought: 'Why the hell'm I doing this, turning this lovely piece of ass loose, for some other joker to play with? Some twenty-year-old, nine hard-ons a day, riding her here to Hong Kong? Ordering room-service Dom Perignon, paying for it out of my money? They'll both think they died, went right up to heaven, and I bought the tickets for them. Now that I've made her what she is, or will have, anyway, if I finish the job and divorce her, why the hell should I finance that much gut-grabbing remorse for myself?'

"So, what he tried to do first was stop short of divorce, just leave her and separate, right? Put Sandra on Hold and spend all of his time, most of it at least, with this hot little new number, Marisa, he'd found, 'ninety-two, down at the mad Mardi Gras. He was taking time out from racing his bloody big boat, *Toreador*, in the Southern Ocean Circuit, whatever the hell that might be. A new piece of ass, as round as a peach, and a dee-*light*-ful person, much closer in age to him, too. His favorite age, not his real age, that is, 'case you might've made that mistake: she was eighteen at the time.

47

"But our Sandra's a woman of character. She will have none of that shit. 'No, nothing doing, no way.' Sandra got smart on the street, keep in mind; she knows what to do to protect her corner of it, and she knows how to get it done, too. She tracks him down to where they are staying, this secluded Bahama resort, calls him up on the phone, and very cool says: 'I'm not puttin' up with this crap. You wanna fuck strange, go ahead and fuck strange. You'll look hard and a long time for better'n me, but I can't do nothin' 'bout that. But then you have got to come home. And if you *don't* come home and live here with me, then what you're gonna find yourself doing is coming back home to *court*. 'Cause that's where I'll be taking your sorry ass, dearie, suin' it here to Poughkeepsie. You know what *desertion* is, honey-child? You know what I get for that? I get what that paper you signed says I get, you divorce me or leave me 'thout getting divorced, so if I divorce you, instead of you divorcing me? That doesn't matter one little bit, babe. That's what the paper says.

" 'You don't wanna believe me, Peter, on that, well, that is certainly your privilege. But if you don't believe me, wanna see if I'm right, all you've gotta do's just try me out.' Oh, motive's a piece of cake, this one."

MEANS

The second thing a prosecutor would've had to prove was that the defendant had what it took to commit the crime. This was definitely not the biggest challenge of the case. The poor woman had been hit from behind with a blunt, not to say amorphous, instrument. The medical examiner had estimated its weight at between two and three pounds, compacted by the force of the blow. Whitlock scoffed. "Half of that, do the job easy," he said. "You get half a pound, maybe a pound, of nice, wet, packed sand—plain old dirt, or gravel, or pennies, but I'd take the sand, myself, and I think the killer did, too— whomp her once with it; there, the job's done, just like that. This killer was no dummy, pal. Dump out a pound of sand anywhere, just cut the sock open and pour. Pile of pennies could attract attention. But anyway, whatever you got, pour it into the sock. A calf-length sock, I would say, it was me, so you can knot it and so forth, keep all

48

the weight at the end. Then all you've got left to do is get behind who it is that you wanna kill and get a good arc on it there, bring it down on his head good and hard. You could blow his brains right out through his eyeballs, I bet, you got the right angle on it. And this isn't King Kong's skull that you're crushing here, a half-ton gorilla or something. This's a small woman, five-four or so. She doesn't have great big thick bones, and she doesn't have an armor-plate skull. A half pound of dead weight in a three-, four-foot arc, the poor kid'd never know what'd hit her."

OPPORTUNITY

That was the third thing that a prosecutor would've had to prove—and that I would have to prove, too, but not conclusively, in my unaccustomed guise of civil prosecutor. Royce: "The long and the short of it is that you can't. This is where this case's always gotten hung up. Here and up in New Hampshire. And unfortunately it's not a matter of a weak case up against an absolute defense. Arthur Dean's got nothing that absolutely proves that Peter couldn't possibly've done it. Peter was in the booby hatch, down here in Massachusetts, having a nice rest. Which of course means he was drying out, or so we're supposed to think. But it's a very permissive sanitorium, Glyndebourne Lodge is. Sanctuary for rich drunks. The keepers seem to think their paying guests're sane enough to treat themselves, which raises the interesting question of why the hell then do they need to be paying four thousand dollars a week for board and room at Glyndebourne Lodge. The food's good, but it isn't *that* good, and the wine list they say really stinks. Most of the guests bring their own, fill their car radiators with Smirnoff and their toilet kits with cognac. But that's what Peter was doing, had been doing for almost five weeks, during the week when Sandra got her last big headache, which at least didn't last very long. He'd come back from the islands about a month before that. And then, after he'd been home for a few days, he started a big row. And then after that, he went down to the lodge and checked in. This's three weeks before she was last seen. But since he'd been the one that checked himself in—said his complaint was exhaustion; exhausted from drinking and fucking and gambling, of course, and sailing his great big boat, not from working or anything like that—no doctor involved and so forth, he pretty much had the run of the place.

"Meaning: he could've slipped out and conked Sandy, and then slipped right back in again. Months went by after she disappeared. All we can prove is when she was last seen, not precisely when she was killed. It's possible, more than possible, she'd gone off with someone else, so maybe that person killed her. She was known to do that, after all, before she got married again. She was a girl who liked a good time. And as far as we know, she hadn't had one of those since Peter went south to go sailing. Long time between drinks, as they say. She's known some shifty lads, and Arthur of course will say one of them killed her, all on his own. And Arthur too's got a problem: he hasn't got a witness who can put Peter in the lodge during the whole time, the entire period, every day and every night, when the fatal blow must've been struck. But I think that's where he was. Pretty unlikely, I'd have to say, that he'd take the chance of slipping out to ambush her, and then in the process maybe get himself spotted.

"Besides, that's not the way he does business. Peter doesn't do unpleasant things himself. This is the kind of guy who hires poor people every winter to have the flu for him. I think that's what he did in this case: when he got back from sailing his boat, he hired somebody else to do her, got the whole thing arranged, picked the fight, and then signed himself in at the lodge."

It sounded reasonable to me, and that was what I said. "It is, and that's what's so discouraging," Royce said. "The DAs tell me, both of them, that I don't have a single lead to who that might've been, who did the dirty deed. This did not come as news to me when they first said it, and it won't come as news to me when you've gone through all the stuff three times, and racked your brains into taffy, and then come back and tell me the same thing. I was hoping the DAs wouldn't notice, but they did, so now I have to think, you start getting into it, you'll probably notice too. That I really don't have any evidence who did it, much less a piece of evidence to link the bastard to Peter. That too, that won't come as news. It's a nest of snakes. Peter could've done it, himself. That's within the realm of the possible, and Dean can't prove that he couldn't. But I can't prove that he did. And until I can do that, or prove that he hired someone else, Dean doesn't have to prove a thing.

"So, where does that leave me?" Royce said. "And where does that leave you, now that you're in it with me?" As though he hadn't been the one who'd pestered Henry into dragging me in, but I let it go. "Right up shit's creek with no paddle, is where. All dressed up with no place to go. I was you I would start with the mother, I think."

"I think I will start with the actual crime," I said firmly. "That means I start with your stuff."

■　　■　　■　　**6**

I started with Royce's testimony at the inquest. He was plainly an experienced hand, the kind of unflappable professional witness lawyers on my usual side of the fence dread to see take the stand, because they never say more than they mean to say, and can back it up if allowed to. If you try to trap them into saying more than that, more than they can prove, they'll say it all again, and just *wither* you, which is not the way it's supposed to happen. In your withering cross-examination, you're supposed to wither *him*. The best you can do with one of those mean old birds is to let him get through his testimony on direct with minimum interference from you, and then stage a per-functory two- or three-question cross, so the prosecutor won't be able to argue to the jury that you let the fatal testimony in without "even bothering to cross-examine," thus implying that even you thought what the cop said—about your client being a low-down dirty snake—was the truth. It was going to be a nice change to have one of those guys on my side.

"The medical examiner after conducting the customary post-mortem"—I could visualize Royce on the stand in Henry's bright courtroom in Newburyport, the light from the tall windows opening to the southeast sharpening the edges of the white moldings and pol-ished dark brown railings; the ursine old cop in a familiar situation, if the surroundings themselves were not; comfortable, at ease, his hands folded in his lap, no documents in sight, speaking thoughtfully (though in fact not thinking at all, but saying what he'd first written and thus memorized; you can prevent a seasoned cop from reading his notes on the stand, but you can't stop him from reciting if he knows them by heart), mostly in complete, if verbose, sentences— "reported that because of the condition of advanced decomposition that the body had been in when he received it, he had been unable to fix with certainty the time and date of death, beyond estimating that it had obviously been more than one month but probably less than six. Our initial investigation therefore as is customary initially centered necessarily around the whereabouts of the decedent's estranged husband during all the period when the crime might have been committed. Spouses, especially when the couple is known to have been having difficulties, being the likeliest to have information useful to investigation of the cause and agency of death. In this particular case, the time when the crime might have been committed comprehended an extended period. Our preliminary inquiries indicated that her husband, Peter Wade, at all times during the period when death apparently occurred, had been a patient at, or a registered occupant of, the Glyndebourne Lodge, a private hospital in Bedford specializing in the treatment and rehabilitation of persons suffering from emotional exhaustion and other, similar disorders, usually attributable to and resulting from substance abuse, chiefly alcohol and drugs. We therefore opened other avenues of inquiry, seeking anyone known to the decedent who might have had a reason to prefer that she was dead.

"We were able to determine that the decedent—whom we referred to as 'Sandra Nichols' for the sake of uniformity in our reports throughout our investigation, though her name'd changed several times in her life, as a result of her three marriages, two of which were apparently valid, at least one of which, apparently without her knowledge, was in fact bigamous, but never dissolved, as we determined, at the Registry of Motor Vehicles—that she had, as I started to say, been definitely seen and positively identified at the academy, this'd be the Strothers Preparatory School, by several persons who recognized her and knew her well. Apparently she'd been quite active in the parents' things and so forth that they have been there, ever since her own kids'd first started going to it, seven years before that. Right after her marriage to her husband at the time of her death, Peter Wade. And this would've been during the morning and into the early afternoon of Thursday, May the twelfth. She'd been one of approximately thirty parents taking part in a conference pertaining to a summer reading list and other preparations for the Scholastic Aptitude Tests to be taken the next fall by members of the incoming junior class. We were informed that her daughter, Margaret Cameron, was a member of that class."

"That was the last benchmark you had, Lieutenant? For when she had been definitely seen alive?" the assistant DA had said.

His name was Duncan Cronin. I'd never heard of him. Royce told me he was "all right. Nothing special. Spent most of his time in the district courts, trying chickenshit local cop cases. Important enough stuff, sure, to the victims, people who're actually involved in it, harmed by it: tippin' over headstones; sprayin' swastikas on temples; battin' down mailboxes from moving cars at night. If it's your mailbox or your synagogue, or your family's headstone that gets dumped, well then, that's important stuff, the most important stuff there is. And Cronin will get you justice, so that when the next election comes, you'll reelect Bob Farr again, 'responsive to the public safety needs of the community. Vote to go further with Farr.' But if it's not your whatever-it-is that got damaged, not what you'd exactly call a prison riot class of case, Cronin'd be nowhere in sight. If Farr'd ever had a prison riot in his jurisdiction, he wouldn't've put Dunc Cronin's name down as clean-up hitter in the starting lineup. If you get my point. So, that should tell you something, Bob putting him on the case. If I'd've really had something, enough to hook Sweet Peter, North Shore–New Hampshire socialite, well-known man-about-town Peter, Bob would've given me a genuine star, might've even called his own number. Which would've been okay by me. Bob was a good old rough-and-tumble ADA himself for eight, ten years or so, 'til Frank Hammond lost his head and ran for AG one year—somebody real good in a scrap, to ram the thing right up Peter's arse. But I didn't have enough. He knew that and I knew it, too, and he knew that I knew it. The inquest was just dealing with formalities, getting it down on the record, where the public could see it, that the reason Bob wasn't prosecuting Peter Wade for murder was because crack state police investigator Royce Whitlock hadn't made a case, a good, prose-

cutable case, in the murder of poor Sandra Nichols. He was hangin'
me out to dry, 'stead of him. For that exercise, Cronin was okay.
He'd do."

"No," Whitlock had said to Cronin, "it was more in the nature of
being the first one, the first benchmark, that we had. We knew she'd
been alive, definitely in good spirits, giving no sign of apprehension or
fear that anyone who saw her could recall observing. So we had her
definitely alive, for sure, on May twelfth, and the body was found on
October twentieth. So that meant we had five months and one week
to account for her movements and those of anyone who might've had
a motive to want her dead during those, oh, roughly twenty-one
weeks."

"A lot of ground to cover," Cronin had said.

"A lot," Whitlock had said, "but we've had cases we've had more,
where even more time was involved between the last confirmed sight-
ing of the victim alive and when we found the body. But we've still
managed to track the matters down to the point where we were satisfied that the case could be closed. Or inactivated. And then, occasionally, reactivated. By our Cold Case division. But it's really *difficult*,
when you have to do it that way. It takes a long time, much longer'n it
does when you've got a fresh kill to work with, 'fore the person who's
responsible's had a chance to wash his hands off, change his bloody
clothes, ditch the murder weapon, get his nerves calmed down, go
over his story. Maybe fabricate an alibi. And so forth.

"But it's not impossible; it can be done. The computers help a lot,
cross-checking all kinds of records—telephone, motor vehicle, wel-
fare, disability pensions—on the CD-ROM files."

"So, when you say that you've reached a point in one of these
tough cases where you were 'satisfied that the case could be closed, or
inactivated,'" Cronin had said, "what do you mean by that? That
you'd caught the killer? Is that what you mean?"

"Oh, no," Whitlock had said. "The only places where the case
always ends with the the killer getting caught're the ones you see on
TV. No, what I mean by that is this: either we've been satisfied that
the killer's either dead himself, or otherwise's permanently left the
jurisdiction. We don't know where he is at all. We're never going to
find him. Or that while we may have a pretty good idea who dunnit, as
they say, put it that way, he was either smart enough or lucky enough,

or a combination of both, to do it in such a way that we can't *prove* he did it. This also happens, time to time, I'm sorry to say. People *do* get away with murder, here and everywhere else. Nothing you or I or anybody else can do about it. And then the chances are that barring a deathbed confession or something of that kind—which is another thing that's lots more common on TV than I've ever found it to be in real life—there probably never will be. Anything that anyone can do about it.

"And then there are some cases," he had said, "there are some cases where we know from the very beginning that we're never going to find out who it was that did it. No matter what we do. I'm glad to say there aren't too many of those, cases where the body's that of a derelict or someone with no known next of kin and no real friends we know about, no one who cared about them. Those damned things could wear a man out. The homeless people, you know? Those kinds of cases could break your heart, you let yourself think about them too long. No way to identify them really, except by the name they went by. Which is often not their own. 'Bobby,' 'Billy,' 'Romeo,' 'Spitball.' Dental charts? Forget about it. Chances are you're never going to ID a guy when a nickname's all the name you've got to go on and his teeth're all rotted out, a long time ago, he's been gumming any food he ate, but mostly drinking the booze, no need to chew white port. Missing person report? What good're they? The bums got no real connection with another person even when they were alive, much less now that they're dead. That was one great idea we had when we let all the drunken, druggie crazies out of the institutions, so they could live free, on their own. Yeah, live free on the streets, like rats. Then die homeless and nameless. Die on the street worse'n most dogs die, even ones get put to sleep. Most dogs at least got names." Royce was going to require a bit of discipline from me before I put him on the stand in any case I brought; otherwise he'd either get it from opposing counsel or the judge, hurting our cause either way. Note that I'd started calling it "ours." It's not a good idea to blow cordite fumes at old warhorses, if you want them to stay quiet and calm.

"But there're still the cases where after a very long time's gone by—in one case I had, we finally solved, more'n eight years'd gone by in that one—after the crime was committed, we've come up with something that tied up the loose ends and allowed us to make an arrest. And then follow it through to conviction. You don't want to make an arrest, charge somebody with murder in the first degree, unless you're pretty sure that you can prove it. For one thing it makes everybody involved in the prosecution look stupid, when someone gets acquitted on that one. And for another thing, once you make your move, if you don't nail him, well, after he's acquitted he can call a press conference and confess to it, if he wants. And there's nothing you can do, double jeopardy and all. Except stand there and look like a fool. I never had that happen to me so far, thank God, but it has happened to guys. I've seen it. And as long as you're doing what I'm doing in these things, you're always conscious of it, always aware that it could. So you're always, you're always pretty careful when you recommend making a bust in a long-term murder case. Mistakes can be fatal, too, you know. Not to just people—careers."

"Yes," Cronin had said. "But now, getting back if we may to the Nichols murder case that all of us're concerned with here. . . ."

Arthur Dean had intervened. "Objection, Your Honor," he'd said. "I assumed that this proceeding, that one of the things that we're all here in fact to ascertain is whether this event in question was in fact a murder. So far there's no proof of that. Let's not assume it before any evidence even comes in."

"Your Honor," Cronin had said, meaning *Oh, really*.

"There're media here, Mister Cronin," Henry said. "*Murder*'s a term of art and Mister Dean is quite right. It hasn't been proven in this case. I don't want to see or hear that word cropping up in the headlines when I read about this in the morning, or see it on TV tonight. If there's ever a criminal case brought on this in Massachusetts, the jury will come from this region. I don't want them preconditioned to think of it as a quote-unquote murder case, think that a murder's already been proven, before they even sit down."

Mister Cronin then had let his temper get the better of him. "Well," he'd said, "all due respect to the court, Your Honor, but I doubt very much that anyone's ever going to contend that Sandra Nichols sneaked up behind herself, hit herself on the head with some blunt instrument, makeshift blackjack or something, hard enough to shatter her skull and kill her with one blow, and then stuffed herself in a green garbage bag and threw herself in a swamp."

"Your Honor," Dean'd said, having gotten to Cronin and now

exploiting the advantage he'd gained—I could hear the exquisite pain in his voice, months after he'd made the objection I was reading— "the judge who tries this case, if there ever is such a case, is going to have to make the Commonwealth try to prove every single element of that case. Whether it's against my client or somebody else. In the interests of saving the court's time and everyone else's as well, I've been letting my learned brother lead the witness here, all over the place, but I can't just sit here like a rubber plant and let him presume facts not in evidence that would establish a felony crime. That would be going too far."

Cronin had then backed down, at least having the brains not to be a sore loser, realizing he'd been soundly beaten. "I'll substitute 'homicide,' Your Honor," he had said. "Mister Dean does have a point, I'm afraid. A most technical point, but he has it. That was a slip on my part. I won't let it happen again."

"Good idea, Mister Cronin," the judge had said. I could see Henry shaking his head and taking up his pen, looking down at his notes. "Completely as you please."

"Lieutenant Whitlock," Cronin had said, "let me rephrase my question. Having established fairly early that Sandra Nichols had been seen alive by several people on May twelfth of last year, what did you do next in your attempt to narrow down the dates on which she had clearly been alive?"

"We followed standing operating procedure in all such cases," Whitlock had said. "This consists first of determining who the decedent's friends and relations were, which you usually do by starting with the public records that you know have to exist, and then working your way through the leads that you pick up until you get the names and whereabouts of her relatives and friends—you get the names of friends from family—that saw her regularly during the period of, usually the last several months of his or her life. Because you don't always see your relatives or all your friends all that often. Some of them for years, if you didn't get along that good, or you had a falling-out, which people will do sometimes, you know; people will do that. Or if one of you moved away. But in this case: a year. Because apparently around five months had elapsed between the time that she disappeared and the time when the body was found. At that point, as far as we knew then."

"I see," Cronin had said, "and if you would please state the names of the persons you thus identified, and how you identified them, and then talked to, in that respect."

"Yes," Whitlock had said. I could guess what he'd done then, because he had done something like it when I'd asked him my preliminary, uninformed questions about the case. He'd unbuttoned his pewter-colored suit jacket—he had two "court suits," as he called them, both gray, one lightweight and one heavy, all he really needed since he was seldom on the stand for more than one day in any trial, and for such emergencies he had two blazers he could wear—and produced a small spiral notebook and a glasses case from his inside pocket. He had opened the case and put on his glasses. He had put the case back into his pocket and opened the notebook. He had cleared his throat. The sound of the mills of justice grinding, exceeding fine, exceeding slow, would have become faintly audible in the courtroom, had anyone bothered to notice. "Having established the identity of the decedent as that of Sandra Nichols, we entered that name into the computerized regional data bank and information retrieval system maintained under terms of the New England State Police Compact, compiled in part from the Registry of Vital Statistics in the State Department of Health, and from that established the following:

"The decedent was identified as Sandra Marie Nichols, DOB August four, nineteen fifty-seven, at Worcester, Mass., mother Evelyn Wynn Nichols, father Andrew Mark Nichols, home address One twenty-four Ridge Street, Clinton, Mass. Father's occupation: U.S. Merchant Marine. Mother's occupation: restaurant employee.

"Decedent recorded as receiving work permit at age sixteen, August four, nineteen seventy-three, at Clinton High School and withdrawing from said Clinton High School, January two, nineteen-seventy-four. Also recorded receiving General Equivalency Diploma, Bristol High School, Bristol, Rhode Island, June eight, nineteen seventy-seven.

"Two records, Clinton, Massachusetts, show issuance of marriage license to Sandra Marie Nichols, home address Eighteen River Street, Apartment four, Paxton, Massachusetts, and Lucas Walter Kyle, home address Eighteen River Street, Apartment four, Paxton, Massachusetts, March six, nineteen seventy-four. Bridegroom's occupation:

mechanic, Wilson Ford, Paxton. Bride's occupation: restaurant employee. Marriage performed by Reverend Harold Clancy, M.S., justice of the peace, Tabernacle Church of All Holiness, Hopewell, Mass., March eight, nineteen seventy-four. Witnesses Danny Hopkins, Linda Lee Merrill.

"Register of Vital Statistics, as I've said, record birth of Lucille Sandra Kyle, May twenty-nine, nineteen seventy-four, Worcester, Mass., mother Sandra Nichols Kyle, Eighteen River Street, Apartment four, Paxton, Massachusetts, father Lucas Walter Kyle, unemployed.

"Now," Whitlock'd said, "that's not where we stopped our initial investigation of records, Counselor. Way before, in fact. But I think it might be helpful if I summarized, or stated, rather, every so often as we go along here, what we were able to determine by our field investigation of the data we'd acquired up to that point. It might make a lot more sense. Because quite a lot of names get involved here, and it's kind of hard to keep them straight unless you've been working with them, you know? It can get pretty confusing."

"Your Honor?" Cronin had said.

"I certainly don't object," Judge Lawler had said. "Mister Dean?"

"Fine by me, Judge," Dean had said, "I'll take all the help I can get."

"If you would, then, Lieutenant," Cronin had said.

Whitlock had produced a thick sheaf of documents, folded lengthwise in half, the ones he had now copied for me. He had said: "We were able to locate Evelyn Wynn Nichols, now known as Evelyn Streeter, wife of one Howard Streeter, at Fourteen Ingersoll Grove, Springfield. In her case, as in the case of each of the prospective witnesses we located, the interview was tape-recorded with the witness's permission, and the tapes were then transcribed in our office. This is a verbatim copy of the transcription of the interview with Evelyn Streeter.

"She identified herself as the mother of Sandra Marie Nichols, born during her first marriage to Andrew Mark Nichols. She informed us Andrew Nichols, and I'm quoting here: 'got himself hired on to a small freighter named the *Biscay Flier*, Panamanian registry, home port of Torremolinos—that's in Spain—bound for Mayaguez, in Puerto Rico, out of New York, in the spring of nineteen fifty-eight,' and that was the last she'd seen of him. 'Got no idea what became of him,' she said. 'Never made that much effort to find out more, either. We hadn't been getting along all that good. I was kind of relieved, as a matter of fact, when he didn't show up again. I was kind of afraid that he might.

" 'Year or so later, I was with Kendall. Or Ken was with me. We was never actually married. Didn't seem like it was necessary. Besides, Ken wasn't divorced. But he moved in anyway, that little place I'd had with Andy. That little apartment on Ridge Street. That was a nice little apartment, very cozy. Comfortable. I kept it very tidy. Had these little café curtains on brass rods in all the rooms. But they was different colors. Red in the kitchen. Dark green in the bedroom, to sort of keep the light out, you know? In the mornings, so you could sleep. And white in the living room–dining room. Blue, light blue, in the bathroom. I made them myself. I was always happy there. Except sometimes because of the man that I happened to be living with there at the time, if we didn't happen to be getting along. But the apartment was always nice. Anyway, Ken just moved in. Not that I minded, I mean. He helped me out some with the rent. But not all that much, 'cause he couldn't. Oh, Ken had a good enough job, I don't mean that, foreman at Miller and Best down in Grafton. I met him one night at the diner. That was a good steady job, and he made pretty good money, but he still had the wife, and she took a chunk out of his pay. And what was left, well, that didn't last long, and it didn't go very far. See, that man was death on the horses. If there was a horse race goin' on somewhere, so help me God, goin' on anywhere in the *world*, and he heard about it, well then, he hadda get down on it. And he was no good at all at pickin' the horses. He couldn't pick horses for shit. He was simply no good at all. I tried to tell him this, tried many times, but he wouldn't listen to me. You know what that is, when a person gets like that, just gambles his money away? I'll tell you what it is: it's a *disease*. That's all it is: a *disease*.

" 'So all of his money, or most of it at least, he ended up payin' to bookies. I got fed up with it after a while, and threw the bum out on his rear end. I'm workin' my own butt off there now, down at Queen City Diner, for nickels and dimes there, you know? And supportin' the three of us there, me myself, and Sandy, and him—because that really is what I was doin', you know; *he* wasn't bringin' anything home, just *throwin'* the money away. I tell you, it began to get on my nerves.

The only reason it took me so long was how good the man was to Sandy. He really treated her good.'

"She told us after she kicked Ken out, she decided to get her life all straightened out, and got divorced from Andy. 'Which cost me three hundred bucks, for what I still don't know. Still had no idea of where he was, or have any in fact to this day. Never heard from him again. I'm not sure what year that was, but Sandy was around six or maybe she was seven. I know she'd started school by then, in first or second grade. So this would've been around, oh, sixty-three or -four, somewhere around in there. And then I didn't live with anyone for quite a while. I didn't have a man. It was as if, well, you know, here I'd made myself all legal, gone to all that trouble and so forth, and then once I'd done it, that was it: the bastards all went away. I didn't have no more new bidders.'

"I'll tell you what I thought, I was talkin' to her," Royce told me, "I thought it might've been because she didn't smell so good, you know? That the men all stopped coming around?" I laughed. "No, I mean it," he said. "This woman didn't smell very good. She'd splashed a lot of perfume, cologne, whatever it was, all over herself, but that just added to the problem. What she really needed was a genuine bath. I don't know if she was always like that, kind of fragrant, before she let herself get fat, when she still had her nice little body and all the boys overlooked what they smelled in order to fuck what they saw, but this woman: when I saw her, she wasn't clean."

" 'I couldn't figure it out,' " the transcript said. " 'I still had my nice little figure; I was just as friendly as always. But I could not get a man. Not even a quick date with a married man, you know? Not even that much came my way anymore. Well, not very often, at least. If I averaged one date every two weeks, that was the best I could do. It was very discouraging for me, because you know, I really like to go out. I never made any secret of that: I like to have a good time. I couldn't figure it out. I got very depressed. I might as well've stayed home, saved my money, all the difference the divorce made to me. I made out better when I was married. More often, anyways. I often wondered if that might've been it, been the explanation, you know? That being someone else's wife like I was all those years, before, if that was what attracted them. Forbidden fruit, you know? Or maybe that they were just thinking: "Well, she ain't gonna take no chances here, get us both in trouble." I never did really know.

" 'But anyway, it was just me and Sandy there, until she was in high school, I think. Maybe last year of junior high. And then I started seeing Rudi.'

"She said she didn't know, that she wasn't sure," Whitlock had said. "She said: "It could've been like that, could've happened like Sandy said. I know that, 'cause Rudi always liked the young chicks. He made no secret of it, that he liked the younger girls. And this was about the time that Sandy started growing up, and it didn't take her long. She had herself a real nice little figure by the time she was fourteen. It would've tempted him, I know, would've any man. But it also could've been that it was nothing like she said. I know her and Rudi didn't get along, never got along at all. Matter what I said or what I did. And it could've been that he didn't do a thing, never did a thing to her, and she wanted him to, and then when he wouldn't, decided: "All right then, you lousy son of a bitch, I'll fix you then with my mother." Because see, I hadn't lost my looks then yet, hadn't put on so much weight so I looked like I do today. Fortunately for me, Howie don't mind, says he likes me this way.

" 'But back then when I was younger, when she was still in school, well, I still looked pretty good. I was *slender*, was what I was. And I know from things she said, Sandy sort of let slip out, that some of her little boyfriends, also, they thought I still looked pretty good. So it could've been, you know, that she thought we were competing, or something like that? I seen this thing they had on "Oprah"—think it was "Oprah" anyway; it was one of them; "Sally Jesse," maybe; know it wasn't "Donahue"—where I guess it's very common that this sort of thing goes on. Mothers and their daughters, you know? Competing the same man? Sometimes they're even *sharing* them. Sharing the man, I mean. It goes on a lot, I guess, and half the time it's going on, they don't even *realize*, or one of them may not at least, *that* it's going on. Don't know they're doing it. Or so they say they didn't, at least, when they're on the shows. I never would've dreamed. And if she couldn't, well, get Rudi, take Rudi away from me, well then she would turn me on him, that he made a move on her, so that I would kick him out. Or also, and I read this someplace, I forget where I seen it, another thing it could've been was that for quite a while there before Rudi came, it'd been just me and her, and she liked it that way. Liked it better'n she did, when Rudi moved in with us. You never know what's going through a girl that age's mind. There's just so much going on in there, sex just starting up and all, and everything like that, all going on at once. I was never really sure. But it's always bothered me.

" 'But anyway she comes to me one night, she's still in school, and I don't know where Rudi was, why he wasn't there, but Rudi wasn't there, working late or something, and she tells me she can't stand it anymore, she can't live like this no more, and she is moving out. She's going to live with Linda Lee, them two was best friends, and Linda Lee's mother'd said that it was all right with her if Sandy moved on in with them. So I said: "*Sandy,*" because naturally I was upset, "why're you doing this, you're moving out on me? I've given you a good home here, taken care of you since you was a tiny little baby, just a little baby girl. It was us two against the world. I've treated you real good. What *is* it, baby, going on?"

" 'And she tells me, she says: "Oh come on now, Mom, you do so know. Don't play dumb with me here. You know what is going on, and why I'm doing this. I told you and I told you: He won't leave me alone. He's looking at me all the time, always brushing up against me, like you know, he just wants some coffee and he though he could get by? He thought he had room enough? But he just happened to've rubbed up against my ass? Or he just happens, pass my room, while I'm in there for five minutes before I go out, just getting my *clothes* changed? Yeah sure, I know, that's all it is; you're right, I'm really stupid. No I'm not—I don't believe that shit. And now it's gotten to the point where I'm afraid to go to sleep, or I'll wake up there in the dark and he'll be in bed with me, and what the hell do I do then? He's bigger'n me, Mom, he's way bigger'n I am, and he's lots stronger than you are, stronger'n both of us. So even if I scream for you, and you come to help me out, which I know that you won't do because you always side with him? All he'll do is knock me down and then he'll beat you up, and then he'll get right back on me, rape me in my own bed. I got to get out of here, Mom, you didn't leave me no choice. It's either him or me, Mom, here, and okay, so you won't make him leave. So well then, I'll leave myself." And that was what she did.

" 'After that I only saw her down Queen City, when we happened to draw the same shift because somebody got sick or something, or we had an overlap from both working overtime. And that wasn't very often 'cause I had seniority, and I always took the day shift because that's when Rudi worked, the plant, and naturally I wanted to be home when Rudi was. He was always very particular about that, that I was there when he got home. But Sandy being still in school and her first year on the job, which I helped her get it there, she was always working nights. And that was where she first met Luke. Her first husband, Lucas Kyle, working the night shift.

" 'I thought she was a really lucky girl, running into Luke like that. He seemed to me like he was, would be, well, a very classy guy. And I know it can happen; it can happen like that, sure. But it very seldom does. That you're serving the pot roast and the custard pie and coffee and then all of a sudden, *well*, look what the cat just dragged in. This classy guy just walks right in, right in front of you. And he's just about your *age*, and he doesn't even have a *wife*, and so you two both fall in love. It can happen that way. But I'd been working in that place a lot of years before that—just like I'm working now, out here; I've worked all my life—and it very seldom does. You very seldom see it. She did bring him around to meet me, at least, when she knew Rudi wouldn't be there, and we had a little chat, made ourselves a little drink, and I thought Luke was great. I didn't even mind when she told me she was moving out of Linda Lee's and moving into his place with him, over Ridge Street there in Paxton; I would've done the same thing, too. I was sure it would work out.

" 'It was even all right with me when she come to me and told me that she missed her period, missed *two* of her periods and she didn't want to have an abortion—Tabernacle Holiness, which he was, so she joined with him; they are really real dead set against that kind of thing—so she hadda marry him. I just said, well, I told her, I said: "Sandy, that's *all right*. That's what I hadda do, you know, when I found out I'm having you. I felt the same way. And lemme tell you," I said this, I actually said it, "Luke is a much better man'n Andy ever was. Even if he was your father, Andy was a no-good bum. But Luke

65

is a good man. If it's his baby that you're having, you should do all right." I even think she was surprised, when I said that to her. Like she thought that I'd get mad. But I didn't, not at all. I was really happy for her.' "

Then there had been a luncheon recess. In my office it was early evening, the early spring darkness hard and more like a held-over winter dusking, a clear chill cover over Beacon Hill. Meredith had left for the day and I was by myself. I got up from my desk chair, went into the kitchenette, and got a Heineken from the refrigerator. One of my new clients the year before had appraised the office and calculated roughly—also accurately—what it was costing me. Then he said: "This's silly, you know, all of this expense. You could have space in our building, eight-sixty a foot, and clerical thrown in. Most of your work you do for us, or companies like us. Which we'll still let you do. So, why throw your dough away on this? It makes no sense at all."

Which we'll still let you do. Nobody *lets me* do anything. "I'll give it some thought," I'd said, without any plans to do so. My father was a small-town pharmacist who categorically refused to sell out and take a salary from a national drugstore chain. He ran his own damned little drugstore, fasting, feasting with the rest of the small businessmen in town. "I know I won't throw me out" was what he always said. "I know I can trust myself, to do a good day's work. I know I'll never fire me, and if I call in sick some day, I won't need a doctor's note. I don't make much money, maybe, but no one on this earth's ever owned me." The blood was coming up in me. I had a brand-new case. I raised a glass to dear old Dad. I mean it; I really did.

■   ■   ■

ow if you would, Lieutenant," Cronin had said, "referring to your reports, tell us whether Evelyn Streeter had any other comments that she offered to you generally on the subject of Sandra Nichols's first husband, Lucas Kyle."

"That's affirmative," Royce had said. "I mean: excuse me. Yes, she did."

"And would you tell us, please, what those comments entailed," Cronin had said.

"Yes," Whitlock had said. "She said, this being Evelyn Streeter, said: 'I still can't figure out what it was that really happened between Sandy and Luke. I thought they was ideal. The ideal couple, you know? Like what I wished I could've been, if things'd worked out right for me. And here they was, they *had* it, had it right there in their hands, and what was it they did with it? Well, they blew it, naturally. It's like, you know, we just can't stand it, something turns out right. We just can't stand to just be happy, and just thank our lucky stars. No, we got to go and screw it up, and make a mess of it, 'cause that's . . . it's like that's the only time we really feel alive. When we're miserable. It's like we've got this *need* for it, almost. And if there isn't any misery in our lives right now, they must've run out of it or something, 'fore they got to us, well then we'll go and make some more, it isn't very hard, and then that is what we do. It's really *heart*breaking. It's enough to break your heart.

"'I talked to both of them about it, Luke come by to see me at work when he knew Sandy'd be off, and I talked to her when she came in as I was going off. But if they hadn't've done that, I would've made it my business, to corner them and talk. I could not've rested. But it didn't do no good, not a particle of good. He said this and she said that, and then he said the other thing, and then she said this to him. And . . . oh hell, I don't know. The more I listened to the two of them, the less I knew about what the hell was going on. Or'd gone on, 'd be better, since whatever it'd been that'd gone on between them was pretty obviously over. You get my meaning there. I mean: There wasn't any fixing it. No possible repairs. Their marriage was plumb over. I seen that happen lots of times, and not just to me either. It does happen, like it, lump it; some people just can't get along, no matter what they do. And no matter what nobody else does, either, they will still not get along. Because they can't, that's all, they just can't get along.

"'Basically what'd happened was he'd done the same damned thing again. That he'd done with Sandy. Not that Sandy was the first one that he done it with, not saying that, but at least as far as we know, she was the last one 'fore he was married. To her. This next time was up in Palmer, and it was *after* he was married. Which is a *completely* different thing. So it wasn't the same thing at all, wasn't the same thing. A single man out scoutin' 'round, doing what he wants, seein' how much he can get and still have time to zip his pants up and take off 'fore he gets caught. Well, there's plenty that'll tell you: He should do it, all he wants. Or all he can, 'd be more like it—all of those guys lie a lot, tell you all the sex they had, and half of it's not even true. That's what I've always thought, at least, and no one's convinced me otherwise, not to this very day. Anyway, that's what they think, and make no secret of it: a man should have all the fun he wants. And I'm not sure they're wrong. Leave him do it, he's still single, probably good for him, get it out his system. Settle him down later.

"'But once he's married then: look out. Then he's got to stay at home. Hang around the ranch. None of this damned *business*, chasin' wimmen every night. That don't go no more. If that was what he wanted, wanted keep on doin' there, then that was what he should've done, no gettin' married there, gettin' some girl's hopes up and all. That just isn't right.

" 'But that's just what Luke there did, what he'd gone and done. Parked his truck in the lot out in the back there and went into a Friendly's restaurant, have himself a cheeseburger. Now there's nothing wrong with that; I'm not saying that. A poor man's got to eat, you know; people do it all the time. Even married people. And there sitting by herself right up at the counter is this perky little number who's the manicurist there, whatever she was, over Chicopee. And he takes one look at her, and all his promises go *poof*. Just like he never made them, man forgot his wedding vows. That was it pure and simple. And *she* forgot what *she* was there for, waitin' for her boyfriend—or her husband; could've been, all I know about it. Just like a couple of hot horny dogs they was, I guess, just couldn't wait to take all their clothes off and get to it, humpin' away. And the next thing you know happened, he was comin' back to Paxton for his clothes and stuff, and goin' back out there and movin' in with her. Men really are such dogs, you know? And women like her don't help none either, come right down to it, in the end.

" 'So anyway, I still did what I could. I tried, the best I could. At first I tried, I tried to see if maybe I could get some kind of sense banged into Sandy's head. I called her up one night when I knew that she'd be home. See, this next-door neighbor of hers, lived in the same building with her and with Luke, when he was there, and when Sandy hadda work and Luke was late getting home—which of course we all now wonder if what kept him late was *work*, or some cute hairdresser, maybe, out in Holyoke, or some other little chippy that he met on one his runs—well, this next-door woman? She would babysit for Lucy. When Sandy hadda go to work and Luke didn't get home yet. Wouldn't take no money, either; did it purely as a favor. Said she liked the little kid. Lucy called her "Rama." I was "Grandma" to her, 'course, but she knew Rama better. Naturally she would've, right? Spent more time with her. But Thursday nights, her and her husband was in these two separate bowling leagues, see? Him in one down at Worcester and her in one right in town. I think it was one in town, may've been the next town over. But that don't matter much, I guess; the net result of all this was she was not available those nights and couldn't babysit. And so as a result of that Sandy couldn't work no

Thursdays if Luke wasn't there at home by six, to take care of the kid. So after he left and he wasn't there anymore, I knew he wouldn't be. So that was when I called her and asked could I come over. And she said, "Sure, come right ahead." Like she didn't care or not. But I went over anyway. It was worth a try.

" 'It didn't do no goddamned good,' she said. 'Didn't do no good at all. Sandy had her mind made up, an' she just wouldn't listen. Sandy was a stubborn girl, even when she was still young, just a little kid. She'd get something in her mind, get her mind made up, and didn't matter what you said, you'd never get it out. "It isn't gonna matter, Ma, it won't matter what you say. I'm not gonna take him back, even if he begs and pleads. He gets down on his bended knees and says he made a big mistake, and will I please take him back? It won't do him any good, any good at all.

" ' "Ma, when we was down in Melville, that time at the base there, Ma? When we're in the Navy? We had that nice little place in the apartment complex down there and I fixed it up myself? Fixed it all up myself? You was down. You saw it. You seen what I did there. Right after he came back from Great Lakes Training Station and he gets this great assignment? That at first I thought was great? Rhode Island, close to home? Well, it turned out after all that it was *not* so great for me. Here I'm having such a hard time, with the new baby and all, and I'm going to classes nights so I can get graduated there, like you always said I should, and you know what he's doing, while I'm doing all of that? Think he appreciates it, all the stuff I do? He does not. He's out tom-cattin' on me, gettin' his damned end wet in some other goddamned broad. He's got this other honey that he met, the Newport Creamery, and when I think he's not home 'cause he put in for another goddamned extra-duty gig that gets him promoted faster, get more pay for us—or so he's always tellin' me, like what the hell do I know?—he's really over her apartment that she shares, two other girls, bangin' her ass off. Just like both her roommates're banging married sailors too, just like she is him. Three whores in the same crib. I tell you, Ma, like you told me, and I wished to God I listened: All men're dogs and we're just hydrants, all we are to them. Can't trust 'em, every time. You should've told me that. And don't tell me you don't know it, either. You've *got* to know it. You *must've* found it out yourself, the kind of life you've had and that now I'm having, too. I don't see why you didn't tell me. Should've told me that.

" ' "Or maybe you did and I didn't get it, had to find out for myself. Well all right, I found out, all right, found out for myself. And I'm never gonna forget. Now he's gone and done this to me, like after he just slapped me in the face or somethin', told me he found somethin' better, then he thinks if he just begs, I will take him back? Well, you know me pretty good: what you think I'm gonna do?" ' "

"I asked Mrs. Streeter," Whitlock had said, "whether if what she was saying, if in fact she knew, that Kyle had hit his wife. And she said: 'No, he didn't do that. Least I don't think he did. That was just her expression, you know? That Luke'd insulted her. But I don't think he ever actually *hit* her. Least she never said he was, doing that to her, and I never saw no sign, he's doing that to her. No sign he was beating her, no sign of that at all.

" 'Keep in mind about her now: She'd seen what Rudi was like, and when she was then still pretty young, but she still made up her own mind, that he was a threat to her. And so she moved right out. She would not have stood for that, if Luke was hitting her. I think she would've thrown him out, the first time he ever did it. And then she would've called the cops and gotten a court order to keep him away from her. And if that didn't do it, if he still came around, well, maybe then the butcher knife, something along that line. Sandy wouldn't take no shit. She never took no shit at all, not from anyone, and she would not have stood for that.' "

Whitlock had evidently paused and cleared his throat. "Would you like some water, lieutenant?" the judge had said. I could see Henry pouring a glass from the carafe on his bench and castering his chair over to the witness stand, Royce accepting it gratefully and drinking about half of it. "Thank you, judge," he had said. "This can be kind of dusty work."

"Yes," Henry had said, "well, you keep that there, and if you find you need some more, I'll have one of the officers supply you with a pitcher. Now, you just take your time."

My guess is that Whitlock had then squared his shoulders and swallowed several times. He had glanced down at his papers and then looked up expectantly at Cronin.

"Well . . . *yes*," Cronin has said, retrieving his wits from wherever they had gone. "And whether, Lieutenant Whitlock, that pretty much completes what Mrs. Streeter had to say about the period during which her daughter, Sandra Nichols, was involved with Lucas Kyle."

"Pretty much," Whitlock had said. "She had quite a lot to say about how 'Sandy was always such a good mother, always took such good care of Lucy, took good care of all her kids, watched them like she was a hawk. Even though it could be hard, all by herself except for them, and working, and like that.' But as far as Kyle's concerned, yeah, that about does it. The only other thing would be that I asked her how much contact Sandy had with him, after they were divorced, and she said as far as she knew the only times they were saw each other had been when he fell behind in his child-support payments.

" 'And every time he did that,' " Whitlock had said, looking at his papers again—I could tell because the quotation was verbatim in my copy of his report—" 'it really pissed her off, that he would do that to her, he would get behind on them. And that would mean she'd have to get docked in her pay so she could take him back to court and get the judge to yell at him, and threaten him with jail. Because, see, that was all she asked of him, when they went in for the divorce, was the child support. And it wasn't even very much, thirty bucks or so a week; that was all he hadda pay. See, Sandy never asked him for no alimony, there.' That's what Mrs. Streeter said.

" 'Her lawyer told her and *I* told her: she was being headstrong, foolish, acting like that with her pride, but she wouldn't listen to us. *"No,"* she would say to you, if you brought it up. "I don't *want* none of his goddamned money for myself. Just for the kid, that's all. If he'll just do that much. *I'll* take care of me." That was what she said. Just let him off the hook like that? I told her that was wrong. That he had the responsibility for her not graduating high school, which she would've done there if he had not've knocked her up. So that now what she had in front of her was the kind of life like I had, after the same thing happened to me when I got involved with that bastard Andy, let him get my legs apart. And after that, when he run out, the only job that I could get was waitressing or something like it, hard work that doesn't pay that good. I wasn't qualified. He got you into this when you let him get into you. And you should learn something from what happened to me that way: you should make him pay.

" 'But she said: "No, I know this guy, Ma, I lived with him for a while. Not as long as I expected, but long enough, you know, to get to know some things about him. And one thing that I know about him's this: You shouldn't ask him for too much. Because in lots and lots of ways, he's still like a little boy, very soft and weak. He goes real easy on himself, and if he gets to thinking someone's making things too hard, well, they don't get nowhere at all—Luke'll be nowhere around—they'll just be talking to themselves.

" 'If he can do what he should do without it *bothering* him too much—so he doesn't really *feel* it, doesn't notice too much pain— then you've got an outside chance that he will do it for you, without too much trouble. But if you ask him for too much, or if he even gets to *thinking's* what you're asking him to do, that he should do for you; that it's more'n he can do or should even have to do, without it inter- fering with him and what *he* wants to do, then well, he may *say* that he will do it, but you can bet he never will. He'll just never get to it. And when you come around and say: 'Well, why ain't this done, then?' he will have a hundred reasons why he never got around to it. And anyway, since you have gone and brought it up again: he doesn't think that he ever should've had to do it in the first place.

" ' "And then you'll have to pull his teeth or something, hit him with a monkey wrench, to get the damned thing done. I don't know. I'd just rather have the whole thing be easier. Have it all just be eas- ier. Just the child support, that's all. That I think he'll maybe do. And then *my* life, it'll be easier, easier for me."

" 'And then, when he didn't always do even *that* much, you could not depend on him, well, like I say, it really pissed her off. And then she had to go and to haul him back in court again, like they'd never left. But that was really just about the only times they ever really *saw* each other. 'Specially after he went north. Got himself another job, with another company, and moved out on the manicurist, left her right there in the lurch, just like he'd left Sandy. And went up to Orange, there. But later on, I think I heard, I heard he came back. To the manicurist. Beautician. Cosmetologist. Whatever she was. But I'm not even sure of that. I could be wrong on that.'

"I asked her what happened when he had his visitation, visitation with his daughter, and she said that 'Mostly nothing did, because most times he didn't come.' Most of the times he never showed up, and never called up, either. Unless he had a special run that took him through the town. And then he might drop in, but without calling first, to see if the kid was home. And then if she was, well she would see him on those times. For a little while. But never when Sandy was there—because of course he knew her schedule and he knew she'd be at work—when he was supposed to, and always just a little while. And then he'd be gone again. Before Sandy got home from work—by then he'd be long gone. Lucy never really got to know him, not that she missed much, but Sandy almost never saw him. Never did hear her complain.'

"And that was just about it," Whitlock had said.

"Lucille is a very self-contained child," Royce said to me later, when something Henry's told me caused me to quiz Royce about his testimony. "She's also still an unhappy child, a lot like my stepsons were when I got them. When I first met her, right off I saw certain resemblances. Keeping the world at a distance, you know? Keeping her distance from every new person, from everybody she meets, until she gets them sized up. Like: 'Sure, you say this, and then you say that, and maybe you're telling the truth. But I make no commitments until I'm sure, and I'm not sure of you yet.' I think it's cost her a hel-luva lot, all of the things happened to her. Lucas Kyle was only one of them. But he was also one of the worst of them, along with being the first, and things like that happening to her her've cost her, cost her and cost her and cost her, like I say, a helluva lot. A tremendous amount, if you ask my opinion. In well-being and all of that shit. Lucy'd rather eat her own shit than tell someone else that she's hun-gry. She refuses to ask for a thing. She simply will not ask for help. She'll stand there and look at you, and say: 'Oh no, I'm fine.'

"So, you'd better get your heart vulcanized or ironclad or some-thing, my friend, for when you come up against this child. She's got a face that angels'd become human to get. And on her legs and on her arms, her shoulders and her chest, if it's so hot a day that she can't bear to cover herself all up, like she generally prefers to do, you'll see if you look carefully little white-lined, spider-web scars, very faint but still there. Where she's carved things and patterns into herself—hearts, squares and triangles; stars and friends' names; lines and just rectangles—any goddamned thing that's symmetry and shape, and cutting it'd also give pain. But *temporary* pain. The kind of pain that comes with blood, and then it goes away. Better than the other kind

74

that stays, and stays, and stays. The kind she thinks she knows too well, because she's always had. So one result's self-mutilation."

"Yes," Cronin had said, "well, thank you. Now, Your Honor, pursuant to the lieutenant's suggestion at the outset of his testimony, I wonder if I might suspend direct examination at this time, subject to resumption, that the court may ask my learned brother whether he desires to cross-examine the lieutenant on any aspect of what he's testified to so far."

"Mister Dean?" Henry had said.

Dean had stood. I knew this because Henry, like most of the judges of the Massachusetts trial courts, is selectively deaf. He cannot hear seated lawyers. He insists that counsel take their feet when they address the court. He's right. They should. "Nothing at this time, Your Honor. Provided I retain unlimited scope over all of the lieutenant's evidence, should I choose to avail myself of it, during any such pauses, or when he has finished."

"So stipulated, Your Honor," Cronin had said.

"We'll take the afternoon recess," Henry had said, standing up and looking forward to relieving the pressure on his bladder. "Resume in ten minutes."

■   ■   ■   **8**

T his guy Arthur Dean," I said to Royce the next time I saw him, "tell me about Arthur Dean. How did he get involved in this thing? What moved Peter to latch onto him?"

"The idea of going up against Arthur Dean bothers you, does it?" Royce said.

"Hey," I said, "how come you guys who aren't even lawyers try to answer my questions with questions? Quit crabbing my act. Yeah, I'm concerned about tangling with Arthur Dean, same as I'd be concerned about tangling with Barbra Streisand, or any other loudmouth I haven't fought against before. Fear of the unknown's a wonderful thing, if it makes you want to find out what the hell's going on. Before it's gone all over you, left tread marks on your back. The transcripts you gave me show a sharp man at work. If Peter's the fool that you think he is, how'd he get so smart? What made him latch onto Dean?"

"Very good," Royce said. "That's the question you oughta be asking. Low animal cunning. Craftiness. Guile. The shrewdness common to foraging varmints. The wisdom he couldn't help but inherit from the predatory ancestors whose greed enabled him to be rich without the damned nuisance of ever having to work. Like I said, Peter's smart. I don't like him, and he sure doesn't work his brain overtime, either, but when he needs it, it's there. The bastard is smart.

You reassure me, Counselor, with that question. Cadillac Teddy was right."

"Cadillac Teddy," I said. He eddies in and out of my life like a mischievous but solicitous ghost. As though now that he's retired, I've become something he does to relax. "Maybe I asked you the wrong question. How did you come to know him?"

Royce spread his hands. "Jerry," he said, "you're a reasonable man. I'm a state *police*man. All of us real ones started off driving the bluebirds. All of us driving those two-tone blue cars had a wallet-sized picture of Cadillac Teddy. Got 'em issued to us with our books of tickets. 'You spot him in a Cad, you can think of one reason, any damned reason at all, that's when you take him down.' You know how I knew Teddy. None of us ever made a charge stick, partly because Teddy was smart enough to steal neat, and partly because, when he slipped up a little, he brought you into the thing. You then proceeded to do what your breed's supposed to do, which is tramp up enough dust to befuddle the judges—and that isn't always a lot, depending on which judge you draw. And Teddy then drove away, clean and green. He used to brag about you to us, whenever one of us grabbed him. Teddy's a professional guy. Treated us like professional guys. He didn't think we busted him personal, and except for Hudson, that fuckin' ass*hole*, no one I knew ever did. But each time we did it, he'd say the same thing: 'Jeremiah'll see you in court.' And dammit if he wasn't right.

"Cadillac Teddy is how come you're in this. Judge Henry asked me, I had someone in mind, take care of Sandra's three kids, who he guessed I'd sort of adopted, and I said I heard of this guy name of Kennedy, not the same guy in the Senate. 'I hear he isn't that bad, he gets the bone in his teeth.' And Judge Henry said: 'Jerry? My classmate, Jerry, that miserable son of a bitch? I've been waiting about three hundred years to do something mean to that bastard, and you call my attention, the obvious fact: I can drive the man nuts and leave him stone broke, without me ever leaving my home.' So that's what you're doing here. As for Dean, he took me to dinner. He was trying a case in the federal court here, and he liked to eat dinner early."

I knew where they'd gone. The Locke Ober Cafe on Winter Place offers the small room to the far right of the stairs on the third floor among several private dining rooms upstairs as suitable for parties of four, but because the rooms were constructed in the early nineteenth century, when Americans were much smaller, a bulky fellow like Whitlock in Dean's barely contained company would have no trouble occupying it all by themselves.

Dean had snuffled—"Hay fever," he'd already told Royce, "although in this case more likely *grass* fever, grass pollen. The way I can tell the difference between seasons is that if I have the sniffles and it's cold out, then it must be winter and what I've got must be a cold. On the other hand, if I have the sniffles but I don't need to wear a coat when I go outdoors, then what I have is allergies and it must be summer"—and had some of his Bombay gin martini on the rocks. He said martinis didn't make him feel better, but they at least saved him from giving a shit.

"I figured the best thing to do with this bird," Whitlock told me, "was take the same approach you have to take with a big stubborn dog. Whack him a good one right on the snout and see if that gets his attention. If it does, then you know how you've got to proceed, and if it doesn't, the bastard takes a lunge at you and bites you, well, that tells you a thing or two. Mainly that the bang on the snoot isn't the way to proceed with this dog, and the best thing to do is clear out. Get rid of that mean-tempered dog. So I said to Arthur: 'Why'd Peter Wade hire you? He see your name in the papers, showboating with one of your high-profile cases, makin' six kinds of public fool of yourself? He thinks you're some kind of a status symbol. He is dumb enough to do that.' Even though I know he is not.

"Arthur got stuffy with me. This caught me off guard. I didn't expect it of him. 'I don't grandstand,' he said, like I'd just accused him of bothering farm animals. 'I make it a practice,' he said, 'to never talk to the media. It's like fiddling around with hand grenades or something. "Seek exposure," if that's what you call it.' Which of course was a barefaced lie. 'So that's why you haven't figured out yet why it is that I represent Peter. Those guys're human explosives, liable to go off any time. And they also lie. I know people that they've lied about and they wanted me to *sue* them. Sue the *Commoner*, or the television station, because the actual reporter's almost always judgment-proof. Doesn't have a fucking farthing of his own, to bother going after. *His* first wife got it all, not that there was that much of it—he's always been next-door, within spitting distance, I would say, of becoming a fucking bum. Like they all are. If it wasn't for the news business, the fucking army of the homeless'd be twice the size it is, and at least twice as stupid.

"Peter hired me because I represented his first wife. I hoovered him pretty good. She didn't get it all, not by a long shot, but she did get quite a lot. They all do. I've often thought there must be some secret school they go to, seminary, something, most likely run by nuns who've got pretty good mustaches and carry knouts or something, that all the first wives go to and learn how to do it. How to do it to us. Because they all *do* do it, every one. Like clockwork, they do it, auto pilot kicking in. It's like the job carried a secret clause that single men and private citizens don't know about, never even hear about. That says: *Provided:* that if you are the guy's first wife, and then you get divorced, you get a fucking lifetime *annuity* for it. But *only:* if you never performed oral sex on him, no matter how much he begged. 'Cause if you did then all of this is null and void, and all these bets're off.' It must require some training. They must have to get it some-where. I just don't know where. But the papers're all rich. Partly because they've got this half-assed First-Amendment-carried-to-an-extreme defamation law in this cockamamie *Common*wealth that denies you punitive damages if somebody libels you in print or slan-ders you on the street. Only compensatory damages, meaning you have to lose your job or something. Which only encourages the news-paper brass to be as slack-jawed irresponsible and slovenly as they like, riding herd on their people. Or *not* riding herd on the bastards, which'd be closer to the truth of it—because they know just as well as I do that nobody their bastards defame can come around and take their fucking building away from them, for not paying any attention and just letting it happen. And the people who came to me're all pub-lic figures anyway, which meant that anyone could fucking lie about them all they liked with imfuckingpunity, and they would be com-pletely fucking powerless to do a fucking thing about it.

"I represented his first wife," Dean had said. "I knew Jeanne from my first marriage. She went to Marymount with my ex-wife, but that didn't make her a bad *per*son. So my first wife, by then my ex-wife, she'd done a good job of convincing Jeanne what a wretched unrecon-structed son of a mean-tempered bitch of a person generally and a lawyer in particular I was. So naturally when Jeanne and Peter got on the outs and she wanted somebody nasty to come up here and cut his nuts off, I was who she thought of. And when I was in fact able to do a pretty thorough job of separating Peter from one of his testicles in the course of that unpleasantness, he took a liking to me."

"Interesting," Royce'd said. "Do you often get clients that way? By destroying them once, I mean? I'd think they'd be more likely to cherish grudges against you."

"Surprisingly enough, yeah," Dean had said. "The smarter clients, I mean. The stupid people that you cut the nuts off of: it doesn't dawn on them what it was that made it so that you could do it; that you were just a much better lawyer than their lawyer was. So the dummies that they are like that, they don't ever come around. But the kind of clients that you *want*, the ones who're smart enough to have a lot of money so they can afford to hire you, yeah, at your outrageous prices: you get a lot of them that way. By beating the shit out of them, so they find out why it is that you can charge so much, and get away with it. And plus which, since they *are* smart, they figure that if you're already *their* lawyer now and someone *else* comes after them, well at least this new bastard won't be able to hire *you*, to remove their nuts again. If they've grown a new set by then."

"Because," Royce'd said, "there was one story around that you'd gone to college together—you and Peter Wade, I mean."

Dean had laughed. "I would've spent a lot less time in college if I had," he said. "About four years or so. Peter and college didn't mix. He was not your basic student. He was in college for about twenty minutes. Well, I'm making it a little worse'n it was, and as usual where Peter's concerned, there's no need to do that. Exaggeration's always superfluous when Wade's involved. Peter dropped out of college Halloween of his freshman year, all right? Halloween. He lasted a little over a month. Cut out for college he was not. The prefects and the proctors and the dons and all them fellows out at Williams College spotted this right off, day that he walked in the door. Hell of a good school. Peter was not meant for it. Peter was not meant for this fucking *planet*, some would say, and indeed he may only be on it on a part-time basis, but certainly he was not meant, designed, or built for Williams College. Pete was meant for many things—perhaps the gallows, some've said—but not for Williams College. And Williams was not meant for him, no-no, no-no, no.

"Keep this in mind," Dean had said. "The Wade family money didn't come from running a textile mill sweatshop Down Maine a couple hundred years ago. Or trading Africans for molasses to make rum to swap for cotton. It came from making clocks and pocket watches; repeating firearms, the kind of guns that won the West. Pump motors, printing presses, and sewing machines. Cash registers; adding machines; punch-card mechanized sorters; power looms and fuel pumps; socket-ratchet wrenches and electric generators: all that nineteenth-century kind of intricate, gear-and-lever, precision machinery with jeweled bearings that ticked and whirred. Or clicked and hummed and clanked and banged, if that's what you'd had in mind. Stuff made in New England, in *America*: that stuff *worked*. It always worked. You could depend on it. Sure, you had to take it apart and clean it every so often, maybe once a year, say, and then lubricate it with an oil so golden light and thin that what you put on your salad even cut with vinegar poured much thicker than that oil did, but when you turned the Wade machine on in the morning, whatever it was, it *went*. Just like you knew it would. It was dependable. That was what you got, and what you assumed you'd get, when you lived in this part of the world. Performance. No excuses. No apologies. It was *dependable*. Bing-bang, bing-bang, bing. You bought this thing to do the thing, because they said it would, and by God if it didn't, well, you didn't keep it to yourself, make a secret of it; you took the damned thing back to them. If it broke, you got it fixed. You didn't buy a new one until the old one was worn out in honest service. And if it broke before it should've, then you took it back and said: 'Gimme my money back. This damned thing doesn't work.' And they gave you your money back, because they were ashamed, and God help the foolish man who made and sold the thing that didn't work. Did he get *his* ass reamed out? You bet *your* ass he did.

"It was a different world then, some'd say, a better, cleaner world. And everyone in that world used to have to have that stuff you made, you Wades, back then in those days. Men in *China* noticed when somebody they'd just met took a Wade watch out of his vest pocket, to see what the time was. They had a Wade watch themselves. So when they saw him look at his watch, *well*, they knew he was like they were, just off the boat or not. He was *reli*able. Everyone, around the world, bought machines the Wades made. Couldn't operate without them. And couldn't get as good of, from any*body* else, any*where* else, in the world. Before the microchip existed. When silicone was something that you waterproofed your shoes with, and nobody'd even heard of silicon, and rational, sane people still thought that when you said 'digital,' you were talking about fingers, the name of Wade was good. Good as gold, all around the world.

"Then Peter came along," Dean had said, "and when the other members of the family'd had a chance to size him up, well, that's when they decided: 'Time's come to sell the comp'ny.' And they did that, too, back in nineteen sixty-two. Although I don't really know for sure that Peter was actually the reason for it. For making that decision. But if he wasn't, he just as well could've been."

"He's always been somewhat unstable, then I gather?" Royce'd said. "Playboy, rakehell, and so forth?"

"There is no vice Peter doesn't have," Dean had said. "No organ in his body that Peter hasn't abused. No sin that he hasn't sampled. Maybe not buggery, though, I would guess; Wade certainly isn't queer. But he doesn't need to be. He's never had the slightest difficulty finding some new woman he can get in trouble with. He's the classic slave-to-his-pecker. He's like a water witch with it. It's his favorite dowsing rod. It's like he closes his eyes and holds on to it, and follows wherever it leads him. Only it doesn't dip down when he stumbles across what he's looking for: it points straight up.

"He could find pussy in the desert with that thing. Unfortunately for him, he has. Repeatedly. And he is *not* reasonable when he picks up the scent of a new one. No indeed, not at all. He's off in full cry, makes up a pack by himself." He had sighed. The waiter had returned with a second round of drinks, served it, and left again. "I like girls myself," Dean had said, "and I've been in trouble too, a result of that. But never trouble like he's been in. Peter's in a class of his own, it comes to woman trouble. He's in it fucking constantly. It's his principal career."

Dean had laughed. "The guy's a fucking marvel. He always ignores the odds. The person who intimidates him hasn't yet been seen on earth. I would no more try to back him down than he'd try it on me. Don't get me wrong here now: I'd rip his gizzard out with my bare hands and *eat* it, steaming warm and slimy-raw, dripping blood all over the rug, in front of him and all his kinfolk—and he knows I'd do it, too—if he made one false move on me. And I know that he would happily perform the same service on *me*, if *I* made one false move on him."

"So what you have to understand, in this case here," Royce said to me, "is that everything in life's a trade-off. Arthur'd like it a lot better if Peter was under indictment for preparing Sandy to go quietly into the ditch. It's pretty clear that *somebody* did it; she didn't get herself ready, and it probably wasn't her first choice of a wonderfully refreshing and relaxing weekend getaway spot. Arthur could fight this one without breaking a sweat, and win it, win it going away. And he'd then collect a handsome fee, which Peter wouldn't mind paying at all. But what Arthur wants doesn't count.

"What you want and I want doesn't count either. You can't just sue *somebody* for wrongfully causing the death of someone that you depended on for your support. You've got to have a proper name. And it helps a lot if the person named either has a lot of money or a big insurance policy, because it's not much fun at all in this world to sue some silly bastard who doesn't have a dime. It's like quitting smoking, you know? What do you do then, after sex? A fucking crossword puzzle? You don't know what to do. So it's not much fun at all.

"Peter's got a lot of money, or access to it at least. Even though he's made a damned career out of screwing and then marrying the wrong type of broads. And then winding up paying them off. He'd be a prime candidate for the honor of being named Sandy's killer, too, if you could prove he was around when she went in the swamp. But I can't, so far, and that means you can't. No one else seems to be trying.

"Which does tend to cramp our style here. Peter hasn't been charged with the crime. It'd make this wrongful death action of yours a whole lot easier, if he were. It'd settle, I suppose, without any doubt. But Peter *hasn't* been indicted, and there's no evidence of any strong enthusiasm for indicting him in either jurisdiction, where at least right now it looks like it could be done. 'So you're gonna have trouble with this one,' Arthur said to me. 'It's not like the other cases that I know you've had so many of. You've got to keep something in mind about the lawyers and accountants who manage family trusts, and the insurance companies that write liability policies: they think it's their money. They really, truly do. They don't want to pay it out. They like to invest and reinvest it and admire it, and look at it and rub their hands, and laugh and laugh and laugh. But when it comes to writing checks for money they're not going to see again, well, they don't go for that shit at all.'

"Arthur Dean was right. So what we're trying to do here really doesn't have that much to do with anyone you represent. It has to do with district attorneys, and with trustees, and with media. It has to do with getting at least one of those groups all stirred up, all lathered up, to do *something* at least to Peter Wade. Make him pay for being in the same hemisphere as his third wife when she went into the marsh."

"Even though Arthur says he had nothing to do with it," I said to Royce.

"Peter's his client," Royce said. "Of course that's what he's gonna say."

■   ■   ■   **9**

It's not that it's hard to learn the tricky part of trying cases; what's tough is keeping it in mind at all times. This is that it doesn't matter what *you* think is the plain meaning of a particular set of facts; what matters is what an average jury of six or twelve people decides to think those facts mean, viewing them as best they can, given their limited intelligence (which, you hope devoutly, has been scrambled into confusion by your best efforts to bamboozle them, if the facts are against your client, as in criminal cases they generally are), against the backdrop of their own generally passive experience, oblivious ignorance, limitless stupidity, free-floating rancor, ill-concealed bigotry, boredom, and general indifference. Now, if you think that's too harsh a judgment, made by an embittered man who's lost too many cases, try this simple test: when you next sit down to catch a ball game on TV, study, instead of merely enduring, the commercials for beer. Then consider that those profound insults to human rationality— "Drink our beer and get bountifully laid"—must sell one hell of a lot of beer. As the screamers for cars must sell cars, and the ones for cat food must sell out the trash fish. So, it follows that at least a merchant's quorum of viewers must be influenced by those tactful messages. Otherwise they wouldn't be made and shown, at great expense, so you get your ball games for no charge except submission to the assaults.

This does *not* mean that there's any such thing as an Average Citizen. The AC's a mythical creature mathematically imagined on the premise that if you fill a room with equal numbers of stupid people with IQs of 80 and run-of-the-mill smart people with IQs of 120, you will somehow have acquired a roomful of uniform people with IQs of 100, able to suffer placidly sitcoms that would bore a smart person into a state of rage but who are, at the same time, smart enough to comprehend trigonometry (which was far too much for me). Anyone who's picked a jury, or had one sit in judgment on him, knows this eternal truth: The "average man" who lets himself get trapped into extended jury duty's way below his own average. If he's above the mean he still won't apply to your case the brainpower he brings to his job, no matter how he strives—he's got no stake in deciding your case; he has in doing his job. And that applies to the "average woman" as well.

So when you try a case, civil or criminal, what you have to keep in mind is that there are only two people in the courtroom who a day after it's over will actually give a rat's ass how it all came out: you and your client. He'll care a lot more than you do, and he'll remember, too. If you lose it, he's the one who'll have to do the time or pay the judgment; all you'll have to do is find your way back to your office and prepare for the next case. But six weeks after it's all over, the jurors will not remember. Several times in the course of a long career I've encountered in a drugstore or a liquor store someone who served on one of my panels; recognized me; flattered me by saying what a fine job I did, saying how I'd impre*ssed all* of the jurors with my swift wit and heavenly eloquence—plainly having forgotten that I'd done such a fine job for my client it'd taken him and the other members of that jury less than half an hour to convict him, enabling the judge to send him away for twenty years or so.

Opposing counsel—now, this may surprise you—also doesn't care, not in any lasting manner, how the cases come out, unless your client's such a trophy, career-making villain that cries of "Give us Barrabas" go up in the land whenever he's sighted at large. Prosecutors are paid by the taxpayers to put all clients, yours or someone else's, through the wood chipper, feetfirst. They're unhappy the evening you finally win one, but their mortgage payments still hit the bank on time; they're still paid the same amount, even though you did manage to hoodwink the jury into letting the defendant go. In civil cases, defense lawyers are retained by the people who insured the defendant but now don't want to pay your guy what they agreed to pay him, or any other victim, if their careless customer fucked up—as now of course he has. Your learned brother may be somewhat dejected the night after you talked the jury into letting you eat his lunch, but he'll recover rapidly. Win or lose or deadlocked jury, he always gets his pay.

Does the judge give a good shit? Sure, but not about you or your client. About what she's going to have for dinner; whether his alma mater's got a chance on Saturday, playing Notre Dame. Or if Freddie the mechanic got around this morning to pulling a wheel like the judge asked him to, to find out whether that spongy feeling on the brake pedal means his car should have new pads he hadn't planned to buy just now, and there goes the new overcoat he really ought to have. You're murdering the Commonwealth's mendacious witnesses on cross, and he's sitting there grumpily thinking no judge should be seen walking around in public wearing a baggy old overcoat that's pilled on the collar and at the cuffs, and the cleaners obviously shrank it, and anyway it ought by rights to've been given to Morgan Memorial two or three years ago, and so what the hell's he doing still wearing it? Goddamn it to Hell anyway.

Everyone with half a brain who's tried a case knows these things. Nobody thinks like he does, and may not even be thinking at all on that day, having gotten out of the habit, and there is nothing he can do about it, nothing at all. What seems to you to be as plain as day can be incomprehensible to the usual collection of nitwits you're liable to get when you cull a jury from a randomly selected pool of people who either really don't have anything better to do and would just as soon get a measly little bonus, but a bonus nonetheless, on their unemployment or disability-insurance checks, in exchange for a warm place to sit, bad coffee, and a stale sandwich, slice or two of pound cake, wrapped in cellophane back in '93, for allowing you to try to entertain them. Or who're so damned dumb they decided long ago to lie back and just go with the flow, see where the current takes them, 'til the quitting whistle blows and they can go and have a beer.

The tricky part of knowing this, which almost everybody soon learns, is how to keep remembering it. That is really hard. Reflexively we tend to be too charitable. Think everybody that we meet is just as smart; just as perceptive; as generous and fair-minded; as we like to think we are ourselves. We're dead wrong. Furthermore, we're deliberately wrong. I knew how I'd been seeing the Sandra Nichols, recently upon this earth, more recently under it, as revealed in the statements Royce took, but that might not be the way that a judge and jury would see her, no matter what I did.

"And whether or not at some time after that fact," Cronin had said to Royce, "you had occasion to interview Lucas Walter Kyle."

Whitlock had pulled the papers from his pocket again. "I did," he said. "One of the other investigators assigned to my office—this would actually be Trooper Morse, who does most of our computer work; our in-house computer genius, best man we have on that: a *magician* with that thing; he can make it sing and dance, do card tricks and feed the cat, and then when it gets through with that, have it walk the dog. Though of course we're all qualified ourselves on it, as well."

He had stopped and coughed. The transcript reflected that, stenographers being paid by the page, greedy ones setting down everything but the complaints of crows and the antics of squirrels playing in the tree outside the window. He had resumed. "Trooper Morse accessed current data compiled by the Registry of Motor Vehicles locating one Lucas W. Kyle, date of birth March fourteenth, nineteen-fifty-four, which corresponded to the DOB stated on the marriage license we had previously found, for him and Sandra Nichols. Last-known residential address: Twelve Monadnock Street, Apartment Fourteen, Athol, Mass."

He looked up at Judge Henry. "The registry data also stated his social security number, but we've been directed not to divulge such numbers publicly unless absolutely required to do so."

"Because of credit card frauds?" the judge said.

"Yes, Your Honor," Whitlock said. "The registry, I understand, is either already giving people the option either to choose another number for their licenses, or else they're about to do that—I'm not sure. But as those of us in law enforcement're all aware, this's become a real problem, people getting credit cards in other people's names, and then running up huge bills. And all they need to do it is the name and the address and a couple of other things. So we've been asked to stop. Unless it's absolutely necessary."

"Yes," Henry had said. "Well, I can certainly see the wisdom of that, Lieutenant. Either of you gentleman have any problem with that? Not having that number on the public record here?"

"I have none, Your Honor," Cronin had said as Dean stood up.

"As I haven't, either," Dean had said. "Although from what I understand, and from what we've already heard about this man Kyle's record on child support, anyone who could get someone to issue him a phony credit card in the name of Lucas Kyle'd have to be a lot more persuasive'n your average common crook: he'd have to be the greatest con man to come down the pike since Charlie Keating went to jail for looting all those S and Ls, pull off a scam like that."

"Does that more or less square with what you learned of Mister Kyle, Lieutenant?" Henry had said, uncharacteristically—and, I was sure, unwittingly; he must've been dozing—assisting one party's attorney to set a trap for the other side. "What Mister Dean just said?"

"Pretty much, Your Honor," Whitlock said, equally surprisingly falling into that trap. "Put it this way: from everything that we found out, it'd be a pretty tall order. The guy's name was apparently red-flagged at least three or four times every year, on the average, up until about four years ago. During the past seven years. Which is all that they report, as far as they go back. Then he apparently got himself straightened out, started paying his bills on time. Or so we've heard at least, I mean," he said hurriedly. "We have no official access to that data whatsoever, under the existing laws, privacy and all." In other words, before going to call on Lucas Kyle, Royce'd had Trooper Morse run the computerized version of a full-field investigation of him, just in case he'd been naughty and therefore would be willing to bargain about just what he knew, and how much.

Danger signals. Henry's reaction had not been verbal, but I could feel the vibrations. The cops are not supposed to go rummaging around in the private lives of witnesses, hoping perhaps to come up with a dirty file of youthful indiscretions that might inspire an otherwise recalcitrant witness to cooperate with the authorities, in order to keep his sins hidden. Maybe even to the extent of improving on the truth to make sure the cops're all happy. The cops still do it, but they're not supposed to. A seasoned judge distinguishes between evident (but undeclared) commission of improper conduct out of court that helps move the cases along, and conduct of the same kind flaunted before him in public session. Judges aren't rebuked by higher courts for scowling on the record. "Yes," Cronin had said quickly—he was an experienced prosecutor, anyway; maybe not the top-gun type Royce preferred to work with, but still, workmanlike enough to extricate one of his cops from a sticky situation that he'd gotten himself into without any help at all. "Well then, if you'd continue, Lieutenant? With what you did then? Or had one of your colleagues do, if you didn't do it yourself."

"Oh, I did it myself, Mister Cronin," Whitlock had said. "On each occasion I would have one or more of the other troopers assigned to the Essex County DA's Office come along with me, sometimes mostly for training purposes, the newer troopers, I mean—but in each instance also to make sure that we would have a back-up witness, who could testify if I couldn't. If when the time should come to do it, I was otherwise tied up, or unable for some reason to appear in court on this. On any case that might come up, as a result of this."

"And is this standard operating procedure, then, Lieutenant?" Cronin had said.

"Standing operating procedure, yessir, to have two troopers in attendance at all interviews in major felonies," Whitlock had said. "But in murder cases, always, unless the circumstances for some reason don't permit it to be done—a spontaneous confession or some such thing like that, at the murder scene; naturally the guy who hears that's going to take it down, advise the guy his rights, and then try to get him, sign the paper that's got on it what it was he just said. Which they don't usually do, because by then they're having what I guess would be called 'second thoughts' or something, about what it was they said. And maybe wished they hadn't, didn't say what they just said. But unless there's some very unusual reason like that why there isn't a lieutenant there, there's always a detective lieutenant on the scene and in full charge of what goes on.

"And in this particular case, as well, on top of that, in addition to the regular procedure we follow in these matters, the DA asked me—

and I agreed completely with him on this—if I would, given the complexity of this one, to give it top priority and make sure I was in attendance at all interviews with anyone who might've had a major role in the victim's life. And I don't mean just potential suspects, either, people who might've had their reasons to think Sandra Nichols ought to be dead. No, this would've been anyone who knew her well, who might've known someone, at some time, who might've had some reason to want her dead. Because most your murder victims, the vast majority of them got killed by someone that they knew. Not someone that they necessarily knew all that well, but most murders're still personal. The killer was someone the victim knew. Not someone who was robbing them, or an intruder in their home, or even one of what we get so much of in the cities now: your drive-bys that just look like random violence there. Those kinds of things do happen, the thrill killings, yeah, they do; but in the bigger picture, they're really only a small part. Most homicides, we find, 're strictly between friends. Or lovers. They knew each other. Before the trouble started. And then the death intervened. So that's who we were after: people who knew Sandy at least pretty well, because that's where we attach, you know, the most importance to when we allocate resources. And so on every interview that we're discussing here, well, I was always present. At every one of them. And I conducted them myself. Every one of them.

"In Kyle's case," Whitlock said, "from everything that we'd already learned about the subject, we thought it might be best if he didn't know when it was that we were coming. We assumed, of course, that when he'd read about the death of his ex-wife in the newspapers, or heard about it on the radio, maybe on TV, that he'd know we'd want to see him. See him and talk to him. So, assuming, of course, that Mrs. Streeter hadn't called him up, the minute that we'd left her place—which from the way she'd talked about him, we didn't think she would—there'd still be some element of surprise, some advantage for us, if we just took our chances he'd be home and we just suddenly showed up.

"So what we did was we called up his company, Homer's Always Freshest Produce, find out what his hours were, when he would *not* be home and we'd be just wasting our time. This Homer's is a company that brings in a trailer load of vegetables and fruit and all that stuff, whatever's available that their customers've ordered. Or they think their customers will want it if they see it and will be able to sell it, even if they didn't—order it, I mean, they didn't know it was in. Out of the Boston Wholesale Produce Market very early in the morning three days every week. Except Sundays; they don't work. I suppose it's about fifty miles or so to this terminal they got, out in Gardner, there, right off of Two-oh-two. And then what the road crew does is they come in at seven A.M. Now this would be the actual drivers, route salesmen, as opposed to the two guys that drive the tractor trailers, that go around the stores in the area—which they do every day, every day 'cept Sunday. Not just three days a week. And what they do is, on the days the trailer comes in, they drive a shorter route those days because they get a later start. They all pitch in and break down the trailer load, and then they reload what they think they're gonna need from it that day onto the trucks they drive. The rest they put in these big walk-in refrigerators that they've got in the plant there. And on the days when there's no trailer coming in, the 'long-route days,' they call them, well, that's what they load their trucks up in the morning from. From these big-bin refrigerators where they put the extra stuff the day before when the truck came in from Boston. If you follow me. Whatever stuff that's been ordered, or they think that their stores might want.

"Now these're not the supermarkets, their customers, I mean. No, not the big stores with everything, stay open day and night. They've got their own big fleets of trucks, buy all their own fresh stuff. These're the local smaller grocery stores, in the neighborhoods. And some of the smaller-chain convenience stores as well. That keep a couple heads of lettuce and some cartons of tomatoes on the shelf, those cellophane-three-packed tray-things of red things, taste like old weeds and chew like cannonballs. For the people who work nights and want that stuff on their way home. Quart of milk, an Instant Game card. Maybe half a dozen eggs. Couple packs of cigarettes. The newspaper. There's a lot of little towns out there like that now these days, don't have too many people, not enough so every town could have its own supermarket, like they used to have markets—they could support them then, that many markets, but they can't do that today with supermarkets. Overhead's too high. And with everybody having cars, now, they don't need to, either. So now there's a lot of little stores. What they are is small-scale markets, markets like the old ones used to be, but on a smaller scale. I don't mean convenience stores. In Baldwinville, Westford, Wichendon, places like that, I'm just giving examples here, of about that size, where people can just go, near where they live, and pick up a few things that they might need. Or on their way home from work. Without having to make a big production of it and driving six or seven miles or so, fifteen some of them, to get to one of those big mammoth supermarkets they have got today, when all they need's just three or four things. And this way they've only got to do that, make the big production, once a week or so, I guess.

"And I would guess they've prolly got, this's Homer's now, I mean, half a dozen or so trucks—what we used to call the old deuce-and-a-halfs, two-and-half-ton trucks, though they probably load more'n that now—maybe eight or ten, and Kyle drives one of them. It's his regular route, so he knows what his people want. Without him getting all the way to the store that's his customer and then finding out he hasn't got it? Instead of that he knows these stores, and what they need, so he's got it on his truck.

"And his supervisor tells us—I recorded this as well, over the telephone, with the man's express permission after I'd asked him if it was okay. Anyway, like I say, he said: 'Kyle comes in seven, he's supposed to, anyway, but he's usually late, up all night makin' whoopee with this woman, that he's livin' with. Dame just can't leave him alone. Or so he says, at least. That's his explanation for it, anyway, is all I mean to say. Sometimes he comes in too late trailer mornings so the unloadin' job is mostly done, the time he gets here. And he takes quite a lot of crap the other drivers, when he does that, but no one gets mad at him. Kyle's a good hard worker.

" 'He makes it up to them in the busy seasons, just before Thanksgiving; Christmas; Super Bowl; Easter, also Easter; all of the big family days all the guys're doubling their routes, goin' to each store, you know, every single day—instead of every two, or three. We're bringin' in here those weeks, four trailerloads a week. Once we even did *five*. Kyle's efficient. He can double up like that and still finish up by eight or so at night. And then what he does is, he will come back in here and just volunteer to take a piece, some other guy's route the poor bastard's never gonna finish, matter he says up all night. And Kyle will go out, do a piece of the guy's route, take care *his* stores. And then he won't take no money for it. None of the other guy's commissions he gets as a result—which come to a lot more, naturally, when stuff's sellin' out like that. Kyle will not take a dime for it, nothin' on the sales he made, he was doing the guy's route. "Nope," he will just tell them, they try to give him something, "this's just for all the mornings you guys did mine on the trailers." So the result is when he's late comin' in on trailer mornings, the guys who're pitchin in doin' his work, they remember those long nights, he did for them, and so all they do when he's late's just razz him, give him a really hard time.

" 'But still, the result of him comin' in late days, when he does that, as most of them he does, trailer days or not, is that he also always gets back late. Kyle may be real efficient, and he is, but there're still speed laws out there, and cops enforcing them, and he still has to finish. So where your normal driver's in here mornings by seven, so he can get out on the road and sellin' the stuff, all bright 'n' early, bushy-tailed, and then he's back in the barn here four-thirty or so, Lucas is generally not. More like six or seven for him. It's hard to know, you know? What makes people tick. Why they act the way they do. I mean, here is this kid, and you look at him, how he lives here under our rules we got here, and at his church, the rules they got there, and then everywhere else that he lives. And they don't match up, you know? The ways he lives do not match up.

" 'See these guys here, legally they're independent contractors, workin' on commission. We got the health insurance plan for them, and they're on the weekly draw if they got to carry someone who needs stuff but there's some reason they can't pay for it the same day the driver brings it in. But otherwise they're on their own. This is a nonunion shop and that's how we plan to keep it. We're all happier that way. We got a problem, we talk about it and we solve it. Get it done between ourselves. My partner's Taft and I'm Hartley. Mister Homer's over us, he's the one that founded this, semiretired now. And that's how we do it here. We all act together. We've got a right to work, or not to, we don't wanna eat. And so've the drivers, the same right. So that's what we offer these guys who drive for us. If they want to come in and get it, it's here, and if they don't, it's okay by us. And by God, that's all we do here. That's how we run our damned business. No goddamned so-called officials comin' in here from the local all the time, comin' in and startin' trouble: and us guys in management like that. And the workin' stiffs on payroll, they do, too, and they should, because it's also good for them. Have to pay no union dues, local, state, and national, send a buncha big fat cats down to Palm Beach every winter, as their personal guests, it all goes on our guys' tab. And there they all are, all the fat cats, on TV at night, our guys get home beat, froze their balls off all that day, and there they are, their officials, drinkin' the bourbon, eatin' the sirloins, takin' some sun, you know how they do. And maybe pickin' up the girls. Acting like they think they're politicians, too, or something. While our guys've been bustin' their humps here, fightin' through the snow, which we get a lot of here, then give part of their paychecks to them? Which the rest of us, who're runnin' the place, have to keep track of, deductions, and then send them all in then for them. Another big pain in the ass. They way our guys think, it's: "No thank you, I don't think so. I earned this and I will keep it; have a nice vacation with it my*self*, me and the bride, and I hope the golf game goes good."

" 'So, anyway, what the drivers take out every mornin' they owe us for, that night. On the slip, is what I mean. Unless they couldn't sell it and we got a carryover. Which doesn't matter really, at least for a day or three; our trucks're all refrigerated—plug 'em in here, overnight—so the stuff keeps pretty good.

" 'So, like I say, most days most of the guys're back in here, back here at the plant, by four, most of them four-thirty in the afternoon. And, so most of them like it, like having it that way: get up in the morning; load the truck; get on the road. Get back here, late afternoon, home for an early supper. Maybe have a couple of beers. Play the kids, you know, like that? Maybe inna summer, you know, am I right on this? They might play a little softball, watch a ball game on TV. And when the cold weather comes, watch a cop show on TV, one of them on every night. And then when that's all over with, go to bed and bang the wife. It's hard work, sure, can get you in the back, but you're still doin' hard physical work all the time, so you stay in pretty good shape. It's really not all that bad. In fact it's actually pretty nice.

" 'Nobody ever quits this place. It's a good, decent life. Guys've been *fired* from this job, sure, for being absolutely hopeless for one reason or another. Stealin' from accounts or tryin', sneak an extra case of lettuce out the door, like maybe Tony wouldn't notice. Skippin' stops to get off early, see a girlfriend, so our customers start screamin' at us, where's their fruit and vegetables? Where the hell's their orders? Something else that's really stupid like that, and it's . . . we always catch them. Then we kick their asses out, put 'em onna road. But nobody gets laid off here, never been a single one. It's a really steady job. If you've got it, and you do it, then it's yours to keep. Until you retire. And that's all taken care of, too—the pension thing, I mean. The Social Security, we all got that, of course—assuming that there's something left when we all get to that point; all those crooks in Washington don't figure out a way to swipe it from us first, before we get our fair share the dough that we've been puttin' in, there, been entrusting to them, all these years we worked. And then on top of that we got the four-oh-one-K here, they call it, this fund the company puts into, everyone works here, and we put into it too, ourselves—we do. *Profisharing* thing, you know? So this is a good deal we've got here. We make a decent living now, and after we're too old to work, so we got to retire, well, we'll still be comfortable. And that's the way that we live.

" 'Except for Luke. He's always late, by at least half an hour, and so the checker, Tony, who's also our accountant, Tony's got to hang around and wait for him, see what's on the truck and settle up with Luke, do the daily settlement. See, payday's not 'til Saturday, but we settle up, *on paper*, end of every single day. So every single one of us knows always exactly how we stand. Who owes what. To whom. That's the way we do it here, so a man knows when he goes home at night, exactly where he is. Whether he can coast along, the last two days the week, or if he's really gonna have to hustle Thursday, Friday, really push the merchandise, if his car payment's due that week and so far he's coming up 'way short. And by then it's close to five.'

"So I then asked this plant dispatcher," Royce had testified, "this is what his title is, if he knows where Kyle goes then: where he goes and what he does, when he gets off work. 'Yeah,' he said, his name was Jenkins, 'I think I do know what he does, and where he goes to do it, too. Luke goes over Valley Gym they got there, over there in Athol, and he builds his body up. Can you imagine that? This's a guy that he's gotta be at least about forty years old, and he thinks he's eighteen.

Or else he thinks if he works out enough—and he does this every single night, after he gets off work. Maybe even Sundays too; I really wouldn't know. But nah: now I think about it, prolly not on Sundays; Sundays he would be in church—other people will think that, think he's still eighteen. And so he'll live two hundred years. He will not get old. Which I don't think will happen, but he does, and it's his life. Man can do just what he likes, it's his own life he's working with.

" 'So after he's put in a full day's work—he always starts it late, but he always gets it done. Like I say, Luke's one of our best route salesmen, always makes a good week's pay, goes out every Monday like it's his car payment week and it's already Wednesday, even Thursday, and he's runnin' 'way behind—throwing crates of vegetables and all that stuff around, and they're not that light at all; it can play hell with your back. Then after he has done all that, *then* he goes this gym he goes to, and he busts his hump some more. He does *look* good, though— give him that. He certainly does look good. And if someone tells him that, he always says: "It isn't really me. *Any*body can look good. You could look this good yourself, too, *if* you paid the price." So not many people tell him that, anymore, tell him he looks good, not after they've done it once, and heard the spiel he gives. Don't want to hear the sermon, if you get what I mean.

" 'Then after his workout, every Wednesday night, he goes over to his church and teaches Bible study. And this isn't kids I'm talking here, Sunday school on Wednesday night, now; this is other adults that joined this little church that he goes to all the time. The church of All Holiness, or something like that there, up in Northfield there. It's not tied up with anything, any church you probably would've heard of, anything about, like all the other ones. Catholics, Episcopals, Unitarians—things like that are, you know? Except a couple other ones, other little churches, maybe six or eight, or ten, that all think the same general thing—about Jesus and so forth. It's one of those Bible-Belting churches like they've got down in the South? I mean, I'm not saying that they handle snakes or anything like that, but they're pretty strict about things. Abortions, school prayers, you know? But I never heard of it, myself, until he mentioned it.

" 'Which is another thing he does: you give him the slightest chance to talk about his church, or maybe you say something he don't think the Bible lets you say, or you're making fun of it, and he's worse about that than he is about the body-building.

" 'The first thing that he wants to do is to forgive you for it, if you insulted God or something—he calls that "blaspheming. Cursing and blaspheming." Luke knows all the official names for things you're not allowed to do. If he thinks you did that, blaspheme, then by God, that's what you did. Even though it's news to you, that is what you did. The trouble is that this blaspheming category covers quite a lot of ground, a lot of guys've found out here. They cursed or something, you know? Told a dirty joke. All comes under it, blasphemy, and he can see he's got no choice, now, being a true Christian: he's got to explain it to you, since you didn't know, how you hurt God's feelings, really made Him mad at you.

" 'This can take a good half hour, Luke forgiving you. Telling you, yes, how he knows you didn't mean it; you just said it without thinking. But he wants you to know *why* you did this, *why* you made God sad. He thinks he's an expert on this stuff. He has got it figured out: it's because you're still a sinner and you haven't been saved yet. And you're taking a big chance there, and he thinks you should know that. Because if you aren't careful and don't start pretty soon to get yourself shaped up, well, pretty soon the world, you know, is coming to an end. You should be aware of that. Because when that happens, *man,* you'll be in one big mess. Left out of the rapture, all that kind of thing, which he knows that you'll regret.

" 'And if for some reason you don't think it's gonna happen, world is coming to an end, well then he wants you still to think what happened to the people who *already* died, okay? These'd be people that you knew—you could say they finished early, 'fore the world came to an end, if you don't like to say they died. They *already* had to go and stand before the Lord, and explain why it was that they lived like they did, if it wasn't completely in the right way. And it won't matter if they knew, or if they didn't know, that they weren't living right: they knew, and did it anyway? Well then, then they go to Hell. They didn't know; they tell God that? Well, that don't get 'em off the hook. God says that they *should've* known, because they knew they didn't know and they did nothing to correct that, to find *out* what they should know. That was their responsibility, and they neglected it. So they go to Hell for that. You hear this speech enough times, you begin to think that everybody that dies, well, he goes right to Hell, no matter what they did or didn't: anything'll do.

" 'That is what Luke wants from you: he wants you to do that. Find out what God wants you to do, and get cracking on it. He will do it with you; he will shepherd you along—I have actually heard him *say* that to a guy: "I will shepherd you through this." Guy said: "I ain't no fuckin' *sheep*. Had a guy make that mistake, once, try that stuff on me, I was in the army. I was mindin' my own business in the shower room, okay? Like he thought that's what I was, I was some damned sheep. And I'll tell you what I did to him, he pulled that shit on me: I kicked the shit right out of him, and this was without no clothes on, and the water pouring down. Broke his nose and make him puke and lost some teeth for him. Pull that shit on me again? No sir, not after that."

" 'All the other guys're laughin' at him, havin' a great time. This did not faze Luke a bit. He went on just like before and finished his whole oration. He just will not give it up, once he puts that record on. Blah-blah, blah-blah, blah. Seems like it lasts a week. So guys around him here, they're careful about that, too. Not only to ignore the great shape Luke physically is in, but also: never mention anything that either sounds to him like what they need is some religion. Or else that they haven't got no respect for the religion that he's got. Because then the same thing's gonna happen; it's the same old way, either way it is: blah-blah, blah-blah, blah.'

"I asked Jenkins if the woman that Kyle lives with is his wife, if he's married to her, and Jenkins told me: 'No. Not so far as any of us here knows, least: lemme put it that way. They could've gotten married without telling anyone, but if they did then that is how, he's married, we don't know it. No, Luke says what she is, she's really a beautician. Works in beauty parlors? But she got laid off, or the place closed, or something—I guess those operations can be pretty shaky sometimes, always going under, 'less you hook up with a good one as apparently she didn't. And it was quite a while before she could get another job—they don't get unemployment, and how they get away with that, I don't understand. Unless they're saying that those girls're like our drivers and're, contractors, you know? This was all right around the time that Luke come to work for us, maybe a year before. And so she was stayin' home you know, all day by herself? And she's watchin' the TV and everything, those home-shopping networks they've got? I guess she ran up a whole lot of bills, on their credit card there? Thousands and thousands of dollars.

" 'Like I say, Luke was honest from day one. We put an ad in the paper about wanting to hire drivers, and he answered it, and we asked him why he should get the job instead of some other guy. And he said, he came right out and said, it was because he needed it more than anybody else. This woman of his, that he loved a lot? She'd had them so deep in the hole they'd never get out, he didn't get himself a better job. I would've kicked her ass out the door, but they're apparently crazy about each other. But they were still deep in the hole. Took 'em three or four years to get out alla way. Then he told me, the day they got out: "Thank God for this job and the church." Because I guess they got programs for this, that train you to have some sense.

" 'Anyway, somebody that she knew asked her to fill in, in a store, just help out a little while behind the register as a temp cashier. And she did it—she needed the money. Well, she found out she liked it. She can basically make her own hours. Take a day off if she wants. So when the first place she worked got their permanent girl back, she was one of the managers' wives, well, word'd gotten around the circuit by then, there was this woman who was a part-time substitute, pretty good, and fast, knows what she is going. And she became a roving floater, really.

" 'So that's what she does now. Goes around from place to place, wherever she is needed, if too many of the regular people who work there either all get sick or want to take their vacations all at the same time: situations like that. All the stores know where to find her when they need somebody fast, but who has also got some experience, so they don't need to train her, she can step right in. And then, when their regular person's had her baby or whatever and she's ready to come back, they won't have to tell her that they're sorry, but her job's been filled. Or else fire someone they hired, as a permanent replacement, someone who'd also been, was also counting on that job. So, when they have to do that, what they do is call her up, and she goes in and works.

" 'Most the guys who work for us met her on the job. She'd be fillin' in someplace, happened to be one of our stores. They all say she seems very nice. You know how you always do, if you're a traveling salesman—which is basically what all of our route salesmen are, although they will not like it if you go and call them that. You're making all the friends you can, everyplace you go, because you want people to like you, so they won't get tacked off at you at some time and go buy from someone else. And especially when you also know that this person that you're talking to gets around a lot. Works in a good many stores, and if she happened to be in one some day when the owner went ballistic about some other produce man that wasn't working out too good, got a crabby attitude, or a fresh mouth on him; never shows up when he's supposed to—which is how you really start to lose most of your accounts, when you start to lose the accounts. Not: your product wasn't good enough, very seldom that. But maybe in this case it *is* that, when she happens to be there, his vegetables *aren't* good and that's what got the owner mad. Well, then, regardless, either way, if she liked you she might say: "Then call Homer's, why don't you. Their drivers're all very nice, that come in the stores I worked, and the food is always good, too, nice and fresh and crispy. That's what I'd do, I was in your shoes—it was me that owned this nice store." Not lettin' on Luke works for us. Her and Luke make quite a team.'

"I said I didn't understand," said Whitlock. "It seemed a little funny. If this guy was that religious, how it was that he could square it, bragging all the time about all the sex that he was having living with a woman that he wasn't married to. And Jenkins said he didn't, either. 'None of us can square it. You have to work with Luke awhile, sort of really get to know him. And that's when you find out that really, you are never gonna do that, get so you do know him well. Most of the guys around here think, and I am one of them—and so is Mister Homer, too; Mister Bob Homer himself thinks this, too, guy that owns this outfit—that Luke has got at least two screws loose, maybe even more. One of them is sex, and the other's body building, and maybe if we knew a little more about his church that he goes to, we would say that that's loose too, his religion screw. "Drinks poison or something." So that would come to three.

" 'But whatever's wrong with him, it's not like it bothers us. He really is a nice guy. Nuts, but a nice guy. He's polite to everyone. Always very cheerful. Never tries to cheat the company, claiming that he got spoiled goods that he hadda throw away, so he shouldn't pay for them—when what really happened was he took them for himself or maybe gave them to some friends of his that buy him beers at night. Doesn't lose good customers, either, skippin' them or what's worse, making the stop but then going in and giving them a lot of lip—and we've had guys that did that, too, had to bring them into line, give them a good talking-to. Mister Homer handles that; that part he does himself. Tells them that he doesn't want to—and he really hates to do it, which is actually true; because I've seen him when he had to: he was actually sick—but if this foolishness don't stop, that is what he's gonna have to: he will have to fire their ass, and then what are they gonna do?

" 'But never Luke like that; he's never had the talk. Knows how he should drive his truck, and that's the way he drives it. Fast, sure, Luke moves right along. But if he gets tickets, it must be that he pays them—we never had none come in here. And careful, too. I don't think he's ever had a single dent in that truck, or made another dent in somebody's else's car. Or tore the padding off the front a market loading platform when he pulled away from it, like we had one guy do four times, 'fore we finally hadda fire him. Couldn't seem to get it through his head, when you drop off a big load of heavy stuff, potatoes maybe, the truck gets lighter on the springs and the rear end comes up under the platform padding. So you get a couple big guys from out the store, stand in the back so they weigh it back down again, and you ease it away from the store. That's the kind of thing Luke does. He takes good care of that truck when it's in here or it's out on the road. Always has it down for service, washing when it needs it—Mister Homer's very particular: wants our trucks to look good when they're out there on the road. Luke notices when something's wrong, something's not quite right, the way it oughta be right off. Comes in that night and talks to Rick. Rick is our mechanic; he works on the trucks for us, nights. That is what he does. And Lucas does that, talks to Rick, what it is that he noticed. Tells him what it is, what it was he saw happening. And that way he gets it fixed, *before* it breaks, and so Luke doesn't lose a day and maybe a towin' charge, like would've happened if he didn't, so he broke down on the road. You'd be surprised how many guys can't get that through their head. That downtime is expensive time, not just for *us*: for *them*. Very careful out there, too, as I say—this is what Luke is. Very careful onna road. Never had a claim against him, nine years on the job. Model employee. So okay, he's somewhat nutty; no one I know's perfect.' "

Whitlock had looked up from his papers. "That's what Mister Jenkins said. What he told us about Kyle."

"Yes," Cronin had said, "well, thank you. For that. And for the next thing, you went to *see* Mister Kyle?"

"Yes," Whitlock had said.

"Excuse me, Mister Cronin," Judge Henry had said. "I know from my own experience how hard it is to accurately estimate how long anything will take, but I do note that it is now after three-forty-five, and I can't help but wonder if you still think it's likely you can finish the Kyle part of the lieutenant's testimony on direct before the court's usual four o'clock adjournment? What is your best guess?"

"I don't think I can, Judge," Cronin had said. "The reason that I asked the lieutenant here to give us so much of the conversation that he had with the dispatcher, this man Jenkins here, at Homer's Wholesale Produce or whatever that firm is, is because unless you have it, it is really awfully hard—to grasp the implications of what Mister Kyle had to say. My feeling when I reviewed all this was that unless I gave the court a context in which to interpret that, what Mister Kyle said to the police, everyone'd be left baffled. It would raise more questions than it answered for the court. Well, I have to introduce what Mister Kyle did have to say, but I also must be mindful that it be, somewhat clear, at least. But since I saw it as that, and no more than that, a mandatory preface to what would follow it, I'm afraid I underestimated just how long it all would take. Prefatory or not."

"Then perhaps it might be better, Mister Cronin," Henry had said, "given the lateness of the hour, if we suspended at this point, and resumed tomorrow morning with what Mister Kyle had to say."

"I think so, yes, Your Honor," Cronin had said.

"Mister Dean?" Henry had said.

"Oh, no objection here, Judge," Dean had said. "Whatever Your Honor thinks best."

"When Cronin turned around and started picking up his papers," Henry had told me on the phone, "he saw Lucy sitting there, right behind the rail. She was smiling at him. One of those old, cold Siberian smiles, if you know what I mean. She was born in this country, and she grew up here, and as far as any living human knows, she hasn't got a drop of Russian blood in her, flowing in her veins, But she's still a Russian child, a two-footed conundrum. What was it Winston Churchill said? About the country she's not from? A riddle wrapped in a mystery, inside an enigma. Something like that, anyway. That is what she is."

▪ ▪ ▪ 10

I mentioned Judge Lawler's remark about Lucille to Whitlock the next time I went up to the camera club to meet him on his day off—I brought my own roast beef sandwich from the deli two doors from my office, the meat so rare it would yelp when I bit into it; and two cans of Heineken from the little fridge, kept cold in a big plastic freezer bag with ice cubes in it. I'd called Royce and asked if he'd like me to bring the same thing for him, but he said he'd already made his own and brought it with him, and he didn't want it to go to waste. Meaning, I surmised, that Royce didn't want to find himself in a reciprocal arrangement that'd force him to treat me to the kind of lunches I like. Royce may savor a lunch of Spam and Coca-Cola. I myself do not. I put the bag on the floor and sat down in what had become my chair across the secretary/treasurer's desk from his.

"I dread a case that's even got a child *in* it," I said. "Kids're like time bombs on the stand. Never know what they'll do or say, no matter what you do, your witnesses or the other guy's: doesn't matter at all. It's like juggling live grenades, dynamite sticks with the fuses lit. You know what it is, and you know what it's gonna do. It's gonna do what it was made to do. Sooner or later it's gonna blow up in somebody's face, and the best you can hope for is that it'll turn out to be somebody else's face. Not yours. Whenever I go through a case, start to get it ready for trial, and it finally dawns on me that I don't have any choice, there's a kid so deeply involved in the thing there's no way I can keep him off the stand, I have to get up and go to the bathroom. Have a beer. Go out and get something to eat. Anything to avoid even thinking about it, having to question a kid. Every time I have to question a kid, I start breathin' just like a damned goldfish. My mouth goes all dry on me.

"Now I've got a case and children're *all* that's in it, far as clients of mine're concerned. All the beers and snacks I'm gonna need to get through it, by the time it's over I'm gonna be so fat I won't be able to walk. And now what I get from Henry is at least some slight vibrations that one of my young client's maybe got problems. That she might be kind of disturbed."

"Well," Royce said, "but they're pretty old children, which is a different thing, you know—makes all the difference in the world, you ask me. Because I'm the guy who knows. What happens. You take on some kids that're older, some other guy's fucked around with their heads, you don't even know what he did? Huh? You got no idea *what* you're contending with, what you've gone up against now. And I'd have to say that on top of that, all right? Even on top of all that, that these kids of Sandra's, they look to me, I would have to say, that they're fairly old for their years. Very old-headed I'd say. But then they really haven't had much choice in it though, I guess, when you think about it. 'Grow up fast or go under': that's been about it. Not that they haven't had problems, getting banged around like they've been. Only constant people in their lives've been Sandra and the grandmother, and now Evelyn's the only one left.

"Evelyn's kind of fun to be with, talk to her and so forth—down-to-earth old broad. But she's not what I'd call the kind of older adult, seasoned person, that'd make a young kid feel secure. Especially if what'd been bothering the kids was the way their mother always seemed to be acting around men—*with* men. At least it wasn't with women. And then when they looked at their grandma, there was Evelyn doing the same thing, and what the hell's going on here?"

"This's mainly Lucy we're talking about here, is it?" I said. "She'd be the one with the biggest problems?"

Royce sighed. "Jerry," he said, "Lucy's just the one who's seen the most of it because she's the oldest. The worst of it, too, I guess you'd have to say. Had the problem right in her face for the longest time. Wherever she went it came with her. Had it on her mind, day and night, week in, week out, ever since she was pretty young, just a little girl, that if everything blew all to hell, all to smithereens; if something happened to her mother, living out there on the edge, where bad things do tend to happen . . . well, she wasn't a dumb little girl. Evelyn wasn't going to be much good if some night Sandy just up and took a hike for a change, ran off with some new guy she'd found, 'stead of bringin' him home like the others. That would mean Lucy was It. She'd have to be the one to do the best she could, take care of the other two. Or else foster care, which Lucy did not want.

" 'I never wanted that,' she told me. 'Get sent to live with some damned fools, no jobs their own so they take in the poor kids; doing it for the money, that's all they do it for. I knew kids in school, 'fore Mom met Pete, school where I went then, in Paxton. Kids who'd had that happen. Had it happen to them. They said it was awful. And I knew if Mom ever died, or ran away or something, sooner or later that'd happen: we'd go in foster care. Youth services. Split up, most likely, sent to three different places, my sister, my brother, and me. I was always scared of that, that that'd be what happened. And if it did, what could I do? Nothing, not a thing. That would just be what it was.'

"And it wasn't just her," Whitlock said. "It wasn't just Lucy that feared that. Mag and Jeff were afraid of it too. Not because Lucy wanted company, clued them in to what would happen. Those two are bright kids themselves; they could see what'd be coming if their mother disappeared. So this isn't just Lucy that we've got to think about here, what harm was done to these kids. It's all three of them we're talking about. They've all of them got some kind of way they just automatically *react*, when they feel threatened or something. They've had a lot of hard practice. Or even when they don't, feel threatened; just so no one *will* threaten them—warding off the bogeyman.

"Lucy's routine is: she cuts herself. Cuts herself with razor blades. Not too deep, just on the surface, so the capillaries bleed. You and I've both cut ourselves deeper a good many times, just shaving your face in the morning. Blade just slipped and blood came out. Stuck toilet paper on it. Pretty soon the bleeding stopped. But we cut ourselves accidentally, didn't mean to do it. We said *'shit'* when it happened. 'Goddamn *bas*tard; *shit.*' She's different. She *likes* doing it to herself. She does it deliberately. On purpose.

"She cuts patterns in herself, hearts and squares and triangles, stars and lines. Sets of lines, I mean. Said she had a swastika once, 'no particular reason, but that one I had to keep covered up. I didn't want someone to see it.' Doesn't want to hurt anyone's feelings—totally unconcerned about what she's doing to herself. I don't mean these're permanent disfigurement. They heal up real fast. They don't leave any scars, no real permanent scars I mean. The way that I found out was when we had that real hot spell, end of October, Indian summer last year. I hadda see her about something, I forget, the investigation. So I drove out, Mount Holyoke, there. It was hot and humid, heavy air, no wind at all: real still. And for some reason I didn't call first. I guess maybe I knew it wasn't important, or wasn't going to pan out, or something, but I was already at my wit's end with this case, and I like to think when I drive—sometimes it helps me to think. Maybe I thought if she wasn't there, off on a field trip or something, well, that'd still be okay, day wouldn't be wasted, 'cause I'd get some time just to think. Away from the phone and so forth. Get things sorted out in my mind.

"So, she didn't know I was coming. Had no advance warning. What I did was take her by surprise, not that I meant to. What I did was go the dean's office and find out the best place to look for her. Showed them my badge and said where could I find her. They said: 'Most likely, the library. Lucy's a hardworking lady.' She was in there, just like they said. Wearing this little vest and a pair of denim shorts. Perfectly decent, I don't mean that, but still, large parts of her were uncovered. You could see these faint white scars, this thin little scabbing, on her chest, and arms, and legs. Patterns, like I said—these're not your minor random razor cuts. And I said to her, first words outta my mouth, just blurted it out: 'Good God, kid, what the hell've you *done* to yourself? What the *hell* have you been doing?'

"She took it right in stride: So I'd caught her. No big deal. It was cool. She didn't mind. It wasn't like it really *mattered* to her, anything. Didn't matter at all. Shrugged it off, really. 'Just something I do,' she said, this calm normal tone of voice. 'Something I just guess I do when I don't know what else to do. I take a razor blade and then I sort of cut myself. It only hurts a little. But it's an *important* little hurt; that little hurt's just enough. It's like the sharp pain, it doesn't last long, but it helps me to focus, and I watch the blood come out, and it gets my mind off of things. For a little while at least.'

"I said: 'For Christ sake, Lucy, do your friends all do this, too?' Thinking, you know, this might be some harebrained college fad, seeing if you can get infected, a really bad infection, using just a razor blade. Maybe someone else used it first. 'You could get AIDS from doing this. You could make yourself sick and die.'

"She looked at me like she pitied me, you know? As though she'd been saying to me: Where the hell've you been, big old tough state cop, you pretending or something? You never heard of this before: pain for killing the pain? As though it was really very normal. 'I feel better when I do it. It's not all that unusual, you know. Lots of people do it. Everyone who really knows me knows that I do it,' she said. 'They don't think it's that strange. And no, I don't go borrow blades, or dig them out the trash. I always use one of my own, one that I opened myself. No one else's, no. And then I take good care of the cuts, wash them off with hydrogen peroxide. And then put ointment on them. So, I won't get infected. I will not get sick and die. Not from doing this, at least. It's like taking aspirin, really, any medicine for pain. If it works for you, well then, do it. Anyway, that's how I feel.'"

He paused. "It sort of knocked the wind out of me, I guess," he said. "I hadda take a minute to catch my breath, get it absorbed. Remember what it was I drove about eighty miles to ask her. I'm not sure I did remember, actually—I know I don't remember now. Whatever it was, either she didn't know the answer either, or else she did but it wasn't what I'd hoped that it might be. So either way it wasn't that important. Of course the result was that on my way back I didn't get much thinking done. Not the kind I'd planned to do at least— thinking about the case. All I could think about was this beautiful child cutting herself up like that. Mutilating herself, really, when all the things that happened to her got too much for her." He shook his head. "I couldn't get it out of my mind. I still can't, to this very day. Every so often I'd be going through the file, and I'd come to those pictures I took, and. . . ."

"You took pictures of the kid in that condition?" I said. "I didn't see any pictures like that in the folders I've been through so far. And for

109

sure, I'd remember them, if they'd've been in it. Something like that I wouldn't forget."

He dealt with his sheepishness by willing himself to become quietly defiant, warming to the task as he performed it. "Well," he said, "There aren't any in there. There's only the one set of copies, I made, and I left them out when I made the set I gave you. Those pictures aren't part of the file, about this investigation. They got nothing to do with who killed Sandra Nichols. Nothing to do with our case.

"And anyway, those're not official pictures. I took those pictures, myself. My camera, my film, and then I developed them, enlarged them, and printed them, all on my own time. In the club lab. The North Shore Camera Club—a private, non-profit org. It is not a state police lab. Using my chemicals and my Kodak paper, I bought and paid for; using the club's equipment that's privately owned. Those are not and were not and never at any time have ever been, official state property. You with me so far? Those photos belong to me."

"Yeah," I said. "Well, I'm not gonna get into a dispute with you on this, Royce. We still've got too far to go, to get where we wanna be at. And we can't be arguing all the way there, or we're never gonna arrive. So lemme just tell you that I disagree, and so would your bosses, I bet. Pictures you took, while you were on duty, driving a state car, on the state's gas, investigating a felony under state law, *using your state police badge and ID to gain entrance to a private institution, under color of law:* now you're telling me *some* of your acts weren't *official?*

"Jesus, Royce, you're worse'n Cadillac Teddy. I'm maybe half as good as he said I was, and I have to admit, or maybe it's bragging, that I've sold a few stories from time to time—even *I* found them hard to believe—when things looked bad for one of my clients. But I'd hate like hell to try to sell that one. The village idiot'd laugh me right out of court if I did."

"Well," he said, looking down at the floor and shaking his head, still trying to maintain defiance, "I still say I don't agree with you. Those pictures were taken months after Sandra Nichols died. Two, three weeks after the body was found. No way in the world could you or anyone else tie in those pictures of Lucy to prove who killed her mother, and why. I'm not gonna give them to you."

"Royce," I said softly, like seduction came next, "this case isn't just about that, who banged Sandra Nichols on the head. It's also about pain and suffering, too, the kids' pain and their terrible sorrow. That's how I pinball the damages up, by proving that suffering, too. If ever I heard of evidence that'd convince even a jury made up entirely of marine drill sergeants that some poor pretty kid was in horrible pain, those pictures'd be what I'd choose."

I stopped and let him munch on that for a while. Then I said: "You got to decide, Royce, my friend, *now*. You got to pick Jesus or Satan, and *right now* is when you've got to do it. You show me those pictures and give them to me, and I'll put them back in the file. You want to keep copies, then make more, for yourself. You've got the negatives, right?"

He was still looking down at the floor. When he mumbled his response the defiance had ebbed a little more, but some of it was still there. "I'm not sure," was all he said.

"You're not sure of what?" I said.

"The negatives," he said. "I'm not sure I still got them. I don't know where they are." Then he looked up. He might as well have had a lighted moving streamer headline on his forehead, reading out in bright white letters: NOW I'M GOING TO LIE TO YOU, WITHOUT ANY TALENT, OR ANY PRACTICE, EITHER. PLEASE BELIEVE ME ANYWAY. He cleared his throat. He spoke with too much firm assurance, so as to convince himself. "I destroyed the prints themselves, when I made up your file."

I let minutes tick off into the silence, dragging the way they do when someone that you've lied to just sits there and stares at you. Maybe two or three. And then I stood up and cleared my throat.

"Royce," I said, sticking out my hand, "nice working with you anyway. Sorry it didn't work out."

"*Hey,*" he said, coming to his feet, "where the hell're you going? I thought we were gonna have lunch. You can't just get up and leave like this. We haven't had our lunch yet."

"Good point," I said, bending down and picking up my lunch. "Would've forgotten my excellent sandwich, you hadn't reminded me of it." I straightened up, shifted the bag to my left hand, and offered my right hand again. "Where I'm going is back to my office. Where I will first have my lunch and my beer and then dictate a strong letter to Henry. Telling him how I'll put up with him handing me a hot rocket of a case if he thinks that's what he has to do, but I can't work with an investigator who's decided he's the shadow lawyer, really the one in charge, and I'm just the jerk out front. Ah, hell, why'm I doing this, anyway? Summarizing all of this for you here now, when I haven't even written it? I'm sure when Henry gets it, along with my withdrawal from the case, as he will, by FedEx, ten-thirty tomorrow, he'll see to it that you're informed very promptly of its contents. In colorful detail."

"You can't do this," Royce said. "You can't get off this case like that."

"Lieutenant Whitlock," I said, "try me. You just watch what I can do. In the winking of an eye."

He sat down like he'd been propped up with a jack and someone'd kicked it out from under him. He exhaled heavily. He shook his head. He rubbed the left side of his jaw with his left hand. He sighed. He said: "Okay, okay, I'll give you the pictures. They're not at my office, the courthouse. I got them in my own file at home."

"That's a promise," I said. "I've got your word on that now."

"Yeah yeah," he said, "that's a promise." He looked at me pleadingly. "But you got to promise me something, too. I got to have your word on this."

"What is it?" I said.

"I can't let those pictures get out," he said. "Get into the papers, TV. I promised her that, that day when I took the pictures. Because she didn't want me to do it. I said just what you said, well, almost what you said, I was just taking a guess. I said: 'Lucy, you got to. You bottle up your feelings. That shows you're a courageous kid. You're not begging pity. But this could be important. What you are going through now. A year from now, two years from now, someone could say: 'Well, she didn't care. Didn't bother that girl at all, her own mother getting murdered like that. Not a bit. Just went right on with her life. And it could be important, we ever catch the man who killed her, for us to be able to show that in fact you were taking it pretty hard. And the pictures I take will do that.'"

Uh-huh. Just about the same thing I'd just finished saying to Royce myself. You don't win every argument with talent and eloquence; it's always possible that the other guy agreed all along, but didn't want to.

"And she said: 'Oh sure, and then someone'll see them, and steal them, and sell them—I know. They'll be in all the sleazy newspapers at the checkout counters when I go in to buy a pack of cigarettes, and I'll have people looking at me, staring at me, saying things to me. I know what will happen. No, I don't want that.'"

He looked at me miserably. "Those pictures," he said. "They're, they're pictures of her breasts. She cut her tits, too, Jerry. I made her let me see them and take pictures of them." He stopped. He resumed. "I shouldn't've," he said.

"Oh nuts," I said. "Of course you should've."

"But that's why I hadda promise," he said. "I said: 'No, it won't. I promise you, that won't happen. The pictures won't get out. I'll make sure that the prosecutor'—see, back then that's what I thought, what I just assumed it'd be a criminal case, like any other homicide—'gets the evidence impounded. So the pictures can't get out. I promise you, I will.' So now, you're not a prosecutor, but you're acting in his place and you've got to promise me."

"Promise," I said.

He nodded heavily. "Okay," he said, "all right, I'll do it. After we have lunch. But I hope you can keep your word. I don't want that girl hurt anymore. She's had about enough."

"Okay," I said, "I guess I'm ahead of where I was. I can't say I like the way I got here, but here is where I guess I am. We opened our bags of lunch. Royce eyed my beerbag covetously as he cracked open his Coke. I gave no sign I noticed, and unwrapped my lovely beef sandwich. "So you might as well show me the rest of the show, get it all over with now. What does *Maggie* Cameron do for pain? And Jeffy Nichols—what's his medicine, human sacrifice? What'm I dealing with here?"

Royce carries a lot of air around inside his lungs. He let it all out, noisily and slowly. "Well, it's a lot of the same sort of thing," he said. "I asked Teddy this. I asked Teddy Franklin, he recommended you. I said: 'Can this guy handle this? I realize you tell me he's great in the courtroom, defending a guy up on charges. I realize you tell me he raised his own kid; far's you know he's a good father to her. But Kennedy's kid didn't have to go through what these three kids've been through. She's got to be in much better shape. And I know from raising two stepsons my own, both of them with a few problems they got from bein' ditched by their old man: it's got to be a hell of a lot easier raisin' a kid startin' out with no problems 'n it is gettin' kids out of problems they got, so you can bring them up right after that. These three kids've been badly damaged by what's happened to them, and they sure do need someone's help. But is he the guy that can give it to them?'

"And Teddy says to me: 'The hell do I know? You got someone else, you think can do it better? Then what the hell're you askin' *me* for, bringing me into this mess? I told you what I think is all, what I'd do if I'm in your shoes.' "

"And did you by any chance," I said to Royce, "tell Henry what was involved here? So he'd know what he was getting me into on this?"

"Look, Jerry," Royce said, "don't be too hard on me here. Henry's no virgin on this one. Henry has sat on this case. He knows what I know, about the people here who're in it. What their problems are, and what mine is, a result, I try to do something to help them. What is it you've been doing, all these years, you've been representing people in trouble? You only take cases of people in trouble, provided those people're fine? They got no problems at all? Is that what you're telling me here? If Henry'd told you the specifics what he was getting you into, you would've gone to work on it right off? Before you really knew anything about the case, and figured out a way to get yourself out of it? Because Henry told me you wouldn't. That's what Henry said. He said: 'If I tell him, before he gets in, what he's really letting himself in for here, he'll be out like a shot before I can grab him. And we'll have to start in again. Is Jerry the perfect choice for the job? Probably not. But if the perfect one turns up later on, I'll ask Jerry if he'd like to get out. And my guess is if that happens, that he will tell me no. And you and I'll both be damned glad he did.'

"So that's the whole story. You know it all now. The two of us weren't truthful with you. You wanna try to find a way out?"

"I'll give it some thought," I said. "Tell me about Margaret now."

He sighed. "A lovely child, Margaret. A wonderful, beautiful child. God's own blessing on this poor world. What can I tell you about her? What can I possibly say?"

"Well, you could stop slingin' the good old stuff and tell me what's the matter with her," I said.

"She's bulimic and anorexic," Royce said. "She binges and vomits and then she starts over. Does it all over again. She's in counseling up at her school. The shrink reports to Henry, not me. You want that stuff, you go see the judge."

"I don't," I said. "Jeffrey."

"For a kid who isn't really sure who his father is," Royce said slowly, "since his mother wasn't when she was alive and certainly isn't now, now that she is dead, Jeffrey is a reasonably healthy boy."

" 'Jeffrey is a reasonably healthy boy,' " I said. "Meaning that so far at least he's satisfied with slitting chickens' throats, hasn't yet moved up to babies?"

"Yes," Royce said. "Well, uh, it's possible that Jeffrey sets fires. Starts fires. Possible, I mean. He may not, is what I mean."

"Fires've had a way of starting around places where he's lived, you mean," I said, helping out.

"Yes," Royce said. "Like that. No one's ever been quite sure."

"No," I said. "Well, good. So now I see I've got a loverly bunch of coconuts. Tell me something else, if you would: did Henry know all these melancholy facts before he roped me into this?"

"Yeah," Royce said. "Say, could I have one of those beers?"

"That's what I thought," I said. "Tell him for me: I'll get even with him for this. And I mean it, too: I'll get even." I handed Royce a beer.

▪ ▪ ▪ 11

In my time I have had some trouble looking at photographs. Not the ones displayed in taxpayer-funded arty museum shows that infuriate southern senators, the postcard stuff that's sold in stores, or the naughty or horrifying pictures reproduced in newspapers and magazines. No, the photos that've bothered me have been frames enlarged from VHS tapes—in the old days, film—exposed in surveillance cameras installed in such places as banks, liquor, and convenience stores. Artistic they have not been, not well composed at all, generally very grainy. But devastating they have been indeed. It's very hard to cross-examine a photograph taken of your client in a credit union with a pistol in his hand—damned near impossible in fact. It's not as hard as trying to figure out a way to discredit a tape recording of your client registering bets without inviting all the members of the jury to think you believe them to be downright stupid, an inference they will not like and will firmly hold against your client when it's time for them to retire and consider a verdict, but it's pretty difficult.

This time there was a difference. The photographs were on my side. The pictures of adorably pitiable Lucy with her vest off and her scars at school that October day were enough to make you wince, probably enough to elicit a few tears (and demands for higher damages) from the more compassionate jurors, if we ever got to trial, but the pictures of her mother's body were nothing short of appalling. The routine black-and-whites and color Polaroids taken by the regular SP photographer were grim; the full-color pictures that Royce'd carefully composed and then painstakingly enlarged were grisly, absolutely devastating.

For the whole five hot and moist New England months that Sandra's lifeless body had been in it, that big green plastic trash bag had been partially exposed to the battering sun and also partially submerged in the warm, shallow brackish water of that protected North Andover wetland. Aging under those conditions had not improved the corpse. "You're a real good photographer, Royce," I said with distaste. "Too good for my sensitive stomach."

Royce was unsurprised, untroubled as well. "I know it," he said, "but it isn't that hard now, being a decent photographer. It's much more the lenses 'n me. That beautiful lens glass they're making these days; the machines they're hitching it up to: you can't make a man sick over a death scene, you've got equipment like that, you should get yourself another line of work. And you decide you want to take some pictures, something, later? Get yourself one of those disposable cameras, just like the first cameras Kodak ever made: a box of film with a cheap piece of glass on it. Don't even bother, get the film processed— what you've got on it won't be any good. Save yourself four or five bucks: just throw the whole thing away."

Royce's carefully arranged sequence began with several wide-angle shots setting the bucolic scene. A couple of early frosts and the late afternoon sun on that October day had combined to dust the tall grasses of the marshland with tones ranging from pale beige all the way to russet gold. The branches of the pines on higher ground to the west of the shallow slough divided the angled autumn sunlight into broad shafts where the outlaw fern lady had stepped on the rubbish bag, making dappled reflections on the still greenish brown water. Here and there on the surface, inverted, circular, one-ring dimples had risen—small fish capturing miniature insects for dinner. Delicately picturesque, had it not been for the almost immediate deduction that the insects were most likely small gray, legless larvae, maggots feasting to housefly adulthood on the flesh of Sandra Nichols. The plastic garbage bag, no matter how tightly the killer had wired it shut, had never been a barrier to maggots. Nothing is. They're God's hardworking janitors. They go into caskets and garbage bags alike, right along with the corpses, eggs laid and left behind by their moms. When they hatch, they eat their hosts and hostesses. Maggots feed on all dead animals, except dead people whose survivors mercifully arrange for their prompt cremation or the kind of hard embalming the Egyptians practiced. As the summer progressed, the bag in the hot sun and water hadn't stayed airtight and watertight; the gases of decaying flesh had expanded inside it, and it had burst. After that it'd been a mere slippery inconvenience to flying and four-footed scavengers.

Predictably Royce'd moved on through the so-called normal lens shots into the close-ups, apparently timing his approach to coincide with the progress of the work done at the scene by the other cops—unseen in the pictures, except for their rubber-gloved hands and fore-arms; the occasional rubber-booted foot and lower leg—lifting the sagging rubbish bag out of the shallow water, then hoisting it up onto a stretcher to carry it to higher ground. Those shots showed the four cops from the rear, trudging up an incline softly deep in the rotted fallen leaves and the brown pine needles of accumulated seasons, their shoulders in the dark blue plastic ponchos white-stenciled STATE POLICE across their shoulders, their backs bowed by their bur-den. Then Royce had zoomed in again as the stretcher was set down and the bag was slit open, going to extreme, frame-filling close-ups of the contents as the plastic was parted wide.

It really seemed as though she should have been larger, given the strain apparent in the posture of the cops who'd taken her up the slight elevation. I mentioned that to Royce: "She seemed awfully *small* when they got the bag open. I assume you weren't using *old* troopers for this, too old for such heavy lifting."

He was undisturbed. "Oh no," he said, "always the young eager lads. But that's what everyone says. Someone who's never had the corpse detail always says 'Those guys with the body look like they were gonna *collapse*.' Yeah. Well, what I always ask those fresh bas-tards is this: '*You* ever do it? *You* ever tried it? No, you haven't, of course not, or you wouldn't think it was funny. But that's okay just the same: use your brain for a nice change of pace. Why you think they call it *dead weight*?' " He stopped and scowled for a moment.

"You're in that situation, you're *always* conscious of it, what it is you're carrying. In that situation you're not a cop: you're a pallbearer. And you know it. It weighs you down. You take four guys who can brench-press two-twenny-five apiece, they could lift a car off of a guy without even breaking a sweat; you give the four of 'em a hundred-eighty-pound stiff, to carry all together? It'll bend their backs every time." He hesitated again, and coughed.

"Besides, in this case, that bag'd leaked some. Well, hell, why not tell the truth here? The bag'd burst from the gas of the original decomposition. Probably about a month or so after she went into the water—we did have a pretty hot summer. But then of course she'd continued to rot, after the bag'd popped there, so there was still a pretty good stench coming out of it by the time the lads had to wade in and pick her up, there. And there was water in that bag, too, makin' a nice gravy for the dish. So add all that to what it was she weighed, too. The whole thing was heavy enough for most people, and it didn't smell very good."

In the pictures she lay on her right side, in the fetal position, the toe of the small white sneaker on her left foot slightly behind the one on her right foot, her bare ankles briefly blackish green and showing multiple punctures below her jeans. Laymen on the jury would assume that was all clotted pond scum, a mistaken conclusion that would nevertheless be enough to make them cringe; I made a mental note not to let them get away with even that, to make sure I had some witness say what it really was: human flesh that had rotted in warm water and warm sun, and then been pecked by feeding birds, crows or maybe seagulls, white and gray vultures going inland a few miles for carrion while the fishing fleet was at sea.

Royce had done his job well. I've defended a number of murder ones; most times I've had a hard time preventing the prosecutor from introducing photographic evidence of death, but thank the Lord the times I lost that point, the proof hadn't had the impact this stuff would have, hitting laymen so hard in pits of their stomachs with their own fear of death that they'd find someone guilty, anyone handy, just so they wouldn't have to look anymore at what happens to us at the Last Stop where we all get off. The sleeves of her greenish pullover—it appeared to be a sweatshirt; "Miami Dolphins," Royce said when I asked him—had been pushed up. Her bare arms, neck, and face were more deeply discolored, blacker than her ankles were. They'd also been pecked.

"More fat and meat on those parts, is why," Royce said. "Flesh rots much faster'n deeper'n muscle does, and your normal-sized females, which Sandra Nichols was, they've got more of that stuff'n males do. Adipose tissue, I mean. And keep in mind this: that's where the blood settles, too, after death. Lividity, remember that? Disappears within a few hours, but the blood doesn't go anyplace; it stays right where it is—no heartbeat to pump it anymore. Tissue with blood in it decays very fast. Starts out reddish white, or chocolate, or something in between, tan or beige or yellow, long's you can stay alive, and then when you can't anymore, it turns kinda blue, cyanosis. That's when you're really getting dead. And then after a little while more, it turns black. Does that when you've started to rot."

Royce'd zoomed in tight on the left side of her head, bowed down chin-tight against her chest as though she'd been napping. "She wasn't a very big kid," Royce said, "no more'n five-four or five-five, but she was still taller'n that green rubbish bag. So whoever did it'd had to kind of fold her up to get her in. Which tells you she went into the bag as fresh kill, almost right after he hit her. Because if there'd been time for rigor mortis to set in, he never could've cramped her up like that. What he did was pull the bag down over her head and then stuff her feet in and close it up and tie it. Just like we all do when we fill a bag in the fall, raking leaves, or when we've got a lot of trash that we want to get rid of—stuff it in, pack it down, twist it closed, and tie it. Very efficient, handy way of getting rid of something you don't want around anymore. Don't normally think of it as a way to get rid a human *body*, no. Hell, we even give dead *bums* a wooden crate, they go down to paupers' field there. But hey, you never can tell; this approach here might catch on. You've got a lot of indignation nowadays, what it costs take care of all the damned poor people, can't take care of themselves. Bags certainly's a cheap way to do it, time comes to drop them off someplace the last time."

I had to clear my throat a couple times. "But these are powerful pictures, Royce," I said. "Yet you claim you've never even *tried* to get pictures that you've taken into evidence, when they come to trial," I said.

"I haven't," he said. "In the first place, you and I both know it'd take a reckless judge to let my photos in. If you were on the other side, you'd be up and hollering good and goddamn loud that they had to be excluded. 'Too inflammatory,' you'd be screaming. "Needlessly prejudicial.' And the chances are, you'd win.

"But even if you lost and the judge let them in, Commonwealth wouldn't gain very much. It'd only complicate matters. I'd be in a position where I'd have to be testifying not only as the chief investigator at the scene but also as the assistant who did the camera work. It'd be too easy for someone to tangle me up, get me to make an inconsistent statement. Or make it look like I must've, at least. 'Now, while you were doing *this* with the camera, you say you were also doing *that* to take notes, and the other thing to direct the investigation. Is that correct now, Lieutenant? Just how many guys *are* you, anyway? All by yourself, a committee?' No, I want none of that. So, like I told you: I take the pictures for the same reason that I take my written notes: I use the pictures to refresh my recollection of what I actually saw at the scene. Also to give the prosecutor a good hard look at what we saw there, because he's seldom with us when we see it. And also, too, not so incidentally, to make sure when I'm *at* the scene that I really do *see* it. As unpleasant as it is to look at. As much as I'd just as soon *not* be, seeing what I see—like to get the hell out of there, in fact."

"But I'm not defending here," I said. "This time I'm the plaintiff, remember? Your pictures go as directly to the issue of damages as I might argue they would not to the issue of criminal guilt. So in a civil case, well, might be worth a try. The impact that they have on someone looking at them, long after the facts of the event've become known . . . it's so much greater than the impact that the 'official' pictures deliver."

"Jerry," he said patiently, "listen to me, all right? *Inflammatory*'s what my personal reason comes down to, when I take those pictures. That's why I take them, so that when I look at them, when the prosecutor looks at them, we'll both get good and mad again at the bastard who did this. We do a better job that way—it focuses our minds. The official SP photographers, they start out as young kids, and one of two things happen to them: either they get so sick and tired of taking pictures of mangled bodies they put in for transfer back to turnpike patrol, or else they harden themselves to what they're always seeing, and're always going to be seeing, if they stay—so they don't really see it anymore.

"I never want that to happen to me, so I start taking it for granted that yeah, this kid, or this old lady, or this poor middle-aged son of a bitch that got caught with another man's wife, or killed by rough trade he picked up, or even this no-good damned gangster, got beaten to death, stabbed, or shot, and that's just the way it goes, ain't it? Everybody so far that I've ever had to look at, every murder victim, well, so far I've been able to treat every one of them, all of them, every damned time, as a recent human being I adopted. To *revenge*. That's kept me hungry, Jerry, helps me to make sure I always do, in every single case, the best job I possibly can. I don't claim I succeed every time. I've still got files open, and I expect I always will, 'til the day that I retire. But I do the best I can. And I never, never forget."

In the pictures, Sandra's wet short hair was all matted down in clumps against her skull, but in an area above and behind her left ear there was a depression, ragged around the ivory edges, about the circumference of a baseball. "That's the broken bone," Royce said. "Shattered parietal area of the skull. The brain in that area would've been exposed, as it was, and consequently decomposed more rapidly than it would've otherwise. Whoever did it hit her a helluva shot."

"And must've been a fairly robust fellow, too," I said. "Hit her that hard and then get her in the bag and drag or carry her . . . how far'd you say from the road?"

"I paced it off at a little over a hundred yards," Royce said. "Of course the person or persons who carted her in there may not've taken the same path I did, but it seemed to be a pretty well defined one, logical choice. People do go into those wetlands for perfectly legitimate reasons. It's not just sneaky old-lady desperadoes out to steal Boston ferns. Birders and just plain nature lovers, out for a nice healthy walk. Butterfly collectors, believe it or not, and every so often, from what they've left behind, young couples, some of them boys 'n' girls, some boys 'n' boys, out in the bushes getting laid. At least I assume they're young: getting mosquito bites on my bare ass's not something that'd appeal to me, or most older parties I know. Don't get *that* horny no more.

"Now generally speaking those good law-abiding people—except for the ones getting laid; they're breaking the law but they're harm-less—aren't going to get their feet any wetter; fight their way through any more brambles, poison ivy, poison sumac, poison oak, under-brush, and so forth; or climb over any bigger rocks, 'n' they absolutely have to. They want to see and hear the birdies; or they want to see the flowers; or they want the exercise. But they're not going to take it to extremes. Well, generally your evildoer dumping off a body feels about the same way. He isn't going to take any more time to do it'n he absolutely has to. Being spotted at his wickedness is not what he's got in mind, and the longer he takes to get it all over with, the greater the chance that'll happen. So, no, I can't say for certain that whoever lugged Sandra into the swamp five months or so before we got around to hauling her out actually followed the same path I did, but that'd be my guess, that he did. Stone killer, for sure, but still: a practical man."

"One man then, you think," I said. "One man killed her and got her all the way in there, but it took four big cops to haul her back out? Gilbert's autopsy report pegged her weight at one thirty-one—I assume that was without her clothes on. Bodies weigh less, they've been dead awhile, after they've decomposed some. How we account-ing for this? The killer was goddamned King Kong?"

"Adrenaline, for openers," Royce said. "A good strong guy, maybe on some other drugs as well, manufactured ones, little Andes march-ing powder, but all pumped up on his own juice even if he wasn't, high-wired and excited at the same time? A guy in that condition, and I'm not kidding here, can rassle five cops or a couple big bears and at least keep 'em all busy awhile. It's amazing how strong a person can get when the situation requires it. Especially if that person was fairly strong anyway, even when he was relaxed."

"Like a bodybuilder maybe?" I said.

"Kyle," he said, "yeah. That's the first thing I thought of myself, I find out what he likes to do. But no, I don't think so. There's just too many things wrong with it, with having him as the suspect.

"Number first: From what everybody says, he's had as little as pos-sible to do with our Sandra ever since he screwed his first big-titted beautician and moved on to the first cosmetician, or whatever the hell all these dames of his are, anyway. If there was more'n one of them. After that he was finished with Sandra like I'm finished with a beer can once I've emptied it.

123

"Number second: Nothing to gain by her death. No money. No revenge, no nothin'. No evidence whatever he ever had any contact with Peter Wade, or even tried to.

"And number third: Absolutely no evidence whatever that puts him in the North Andover area at any time during the period when she was last seen there. None. But much evidence indeed that puts him elsewhere during that time, regular as ever, work, gym and church, then go home and fuck the broad, the one that's gone straight and become the cashier. This man is a pain in the ass, absolutely, but set-your-watch-by-him dependable.

"So, I don't think he's our man. The man I think we're lookin' for is someone who (A) knew Sandra, before she hooked up with Peter. He didn't see her that much after that, but he was still on good terms with her. So that after the dream dies with Peter, if this old flame of hers got in touch with her and said: 'Hey, let's have a coffee,' or: 'Meet me for a drink?' Sandra, trusting soul she was, lonely and upset, most likely would've said to him: 'Yeah, sure. Nice a you to call.' And who (B) also knew Peter, who'd called him for that reason, because they both knew he'd known Sandra before, and our Pete said to him: 'Here is what I want from you: I want you to kill Sandy and I'll give you money for it.' And our man did not say: 'Hey, not on your fuckin' *life*—I'd *never* harm a hair on that girl's *head*.' No, she'd dumped him for Peter, tough shit for her; he's gotta be practical now. So he said: 'How much, Peter? How much're we talkin' here?' And Peter named him a price. Which if it wasn't enough, and this guy haggled with him, Peter, knowing what the stakes were, would've gone the sky's the limit. Whatever he had to to get this guy's solemn promise to do the deed he wanted done."

"Its just that you don't know, offhand, who this guy might be," I said, somewhat sarcastically.

Royce was not perturbed. "As a matter of fact," he said, "I think I prolly do know. It's just that so far at least I haven't figured out a way to prove it, beyond a reasonable doubt. I've begun to think, in fact, that I agree with the DAs—that that can't be done." Then he smirked at me. "But you don't have to do that, do you, Jocko, now? Prove it to that great extent. All you've got to do is prove he's probably the guy. And that is why you're in this case—because Henry and I think that that can be done. And we think you're the guy who can do it."

124

"Got any idea *how*?" I said.

He nodded emphatically. "I was thinking it over last night. Don't waste any more of your time with Saint Luke, the Hairdresser's Bedtime Dream. Read the Cameron background. Then my interview with him. I thought at the time that he'd given it away, and damned if I don't still think the bastard did. But not far enough so I could get a grip on it, and yank it the rest of the way out of him. But I'm not gonna say any more on this. You go in and make up your own mind. Don't go into it with my ideas. Read it with a clean slate of your own, and then tell me what you think of it."

▪ ▪ ▪ 12

Whitlock had testified at the inquest before Henry Lawler that Trooper Morse had located Hugh Cameron through the computerized records of the Registry of Motor Vehicles. "The last-known address given for Hugh Cameron, date of birth May fourteenth, nineteen forty-one, was Seven thirty-one Federal Street, Avon, Massachusetts. The decedent's mother, Evelyn Streeter, had told us that the Hugh Cameron who had become involved with Sandra Nichols had met her in the Queen City Diner shortly after 'he'd been through a real bad divorce. It was country music that brought 'em together. He was a big fan of it, always played it on the jukebox, whenever he came in, and Sandy, well, you could always tell exactly where she was if she was in the house, whatever—there was country music playin'. She played it in the car. She just played it all the time. So she knew all the words to all the songs, and when she was his waitress, whichever one he played, she'd be singin' right along. And that was how that happened.

"'Not that I'm saying that there's such a thing as a *good* divorce, but I guess him and his first wife's'd been pretty bad. I never did find out what it was brought it on. They had a child, lovely little girl, about seven then, I think. I saw her a few times while him and Sandra was living together. He had her up for the weekend. She was an angelic child. A little angel she was. Tiffy. Her real name was Tiffany but everyone always called her "Tiffy." 'Cept for her father, that is. Hughie always called her "Tiff." Lived with her mother, of course.

" 'I guess there was trouble every time Hugh went to pick her up. His first wife didn't want him takin' her to where she'd be with Sandra. Didn't think that was right, her daughter spendin' much time with Daddy's girlfriend; she was supposed to be visitin' *him*. I guess she didn't think Sandra was good enough for Tiffy. Said Sandy was poisoning Tiffy's mind against her mother. Hugh had his part in the fighting, too, though. Tiffy said he was pretty bad, get real mad and then called her mother bad names. She said they made her frightened, the two of them, warrin' like that, hollerin', yellin', and screamin', and sometimes she didn't know if she wanted Daddy to even come, even though you could see they was close. She missed him since he left, and she wished that he'd come home. So she depended on those weekend visits. But then she was afraid that when Daddy did show up for one of them, there'd be one of those terrible fights. And generally, I guess, there was. Him and his ex-wife, they just couldn't seem to let *go* of it, just realize it was all over with and put it *behind* them, once and for all. Always had to be *at* each other, all the time. Never could give it a rest.

" 'But Tiffy just rode it out. She didn't have no choice, if she wanted to see him—and she sure did. Tiffy just loved her daddy. She *loved* bein' with him. She didn't mind it that Sandy was there, when he brought her back the apartment. And just where was Sandy s'posed to go, when he brought her, anyway? It was *her* apartment. Hugh was just livin' there with her, though he was payin' his half of the rent. But Tiffy didn't mind it. Sandy was just fine with her. And Lucy was only four or so then, but it was like she was a little sister Tiffy'd never known she had, and Tiffy was her big one. So the two of them got along just fine. It was really cute seeing them, how they acted and all with each other, just as natural and happy and everything, as you could possibly dream.

" 'So generally it was Sandy and Lucy and Tiffy. Hugh was a good father. Good as gold about making sure he always took advantage of his visitation days. He made sure he always used them, so his first wife couldn't haul him back there into court and start in complaining about he wasn't showin' up and she couldn't ever plan. He wasn't gonna let her do anything like that, give her another, different, way, start harassin' him again? Which she just *loved* to do—he said it was her favorite sport, "makin' my life miserable." Oh no, forget that. Not on your life. But once he had Tiffy with him and they's back at Sandy's place, he didn't really know what to do with the kid—'s only natural. He loved his little girl, no question at all about that, but what's a man his age know about playing with little girls, anyway? Little boy, sure, he'd've known what to do then, if Tiffy'd been born a boy. Take him right in the living room with him, start teaching him all about football. But with Tiffy he didn't know what he should do. And so he didn't do very much.

" 'So Sandy would have to step in and take charge, and he would turn Tiffy over to her, grab a can of beer, go into the living room all by himself, and he'd sit down in the big nice reclining chair that Sandy'd bought for Luke for Christmas one year when they were married. It's real Naugahyde, if you know what that means; looks and feels just like it's real leather, only it don't wear out half as fast. It cost a lot of money. She wouldn't let Luke take it when he left her, and that really pissed him off. Just his clothes was all he got, which was really all he'd brought with him when he came, before they got married, and as I say, that pissed him off. He really liked his chair. And it is, it's really a nice chair, and that's why I didn't blame Sandy one damned bit for hangin' on to it the way she did. She didn't pay all that money so he could just take it with him, park his no-good cheatin' ass in it, some other woman's place. That was not in her mind at that time at all. And so Hugh would sit himself down in that chair and watch whatever kind of ball game would be on, that time of year, and at some point he'd get up, go into the kitchen, fix himself a sandwich, get himself another beer, see what they was doing, Sandy and the kids, and then go back and watch the game. Or watch another game, if the first one was all over. There was always lots of games and he seemed to like them all, so he was always entertained. It kept him occupied.

" 'And unless Sandy hadda be at work or something, in which case it'd mostly be the two little girls, just on their own, playin' with their dollies, Sandy'd be the one that was with the two kids. The three of

128

them got along together perfectly fine. They would make pies and cakes, "and brownies for Daddy"—although I don't think any of the ones that Lucy made her daddy ever ate, because her daddy never came around; she almost never saw Luke—and cookies and so forth, like that. Sandy said they were almost best friends, Lucy and Tiffy, the two of them got along so good. She told me she figured when her and Hugh married, she'd have no trouble at all bein' with Tiffy. And then, of course, what'd he do to her later on? What'd he do but he went back to his first wife there and they got married all over again. You see what I mean about just letting go. They couldn't seem to do it. They was just meant for each other, I guess. Hated each other, but what could they do? It was just their destiny or some other thing. They was fated to do what they did.

"'This would've been sometime during the spring of seventy-seven, I believe it was, when him and Sandy started getting together. I'm not really sure *when* it was, exactly. Well I mean, I know what the *year* was, it was seventy-seven, because she had Maggie the year after and Maggie was born in seventy-eight. My God, that'd make Tiff, what? Twenty-four or so today? Doesn't the time just go by. Just takes your breath right away.

"'Anyway, Hugh Cameron was Maggie's father. There was never any question about that. But I never was quite sure what the month was, two of them started getting together.

"'See, she kept it from me quite a while, I know, as long as she could, because she knew how I felt about Lucas, that I liked him quite a bit. Even after he'd done what he did to her, runnin' off like that. In my younger days I would've gone with a Lucas, if I'd ever had the chance, which I didn't. Even if it turned out for me the same it did for Sandy, and the bastard ran off on me. I have to admit that's always been one of my weaknesses. I've always been willing to see what might happen and then say to myself: "And it also might not. So the hell with it then, take a chance." And go do it. And I would've done that, with Luke.

"'But anyway, Sandy figured I'd be mad at her if I found out she was seeing this new man she'd picked up for herself, so she just put it off, me finding out, for just as long as she could. She got that from me. We've both always been like that. Although of course she's dead now, and all. Even that she kept from me, long's she could anyway. First she disappeared for all that time, nowhere to be found. Like she was making sure I had some time, get used to the idea and all, she might not be coming back. And then when I finally found out that she was really dead, well, I'd be used to the idea. In her own way, she was kind. Sandy was always kind. Mind you, I'm not sayin' that. Don't get that idea. But if she could've planned it that way, that's the way it would work out, that's the way she would've planned it, ease the blow on me.

" 'And she always was that way, too, ever since I can remember. Took after me on that; just alike on that we were. Go ahead and do something that we know'll make somebody mad—like: "Well, but too bad for them it's my life"—and then turn right around and just do our damnedest to try to keep them from finding it out. That we really did it. For just as long as we can. It don't make no sense at all.

" 'But she was right about that, of course, when she did it. I probably would've jumped the tracks, gone and said something to her that I probably would've regretted, if I'd just found it out and didn't have any time to get used to the idea first. A little bit at a time. So I guess when you come right down to it, Sandy was right, and she went about it in the right way. Instead of just coming right out and telling me: "Ma, me and Hugh now're living together," she just let me sus*pect*, and suspect and suspect, until I just figured it out. So that by now I'm all used to it, all by myself, and then when I ask her, she admits it. So by then, you know, I'm not really all that put out about it. It *is her* life, after all, and if this new man, this Hugh fellow, is the one she feels like she wants now, spend it with and all, well, okay. See by then I'd come around so I reckoned it was her choice, really. Wasn't mine to make. Even though she still wasn't even twenty-one yet. But I knew she needed a man, and I told her I knew that. That I understood how she felt. So then it was all right, more or less.

" 'Even though he was quite a good deal older'n her. She would've been just twenty then, and this Hugh fellow, he was already thirty-six. Now I've never been a one to say that, you know, "Well, it's okay if the man is three or four years older than the woman he's with, but it's not okay if he's eight, ten, or twelve, because those things don't work out. They just never do work out when there's an age difference big as that." Because I've seen ones that *did* work out, and worked out very good, too. Very nicely, in fact. Several, in fact, quite a few. But still I thought that sixteen years was quite a lot and all, especially seeing how young she still was. He was literally old enough to be her father, at his age—he literally could've been that.

" 'I might've seen it differently if she'd been thirty years or so old, say, and he would've been . . . well, then he would've been forty-six. She'd've been lots more mature then, if that'd been the case, if they'd met about ten years or so later. Would've had more experience. Would've had more of an idea what she wanted from her life. What it was she *wanted*, in a *man*. And where she was so young and all, and him movin' right in, as fast as he really did, didn't waste no time at all doin' it, well, even if she had known, did know, she didn't have no time to think: "Is this guy really what I want?" Hugh didn't give her none. Like he was afraid, he did, she would change her mind and say: "No, you can't do that. I'm not ready for that yet." But anyway, don't matter now, because he didn't do that.

" 'I thought at the time, and I think so now, too, there was a certain amount of the old ricochet-romance thing that was involved in this Hugh thing. A certain amount, gettin' even with Luke. "I'll show him, I'll show that bastard, I can still get a man. It won't take me no time at all." But of course I don't know. You never know what's in another person's mind, what's going through it when they do something like that. Sometimes they don't, themselves. It's just something they end up doing. But whatever it was, she didn't see this new man the way I saw the guy. To me old Hughie was no bargain. Divorced himself, they started out, a kid his own, bringing her out for weekends. At first, when they first met, he had this apartment in Leominster he'd been living in, since he left his first wife. But before you knew it, *bang*, like *that*, he'd moved in with Sandy.

" 'So I just had to wonder just how serious he was. Or if he wasn't serious at all, maybe—that could've been also. Simply after . . . well, you know what I mean—some of that hot young little chickie-poo she still was then. All he could get, even though she'd had a kid, too. Man his age'd go for that, say anything, do anything it took to get her out of her pants and into bed. That's just a very normal thing.

" 'Or maybe, and I also have to admit I did think this, that he was just pretending *that*. That he wasn't after even that, hot sex and plenty of it, but just someone to split the rent with. 'Cause things had to've been fairly tight with him, moneywise, by then—him with the child support and alimony and so forth. Just tryin' to cut a few corners, you know? Save a few bucks here and there, or wherever else that he could. He did kind of look like the type who would do that—very dark, heavy-beard kind of guy. Like more'n one of mine turned out to be. Like that poor bastard, Ken, I lived with awhile: not that he *meant*, or *wanted*, to be, you know, not pullin' his share the load, but between still havin' the wife, still takin' care of her and what it took to keep her quiet, and playin' the horses, same time, that's what he turned out to be. A money grubber, always hittin' me up for some cash. Gold digger with a dick in boxer shorts. Bad thing, I know, to call any man, but it still has to be said: that's what he was, all the same. And Hugh looked to me like he could be one, too. But I didn't say anything of that stuff to her—I kept all of that to myself. Half a mother's job in this life's keeping her mouth shut.'

"We located Mister Hugh Cameron at his home address in Avon where he had resumed living with his first wife, from whom he in fact'd never been divorced."

"Cameron was a bigamist, in other words, Lieutenant?" the judge said. "That what you're telling us here?"

"That's the way it looked to us," Royce had said. "Notwithstanding what Mrs. Streeter'd told us, which we believed at the time, as she told us subsequently, she mistakenly herself'd believed. He told us his first and only wife had accepted him back on the condition that he give up his previous occupation, which had been that of driving a truck owned by Atlas Auto Parts of Attleboro, Mass., specializing in supplying tools and automotive parts to independent auto repair shops located throughout northern New England. Which according to him would've been Massachusetts, southern Maine, New Hampshire, and Vermont."

"Yes, Lieutenant," Judge Lawler had said—I could hear him grinding it out—"and also according to the rest of us, too, as well as most of the maps that I've seen. What did Mister Cameron tell you? Can you just tell us that, please, if you would?"

"Yes, Your Honor," Royce had said. "Getting right into that, here.

We found Mister Cameron at his home at five-forty-five in the evening, that being his customary time of returning there after his regular day's work at Cobra Consolidated Auctioneers, where he had obtained employment subsequent to his reinstatement—reconciliation, I guess you could call it, in his marriage—as what he called a shipping and receiving specialist. Or boss. In East Bridgewater, Massachusetts, which isn't that far from where he lived. In Whitman.

" 'It was the traveling that got to Edie,' he told us. *'My* traveling, I mean. She said the traveling all around New England was what'd caused me to get into the trouble with Sandra, and all, and if I hadn't've been doing it in the first place, and staying away from home at night, I wouldn't've ever even been in a position where I got involved with Sandy. And she figured if I kept on doing it, even though me and Sandy're all finished and over with long before I come back and got back together with Edie and so forth, sooner or later I'd do it again.

" 'So, to make my peace with her I had to find myself a job that didn't require me to go away too far from home, and that basically is what I did. And I don't do that anymore.

" 'Basically what I do now is I work for these professional auctioneer types and appraisers and so forth, and they get hired to liquidate estates, that kind of thing, and what they do is they go in and decide what something's probably worth, all the stuff in the dead person's house, for the family members and so forth, and they give them a figure as to what they think it's probably likely going to bring in when they put it up for sale. Less their commissions and what it costs them for the warehouse and work I do in it. What their stuff looks like it would bring. Although of course that's not guaranteed; just an educated guess is all it ever is, never guaranteed. You never can say for sure what a thing'll sell for, just what you think it might. And it's time the actual sale, and what the hell do you know? Sometimes it's more, sometimes it's less, who can tell in advance? So we never guarantee, and we tell the people that. And then the person who's inherited the stuff, or one of them at least, will either say—or *not* say; because they also can say that, "Nothing doing, pal"—"all right," and you can go and sell it. Or you can't and that is that. And what it brings is what it brings. We haven't got no side deals going for ourselves on the side of this, either, where the auctioneer's tipped off his friend who's in the antique business and they keep the bidding low so his friend can scoop it up real cheap.

" 'So if they do that, these outside people, owners of the stuff, if they say, "all right," then what they do, these are the actual appraisers and auctioneers that I'm talking about now here, they will then come back to me and say: "*Oh*-kay, Hugh, here's where it is, all the stuff is here. And you can take a guy, Jackie, maybe, someone, and go and pick up all this damned *junk* here, on the list, anything with our tag on it, and the crap and stuff like that, and I said you'd be there next Wednesday at eleven in the morning," or whenever it might be, the next day on the board that was clear when they went out. "And they'll have somebody there who'll be expecting you." And I get another guy to go with me in the truck, and I get the stuff and bring it to the warehouse, and I put it there, all right? And then when there's enough of it, when they've got enough of it backed up, so it looks like it's worthwhile, then they put an ad in the Sunday newspaper and they announce the auction, and then they sell it off. And so that is what I do now. No more nights away from home. No more those long nights on the road.'

"We asked him about his daughter, Margaret, and how often he saw her and so forth, and he said: 'Well, not that often, actually. As a matter of honest fact. Now it's not that I don't care about her, or anything like that, because I do think about her. I think about her a lot. But you know how it is, one thing and another, and besides, she's been a long way away from me here, most of the time, a long way away, since me and Sandy broke up there. It's not like she was living next door, or even the next town over. She lives in another damned *state* now. I'd have to drive a long way. And then anyway, as soon's I started thinking, well, that I should go and see her, well, then I start to think: "Why should I do that? I never hear from her, do I? I don't even get phone calls, the kid. Lousy card on Father's Day—don't even send me one of those. She's got a rich stepdaddy now. He prolly gets the card. What does she need me around now for? Poor workin' stiff like me." So then I end up not going.

" 'I know how it all sounds to you. It sounds to you, or someone else, I don't care what happens, the kid. But I do care, I honestly do. It's just that it's not as easy as it looks, you know? You think: "Well, I should've done this. I should've done that. Made some kind of an effort. Or something." But then when you actually start to think about it, about actually going and doing it, well, then, you know, you just don't. It's too fuckin' much trouble is why, and that was why you didn't do it. That's the way all of us are. All filled up with good intentions and so forth, but then when it comes time to do them? Well, you don't. Because they are a pain in the ass. Guy said to me once, I forget why he said it: "Friend in need is a pain in the ass." He was right, whoever he was.

" 'And besides that, there was the Brian thing, the thing she had going there with Brian and all, and I really do have to admit, that one did piss me off. That one really did piss me off.'

"Mister Cameron," Royce had said, "Mister Cameron was really quite adamant in expressing his feeling about this Brian gentleman. He didn't like him a bit, and he said that, he told us that. He said: 'It was one thing, more or less, that after the two of us, we weren't getting along so good together. That she'd be late getting home from the job, and of course I knew what she was doing. It was the same thing she used to be doing with me—all right? When she was still married to Kyle and I was still married to Edie here, as I was then and I am right now, but that wasn't what I was saying. Because I didn't think I would be, very long. I was sort of getting ahead of things there, but that was all that it was; I *thought* we was getting divorced. We had the legal separation and all, court orders, everything like that, how much I hadda pay and all; when I could see the kid. *I* thought we were gettin' divorced. You'd've asked me, I would've said that. I would've told you that. I couldn't tell you, give you one single reason, right here this very minute, why we didn't get the divorce. Because we sure were headed that way. It's just that we never got there. Just turned out we didn't get one, that's all. Down near the end, just looked at each other one day, I guess was it, and said: "Oh what the hell here, maybe we should just go and give it one more try." And that time it finally worked out. But that was what I thought at the time.

" 'But anyway, back then it was all right with me. She was out in the back doing guys in the trucks, when I was the guy she was doing. But then when I wasn't, I was the guy at home, and she was back out in the back, then it bothered the hell out of me. But what could I do about it, you tell me that? What the hell could I do. I'll tell you: I couldn't do nothin'. She was back to picking up extra dough in back, just like she always'd been doing, and that's what she was doing again.

" 'Well, okay, and I can't be surprised. I knew she was like that. That's how I ended up with her, after all, and you can't go an' unteach an old pussy any new tricks that she didn't already know how to do, before you got to her there. But what got my goat, and I mean it really did, was when I saw the goddamned tattoo. I mean that was going too far, *way* too far. I saw that and I went up in *smoke.*'

"Mister Cameron told us he hadn't seen the victim since the time he left her and the time she turned up dead. That was over five years. He said: 'I mean that. That's the truth. I didn't bother her and she didn't bother me. And we didn't bother each other. It was about as good a deal as you can get. We broke up when I found out about this Brian person, and I just got completely mad. And then I said: "Well, if that's the way you want it, babe, or even if it isn't, that's still the way you got it, and the way it's going to be. And I left, completely pissed off. And I never went back. I never go back. Not to anythin'.'

"At this point," Royce had testified, "Mister Cameron's real wife, Edie, who was present throughout the interview, interrupted him and said: 'Well, you came back here, Hughie.' And he then said to her: 'You just stay out of this, all right? I can handle this by myself. And that's the way it's been ever since, with me and Sandy. I left and I never went back. I come back to this house instead. That was the way we both wanted it, I think. We must've, if that was what we both did.'

"We, I, asked him if he knew where Brian was, since this was the first official word we'd had about him," Royce had said, "and he said he had no idea. He said: 'First I heard about him was the morning I saw that damned tattoo, and I asked her, and she said, well, that he come into the diner one day on his way up to New Hampshire or something, and business was slow, so they struck up a conversation. "And, you know how it can be sometimes, it just went on from there. One thing leads to another, you know?" So she started going with Brian. When her and I was supposed to be, well, you know, a partnership for life. And I was pretty damned mad about that, her doing that to me, sneaking around on me, at the time. As you probably could

136

guess. But I only had myself to blame, I guess, you come right down to it and all. Because I guess I should've known if she would sneak around on whoever the guy she was with when I first met her, when I was the next guy along, well then naturally it stood to reason she would sneak also around on me. That girl, she would've been a great whore in her time, if she'd just stuck to that one thing, doing what she liked to do. Sandra Nichols, really, she *really* liked to fuck, and that was why, when she was still alive, you could not trust her at all. You could enjoy the hell out of yourself, but you just could not trust that girl at all.

"'And if you don't believe me, well, go and ask Brian. 'Cause the damned thing happened to him. She did the same thing to him, when his turn came around, she met a new guy she liked better. Brian met him at Queen City one day, and I guess he introduced them. That was Brian's big mistake. She dropped Brian off like a sack of returnable cans, like a big bag of Coke cans or something. The other guy was the one Brian'd been driving through Queen City all the time, to see him at his home in New Hampshire. And this guy had something new for her to try out, she had had before: big bucks to go with his cock.'"

At that point in the inquest, Henry had gone off the record. As far as the transcripts I had showed, he'd never gone back on again. I went to the raw interview report Royce'd recited in court. That had a little bit more.

"Mister Cameron was asked whether he knew the name of the fellow who knew, who was doing this business with Brian. Who the rich fellow was, and he said: 'Sure do. It was that rich Peter guy she finally ended up married to. Which also stood to reason, I guess—that she'd end up with someone named Peter. Or could've also been one named Dick, I guess, too. Something along that line. Sandy wasn't a bad girl at heart, and she was a peach to her kids. A very good mother, I mean. But she did have that weakness of hers, all the same—she sure was a one to get around on a man, just as long as she was alive. All it took was for some good-lookin' young stud to just look at her cross-eyed, and *bang*, she'd be off like a shot. It's too bad she's dead and all now, not saying it isn't, but . . . well, I got to say it, can't help myself: the last guy she was married to, there, the rich one, he's the first one to ever at least know where she is, when she don't come home on time. That she's not off with some other guy.' "

That was the end of it. No follow-up, follow-on report of an interview with Brian. After the treasure hunt adventure I'd had with the pictures of Lucy, I was more than a little suspicious. I went to see Royce—no call; face-to-face; you can't beard a guy in his den on the phone—for the fill-in of what had come next.

"There wasn't any next as far as Brian was concerned," he said. "I'd alerted Cronin, and he'd tipped Henry off, that what I'd found out about Brian I didn't want on the public record. I didn't want him to know, to ever find out, get tipped-off by someone and right away, bolt for the border. I didn't want Brian to know."

"Well, you found out where he was, I assume," I said. "You went and interviewed him. Wouldn't that've all told him, pretty damned clear, that you had an interest in him?"

"One-third right," Royce said, "not even half. We did find out where Brian Ross lives, where Brian Ross works, and what Brian Ross drives between places. But we did *not* go there, either place he frequents, and sit the guy down, have a nice heart-to-heart with the lad. We gave him a good leavin' alone."

"You don't think he might be a good, useful witness?" I said. "It sure sounds to me, so far at least, like he might have something to say."

"No, I *don't* think he'd be a good witness," Royce said. "What he'd have to say'd destroy anything that's left of the dead woman's reputation. And demolish those kids, all over again. Out in front of God and all the people. And he'd do it without batting an eye. He's a bad man, Jerry, a very bad man. If we'd gone and interviewed him, he'd've been able to guess how much progress we were making, if any; in what direction we were making it; and then spew out a lot of damned lies about Sandra. We'd *know* they were lies, but we could never disprove them. So that if we ever did reach the point of actually charging his pal Peter Wade with the crime, Peter and his honorable mouthpiece'd know damned well that when they asked for any exculpatory evidence we might have—which of course we've got to give them, plus a list of any prospective witnesses we'd interviewed and talked to, but we *don't* expect to call, because obviously we think they'd hurt our case— they were going to get a bomb. Brian's unexploded mine would be right there in those papers waiting for them, right there all in place for them, just like they'd know all along it would be—to set off right under our ass. No, we don't want to interview him. No Brian for witness for me. I don't see him in that role at all." He paused and then said thoughtfully: "On the other hand, though, I think he would make a truly *excellent* defendant."

■ ■ ■ 13

Ipondered that one for a moment or two, wishing I could clear my throat and truthfully claim I'd seen Brian as the leading candidate for culprit from the very start. But I hadn't, so I couldn't. In fact, I still wasn't sure I saw it even then, after Royce'd told me where to look. "You think he was the guy then, that did the actual evil deed?" I said.

"Yes, I do." Royce said. "Brian Ross was the ultimate, terminal marine. Joined the corps right out of Dorchester High. Where he had not distinguished himself, academically, but'd played gutty-enough, no-talent ball to letter in football and basketball, both. What he'd done, in every respect there, what he'd done was get by. So when he'd finished, he could do what for him was the logical next thing. He didn't *leave* home; he signed up and *went* home to the corps. And that's where he's lived ever since. Even now that he's out and retired, the corps is his domicile still, his permanent lifetime address. It'll always be where he lives. He got in and he found out he was right: he'd been a marine all his life. He'd always been a marine. Thought he'd died and gone right to heaven. He never had so much fun in his life. And they recognized him right off. He was one of their own. When they saw what they had in this kid, they wasted no time at all. They said: 'Shit, this one's a killing machine. Give him a goddamned machine gun.' And he *loved* that fuckin' thing. Killing was his true profession, that machine gun the tool of his trade. It was what he'd been born to do. And it was all *legal*, too.

"He got out of the corps because he had a full thirty years in on the pension. But the sheer joy of killing—that he never got out of or over. He never should've gotten out. They never should've *let* him out, much less tell him he hadda get out. Should've let him re-up and re-up and re-up, as long as the rules let him do it, like they did. And then if he's still living, as we know he was, when that dark day came to pass and the rules said he'd gotten too old, that's when what they should've done was change the rules, just a little, right then and there, on the spot—*Except:* this here rule don't apply to Sergeant Ross, only to everybody else'—and let him re-up again, and again and again, long as he's still on his feet. And that's what I think he would've rather done, too, if we hadn't run out of wars for a while there. A marine by birthright with no war to fight? He got bored, naturally; no more damned enemies to kill."

"So did he find new challenges stateside?" I said. "Moonlight in private contracting stuff?"

Royce shrugged. "He could've," he said. "Hard to think he would've turned anything down. He certainly knows how to do it, and he's got the free time, his regular job, so he could certainly handle a little piecework now and then—no family; lives all by himself.

"Brian makes Sandra all giddy. Sandra just knew, before she met Peter, that she'd never get over Brian. So, to prove her devotion, she had this little globe and on top of it a fouled anchor—you know, the marine insignia: globe and anchor with a hank of rope sort of wrapped around it; some small blue stars, six, I think; but they may've been red—arranged in a semicircle over it, tattooed on her left cheek. Her buttock. And below that, BRIAN, and below *that*, SEMPER FI. Must've given her a little tingle, whole lot of little tingles, gettin' that decoration.

"That was the tattoo Hugh saw. And got offended by. She got up with no clothes on one morning, no doubt having spent much of the previous night doing with Hugh what she liked to do best, and he saw it on her ass in the light, which she didn't mean him to do. And this was also what the medical examiner, Doctor Armand Gilbert, found on the body of the decedent. You couldn't see the design on the surface of the skin, all rotted like it was, but under a microscope or some-thing, I assume, they could make out where the tattoo pigment'd been injected, and trace out the pattern. So even if we hadn't've had the dental charts, as we did—fingerprints were long gone, time we got to the body, of course—we would've then been pretty sure who she was.

"Brian lives in Central Falls, down in Rhode Island. One thirty-two Abrams Street. Abrams Street's a private cul-de-sac way, not on a map, and Central Falls's sort of an afterthought little blue-collar burg attached to Pawtucket. He's got a one-bedroom apartment on the sec-ond floor of a two-story, wooden-frame, two-family house. The people who live on the first floor—nice retired couple, he used to drive a truck for the Providence Public Works Department—didn't seem to know much about him. Morse went down there and knocked on the door after he was sure Ross'd gone to work at his regular job, week-ends plus Mondays and Tuesdays, bartending Franco's Club and Lounge in Cumberland, mile or so up the pike. Morse's good at lookin' like a young and eager salesman, being as how he *is* young, and he's eager to get something—even though it's not really what he tells you that it is. Said he owns and operates this kitchen-remodeling out-fit and one his customers'd told him Brian was a man who might be interested in having something like that done.

"The old people sort of laughed and said they doubted it. The wife said: 'Can't imagine *why* he would. For one thing, it's not his house; he rents here, just like us. I don't expect the landlord'd *mind* if he was to ask him if it was okay to put in a new kitchen—probably raise the rent then, if he did: "This place's got a nice new kitchen now. Worth a lot more money." But I can't think why he'd *want* to do that, even if he owned the place himself. He's almost never here. He spends no time here at all. He works five nights, I know, and he isn't on the job, well, he sure isn't here. Don't know where he goes then, but he doesn't stay at home. Some nights he doesn't *come* home, even. Not 'til the next night. Now and then, a few times, every now and then, he'll be gone for two or three days. Where I couldn't say. Finds a girl-friend, I expect, stays with her a couple nights, 'til he needs to change his clothes. Then he comes back here. The nights he does sleep here, though, he always sleeps late, ten, eleven in the morning. Like you'd expect he would, of course, working the night shift and all. Doesn't snore, though, like the last guy did, had the place before he died. *Man*, did that guy snore. Sounded like someone tearing burlap, real thick burlap, the first part of it at least: *rowwrrrrrrr*, and then this little whistle, like a teakettle going off when it gets to boiling, *wheeeeeeee*; that was him gettin' set to do the next one. Hear it through the ceiling, him and his damned snoring—probably clear across the state line if your hearing was real good.

" 'That's what made me think, the night he passed away, "Why, Joseph isn't snoring. I wonder if he died." In the morning I told Ed, here. He just laughed at me. But sure enough, next morning, still without a sound, I went up there and knocked? Called his name out loud: "Joseph? Joseph? Joseph?" And he didn't answer me? I didn't hear a sound. So that was when I called the cops, and they came and broke the door down. Sure enough, that's what he was: just like I suspected. He was dead in bed. Right after that, the afternoon of the same day he was buried, which was the day after he died, landlord got his place cleaned out, like he was never on the earth. It didn't seem decent, somehow. Man's ghost hadn't had time to leave, pack a few things and clear out. He couldn't've even waited a week? I guess he could not. "Can't have it idle, just leave it standing vacant, you know." That was what he said to me. Joseph went into the ground in the morning, and that same afternoon his stuff went out the window, down into the truck on the street. Landlord just parked a dump truck out there in the front, and him and these two kids he'd hired threw Joseph's stuff right out of the windows, crash-crash-crash, down into the truck. Wasn't much else he could do though, I guess. No one else to do it. Joseph didn't have no relatives, fight over what he had, which wasn't very much, enough to bother with. A little money was all, three, four hundred dollars, in a credit union account that the landlord could sign for, case if something like this happened. And that was all there was in it, because I seen the bank receipt—landlord showed it to us, 'long with the undertaker's bill. Burial took care of that.

" 'Brian moved in right after that. Brian's very quiet, answer to my prayers. Havin' him livin' above us, it couldn't be more peaceful if they'd just left Joseph where he was until he disappeared into the air. Brian don't snore at all. He don't make *any* noise, of any kind; not a sound comes out of there. I think when he gets home, he likes to take his shoes off. The ghost on the second floor; he don't live on it, he haunts it. On his feet the whole night long, workin' at the bar, I'd guess they probably hurt. But the reason that I say that, he must have his shoes off, is you can't hear him walkin' up there, walkin' room to room. We know when he's up in the morning 'cause we can hear the water running, for the shower and so forth. Then it's quiet for a while. I guess he makes a cup of coffee, has that, then goes out. By noon most days he's gone. I don't know where he goes. Doesn't get home any night until two, three, four o'clock. For us it's just about as ideal's you can get it. We got the whole house to ourselves most of the day and night, and when the guy upstairs does finally come home, he doesn't wake us up. I hope Brian stays forever. I hope he never leaves.'

"Morse said the old man said they never had much conversation with him. 'And he's lived here for nine years, moved in in May the year that I retired. We know his name and he knows ours. We say hello, we see him, ask each other how we're doin'. And that's been the whole of it. He's never asked us for a favor—bring his mail up; water plants; bring his rubbish barrel in on trash day; anything like that. And we've never asked him, either, to do us a favor. I would, I guess, we needed one. I wouldn't hesitate to ask, and I think he'd probably do it. Seems like a nice guy. But we like it like it is, nice and quiet. Peaceful. Like Carol says: the best kind of upstairs neighbor you could ever hope to have. Quiet, like I told you; doesn't play the TV loud after you've gone to bed—how could he? He's not even home. But for *him*, a brand-new kitchen? Hope you didn't come too far, son. Someone's played a joke on you.'

"Brian goes to work at five in the afternoon. Gets off at two A.M. Morse found out where he goes in the afternoons, working days or his days off, that he never spends at home. He leaves the house and gets in his car. It's a black eighty-nine Chevy Monte Carlo that's seen better days. Been hit a couple of times, just minor stuff when it happened but it's never been repaired. Looks like the salt's been eating it—it's starting to hole out now, like the metals' getting frayed. Morse says it could also use a new muffler. It's registered in Rhode Island and it's kosher.

"His first stop from the house is a quick 'n' dirty, Elmer's, two blocks away. He buys the *Herald* and the *Journal* from the coin machines on the sidewalk. Sometimes the *Herald*'s machine's sold out. When it is, he gives it a kick, but so far it hasn't come up with an extra paper for him after he's done that. He takes the papers inside. He sits at the counter. He takes up three places, spreading his papers out. Nobody minds—breakfast for everyone else is over; no one's come in yet for lunch. He doesn't order. He doesn't need to. Has the same thing every day. One the waitresses—there's three of them; they all do the same thing—comes over with his setup and a mug and puts them down where he is sitting. Then she gets the coffee pot and fills the mug. He starts drinking it right off. He drinks it black. The cook fries bacon and three eggs over easy, and makes him a short stack— three buckwheat pancakes. A big serving of hash browns. White toast, two slices. Brian reads the paper. The cook puts all the food except the toast and the potatoes—those go on separate side dishes—on a platter and the waitress brings the chow to Brian. He eats it. He eats every last scrap of it, mostly because he eats only two meals a day and this's the big one. The other one's a sandwich, roast beef, corned beef, something like that, 'nother couple mugs of coffee. That he has Franco's kitchen make up for him, and he eats it on the run while he works the bar, alone. It's a very busy bar. They do a lot of business. They really need another man, but I suppose he doesn't want that— then he'd have to split the tips. So anyway, breakfast he eats hot and slow and easy, takes his own sweet time about it. He reads the paper. The waitress keeps an eye on his mug. When it's empty she refills it. When he's finished he stands up and puts the papers back together. He takes his wallet out, puts a five-dollar bill on the counter, and goes back out to his car. The waitress buses the dishes and puts the papers under the counter for anyone who might come in at lunch and want to read them. She goes to the register and rings in three seventy-five. She puts the fin in and takes out a buck and a quarter, which she puts into the tip jar they all share. Thirty-three percent tip: no wonder he gets such good service. It's now close to noon.

"Workday or day off, his next stop's Competition Engines on Route One in North Attleboro. The owners're two guys who apparently're ex–Third Division marines. Tankers. Whether he knew them from the service or just hooked up with them by chance, some reunion thing or something after he got back, is something we just don't know. Just what he does there's something of a mystery, too. He doesn't seem to have a definite assignment you could point to and say: this's what his job is. He's not on the payroll there. But he's not just hanging out either. He more or less informally serves a purpose for them.

"See, Competition's sort of a specialized garage-showroom kind of thing, I guess," Royce said. "They don't have any brand-new cars. All they've got is exotic stuff, gray-market high-performance machinery that came in from Europe needing one hell of a lot of expensive modifications to the exhaust system before it can pass our emissions. The BMW M-One, little two-seater crop-duster so low to the ground it wouldn't come up to your belt—never imported here by the manufacturer. Aston Martins. Morgan Plus-Eights. Lotuses. ACs. TVRs. European market versions of Porsches and Alfas, Ferraris; Lamborghinis and Mercedes; cars that cost three and four hundred thousand dollars ordered two years in advance; mostly by European and Japanese playboys, Arab oil sheiks, tennis and rock stars. Imported to the U.S. later, but only after they'd been assembly-line detuned and desmogged, which hurts performance, and these ones that they got down there weren't. These they custom retrofitted, which costs a lot more money than the factory methods, but it makes the car all legal and perform just as well or better.

"But it seems that that's just the dessert, the way the Comp boys get their jollies. Apparently the meat and potatoes of the business, what really keeps it going, is restoring, maintaining, and repairing classic cars. From all over the Northeast, far away as western New York. Rich people who collect cars give their name to each other, what wonderful work they can do, what miracles they can perform with some old bucket of rusty bolts and frozen gears, and the next thing you know, the new recruit's on the phone to North Attleboro, asking one of these two guys if they could fix his prewar Jag, which wasn't even Jaguar then—it was a Swallow Sport. It isn't running right now, hasn't been since nineteen fifty. He suspects it might be something more than just a dead battery that's causing all this problem. They tell him they're putting him on the speakerphone so they can take some notes, and will that be okay? He says 'Sure,' there's this note of anxiety in his voice, and that's when the full treatment starts. They won't know if they can take the job on until they see the actual car and take a good close look at it. Unfortunately, just taking a quick look here at the way their near-term schedule's shaping up, it'll be at least two months before one of them'll be able to pull himself away for two or three days and get all the way out there to do that.

"Rich people're all alike. They tend to be impatient. And having dealt with so many of them, these two guys know what he'll say next. The rich guy says he'll hire a flatbed-trucking guy to bring the car to them. They can look it over in their own garage, at their own convenience, run any tests they want, and then give him the rundown, what it's all going to cost. Which they know is purest bullshit 'cause cost never matters to him or anyone like him, any one of his rich playmates. Money's what he's *got*; his car fixed is what he *wants*, and therefore, much more important. He's been a spoiled child all his life. The only difference now is that since he's been old enough to vote for thirty years or so, he's now a bigger brat, with more experience and therefore even more demanding. He wants that car *fixed*, and 'right now' will be quite a bit longer than he really plans to wait. He's the kind of a guy who comes into a fancy restaurant for the first time with a new trophy girlfriend but no reservation, and tries to buy the best table by the window by telling the maître d' that he'll treat the folks who have it to their dinner, if they'll move. And really has no idea why it is the maître d' shakes his head as he goes to ask them, and then comes back this little smile and says no, they think they won't, thanks just the same. When what they really said of course was: Tell that jerk to take his dough and shove it up his ass. If Competition quoted him an estimate for what it would cost to *duplicate* the goddamned car, by fabricating all the parts brand new, from *scratch*, counterfeit the bloody thing; if they also swore to him that they could match the numbers on the new parts so perfectly to the numbers on the old parts, so no one who didn't know the actual story could ever tell the new car was a fake, he'd okay it without blinking.

"So what they do is sigh and say no, they don't want him to do that. Spend two or three thousand bucks getting the car flatbedded to them so they can look it over. They tell him that they're very careful never to take on a job they don't think they can do right, or one that even if they can do it right, it ought not to be done because after they get finished what the owner gets back from them won't be worth as much rebuilt as what he's just sunk into it. And that they also don't take on jobs unless they actually meet the guy who's going to pay the bill and get their own impression of whether he'll *be* satisfied, and then *stay* satisfied, after the job's been done.

"The rich guy now is frantic. Not used to having people playing hard to get with him. He'll try a little soft soap, see if he can smarm them up, and what effect that has. He says he knows their reputation, and he's sure he'll be satisfied. They tell the guy flat-out that that's what everybody says, when they're in his situation, but six months after the job's done, turns out they didn't mean it and they call the lawyers out. They tell him also that they got more work than they can handle; that they're booked right up through the first two months of the coming year; that they turn down far more jobs'n they accept; and that even if his project's one of the three or four out of ten that they do take on, they haven't got any space to store his sled in the shop until they can get to it, and they sure don't want it sitting outside on the lot, exposed to all the little Route One vandals with their cans of spray paint who do windshields, ruin paint jobs on new cars left out on lots at night with no wire fence and killer dogs to keep them safe from harm. Then there's the New England weather, making the job even harder when they finally do get around to it. And besides, if they tried to carry enough insurance to cover many cars as valuable as his most likely is, Lloyd's of London'd be the only company on earth that'd underwrite it, and it'd probably take what the business's worth to pay the premium.

"All of this palaver of course makes the rich guy crazy. He'd torn most of his hair out already, finding out who to call, and now that he's finally found these genius artists, it begins to look as though they might not take the job. The longer they talk, the more upset he gets— now he's starting to pull out his eyebrows. He pleads with them. He wheedles. He lowers himself the way he expects to have people grovel for him, they're trying to get fifty grand out of him for their new college library, their favorite disease, whatever it happens to be. He gift wraps his pride and his dignity too, and humbly offers them to this pair of boutique mechanics, who'd be common ordinary grease monkeys if they didn't happen to be also the guys who've put together this *marvelous, blinding* line of the purest bullshit. What the rich guy does is *beg*.

"Now they've got him where they want him. They will take pity on the guy, show him a little mercy. Everything they said still goes: their schedule's really tight. But they would like at least to make it possible for him to know sooner'n two months from now, whether it's a job they'd even want to tackle. So at least he will know, and if it isn't, well then, he can start looking that much sooner for another shop to do the work. So what they suggest is that if he really has to get an answer right off, they have got this guy that they occasionally work with, use to inspect prospective jobs for them, when they just can't get away. He doesn't work for them directly—he's got his own full-time job. For them he works on referral, strictly on a fee basis, for the owners of the cars. But he's totally familiar with the kind of work they like to do, and the kind of work they *can* do, and if the rich guy's willing to pay his fee, which isn't cheap, well, they could give him a call. But he should know, going in, that the guy gets four hundred bucks a day, whole or partial, portal to damned portal, and his expenses, too. And he will not fly. So almost every job he takes on outside southern New England is at least eighteen hundred bucks, and where you say you're calling from, well, that's a real long drive. He'll try to get it done in two days, but you may find you wind up payin', all tolled, fifteen hundred bucks or so, plus mileage, hotel, and meals. Sure you're prepared to do that? And if the rich guy says he is—as of course they know he will because those rich guys always do, full treatment gets them into the tent every time—then what the Comp guy says is they will get in touch with this guy and see when he can get free, and find out will he take the job.

"Of course this isn't going to be too awful difficult for them to do. Because Brian's been sitting right across the table from his pal the whole time, listening to the entire conversation on the speakerphone. Brian's the one who's taking the notes, and by now he's taken a lot of them. This's when the car artist-genius sinks the hook. He says to the rich guy: 'Now what I'm gonna do, if you authorize me, I will get in touch with him. Or he may come in first, on his way to work. His name is Brian Ross, and I will tell him what you said, and make a copy of these notes. If he's agreeable, he'll be the one who'll call you back. If he tells me that he can't do it, or he doesn't want to—completely independent; he can be a funny guy—then I'll get back to you, at least, and tell you he can't come. But if he says he can fit it in, I'll have him call you direct. Want to give me your numbers, day and night ones if they're different?'

"The rich guy falls all over himself giving numbers. He gives numbers for his home and office, car and plane, yacht and pocket phone. And those of his next of kin, and his two best friends, the vet who takes care of his prize horseflesh and dogs, and the foreman of his little spread all the way out there in the high plains, big sky country, where he goes to play Clint Eastwood, ride a horse, smoke El Ropos, squint a lot. He says if Brian can't reach him at one his own numbers, he should try all of those, and someone will know where he is.

"And the Lord High Mechanic says, when the rich guy asks for it, as the rich guy then always does: 'No, I can't give you Brian's number. He won't let us give that out. His decision's final on whether he takes an assignment. He doesn't want people bugging him at home or at his regular job. Like I say, he can be a hair eccentric, a little off the wall sometimes, but he's a dedicated amateur, really knows his cars. We call him our extra eyes and ears. If we can't get to a car to estimate it ourselves, well, we can trust Brian completely to do it. He's just as good as we are. We've often tried to bring him in here, in fact, as a salaried staff consultant, but Brian likes his freedom and he's always turned us down."

"And an hour or so later, that same afternoon," Royce said, "Brian does call the guy. On Competition's dime. Just happened to drop by on his way to somewhere else. And yeah, he'll come and take a close look at this guy's antique classic car, his Delahaye, Bugatti, Cunningham LeMans Ford, whatever the thing is. How does next Wednesday sound? And the rich guy's so happy he's practically wetting his pants while he's giving Brian directions, how to get to his place.

"Back around the last part of nineteen eighty-one, the beginning of eighty-two," Royce said, "Peter Wade bought a nineteen thirty-four Mercedes Benz Five Hundred K, subseries A, cabriolet, body by Daimler Benz Sindelfinger, not one but *two* spare tires mounted on the trunk, chromed wire wheels and a camel-colored leather interior. This car was so outrageously expensive even when it was brand new that the company suspended production when the Depression swallowed its first big bites, belched and liked the taste, and really settled in to gnaw on everybody's lives. Fear of the guillotine, no doubt. They didn't put it back on the market until the Little Paperhanger'd taken office and made everyone feel so much better. Everyone at Mercedes Benz, at least, few of those chaps being Jewish.

"Anyway," Royce said, "I don't claim to be an expert on this stuff now, any kind of connoisseur, but with permission from Peter Wade—which I got through Arthur Dean, Peter being in the deluxe booby hatch at the time and all, not receiving visitors, especially state cops; I said my interest in taking the pictures was personal, part of my hobby—I took some 'after' pictures of his car, as rebuilt by Competition. I don't have any 'before' pictures of it, but it must've been a near wreck because the rebuild/restoration came in at a total cost of two hundred and three thousand, six hundred and forty-one dollars. And seventy cents. I said to Morse: 'Look at that: can you beat it? They wouldn't even cut him seventy cents' worth of slack.'

"Those pictures were never in the file. I did those for me, thinking maybe I could work up a collection of fine automobile pictures, sell them to go into one of those coffee-table books, and so kept them at home. I'll get some copies made for you, one or two of the best. I showed them to a club friend of mine who's done some salon photo work for the Larz Anderson Museum, that one down there off the Jamaicaway in Boston where they have the classic car shows? And he took them with him, next time he went down there. That was what made what I told Arthur Dean about my interest in the car was personal into God's gospel truth. My friend was trying to find out from a guy he knew there if the museum'd be interested in buying the negatives from me. They were not, but they said what that kind of people always says when you try to pry money off of them. That mine were very fine pictures and they'd be delighted to have several free copies to show, if I'd be good enough to make them. I wasn't. Never had any trouble at all, giving my work away; it's getting people to give me money for it; that part's been kind of hard. Anyway, this friend of mine asked the man at the museum how much this car would be worth, and he said he doubted you could even find one that someone'd be willing to sell, to you or anyone else, but if you could, it'd most likely turn up in a Sotheby's or Christie's estate sale, and the reserve price'd probably be at least a million dollars. So, you see, Peter may've spent one shitload of dough on that restoration, but without knowing what he'd paid for the hulk in the first place, if it was a half a million or less, it seems to've turned out to've been a fairly wise investment."

"Just the same, no thanks," I said. "I'm not in the market just now. Just the other day I hadda sink all my ready cash into several sets of brand-new underwear and some socks I really needed. Call me in a couple months."

"Yeah," Royce said. "Well, the rich have all kinds of different problems'n we do, but as long as Peter continues to believe no one can get him on this thing, he won't be looking to sell, anyway. So you can just put your checkbook away.

"Anyway," he said, "Peter's first face-to-face human contact with anyone from Competition was, guess who? Brian Ross. That was a real good day for our Brian. For one thing, it was probably the day he met Sandra. Stopped to get an early lunch and take a leak at the Queen City Diner, on his way to Wade's place in New Hampshire. On his way back that night, after dinner with Peter, he dropped in again, take another leak, probably, and sure enough, she was still there. Workin' a double to help out a friend. She did him that night, in the Monte Carlo, out in the back parking lot. Brian was very impressed, you can bet.

"And Brian and Peter had hit it off too. In just one short afternoon they became the best of friends. Brian could tell right off that Peter was a high-class, first-class guy. After he'd seen the other cars in the Wade collection, all six or eight of them, and all in perfect shape, ready to be driven; cased the entire joint that Peter owns up there in Enfield; toured the main house; seen the pictures and models of *Toreador*; and the trophies that she's won, well, as you can well imagine, even *before* Peter slipped him five hundred extra on his fee to put in a good word with his pals on Route One, to move Peter's car to the head of the list, if something should happen to happen, Brian knew Pete was a prince. And Peter knew Brian to be a reliable man you could trust, because just two days later they called him from Competition and said: 'Guess what? You're never going to believe this. This guy we had waiting in line, his Hispano Suiza was our next job to start; called us late yesterday, said not to do it. He's taken a bath in the market, I guess, had a lot of his money in Wang computer stock, and since that crashed and burned, he can't swing the job. You want us to come get your wheels?'

"After that Pete and Bry were buddies for life. That car restoration took over two years, tracking parts down, making new ones when no old ones could be found, mixing paint to the precise specifications that Mercedes paint met in nineteen thirty-four. Matching leathers and carpets to what they were then, replicating the original steering wheel. Tailoring the canvas, keying the color of the stitching to what it would've been about six years before Hitler told his panzers to ride.

"During all of those two years, anytime there was to be a major subcontract let out, Peter had to okay it and pay money down, every single major proposal. The tire guy was typical. When they located a company that could replicate the tires, all six of them plus four more spares, guy wanted all of his money up front. He wasn't going to get molds made and adapt modern compounds to them for a one-off job unless he got his money up front. Peter was tied up with some other things. He was driving to Albany, some New York State thing he thought that he oughta sit in on, and could Brian maybe meet him somewhere, with the work order papers, he could okay them on his way and give him the check? Peter would pay him for his time. And Brian, maybe to his sorrow, later, maybe to his great relief, said: 'Queen City Diner,' figuring to make a payday from old Peter, get the check and boff old Sandy back at her apartment 'fore the kids got home from school. And for all we know, that's what he did, but if he did it was close to being his last dance with her. Because once she and Peter met each other, that was it for both of them. For a while, at least. Sporty as they both'd been. But then, we shouldn't knock it, should we—that's all life itself ever is, really: something for a while.

"Now," Royce said, hunching over his desk at the club, "I can't tell you why, 'cause I don't know myself, but I have got this real strong hunch that at least one of those kids, if not two of those kids—could be all three of them, in fact—saw or heard something they haven't told us, something that'd hitch Peter Wade to Brian Ross to bring about this murder of this woman that they'd both told that they loved, and really meant it at the time. Well, at least Peter had. Brian? Probably not.

"I haven't been able to worm it out of them. I think I know why that is. They look at me and they see a guy who's got something to gain from this case, from hauling in Peter, the scruff of his neck, and pinning their mom's murder on him. I'm a cop, those kids figure. That makes me look good. But it cuts them adrift once again. These're cynical kids. They've had a hard life. Peter is what they've got left. If Peter goes down, and I get commended, well, that's very nice, but it doesn't leave them a damned thing.

"That's silly," I said, "nothing'd change for you. You'd get some satisfaction, sure, knowing you'd done a great job. But what do you need kudos for? You're full of age and grace."

"They don't know as much as you do," Royce said. "This's natural. They're not as old as you are. They see me the way they do because I'm just doing a job I have to do for the money I get paid anyway. You they see different. They see you as the white knight with the white plume, riding on the big white horse, the goddamned Lone Ranger, for God's sake. Just doing Judge Henry a favor. The goodness of your heart and all."

"Hey," I said, "if there's rumors circulating that I'm doing this for nothing, whoever's spreading them is telling bald-faced lies. Don't believe a word of it. If I make a case and take it in, then I'm a tort lawyer and I get my share. I'll give the little urchins an even break— twenty percent of the take, not a third. If I don't make a case I can take into court, then I'll take the usual bath on the thing, and beat Henry up every time I see him for the rest of his natural life."

"I told them that," Royce said. "I told them you got an office to run, and salary to pay, and a living to make, and you can't spend time like this free. They just looked at me and said yeah, they knew that, of course, but still, you were takin' your chances. They didn't say to me: 'You're not takin' chances. You're gonna get paid anyway.' But they were thinking that, sure enough; I could see it right in their faces."

"Why're you telling me this?" I said. "Just what's your motive in this anyway, loading all of this hogwash on me?"

"I'm doing what you guys always say that you're doing, when you start being mean to a witness. I'm refreshing your recollection on this, Jeremiah, making sure that you don't forget. Henry dragged you into this because of me, and I asked for you for a reason. Sandra Nichols had a hard life, a tough life, a full one to be sure, but still, until quite recently, a very hard one. Until against all the odds, she got a good one, and then someone killed her for that.

"Well, that doesn't seem fair to me. I can't bring her back, to have what she lost, but I want those children of hers to enjoy the kind of start in life they would've had if that hadn't happened to her. They may turn out to have very unhappy lives; there's no guarantee against that. But they should at least have what she lucked out and got, got for them as much as for her.

"You've been shying away from them, Jerry. Shying away from those kids. You've had no contact with them at all. You're the ghost they've never seen. For all I know, they're comfortable with that. They're very self-reliant kids, as they've always had to be, and maybe they like it that way. But it's started to bother me some."

I gave him the usual shrug. "I told you already, Royce," I said, "a lawyer for kids I am not. I don't have the talent for it. And from what I've seen so far, learning this case, I doubt they can help me much. To do what it is you want done."

"I disagree," Royce said. "I think one of them knows something that we need to know, that'll hitch our pal Peter to Brian. I've done everything I can to get it from them, separately and then together. I haven't gotten it. Like I said, they don't trust me completely. If they give me something that'll mean I nail Peter, and then that's it: their lives blow up. I can't do a thing to preserve what they've got. Unless I can, I get nothing they got."

I simulated a shiver. "Damned chilly in here, all of a sudden," I said. "Bet they're fierce little sharks at seven-card stud and five-card, hold 'em and draw. I'm not sure I want to see them."

"Oh, I'm sure you don't, Jerry," Royce said to me. "I think you're afraid of those kids. I think you've been shut up in yourself for so long now you don't wanna come out. I'm telling you that you've got to break out, if for this case and no other reason. Got up to Strothers, see Maggie and Jeff. They won't intimidate you. Make allies of them, and then go see Lucy. But get started on it, for God's sake. This's something that needs to be done."

I didn't have any reply. I did live an odd life of my own after Mack, I guess. People've recently started telling me this. Now that it's changed, they feel safe, and bold; before they'd been holding it back. I haven't argued with them. They've been right. I lived almost completely by myself, every day of the year, weekdays and weekends, Sundays and holy days of obligation—didn't matter at all. In the morning

I got up in my two-bedroom condo on Pinckney Street at the foot of Beacon Hill—"riv.vu, [one-car] ind. pkng," for a paltry $335,000, fifteen or sixteen times what Mack and I paid for the four-bedroom house with a one-car garage on Kevin Road in Braintree, all those long years ago—and I shaved my face and washed my body while the coffee brewed. Then I sat in my bathrobe in my "dining area," meaning that part of the big room that isn't the "living area," and drank some coffee, having toast with it, same as the Duke of Wellington did—he was also a creature of habit, except with his toast he had tea. Same as always. I read the newspaper, same as always, and then I put my clothes on and went to the office. On nice days I sometimes walked, but not very often; it makes me uneasy not to have my car downstairs, since I never know when I may need it to go out of town on something. Same as always, in either event. At night I walked or drove down the hill and went home, generally around eight or nine. I'd usually provided for the light evening meal by shopping on the weekend. I'd have something elaborate, such as a ham-and-cheese sandwich or American chop suey, refrigerated fresh linguini with refrigerated fresh meat sauce and Parmesan cheese. Occasionally I'd botch an omelette. I'd have a beer. Maybe two beers. Maybe three. Or share a bottle of wine with myself; whichever suited my mood. I'd read a biography and listen to some forties big band music. I'd watch a little TV, catch the late news most nights, and then I'd go to bed. Man has to get his rest.

On the weekends in the fall I'd watch some football. I still have an emotional investment in how Boston College does. I went there twice, for seven years, college and then law school; you don't forget seven years of your life, even some years you might wish you could, and those seven I plan to keep. As spring approaches I'd get interested in the NCAA basketball tournament, and in days gone by spring training and the start of the baseball season used to bring the Red Sox fan in me out of hibernation, at least until the Red Sox got their annual attack of the bends and once again got satisfied with going through the motions, usually around Arbor Day. But not even that anymore. They ruined it for me with their last strike. In the summers, when Mack and Heather and I used to move to the beach house at Green Harbor, I'd watch everyone else go on vacation, and I'd go to work, and in the fall I'd watch them all come back, and I'd still be there at my desk. Same as always.

In other words: I was as close to being the direct opposite of my posthumous client, Sandra Nichols, Friend of Those Who Have No Friends, Safe Harbor in the Storm, as it is possible to get without getting dead myself. The only time my shirt went unstuffed was when I wasn't in it. That was okay; it was quiet.

■ ■ ■ 14

The Strothers School *is* in Andover (it's on the wrong side of the superhighway that divides the southwesterly third of the town from the two-thirds the elite have in mind when they mention it, but it's still within the boundaries), so when semistrangers idly inquire of social-climbing Strothers moms and dads where their perfect children go to school, the parents are within their rights when they reply "Andover." It's certainly not their fault if the strangers mistake that geographically accurate response to mean Phillips Academy in Andover, or "PA." One of Heather's more irritating boyfriends, a PA alumnus she'd met at Dartmouth, would languidly roll out those initials in reply when asked where he'd prepared for college, hoping to elicit still another question further betraying his rustic interlocutor's appalling lack of sophistication. After Heather and he had broken up, with some hard feelings, I gather, she reported to me with some relish a social occasion when David'd pulled that routine on an older gentleman with a bad haircut and the baggiest brown corduroy pants she'd ever seen in her life, and the old geezer like an all star shortstop'd fielded the trapper smartly on one hop and gunned it right back at the little snot, drawling: "*Rawly? Excellent* school. I take it your grades weren't sufficient to get you admitted to Harvard?" "Leaving David speechless," she said with satisfaction.

Strothers itself forthrightly declares it wasn't established to compete for enrollment with the classic New England prep schools, has never done so, and has no plans to do so in the future. Nor do its recruiters go head-to-head with other scholastically demanding private schools, secular, sectarian, or military, offering strenuous private education stressing study and enforcing insofar as possible rules of good behavior. Strothers people are relaxed and realistic; they will tell you informally that "our mission here isn't to *build* good character; it's to try to *rebuild* character, after it's been damaged by real life. That does *not* mean we always succeed."

From the first the school was intended, established, designed, and built to address the needs of young people whose lives have been buffeted by heavy emotional or psychological weather. It's not a quasi-psychiatric school for seriously disturbed young people, or a hospital for severely handicapped kids whose learning disabilities border on autism. Nor is it a haven for druggies. It's for the kind of children who, but for very bad breaks that derailed them, would've been well into the process of becoming well-rounded, healthy, normal young people, and who if given a chance to catch their breath and feel safe, will have a pretty decent chance of getting back on track again.

The kind of children and teenagers Strothers takes in are the kind that Olive Matthews Swann Strothers took on in their early adolescence back in 1931, when as a young widow at the age of twenty-eight (her first husband, nationally known Boston organist—Trinity Church—organist Edgar Fulling Swann, had died of tuberculosis at a mountaintop sanitarium in Arizona just two years before) she decided to remarry. Returning to her hometown to recover from Swann's death, she'd rekindled a big girlhood crush she'd had years before on the town's then-most-eligible bachelor, Thomas Clavell Strothers.

By the time Olive came back in widow's weeds, he was forty-six, no longer the dashing, courtly swain but somewhat damaged goods, and Olive, initially bemused by her own behavior, had little competition to become his third wife. His first wife had died giving birth to their fourth child, the conception having directly and deliberately contravened the strongest possible medical advice against further pregnancies. His second, hastily wed during a wild, desperate two-week revel all over New York City, had divorced him for a younger, richer man—who'd thereupon promptly ditched her.

Olive must have concluded—correctly, as it turned out—that that headline-making period in his marital history was a temporary aberration most uncharacteristically gaudy. It belied the essential *gravitas* of the man who'd blundered into it when he'd been blinded by his grief. Devoted to his first wife; said by his mother, fondly, to have celebrated his thirtieth birthday the year after his twelfth, he had faultlessly succeeded his father as the third president and chief stockholder of the family business, Strothers Textiles, its red-brick three-story mills sprawling along the Methuen and Andover banks of the Merrimack River, without a beat being lost. When death put an end to his first-marriage love-match, the man'd simply gone all to pieces, consoling himself with booze and high living, becoming in the process easy, tempting prey for the Manhattan gold digger. By the time he'd come to his senses, after close to five years of hell raising, he'd long since gone and married the wench. Years later, long after she'd left him for the younger, richer man, he would say without hesitation that he knew there was a God, one who'd taken mercy on him, when He sent down her seducer, rescuing him from his folly.

I learned all this history from Allison Bassy. "He apparently loved Olive very much," she said, over a candlelit dinner of roast pork with apples and cinnamon—we'd moved on to it after drinks in the oak bar of the Mulberry Inn. ("So named," she told me, "for the trees they planted around here in the nineteenth century, to feed the silkworms for an industry that was going to make all of China and Japan's hard-working worms completely obsolete. Didn't work for some reason; what it was, I couldn't tell you. But like the lilies of the field, they toiled not, and neither did they spin. Homesick, maybe, you think? Anyway, the net result of that disaster is that by default PA's really just about the town's only attraction, its sole claim to fame. Sort of scary, isn't it? All you have to do is open for business a couple years after the Declaration of Independence, ten or eleven before the Constitution's ever written, survive, and then thrive for a couple hundred years or so, training many of those who seek and win power of every variety, and first thing you know, you're pretty well known. There's no secret to it at all.)

"Obviously there was some passion behind the serious public personality of that no-nonsense man, who saw his duty and did it. The excesses, good and bad, of his love life up 'til then were proof enough of that. So it shouldn't've been too surprising when he began to feel very much attached to Olive, with her winning ways," she said. I'd left the wine list to her; having learned in the bar that her ex-husband was a managing wine buyer, shipper and importer employed by Heublein, I'd figured that whatever their differences had been (chiefly arising from her discovery that on his semiannual six-week solo buying tours of chateau vineyards in France he hadn't limited his connoisseur samplings of the pastoral countryside's delights solely to the *vins du pays,* the discovery coming when one of another variety, a comely blond baroness from Bordeaux, nineteen, born in Tuscany—"young mountain ghinny with big boobs," Allison growled felinely to me much later, when we'd gotten to know each other better—told a writer from *Bon Appétit* that her favorite among all of the *negociants* she eagerly looked forward to seeing *every* year was "that charming, very sexy, Boston bachelor, Paul Bassy") she hadn't been deaf to his expertise. She'd handled the chore beautifully, selecting a 1990 Nuits de St. George that tasted wonderful but wasn't priced so high as to give a man the blind staggers.

"Olive was an easy woman to admire, when I met her, and I'd have to think she must've also been an easy one to fall in love with, when she and Tom got together. She took that big house right over, what's now the administration building, and here were these four kids in it, basically nice kids, but undisciplined, neglected, just allowed to grow like weeds and run completely wild all those years their dad'd alternately been despondent and then off somewhere playing the rakehell, in both conditions being something that he really wasn't, and as a result by the time Olive arrived they were headed hell-bent for election straight down the old primrose path. The oldest of them, Tom the Third, was seven when their mother died. The youngest of course was newborn at that time, but by the time the bimbo'd left—she'd lived with them, if you could call it that, less'n two years, but they were eventful years—Tom the Third was nearly thirteen, taking his cues from his father and headed for very big trouble. The other three kids were taking their cues from big brother. They'd be going Dad's way as soon as their time came. They were impatient for it to come, and it was going to, very soon, 'less someone stepped in and did something first.

"And that was around when Olive's first husband died. So she'd come back here to Andover, lick her wounds for a while, and when she'd recovered from mourning she decided she'd like to remarry. Well, Olive was a practical woman. If she was back in the market she certainly ought to take the kind of close look at Tom Strothers the Second an appraiser would give an estate diamond. Stood to reason. He was certainly available, and she *had* known him since she was a girl, of course, but now she was a woman, more hardheaded about things. Still, apparently she decided that he might still have some promising, husbandly possibilities; might yet be put to some use. So she moved in and rounded him up. Shaped him all up, and then, when she had him all dusted off, married him and moved in on the kids. Olive was a remarkable woman."

Allison Bassy that night was forty-seven years old. She admitted to weighing twelve pounds more than she had when she'd turned thirty, "convinced that death would come next; there could be no life after thirty; thirty was old age," four pounds more than "my real fighting weight"—I told her she looked fine to me. That was a bald-faced lie, of course; at that point I'd scarcely looked at her, studied her body (it turned out to be entirely satisfactory, by my lights; active, too). She'd halted me right at her wonderful eyes.

Eyes've always been my weakness. Mack's dazzled me years ago, when I was a mere lad, and when I saw how Heather used hers, heredity no doubt, I knew she'd be a caution too (not that that's an unmixed blessing upon the woman who has that kind of expressive eyes; they can express her right into the gravy, if she isn't careful with them). The color doesn't really matter, gray or brown or blue—Allison's're green, I think, sometimes; at other times dark gray, depending on the light. What matters is the life behind them. The windows of the soul, perhaps? I probably wouldn't go that far. But I can almost always tell when I've just met someone whom I'm really going to like, so much that I'm grateful we don't have adjoining desks—we'd never get our work done; we'd be talking all the time.

Drinks and dinner with Allison (Wagner) Bassy had not been on my agenda that afternoon. If that had been an entry on it, I would've been in a much better mood that afternoon soon after lunch, checking my wallet to make sure I hadn't inadvertently exchanged my Board of Bar Overseers ID card instead of my claim stub for my last batch of clean shirts; taking the precaution of having my secretary Xerox three copies of my appointment as guardian *ad litem* for Lucille Kyle, Margaret Cameron, and Jeffrey Nichols in the pending Essex probate matter, *In re Nichols;* and left my office after lunch. My dreary purpose had been to drive forty miles, plus or minus, up Route 93 north, taking exit 43 east onto Route 133, Andover Street, hunkering well down in the driver's seat as I passed the lair of the law-abiding northeastern American citizen's most hated and feared, all-devouring monster, the regional office of the Internal Revenue Service ("We don't eat *our* young—we eat *yours*"), turning right onto Haggett's Pond road, then onto Wood Hill, and thence onto Strothers School Road, formerly the main gate drive leading to the Strothers' massive white three-story clapboard mansion, Woodleigh, as they called it then, now become the operations center of the Strothers School.

The first Strothers to become wealthy, Olive's husband's grandfather, had had an eye for scenery. The plateau he'd chosen and landscaped for his homesite overlooked Haggett's Pond, with a panoramic view of the woods beyond. It'd been even lovelier, of course, when he selected it, back in the 1870s; there'd been no Route 93 then to interfere with his view of the sunsets from his western verandah, "but it's still really something to see in the late afternoons," Allison told me, "especially during the foliage season. Really something to see."

"I'll drop by next October, have a look, if you don't mind," I said.

"Not 'til October?" she said. "October's a long way off."

There was a rectangular black sign planted kitty-corner on a stake in the lawn bordering the maple-shaded parking lot of crushed white stone, to the right of the broad front walk of the main house. It was gold-lettered ADMINISTRATION, with a small gold arrow pointing toward the door. Around 3:30 that mid-May afternoon I grabbed my portfolio of copies and the small tools of my trade off the passenger seat, locked up my T-bird, and followed that sign's direction.

The double front doors were open behind two green-framed screened doors. I went into the foyer, a cavernous two-story, darkly polished, oak-paneled hall framed by broad staircases, right and left, leading to a balcony made for delivery of grand welcomes, proposals of exuberant toasts, and expressions of sad last farewells (exactly what the Strotherses had used it for, Allison told me, hailing guests into great fancy-dress shindigs; hefting bumpers of champagne as wedding receptions began and ended; condoling with family and friends as the body of a newly departed Strothers lay in state below). High above, a huge wooden four-bladed fan turned slowly in the soft May air. The light was dim but I could make out one of those black ribbed-surface directory boards, silver framed, encased in glass, on the wall ahead of me to the left of the doorway opening down a long green-carpeted hall paneled in wood like the foyer. The door to the office at the very end of that long hall was open, and beyond it through the southwest window, bordered in stained glass, spilled a golden light partway up the hall, sort of like a Cecil B. DeMille–staged piece of corny-movie hokum meant to illuminate the hero's entrance to Valhalla, or the Promised Land.

I didn't know what exactly I was looking for, but whatever it was, it was probably in some office down that hall. I'm smart enough to know a middle-aged fellow who can't help looking shifty had better not go wandering aimlessly around a campus full of young people, whistling a happy tune, even in a fine suit, without first reporting to someone in charge. Establishing his bona fides, and obtaining permission, ideally plus an escort but at least some kind of badge, enough to prevent his otherwise certain detention by private police security guards on the lookout for child molesters and worse: yes, I was sure I was looking for something.

There was a line for "Headmaster," which at last resort I'd come back to—but it would be a last resort; even after all these years, I still shrink from being told to go to the principal's office. There was a list of deans' offices. "Admissions" and "Management" didn't fit the bill, and neither did "Curriculum." "Dean of Students" looked like it might. I took note of room number 107 and started down the long hall. Small black iron signs with scrolled gold numbers hung on brackets over each door. The numbers alternated, 101 on the right, 102 facing it on the left. All of the doors except 103, the last one on my right at the end of the hall, were open and the sunlight came through the windows on the polished floors of what appeared to be fairly large apartments subdivided into cubicles partitioned off with wood paneling and frosted glass. Allison would explain it, giving me the tour as she took me to meet Maggie. "The first floor of the house when it was built was a music room on the left of the hall and a ballroom on the right, and then down at my end, what they called a dining room, you and I would call a hall or a banquet room. After Tom the Second died, Olive decided there was no need for anyone to wait until she also died—after all, she was only sixty-one, a *vigorous* sixty-one, when he had his heart attack at the age of seventy-nine. She still had much to do, and certainly no intention of dying for a good many years to come, to complete the conversion of the main house entirely to the uses of the school. Tom'd insisted that they retain half of the first floor, and all of the upstairs, for their private living quarters, which as a practical matter put a ceiling on the number of kids she could accommodate, and also meant most of them had to come from nearby, and commute—the carriage house was only big enough to house eight boarding students, really, and they were pretty cramped. So she thought if that was what she was going to do, convert the whole main house, and it was, then there was no point in waiting—she might as well get started on it. Besides, if it was put it off until after she died, she wouldn't have any say in the way it was done, and that didn't suit her at all. Olive did like her say. So she had the carriage house refurbished and redecorated—and very nicely, too; Olive had good taste—and there was room enough in it for her maid and her cook; she had all her favorite things moved out of the big house into it; and she lived there while she ran the whole show from her office here.

"The rooms along the hall on either side, the ones made from the music room, and ballroom, were the original classrooms. Olive believed that when you were working with the kind of children she brought here, age shouldn't determine what grade the kid should be assigned to. She thought the kid should attend the classes that a kid who tested at his level in that subject ought to be taking next. Sort of a one-room schoolhouse, but with six rooms in it. There weren't any hard-and-fast age requirements for admission—or exclusion, for that matter. It was all what the jargoneers today would probably call child centered, or some stupid thing like that. But it was basically an unstructured environment. So you'd have twelve-year-olds from bilingual households taking advanced French, Italian, Spanish, with fifteen-year-olds who were taking college freshman calculus with seventeen-year-olds. There wasn't any conscious effort to attract particularly gifted children whose intelligence'd been suppressed by intellectually hostile environments; it just seemed to turn out that very often children with that kind of background opened up and sort of bloomed when they came under Olive's wing, and then lo and behold, seemed to *become* gifted up here.

"She was on her last legs when I first came here, fresh out of Wheaton, looking for a job. Pretty frail and pretty feeble, had to use two canes to get around at all, but she was ninety-seven, after all was said and done, and even she said she supposed it was natural, she was tired. I was all atwitter when I met her. My parents had a house in Ipswich, up near Crane's Beach; my mother was in education, so I'd heard a lot about Mrs. Strothers and her ways. Naturally I gushed, tried in my young way to pay her rightful homage, and naturally I made a proper mess of it right off, and she said, putting me at ease: 'You know it's all quite simple, really. If you're someone who's important to them, normal people, not deranged, tend to meet your expectations of them. Not all of them. Not all the time. But pretty generally they will. If you degrade them constantly, they'll degrade themselves. If you tell them you expect good things to come from them, and if they believe you, then pretty soon you'll start to see good things coming from them.

" 'That's all we really do here. We put them into nonthreatening surroundings and make it clear to them that all they have to do to please us is the very best they can. A phenomenally large number, slightly over eighty percent, do exactly that. The other eighteen, nineteen? Well, no system's perfect. Ours is pretty good.' "

Room 107 was the one at the center of the back corridor crossing the T of main hall. There was a counter waist high across it about eight feet inside the door. Five captain's chairs, black, flanked the door. Beyond the counter there were five desks, arranged in an H, two on the left and one on the right unoccupied. Two women to whom I paid little attention operated desktop computers, one on each side of the room, and a young woman who appeared to me likely to be one of the older students got up from her chair at the desk that completed the H pattern in the middle of the room and came to the counter to greet me. She seemed a bit nervous, but since I hadn't done or said anything to give her the jitters, I figured that was her normal state. I told her who I was and what I wanted. I put my portfolio onto the counter and pulled the documents out of it. I started to pull out my wallet ID, but she shook her head quickly three or four times and said: "No no no, I'll get Mrs. Bassy. Mrs. Bassy's the dean. She can help you."

She fluttered her left hand at me over the counter and backed away a couple of steps, as though fearful I might vault the counter and pounce if she turned her back on me within range, and then when she felt far away from me to be safe, half trotted, hobbled knock-kneed by her tight short black skirt, to the door opening onto another office on my left. She rapped on the door frame twice; I heard a "Yes? What is it, Janie?" and then she moved in to stand in the doorway. I recognized the sound of my own name but otherwise could hear only an undertone of the low-voiced conversation she had with the person in that room. Then I heard quite clearly: "Well, ask him to please take a seat and I'll be with him as soon as I finish this call. Tell him it won't be very long."

The girl backed away from the door as though she'd been reprimanded and came back to her desk looking dejected. "Mrs. Bassy said to ask you to please have a seat," she said sadly. "She'll be with you as soon as she gets off the phone."

Allison emerged from her office before I could move from the counter to any of the chairs outside the counter. She was wearing a pleated reddish orange skirt of lightweight wool, I guessed, and a white silk blouse with a gold pocket watch suspended from a gold-chain necklace just below her breasts. She tousled her short dark hair carefully into an arrangement that would have looked perfect under a black beret but looked damned good just as it was. She had a smile that she had obviously practiced, often needing one in the kind of job she had, but she had equally obviously enjoyed the practice, because she liked to smile.

I was completely dazzled. I didn't know what the hell I was doing, or what the hell I ought to do next. I could feel my face was getting red, and that if one of those adult females at the computers happened to glance up from her work at me she would know instantly that either I'd had far too much to drink—"and mind you, Mildred, this was just midafter*noon*"—or else I must suffer from some socially disabling condition that would explain why I, a fairly well dressed man of fifty-six seasoned years who appeared to be in his right mind, nevertheless plainly appeared to be on the brink of making a colossal, blabbering fool of himself. "He just came in there, looked normal as you please, and I tell you, Mildred, Allison came out of her *office*, and everything about him changed. I thought that he was either drunk and passing out, or else he must be having some kind of an attack."

I have told her many times since we met that day that while I know she's very happy in her job, and at that school, on her performance that day I have to insist that I think she missed her true calling. Allison Wagner Bassy should have proceeded out of Wheaton directly to the Fletcher School of Law and Diplomacy at Tufts, the International Law center at Georgetown, or else to the next scheduled examination for U.S. State Department foreign service applicants. As the fastball was Roger Clemens's birthday present from God, so spontaneous natural diplomacy was her natural gift. "Because if you had said anything but what you said to me that day, maybe 'Can I help you, sir?' or 'Would you step this way?' something threatening like that, the next sound you would've heard coming from my mouth, assuming I could've made any sound, my mouth was so dry, would've been 'abba, ababbaba, ba ba . . . ,' gobblings to that effect."

She always laughs and waves it off, but that's the solemn truth. I'd been struck completely stupid. The only thing that saved me from making an utter, abject, gibbering spectacle of myself was her inspired opening patter, coming out of that besotting smile: "Not *the* attorney Kennedy? *Jerry* Kennedy?" I guess I must've gulped and nodded, swooning eight grader I was again, in love with his pretty new teacher. "My father hates your guts."

· · · **15**

That sharp hard shot, completely unexpected, was exactly what I'd needed to snap me out of my addled state. Like the short push start a college friend would give your old jalopy, when the starter motor froze dead center and the damned thing would *not* turn over; when he got it rolling, you'd turn on the ignition and drop it into gear, and the engine would come to life. Piercing sexual attraction hadn't been a regular feature of my late middle years (once I heard a man say sorrowfully that when he'd been in his thirties, he'd just assumed that people in their fifties seldom thought about sex anymore, and "never did it at all. And now that I'm in my fifties," he said, in the mournful tone bloodhounds would use if they had the habit of talking, "I'm finding out I was half right"). Concealing hot desire with dignified bearing (or at least deferring action on it for the decent interval required to ascertain whether the object of it desires to be pursued) had therefore not been a skill much demanded of me for several years, so I was somewhat out of practice. But, sudden unprovoked aggression? *That* was an entirely different matter, a whole 'nother bag of cats. *That* I know how to respond to.

"Oh-*hoh*," I said, suddenly no longer afraid that I might wet my pants, "and what've we got here, now?" That was another good sign: my voice registered in its normal baritone, not the squeaking thirteen-year-old's falsetto I was sure I would've piped one minute earlier, if forced to reply to a question. My pulse rate was declining, down from jackhammer pounding above the red line on the meter that warns the medic checking your pressure: *big fat vegetating stroke impends*. "Another in a long line of satisfied customers? How many years did the old villain get? Much less than he probably deserved, I'm sure— and would've gotten, too, if I hadn't been there with my skills to get him off easy. What was it that he thinks I got him convicted of doing? Mugging old ladies? Taking candy from babies? Robbing the poor box or something? Something he did, in any event; something he shouldn't've done."

The two women at the computer keyboards had abandoned all pretense of work; they were openly staring. The kid at the center desk looked to be scared out of her wits. If she'd had a silent alarm button within stealthy reach at her desk like the bank VPs and the jewelry salesmen have (and now the abortion clinicians as well), the SWAT team would've been rolling even as we spoke.

"Oh, it wasn't a con*viction* you got that enraged him," Allison said, "his or anyone else's. It was an *acquittal* that set my dad off. Went right straight up through the roof. Seven, eight or so years ago now, and still he's not all the way down yet. Even today, if you mention that case anytime in his hearing, he'll go into orbit again. The night it came on the news, you'd gotten Billy Ryan off, Dad exploded, right there on the spot in his chair. He's been retired for sixteen years now, but he spent his whole life after the Seabees in the state DPW, career highway-planning and design engineer, all those years when Ryan was running it, and robbing all of us blind. The *language* he used—it was awful.

"Now block your ears, ladies," she said to the others, without taking her eyes off me, "you especially, Janie. Don't want anyone gettin' shocked in here now." They of course did no such thing. "And keep in mind now, I'll just be giving the *flavor* of it here. What he *actually* said was much worse.

"He yelled '*Son of a bitch*,' and belted the arm of his chair, and then he really warmed up. 'That just goes to prove it—the law's a damned big joke. Those idiots never convict anyone. It's all just a big goddamned *act* they go through, a charade they put on, make it look like they *are* doing something. Then the guy gets acquitted, and they all just shrug, tell us they did the best that they could, and hey, what can they do? All *they* can do is get charges brought—it's juries that have to convict. And then everybody all goes right back to doing what they were doing before, only now they do more of it—we've increased their confidence.

" 'No wonder it all just never ends, all this thieving, conniving. Why should it? What is there, really, to be afraid of? No one ever gets punished for doing it. Steal a million dollars, five years later they catch up with you, and then what happens to you? Well, really, not very much. What does happen's not *fun*, I will grant you that, but it's not like they were tarring and feathering you. It's just kind of embarrassing, really. Your name's all over the papers and your best friends all tell you you'd better resign your position—don't wanna lose those pension rights there, as you could; it's possible you could get convicted. Not that anyone ever did yet, least that anyone else alive can remember, but it isn't worth taking the chance. So you do that, and then you do the next thing, what your heroes did, the crooks who came before you. Stole us blind and then got away clean: you get yourself some damned slick lawyer, and you go to trial on it, and that bastard gets you off.

" 'And that's all there is to it. You can get through that for a year or so, you get to keep all the money. All you got to do, you want to steal a million bucks—maybe two, if you're really greedy—is put up with people callin' you a crook for a while, and that's all there really is to it. After awhile they forget. Not a bad deal at all, a million or so for a red face, people makin' fun of you on the radio talk shows, takin' pictures of you goin' into court. Not a whole lot of fun, I admit, but there's no way you can beat the pay.

" 'That bastard Ryan was stealing from us for upwards of thirty years. Everybody knew it. But of course nobody who was in it with him was going to say anything; they're busy rakin' *their* shares in. And no one who was honest and knew what was going on, actually had the goods on him, or where to look for them, none of them *dared* to say anything, for fear of losing their job. All scared to death of the guy. And then now, when the day comes at last, when it *finally* looks like they've got the old son of a bitch, cornered the old crook at last, then, what happens then?' " She dropped her voice down into disgust at least a foot deep. " 'What happens then? He goes free.

" 'They should throw a big party, the son of a bitch. Issue a damned-fool proclamation, and have a goddamned parade. Declare it another paid state holiday, celebrate every damned year: "All ye, all ye, in free; Billy-Ryan-Goes-Free Day." ' 'Goddamned' was not what he actually said, but you get the general idea."

I grinned what I hoped was an aw-shucks-'twarnt-nothin' smile and said: "Well then, this is a first. The first time in my life I've been hammered for actually winning a case. Many times, I admit, I've been slandered for *losing*, harshly libeled and scorned; reviled and abused; defamed, insulted, in terms I never read in the Bible. But until now never, no, never before, for actually having won one."

She came up to the counter and rested her forearms on it. I held my distance, hiding my insistent erection by keeping that counter between me and Mrs. Bassy. I was feeling a little light-headed again, but still figured I'd be okay, if I could only manage to stare at something besides that gold pocket watch and its immediate surroundings. (Mack told me once, back when we were friends, a very long time ago now, that she knew why it was one of my friends, a perennially frustrated lecher, never got anywhere. He made Mack and all her women friends laugh. "He thinks he's being so smooth with you, hanging on every word that you say, and then when it's his turn to say something back, why, he looks you right in the tits and he says. . . . And by then, who's still listening, huh?") The ring: that was something to study. Talk to her but look at the ring, at least until you can stand up straight again.

Mrs. Bassy wore a very good white diamond ring, four-prong white gold Tiffany setting, on the third finger of her left hand; about three-quarters of a carat, I should say, excellent color, brilliance, and fire. I sort of know what I'm talking about here; I was tutored about diamonds and so forth by a client who made house calls on prosperous people he'd never met and didn't know at all. All he knew was that they had a few bucks and weren't home. To pass the time while he waited for them to return, as a free service he'd examine a few of their assets.

"A favor, really," the visitor called it, "a random kindness, you know? Lots of times you've got these well-to-do families that've been pretty well fixed now for two or three generations, and quite often they will have some item in the family they inherited, it's been in the family a long time, one of those things that's just always been around, they never gave it much thought, and it's become valuable now? They got no idea its real worth. If they did they might want to sell it, you know, and then maybe I'd make a commission." He'd inspect any gold jewelry and precious stones they might have left lying around—along with sterling silver, paintings and engravings, collectible antique firearms, other bric-a-brac they might have on display—and when he was uncertain about the value of a piece, he'd take it with him. In a quilted, pouched gunnysack he was always sure to have along, for just such emergencies. "So nothing rattles, gets banged up, you know? Scratched, dented, or chipped, or like that. You don't want the stuff to get damaged."

Then he'd have it appraised by a friend who'd been a certified gemologist long before the two of them had first met up in the Plymouth County House of Correction ten or fifteen years before, the gemologist vacationing at government expense for writing inflated insurance appraisals of jewelry soon afterwards reported "lost," for a third of the falsified markup. "But I never meant to *keep* it," he would tell me when he'd gotten caught again. "I was just *borrowing* it, purely a matter of curiosity, see if I was right about what it was probably worth. Because why should the owners believe what *I* said, what I said that something was worth? Why should they take my word for it? How the hell do I know? I could be tellin' them *anythin'*, right? Anythin' that comes into my head. Who am I to say what something is worth, that was never a licensed appraiser? So that was the reason for that.

"And then I had this small emergency come up, friend owed me some money, and *he* couldn't pay, and *I* had some bills that *I* hadda pay, so what do I do about that? I needed that money he owed me real bad, but what I could do? Guy was tap-city, stone broke. So *I* hadda go and take out a loan, hadda borrow some money myself, those bills I had just hadda be paid. And so what I did was—see, my credit's really in bad shape, those times I went to jail there and so forth; it's hard for me to just borrow money. I got to give some, some whaddayacallit, *security*. So I guess what I did is, I must've used some of that stuff I borrowed as collat'ral to get the loan. You know? That's what I must've done. So I could get myself a loan. And that's all it really was, honest. Whaddaya think about that, huh? And that's how I get into this mess? Jesus Christ, man," shaking his head, "I mean, I gotta tell you, I just don't know about this. It don't make no sense at all, and I'm tellin' the God's honest troot to you here. That as soon as I got that dough from my friend there, I would've gone to the guy that loaned me, paid him off, and I would've gotten it back. I would've brought the thing back, honest. No harm would've been done at all."

He performed that song and dance on the occasion of the second of our excursions—I represented him four times. I was not his only lawyer, and those were not his only brushes with the law. He hired other lawyers for minor offenses when jail was not on the menu; he sought to flatter me by telling me he saved me for "the really big shit. When it's serious, you know? That's when I really need you." What that meant was that when he could get a lawyer cheap, and a cheap lawyer would do for the job, that was what he got. But when it looked like this new scrape might be a costly one for him to lose, in terms of real years, not mere money, then he called on me.

On our first outing the Middlesex docket was even more crowded than usual, and I was able to bargain the assistant DA down from two years to be served to five suspended and three years' probation, in return for a blindingly quick plea. Our second adventure involved a caper committed two months after expiration of the probationary period from the first one; the old five years SS was therefore off the table, just barely, but still, off the table. After much blood and sweat I got the Suffolk assistant down from a new five years to a Concord ten, meaning my guy got out in a year.

The third rap I beat for him. It was a weak case made out of a strong one, just plain screwed up by an impatient, careless cop who was in a hurry just to make the damned arrest and get it over with, so he could go off duty and bang his fifteen-year-old girlfriend before he went home to his wife. So he hadn't taken the time to get a search warrant. The judge agreed with me; he'd needed one (and after his reason for not getting one'd reached the ears of the commissioner he was also in the market for a new job, and a public defender to handle his statutory rape case. Talk about shitting the bed). That left the prosecutor with about enough evidence to convict my guy of breathing in and breathing out, and cursing all horny cops in the world, he moved to dismiss my guy's problem.

But luck is a thing that runs out, especially when you squeeze it too hard. His last time Gary'd played with the pros and got fifteen years of federal time: interstate transportation of stolen property, to wit: a green leather case, lined with white satin, marked "Fred, Joailleur" on the inside top, containing a twenty-four-inch necklace of emeralds and diamonds, valued at about $43,000, being the property of Mrs. Roger Amelia of Saddle River, New Jersey, sold by my client in a Saugus motel room, under video and audio surveillance, to exemplarily patient, meticulously careful, unexcited Special Agent Farley Green of the Boston field office of the Federal Bureau of Investigation, acting in an undercover capacity. Gary at fifty-eight was inclined to be philosophical. "Well, I guess I can't complain too much," he said. "Even with you, you still can't win 'em all. Our mutual friend Teddy, even, and you know how much he respects you, all the things that you done for him? All the times that you got his ass out of the crack? Even he never went so far's to say that: that no one could ever beat you. That would be asking too much." I saw him off to Leavenworth. I haven't seen him since.

Anyway, when I say Mrs. Bassy's diamond was impressive, I know pretty well what I'm talking about, three or four thousand bucks easy. And even more impressive, to me, was the fact that she wore no wedding band above that beautiful jewel.

■ ■ ■ 16

I'm not sure exactly long it took me to go wherever I'd gone and then get back again, but when I did regain my wits I at least had the presence of mind to surmise that Mrs. Bassy might've said something to me while I was away, and therefore might also be somewhat perplexed by my failure to respond. Like the man who talked about sex after fifty, I had about half of it right; she had said something, but she wasn't a bit perplexed: she knew the explanation for my unresponsiveness, and she was thoroughly enjoying it.

"I'm sorry," I said, deceiving her not at all, "I was just . . ." There seemed to be something in my throat and I had to pause and clear it. "That's, ah, that's a beautiful ring you've got there. I had a client who taught me how professionals look at stones like that, what they see that most laymen don't. Because they don't even know what to look for. So that's what I was doing. I was admiring your ring. That's a very valuable ring."

This was obviously getting me nowhere. I had no real choice: I could either ask her to repeat what I hadn't heard, or else continue blithering on and risk having her ask me how often I behaved like a gibbering idiot. I capitulated. "Did you, ah, did you say something to me?"

"Oh, swave, yes, very swave," Welden Coooper used to say when

he saw or heard about someone clumsily doing something mortify-
ingly stupid, "the very *ep*-ee-toam of swave." At least the women at
the computer keyboards appeared to be satisfied that the dramatic
entertainment seemed to be over with and had returned to their
work. The frightened kid at the center desk was still struggling to pull
herself together (I surmise she's probably going to spend most of her
life trying to do that), so she was occupied as well. I looked for help in
Mrs. Bassy's face.

She was a good sport. She'd play along with the gag. Besides, she
was having fun. She was having the time of her life, as she admitted
much later, when we knew each other much better. I asked her how
often she'd bewitched men as she'd done to me, and God bless her,
after she'd airily said, "Oh, hundreds of times, six, sometimes seven
a day, one loses track after awhile, leave them all fainting there in
my wake," she'd laughed and said, "No, I'm just kidding, of course.
Not all that often, I'm sorry to say. Oh hell, only once, if you want
the truth, and probably not even that—it's more than just possible
Timmy was faking, and lying, as well; he was real good at that sort of
thing. Spotted a fresh divorcée on the hoof, healthy but still, moving
slowly, limping, ego all lamed up—why not put on a little act for
her, huh? Might as well give it a try. Not like it could do any harm.
'Oh Ally, Ally,' much heaving breathing, 'why couldn't I've met you
first? Sally's a wonderful, wonderful girl, a great mother to our little
kids, but she never did this to me, what you did, never affected me
like this. I know, I know, it'll break her poor heart, but I can't do anything else: I'll just have to leave her for you.' He might just as well've
said: 'Or Vegas, maybe, if I can get on a plane. Always some action out
there.' No-good, lying snake.

'Paul? Uh-uh, not a chance. Certainly never happened with Paul.
He would't've allowed it. 'How jejeune,' he would've said. He
would've been amused; he was far too urbane for that. Or he would've
tried to be that anyway, pretended that he was amused. Dashing, cos-
mopolitan, boulevardier, and man of the world: that was the role he'd
selected. 'May I suggest, sir, our thirty-nine regular; Italian-cut, urban
sophisticate model? I think you'll find it will suit you quite well, look
very handsome on you.' 'Why, yes, Maxwell, I do believe you're right.
Have a dozen made up for me if you would, solids, chalk strikes, and
pins; grays and blues; three summer, three winter, six midseason

weights; might make one of those in a glen plaid. That should get me off to a half-decent start. Oh, and a couple of blazers, or shall we say: three? Three pairs of odd trousers, gray flannel worsted, I think, one weight for each kind of weather. And two Harris tweed jackets, of course, a gray and a glen, and black tie ensemble as well. I think that'll fill the bill nicely for now, Maxwell. Many thanks for your excellent taste.'

"Paul did not *start* things. He did not initiate anything. None of that was incumbent upon him. All he had to do was attend. If he wished, and then if he happened to be present, and *you* fell for *him*, well, he might deign to accept your homage. But it was *you* who courted *him*, not the other way around. If he also happened to be in the mood; decided it could be 'rather fun,' then he would guess he'd take part. And then again, he might not. But forever after that, if he did notice you, panting and pawing the turf, well, as long as it might last, it'd never change: you'd always be the one who got the hots for *him*, not he the hots for *you*. That is his role in this world, serpent-bastard he is.

"But still and all: the scaly, slithering, son of a bitch does play his part very well; I have to give that to the guy. Not knowing then, of course, back when I fell for him, that he couldn't *not* play it, his role. That's why he's so damned good at it. Even back then he'd *become* his own character; designed himself from scratch; written the script, all of the lines—giving himself the best ones, of course; and then practiced and practiced and practiced; until he'd become what he'd set out to be: a variorum Charles Aznavour, a master forger's Yves Montand, good enough to fool the counterfeit detectives at the secret service. An ordinary amateur wouldn't've had a chance of telling them apart, the real toff thing from the beautiful fake. I really was quite impressed. As his first wife was, too, not at all favorably, when she found out about me. And as *I* was impressed, and not pleasantly, either, when the baroness Christina surfaced.

"Which was why, still all bruised, I was such easy pickin's when Timmy declared himself smitten. I really did want to believe him. But by the time it'd begun to dawn on me that it was very possible he was lying to me, he'd already started growing tired of me, needed a new conquest to get him pepped up. So before I could give him the heave-ho, bum's rush, get at least that much bitter satisfaction for the damage he'd done, Timmy of course'd cut *me* loose, like the cad and the bounder *he* is."

I murmured something meant to be soothing, and she laughed and said: "Cut it out. I'm not looking for sympathy here. I'm in full gloat right now. That was the best tactic you could have used, making a complete fool of yourself like you did. It was just so impossibly *sweet*. What woman could ever resist that? It's really quite exciting, intoxicating even, for a woman when that actually happens to her; a grown man, supposedly mature, successful, and *responsible*, goes absolutely gaga, turns into Silly Putty right before her very eyes—and the only explanation is that it was her effect that did it.

"*God*, what a feeling of *power*, raw power: now I know how Helen of Troy must've felt, when she got all those guys to set sail and start fighting. 'A thousand ships? Thousands of guys? All for just poor little ol' *me*? Am I a dazzler or what? Hot damn, will ya look at me now.' At least for the women that're fortunate enough to have it happen to them.

"Most of us don't ever have that much good fortune, I think, and those of us who never did really resent those who do. Katie and Jinx in the office the day after you came in, they let me know they disapproved. Not in so many words, of course, didn't come right out and say it; they know what'd happen to them if they did: find themselves on KP; groundskeeping maybe, raking leaves, pulling weeds; they'd started giving me any shit, just because they were jealous of me. Assuming of course that I would've even noticed if they'd started in sassing me—most likely I wouldn't've, floating around a foot or two off the ground myself like I was, playing the fool to your sap. 'La-di-dah, la-di-dah, ain't love grand?'

" 'Jealous'?" I said. "Who am I, Paul Newman, or whoever the newest hunk is?"

She was indulgent. "Mel Gibson, I guess it'd be now, but Paul Newman wouldn't've been bad." She spoke thoughtfully, nodding. "Yeah, I could've taken Paul Newman, good looking and rich as he is. Little old for me, maybe, coming up on seventy, paper said the other day, but if it'd been Paul Newman I'd put into a trance? 'Who, *me*? You mean *me*, you mean: I'm the one that did that? Morgan le Fey, now dean of students at the Strothers School, long way from Camelot in my new incarnation?' Yeah, I could've lived with that, I think. Kind of tough luck for Joanne, of course, bit rough on the lady, all those years that they've been together, but I'm sure I could explain it all to her, so, you know, she'd understand. 'Paul just couldn't help himself once he'd come under my fatal spell.' She's a woman of the world; I'm sure she'd understand. She'd want us to be happy. 'It's not like it was something he could've helped at all,' I would say. 'Or I could've stopped happening, either. We've simply got to be adults about this, and just do the best that we can. Fate. Kismet, Joanie baby, this's our *dess-tiny*, babe. I'm sure we can all stay good friends.' Hey, you know how it is: *go* with it, if it ever happens; well, that's what you've got to do.

"But no, that's not what I think happens, when somebody acts like that. That if it's you that it's happened to, it would ever even cross your mind to think: 'Well, this isn't bad, it's not like I mean that—and I don't really want to complain—but did it have to be *this* guy? I picked to enchant, to stop in his tracks just like that? I mean, I know he's not *attached* or anything, so that's one point in his favor, makes the whole thing so much neater when there's no wife to pick off, and it's not like I'm not grateful, don't appreciate it. But just the same, couldn't it've been, say, JFK Junior, some guy closer my own age, like twenty-eight or so?

"Twenty-eight *is* my age, you know. Just like it was Olive's. Olive's the one who told me that, first time I ever met her; I was still just twenty-two. 'You get to pick your own age, you know, my dear, and that's the one that I picked out because of all the many years I've had, that one's always been my favorite. That's the year that I decided, after Fulling died and I was just so devastated, that I would come back here and pull myself back together, so that I could get on with my life. And that was what led eventually to my second marriage, to that wonderful, fine man my second husband was. So that will always be my age. That's the age I am today. You look at me and think you see a frail old lady, I know—of course you do. But wrapped up inside this old sere leaf, this fragile husk you're looking at, is still that strong young woman. When she goes, I'll be gone too.'

"So I followed her example and after I'd been twenty-eight, tried twenty-nine and thirty, maybe one or two more years after that, one day I found I'd decided: 'Nope, no need to put it off any longer here. Olive had it right. Twenty-eight's the age to be.' So that's the one I picked. By the time you're twenty-eight you've got a few miles on you, so you now know what you're doing, but you're not quite thirty yet. Nothing's that's supposed to be up north's really started south yet, down toward the equator. Course you have to work like hell to keep it *up* there, sit-ups, exercise machines, but no bold young hussy, twenty-two or so, 's going to take a man from you, you aren't quite finished with him yet—still want to keep him around a bit longer, case you or a friend needs a spare."

"Nothing too important," she said that day I'd showed up in her office and started maundering right in her face. "Just what we can do for you, what you came here for. Busy man I'm sure you are, you couldn't've driven all the way up here without having some pretty good reason" (leaving out, bless her, what she might've added: "I mean, besides just intending to swoon over me"). "You practice in Boston, don't you? Didn't I read that or hear it somewhere? 'Prominent Boston attorney Jeremiah Kennedy'? Maybe in connection with the Ryan case or something?"

"Could be," I said, as casually as I could with the only instrument I had to work with, a partially strangled voice. "Once they paste a label on you, it generally stays stuck."

"Yes, but that's a pretty nice one to have," she said, "if you have to be labeled at all. As I'm sure you must agree. And so recognizing you as being that, big-time lawyer down in Boston, I have to assume you didn't come all the way up to this part of the forest just to pass the time of day."

"Yes," I said, spreading the documents on the counter between us. "This's the original, and I had my secretary make these copies for you, for your files and so forth, or whatever, and as you can see I've been appointed, very much against my will, not that that matters much, by Judge Henry Lawler of the Essex County Probate Court, to look after, protect, conserve, or whatever you want to call it, the legal interests of the heirs to the estate of the late Sandra Nichols, as they are the decedent's children, and make sure they get their just due. And because it's my understanding that the two youngest're still students here, I thought before I sign myself up for the long hike out to western Massachusetts to see their half-sister Lucy, I'd be better off starting out by coming up here, a shorter distance, and talking to the two kids that you've got."

Having read my document of appointment while I was off in some other galaxy, she said: "Yes. We're aware of Judge Lawler's strong interest in the children. He's been here himself, on two or three occasions, to see them, talk to them, and so forth. His appointment of you we did *not* know about, which means somebody must've screwed up, but . . ."

". . . that's a common event in court cases," I said.

". . . and in private schools, too, I can tell you," she said. She raised her voice slightly, so that anyone else in the room would've had to be asleep or deaf not to've heard it. "It's entirely possible the screwup wasn't in Judge Lawler's court at all. That it took place right here, when someone misfiled a paper. Or perhaps didn't file it at all. And not for the first time, by any means, no. This's a little Bermuda Triangle of papers. They disappear around here all the time, without leaving the slightest trace, and nobody knows where they are." Both women at the keyboards kept on typing, but the one farthest from the counter got very red on the back of her neck.

Mrs. Bassy dropped her voice back to normal conversational level. "Maggie is no problem. You can see her today. She's finished classes for the afternoon. She'll be in the library doing research for a term paper on the poetry of Elizabeth Bishop. Which most likely means she'll be sitting with her back against a tree out on the terrace lawn in the sunshine, a beautiful spring day like this, now and then snapping herself out of her reverie to read a paragraph or two out of the book she's got resting on her legs. But most of the time simply dreaming. Like all young women her age."

"Sixteen," I said. "Do you know all of your students this well, in this much detail?"

"Hardly," Allison said. "But then it's fairly unusual for one of our students to have a parent get murdered. I'm sure a good many of our parents would've *preferred* to murder each other, at various times, but murder doesn't seem to be the done thing around these parts. Divorces are so freely granted, you know, no damned need, all that *gore* anymore. So homicide just isn't *done*, and that's simply all there is to it. Therefore, when this news came out at last, that the poor woman hadn't just run off impulsively, her head turned by some rogue cavalier—she was been known to've been rather footloose, of course, before she and Mister Wade got together, so that was what most'd suspected—but'd been in fact *chastely* and *honorably murdered*, well, I tell *you*, that sure grabbed our attention. Big doin's ensued around these parts. We had the police, and all the reporters, and not just the local folks, either; there was at least one of the network guys here, too. I think his name's Fred Briggs? TV cameramen and their satellite dish trucks, swarming all over the place; the first traffic jams that'd ever been seen on the little humble two-lane blacktop in here, and all because the Strothers School was the last place on earth that she'd been seen alive. By anyone but her killer, at least.

"We lead sheltered lives here at Strothers, Mister Kennedy. Inward looking, insulated, introverted; we're primarily concerned about what happens to each other, and what happens at the school. That takes up all our time. It's more of an obsession than a career sometimes, I guess. We become somewhat cloistered in here, not so much renouncing the great world outside as ceasing to care much about it. So when some rare event here makes the news for one night or one edition out in the real world, and then fades away, disappears, it becomes and remains historical for us. Local folklore. When it happens *to* one of us, to anyone who's still here. We've had lots of parents with colorful histories—many more, I'm quite sure, than we ever knew about—but as far as we know, none of them had pasts, or presents, for that matter, quite as gaudy as hers, ending up in such dramatic fashion. You're a man of the world, Mister Kennedy—I'm sure you can understand that. Mere common pedestrian scandal's enough—it's too bad, but still true—to heighten the interest that's paid to the children involved at the school. And of course, since Jeffrey's here too—sorry but you won't be able to see him today, I'm afraid—we had not one but *two* such students. If it'd happened, if she'd dropped out of sight three years ago, then Lucy was still here, well, then it would've been all three.

"So, since we don't want them set back or derailed from the progress they've made since they came here—and they've made a lot of it; they've done very nicely here—and since for all practical purposes, they're all alone in the world, without a real parent or relative who can look after them—Grandma's an old chippy herself—we've tended to keep a close eye on those kids. They've had bumpy lives up till now, and we not only try to do what we can for them, but the very best we can. We give them our most special attention."

"Why can't I see Jeffrey?" I said.

"Oh, my good man," she said, "because you don't *want* to see Jeffrey. If we let you in to see Jeffrey today, sure as shootin' you'd sue us two weeks from now, and we're a nonprofit institution. We consider ourselves lucky any year we manage to be a non*deficit* institution, and we don't see one of those very often, either, I regret to say. So, we can't afford any sort of that suing kind of thing people of your habits do. Jeffrey's in the infirmary with a galloping case of the chicken pox, in quarantine, contagious as all get-out. He'll throw it off in a few days, being young and all; for a kid of eleven, it's not any fun, of course, but all it is for him is just a heavy cold, plus a lot of itchy scabs. But for us older kids, people of our age, it's more than a damned nuisance—it can be quite serious. No, you don't want that. Save him for another day."

"I had chicken pox, when I was a kid," I said. "I'm immune to that plague."

"Maybe you are and maybe you aren't," she said. "The age that makes afflictions worse also changes the immune system, among other things, you know. And chicken pox is a form of herpes? As you may also know?"

"Ah, no, I didn't," I said.

"No," she said. "Well anyway, we're not going to take that chance here today. But what I will do, instead of giving you directions, is have someone walk you down to where I'm sure you'll find Maggie daydreaming. So you won't get lost, which many visitors do. But also because, as you'll understand, I'm sure, we do have certain rules here that we do insist upon. Unless it's a parent, or other family member who comes here with a parent, or a letter from a parent, to see a student for the first time, someone monitors the visit. In certain circumstances, in fact, this can even apply to parents. There've been fierce custody battles in the past between Strothers parents fighting the divorce wars, and we're all to aware of cases involving other schools where the children were taken and then spirited away, and the school in question was severely criticized, two or three were even sued, for allowing it to happen. We're determined nothing like it's going to happen here.

"But assuming nothing like that is involved, after that first visit, if we're satisfied the student hasn't been troubled or upset in any way, by the visitor—and in addition to one of us sitting in on the first meeting with any stranger, we have the student in here after the visitor's left, and I interview him or her to make sure everything that may've *looked* okay, really *was* okay—we note the visitor's name on an Approved Visitor card in the student's file. And when that visitor comes back, all we ask him to do is check in here and get a badge. And please, no disruption of class schedules except in truly dire emergency. But we don't sit in again unless the student either says something or does something that makes us think perhaps we'd better. Or else exclude the visitor, the next time he shows up."

"Well, yes," I said, "I certainly understand the policy, reasons for it, so forth. But whoever comes along with me has also got to understand that this is an attorney-client conference I'll be having with this kid, strictly confidential. So you can watch but you can't listen; no third parties can be present, close enough to overhear." She frowned. "And if you can't or won't agree agree to that," I said, "because of this school policy of yours—which I can certainly understand; reasons for it, I approve of—we will then have a conflict between two strong policies, and my only alternative'll be to go back before Judge Lawler and get an order from him, directing you to let me see my clients by myself. And he will give it to me, too, because as the court's appointed guardian, I outrank you on this. That I do not want to do."

"No," she said, "nor do we want you to. So, what we will do is this: just give me a moment to get my jacket here, and I'll appoint myself to be your escort. If Maggie's outdoors under her favorite maple tree, where she's usually to be found on a pretty day like this, I'll take a magazine from the library and a chair on the terrace, where I can keep an eye on you, but too far away to hear you. And you can have your conference in private. And when you've finished, I'll walk you back up here. Will that be satisfactory, sir?"

"I don't want to take up your day," I said, wanting to add: "Your night would be a different matter entirely."

"I could use a break," Allison said. "We could all use a break in the routine today. Don't you think so, too, Kate and Jinx?"

I didn't know which one was which, but the typist whose neck hadn't reddened, the one seated closest to the counter, said without turning around: "Oh, you bet. I could sure go for that about now."

"Okay, Mister Kennedy?" Allison said.

"Just terrific," I said, meaning it.

▪ ▪ ▪ 17

Allison emerged from her private office shrugging into a rumpled beige linen jacket. I knew enough (from a dash of my new secretary Meredith's petulance: "Oh for heaven's *sake*, Mr. Kennedy, it's *supposed* to be wrinkled like this—don't you even know *that*? This's what the style *looks* like." Meredith at twenty-six no longer even makes an effort to disguise her conviction that I most likely don't have a TV set yet because I'm still waiting for them to bring out one that runs on coal) not to take it as a sign of slovenly habits. "We'll go out down the end of this hall," she said, walking briskly, turning left as we left room 107 into the rear corridor. Down past three doors closed on the left there was a screened door opening onto a terrace, and beyond that a broad lawn sloping away toward a fringe of trees bordering the pond. Before the screened door whispered closed behind us, restrained by its pneumatic piston, Allison had pulled a flip-top box of Marlboros from her right-hand pocket and a translucent blue-plastic disposable lighter from her left, opened the box, selected a cigarette, lighted it, dragged deeply on it, and started to sigh "ahhh" as she exhaled. The door at last latched itself shut as she took a second drag, slower.

"I see what you meant by needing a break," I said.

"Will this bother you, even outdoors and all?" she said warningly. "Good lord, I sure hope it won't. Assuming you don't smoke yourself."

"It wouldn't bother me indoors," I said. "I can't think why the hell it would out. Your smoking's your problem, not mine."

"Well, thank God for that, at least," she said, taking another pull on the Marlboro. "This's been one bitch of a day." She laughed. "And I've been one bitch of a bitch. Kate and Jinx, when I said that, about needing a break, and Jinx agreed right off with me? I meant they needed one as much as I did. We've all been driving each other plain nuts. Little Janie, poor kid: I feel sorry for her; she doesn't know what the hell to do, except try to stay out of the way."

"What the heck happened?" I said. We had left the flagstoned terrace and were walking in a southerly direction parallel to the shore of the pond, but high above and a long way from it, and the lawn felt like plush carpet underfoot.

"Oh, nothing new, really," she said. "What happened today's the same thing, no different, as what's been happening every day for, what is it now? Coming up on three weeks now, it is. Ever since the headmaster, our Miss Jean Brodie dressed up in a man's coat and pants, David Greenwood, unilaterally decided that Strothers ought to follow the example of Harvard, of course, where *he* went to school, and public schools, too, and government agencies, everywhere really, and put in a complete ban on smoking. Total, complete ban on all indoor smoking. All rooms in all buildings, anyplace on the campus, including the toilets and the equipment sheds. Not even set-aside smoking rooms, dedicated areas, lairs of foul air which some people asked for, once they found out what David was up to.

" 'No,' he said, 'I don't want to have that. It'll just be a stop-gap way for people not to stop, if they know they have someplace they can go and maintain their filthy addiction. They know it isn't good for them, that it's very bad for them, and also everyone around them. Well, if they're that badly off, they can just go on outdoors, and I don't care if they get cold or if they get wet; maybe that'll be their incentive to do what they ought to do anyway; maybe that way they'll finally quit.'

"And then all the trustees—five out of twelve of them smoke, and you know and I know and *they* damned right well know, there's still going to be ashtrays around the boardroom table when they come to the campus for meetings; fat chance Miss Priss'll enforce it on *them*. He won't even notice they're doing it. Because he knows if he gets shirty and reprimands them, he'll endanger the ten grand a year *each* that they give. Do the school out of at least fifty grand, and that's the minimum, mind you; most of them give a lot more. So what difference does his big crusade make to those fat cats? It doesn't make any at all. They all sort of said: 'What the hell then, if that's what you want. You're the one has to work with the inmates.' And the next day the signs started going up all over the damned place, just like *that*." She snapped her fingers.

"All those who smoked were just going to quit, have to, cold turkey, or else they could look for new jobs." She took another deep drag. "A couple of men on the buildings, grounds, and maintenance crew did exactly that, said okay, then they quit; they'd claim unemployment awhile. Take the whole summer off for themselves, let these beautiful lawns go hell, weeds and seeds, see how Little Miss Muffet liked that. Well, he didn't. Mister Greenwood didn't like the sound of that at *all*. He relented a little, to the extent that he said they could smoke in the sheds and garages, and the boiler rooms, too—as though he would've had some way to stop them, if they'd defied him on the sly—but nowhere else indoors on the campus." She snorted.

"So, we unreconstructed but educated nicotine junkies've been making do, best we can, smoking outside of our buildings. Smoking much more, I suspect, because under this new, *health*-conscious rule, it's on our minds all the time now. At least it's nice outdoors this time of year. I've got an idea when the cold wind starts blowing and the white snow starts falling, those buildings and maintenance guys're gonna find out that they're much better friends with the staff and the faculty types'n they ever dreamed in their lives. Pretty soon they'll be offering freshly brewed coffee, selling doughnuts, putting tables and chairs in the basements and sheds, maybe piping in cable TV. Dunkin' Donuts'll grant 'em a franchise.

"In the meantime," she said, "I guess all we can do is snap and snarl, and do our best not to start killing each other. Morale's gone right down the toilet, at least in my shop. It's been *rough*. Not quite open warfare, at least not as yet, but a good deal of plain open hostility. That makes Jinx the skunk that decided to winter in the crawl-space under the master bedroom. Her life's much more at risk now from the homicidal addicts than it ever was when all she had worry about was breathing secondhand smoke.

I said, "Jinx never approved of your smoking."

"You got it," Allison said. "She was restrained, didn't show it *too* often, she still made sure whenever Kate or I lighted up, we still *remembered* that she disapproved. Little ladylike hacking, smoke drifted her way? The hand-fluttering frown as she came into my office? Nothing really *ostentatiously* obnoxious, but no mistaking it either: it was martyrdom we were inflicting on her, and she wasn't going to let us forget it. So when our headmaster sounded his clarion call, she led the cheering. Made it clear it was with her wholehearted endorsement, even though, as she said, she knew it'd be hard for us. But she hoped we'd remember when we went through it, how hard and uncomfortable we'd made it on her, to work in that polluted air. As relatively restrained as she'd been, when she was outnumbered before his decree came down, after he announced it she made no effort to conceal her delight.

"You can imagine where that's left us. In the usual crush of work just before commencement and all, which always makes everyone cranky by the time the quitting whistle blows, we're now starting *off* the day already at swords' points with each other. Katie and I, nicotine starved and vicious, but helpless to do anything, snapping at each other but united against Jinx, we'd kill her if we could; and Jinx all smug and happy, curled up snug in her new little law. I'm thinking of putting some posters up over her desk, and also on all the other walls. Full color prints of the Eskimos hunting, clubbing the seal pups to death. Trawler nets bursting with tuna, and dolphins, coming up fresh from the deep; a Japanese whaling ship firing a harpoon gun at a spouting blue whale; liven up the place in general with a lot of shots of death. If war there must be, then let it begin here. I'm thinking of getting a musket."

She had me laughing, of course, which in turn started her laughing too, as she finished the first smoke and promptly ignited another. "Got to take full advantage," she said, "every available minute, every chance that I get. Maintain those normal levels of nicotine supply. I was sure glad to hear those tobacco kings tell our Congresspersons it's not addictive at all. If it were I'd be worried I might be hooked. Those people made me an atheist. If there was a God they'd've been struck dead on the spot."

The warming sun shone on us and the air was still around us, and the thought first came over me that the only way that I could ever possibly have done this was the way that I was doing it, unintentionally, without planning, just by going out to do a job and letting it happen to me. Because by now my head was clear enough to let me see ahead perhaps a hundred years or so, and I knew that as many of them that I had remaining I was going to spend with her. "Tell me about Maggie," I said, sticking to the formula of spontaneity, doing what I'd come to do, letting mundane legal business take up all the space that clumsiness and nervous jitters would've filled if I'd ever deliberately set out to do this wonderful enormous thing on purpose—and probably therefore never would've tried to do, knowing it would never work.

"Maggie, yes, our Maggie," she said. "Margaret Nichols Cameron. How *are* we to describe this child? Her physical appearance you'll soon see for yourself. Whatever you might say, meaning to compliment her, please do not mention her weight. Or the lack of it. Back in the office I said she's dreamy, as most sixteen-year-old girls are, but back in the office Janie was listening, and Janie's in Maggie's class. Teenage girls can be cruel. Maggie's dreaminess is excessive, and for that reason it worries us. Quite often, I think—most of us think—it's due to the fact that she's hungry. She doesn't think that, of course; she thinks she's perfectly normal. But her body thinks it never gets enough fuel, so it runs at a speed that's abnormally low. Her metabolism seems to've adjusted to consistently inadequate nutrition by dropping to a rate that for the time being will keep her alive, but only just barely, and not indefinitely. So she isn't dreaming, really, although we call it that. She's gone way beyond dreams of a lusty young swain come to bear her away; what the child is is basically listless. She doesn't have much energy. And the reason she doesn't is that she doesn't eat much. She's developed an aversion to food. As a result, her stomach's shrunk. She's been able to will herself—browbeat herself really—into believing if she eats normally, she'll become grotesquely obese. We're concerned enough that if she had just one parent, or even a relative who looked reliable enough, we'd call him in for a conference. But of course this kid doesn't have such a person, unless that's part of *your* job."

"I suppose I could make it part of my job, if I wanted to," I said. "And if I thought there was any chance that doing that might do some good. But the fact is I guess I've never really been very good with young people. My daughter turned out reasonably well, but looking back on it now, I have to say that was mostly her mother's doing. She had her shortcomings at being wife, but she was a good mother to Heather. And anyway, you must have someone this kid here can talk to; someone who could talk to her?"

"The psychologists," she said. "Mrs. Glennon's the full-time staff counselor. She has a master's in psychology, and she's trained especially in treating adolescent anxiety and depression, which is obviously at the root of Maggie's problem. The poor kid's had a life that'd be enough to make anyone—the strongest, healthiest, mature adult—anxious, afraid, and depressed. Tricia's very good with young girls, which we desperately need here, of course, because our stated mission's to help children whose lives've been catastrophically disturbed, the damaged kids. Even normal girls often have a harder time going through puberty than healthy boys usually do, and our kids are not normal. That's why they've come here. We've had kids who were literally afraid of the primary colors, for heaven's sake. You hear something like that for the first time, and naturally, you just can't believe it. 'This kid's afraid of *red*, for God's sake? Is that what you're telling me here?' Until you've looked into it a little deeper, and it turned out to be true. Because they associated yellow, or red, or blue, whatever it happened to be, with the color of the wallpaper of the room where one or the other or both of their parents first sexually abused them. Or the place where someone attacked them. Or the car the man drove who came to tell them their father'd been killed on the job. So that now when they see that particular color, all they want to do is curl up in the fetal position, cover up, until the bad thing that they know must be coming gets over and done with.

"And then if Mrs. Glennon can't get anywhere, which doesn't happen very often, because she's very good, then we have our psychology teacher, Mister Plough, who more or less doubles in brass as Mrs. Glennon's backup. If the rapport isn't there, if Tricia can't establish it with a given kid, maybe it's a boy who can't bring himself to talk to a woman about some sexual problem he has, then she calls on John. He refers to himself as 'Tricia's bullpen,' but he's really quite good in his own right.

"So far, at least, Maggie hasn't responded to Tricia," Allison said. "She refuses to talk to Johnny at all. Won't even hear of the idea. The temptation normally would be to say that, well, this kids' not responding to the in-house people we have here, and she's obviously at some considerable risk, so it's time to confront the parents here, or the custodial one, if it's one of those situations, and just say to them: 'Look, we've got to face the facts here. As much as we ourselves don't like to say it, and we know you don't want to hear it, we're not getting anywhere with this kid. What we're thinking now, because we don't have any choice, is that she needs intensive therapy, her own shrink, regular hours, every week, for as long as it takes, until someone gets to the bottom of this and exorcises her demons. Drives out whatever it is that's bothering her. We've got to get her out of this.' Or him, as the gender may be."

"Maggie's a severely disturbed kid, you think, then," I said. We were now a couple hundred yards away from a somewhat retro-design, two-story brick building with a white-columned verandah and too many palladian windows, the building dappled by light reflecting off the windows as the sun sank down to the tops of green maple trees arranged in a gentle curve along the edge of the plateaued knoll, before it sloped down and away into woods.

Allison stopped, turned to face me, and put her right hand on my left forearm. "Now look, Mister Kennedy," she said.

" 'Jerry,' please, Mrs. Bassy," I said. "I'm not used to much formality, and I don't want any from you anyway."

"No," she said, "no, you're quite right. I knew that. You call me Allison, or Ally, if you like." I nodded. "I know the history of Sandra Nichols. How she was the lonely guy's delight at the Queen City Diner. How she never caught an even break. How, compared to her, the life she'd had to lead, Horatio Alger's luck 'n' pluck boys had it very easy. But it wasn't just pity and sympathy I felt for her here, not at all. I went into it having made up my mind that I wasn't going to prejudge her on the basis of what she'd been, which was a shameless tramp. I was going to treat her the same way I've treated every other mother I was meeting for the first time, make her give me a reason not to like her very well, and a mental note to keep her at arm's length. But until such time's she did that, gave me that kind of reason, I'd treat her with the same respect I give to everybody else. I didn't really expect she'd turn out to be a cultured, cultivated woman, one whose company I'd seek out, every chance I got, as she didn't; all I really hoped for was that our dealings'd be reasonably pleasant, and that we'd get along.

"But I found myself genuinely liking Sandy. As did everyone else who came in contact with her here; they all liked her too. Here was this woman with a history full of potholes, and everybody knew it. She'd been a wanton and a slattern, and the whore of Babylon. But she was a trouper, and she didn't look like what she was, what she'd been. Somehow she hadn't been hardened by the life she'd led. For all the wear and tear on her, she still looked like a teenager, bubbling with this natural charm, as though the world and life in general'd never hit her with a left hook. It would've taken real determination to dislike her, and none of us felt like making the effort, because we all really liked her. Yes, including all the women, before you have to ask, even the puritans. Because when you thought about it, it was very doubtful she'd been any more promiscuous than several of the ladies who dressed very nicely and came to parents' teas and other functions, having taken multiple partners, sometimes marrying them and sometimes not, depending on their mood at the time. 'Serial monogamy,' I guess we call it now, regardless whether any clergy were involved. Ladies who've taken their fees, their honoraria, if you like, in expensive jewelry, glamorous lifestyles, and alimony. The only difference was that Sandy, until Peter wandered into the truckstop, had never been able to fish her baits in the waters the rich catches swam in. That was the only real difference.

"But even though we all liked her, we still had to face some rather nasty facts here. Hearts of gold or not, Sandra Nichols'd been a bad mother to those children. She was at least instrumental in causing their chaotic childhoods. She brought them into this cold world without having any means to assure she'd be able to take care of them. And then while they were growing up, she left them unattended quite a lot and repeatedly treated them to the spectacle of a mother who was hooking on the side, bringing her favorite best customers home.

"Kids're not stupid. Even when they're little, they study other people. They compare the way they're living to the way that others live. They may not be able to put it into words, but they know the difference between order and disorder, security and insecurity, and they know which one is better. They know it when people look down on them, or pity them, and they can figure out why. If it's because of the way that their parents are acting, they deduce there're certain kinds of conduct decent people find disgraceful, shameful, even contemptible, and therefore the kids are ashamed.

"Lucy's response was to withdraw, to trust nobody else. She was ten when she came here. She'd already gone inside. Nothing we could to do was enough to lure her out. She'd withdrawn before she came to us. When she left us eight years later her condition hadn't changed. The mask was still in place. Her personality was closed. When she's come back here since she graduated, to see Maggie and Jeff, and she's encountered one of us, someone who was here when she first came, she acts just like she acted then, formal and polite. Aloof. Meets your eyes, and what she meets them with is what Tricia Glennon calls 'that cement gargoyle stare.' Her mother had a real tough life, but when she finally lucked out, she wasn't hard at all. Lucy'd had a tough life, too, but a much shorter one, and her own flesh was not involved, as her mommy's'd been in hers. After Mommy made her bail, Lucy's life'd been a fairly cushy one. But Lucy was diamond hard. Funny how it happens, huh? Those young years really count. Kids get calloused faster'n adults, I guess. Must be they have tenderer skin.

"Jeffrey, when you see him, will look like Lucy's copy. Jeffrey's clamped down tight. He trusts no one; eyes the whole world warily. You say you're his friend today? Okay, he'll accept that, take it at face value. But come tomorrow he won't be a bit surprised if you act like you don't recognize him. And he won't be disappointed, either; neglect and disregard are what he expects. That's what the kid's used to, and that's by far the sadder thing.

"Maggie isn't quite as far gone, yet, as she plans and hopes to be. But we're all apprehensive that what we've really got on our hands with her here is a chronic suicide. One of those people who never says anything alarming, never collapses, writes any notes, never stockpiles any drugs or gives broad hints or anything, but who's quietly determined to die. No hurry or anything. Just: as soon as possible. By willing her own death, and if no one gets to her, she will surely do it. She'll bring it off. I hope to God you can reach her. None of us've been able to do, and Judge Lawler hasn't, either. If her mother could've done it, while she was still on the earth . . . well, the fact is that she didn't, and neither did her natural father—who I gather's just a selfish jerk, not worth looking up—or Peter or anybody else. And that's what we've got to deal with now."

"I'll do my best," I said. "Other than that, though, I promise nothing. This stuff's not my specialty, not at all."

"But if you do get through, you'll tell me?" she said.

"Anything that doesn't come within the privilege," I said. "But I have to tell you, my definition of it errs on the generous side."

She sighed and lit another cigarette. "Well," she said, "I do the best I can, God knows. And the rest I sweep out on the weekends.

"Maggie'll be around the corner of the building there," she said. "There's a patio-terrace out in the back, and a big black maple—the Boss Tree, the kids call it—down below it on the lawn. That's where she likes to hang out. I'll introduce you and then I'll go up there. It's way too far away for me to hear."

"Thank you," I said.

"You will tell me," she said, "at least how she seems? How her mood strikes you, and so forth? Because we do worry about her. We don't want to lose this poor kid."

"Well, I was sort of hoping," I said, "that we could do that late today, over drinks, and then maybe continue, with dinner. If there's someplace you can recommend."

"Actually," she said, hitting me with that million-candlepower smile again, "what I was sort of planning on, if things worked out and all, was to go to the Mulberry Inn. They do pour a nice drink, and serve very good food. Nothing fancy, just regular stuff, but it's here, and close by and so forth. I thought that would be a good place. I can make a reservation while you're talking with Maggie. Shall I say seven-thirty, for dinner?"

"You're way ahead of me, I see," I said.

She patted my arm once again. "Not to worry," she said. "You did take a little time out, there. But you seem to be back, and you also seem to be a quick study. You're catching up fast. By nightfall we ought to be even."

▪ ▪ ▪ 18

Ordinarily I'd say the age of sixteen would probably bar any further reference to that person as a child. But that was what Maggie Cameron still clearly was, midway through the afternoon that I first met her. She was a girl-child dozing in the shade of the enormous overspreading old black maple, her soft, frizzy blond hair disheveled against her pale skin, her torso femininely formless under a white mesh short-sleeved polo shirt, her legs still thin in her Levi's. She breathed shallowly but evenly, exhaling with the faint whistling sound that often embarrasses people whose false teeth don't fit properly. Her skin was semitranslucent; through it I could easily make out the faint blue tracks of the larger blood vessels of her neck. There was a book open on the ground next to her left leg, the text of it set in verse; her left hand, palm up, fingers loosely cupped, rested on the inside of the building.

Allison crouched down in front of the child and reached out with her right hand to touch her on her left knee, saying "Maggie" softly as she made the contact, then waggled the knee a little.

At first the kid awakened calmly enough, even smiling shyly at Allison, stretching a little, but then the shape of the male stranger looming over her took her by surprise and startled her. She raised her right hand jerkily partway to her face, as though she feared that I might hit her. I hunkered down like Allison and stuck out what I hoped she'd take as a trusting paw proffered like a big, perhaps strange, but still friendly dog. Evidently she lacked experience of big friendly dogs. She shrank back from my hand, fear on her face, her back hard straight against the smooth bark of the tree.

Allison rubbed the kid's knee, crooning: "Easy does it, Maggie. He's not here to hurt you. I'm not here to hurt you. No one's here to hurt you. This is Mister Kennedy, and he's come here to help. Judge Lawler sent him, just like he said he would. You remember what he told you, last time he was here, when he saw you and Jeff that time and told you what he planned to do? Get the two of you and Lucy a good lawyer, to look after you in court, just like we do here at school? Well, this is the man he chose. Jerry Kennedy. The judge's known him a long time. They went to school together. They were classmates in law school."

"And as you can see just by looking at me, this old geezer," I said, mustering my best phony, condescending, ingratiating smile, "that has to be a good long time, that Henry and I've been friends."

She seemed to relax a little, but not enough to risk making any sound. She looked inquiringly at Allison, apparently to see whether there might be some more information forthcoming. "Mister Kennedy's been appointed by Judge Lawler to be your legal guardian, yours and Jeff's and Lucy's."

"The actual term is guardian *ad litem*," I said. "Meaning I'm to be responsible for making sure your interests don't get overlooked during the judge's inquiry into your mother's death." That seemed to be acceptable to her, although I wasn't yet sure whether it was her habit to react audibly to any new information, agreeable or not. She raised her knees now and hugged her legs together, gripping her left forearm with her right hand. She seemed to have decided that her chances of avoiding harm at this intruder's hands would be better if she gave Allison and me as much time as we might need to deliver, at our own pace, all the news we might have for her, not because she wanted to know what he had to tell her; because she had resigned herself to the fact that she could not prevent anyone, including me, from doing anything to her that he'd decided he wanted to do. I found this attitude unsettling.

The only intensive experience I'd had with any kid at close range—

at least since I'd finished being a kid myself, hanging out with other kids my age—had been with Heather. We got along gloriously while she was an adorable child and then little girl, sitting on Daddy's lap on the nights when I got home early enough to read her a story—by the time she was seven or so, those'd begun to happen more regularly, as I learned enough about my trade not to have to stay in the office 'til well after dark, preparing what I had to do the next day. But once she'd become an adorable adolescent girl, equipped with breasts and so forth, all of which attracted boyfriends, things became a little edgy. While we remained fond friends, Heather and I also began to have our share of quarrels. Virtually all of them arose from her choices of male companions (most especially her now-estranged husband, Charlie, who in justice to him may not always've been a world-class complete asshole, but who, in justice to me, had certainly become one by the time he mesmerized Heather, necessitating that he meet me). But since Heather and I'd known each other all her life (going back at least all the way to those infuriatingly precious favorite stories of hers about the adventures of Babar the cloying elephant, and his sickeningly good queen, Celeste), we had a reserve of good will to fall back on. So while our discussions sometimes became a bit heated and noisy—well, tell the truth here: as they quite often did, most likely because there may be something to this heredity stuff; Heather takes and defends her positions just as strenuously as I take and hold mine—one of us would still generally have good judgment enough to call for a cooling-off period, and the other one enough good sense to agree to it. So goodwill in time would accomplish what loud argument had not; not a perfect resolution of the matter but at least a quiet reconcilement to the fact that it could not be resolved.

That afternoon I met Maggie I felt almost nostalgic for those old knock-down-drag-out tumults with Heather. Those I understood, and had some idea how to wage, so that while I can't claim that I usually handled them well, at least I knew what to do. With this kid I could see no possibility of ever having any kind of confrontation with her (what pompous name have they got for what I mean by that now? "Interaction" or something like that?), of ever getting a reaction out of her, of any kind, pleasant or very unpleasant. She was utterly passive;

the kind of person who chooses not to act, usually citing fear of failure if persuaded (only with great difficulty) to give a reason; but apprehensively expects to be acted upon; what the witch doctors call a low-affect personality.

"Now I'm going to excuse myself here from you for a while, so that you and attorney Kennedy can talk in complete confidence," Allison said, maintaining tactile contact with the kid, looking her straight in the eyes. "He says this's the way he always insists upon conducting all conferences with his clients—no one else present during the conversation."

Maggie looked alarmed and stopped hugging her legs, freeing her left hand to grasp Allison's right and hold it on her knee. "It's perfectly all right, I assure you," Allison said. "I'll just go on up there to the library and get a new magazine off the big round table in the reading room, and then I'll come back out and sit in one of Mrs. Carpenter's famous green lawn chairs, and read and smoke, and smoke. To my little heart's content. Or maybe to its *dis*content, if Mister Greenwood's right." Maggie smiled a little. It was tentative, and it didn't last very long, but I did see its brief glimmer. Apparently the conflict between the forces of mandatory abstinence and the legions of the addicted was a matter of common discussion around the school. "So except for the time I'm inside, picking out something to read, you won't be out of my sight. If you need me, should you start to feel faint, or light-headed, or nauseous, or anything like that, all you'll have to do is wave, and I'll come and get you. Did you eat some of your lunch today, by the way?"

Maggie looked down at the book and traced the first two fingers of her left hand over the verse. She chewed her lower lip. "Did you?" Allison said, gently enough, but plainly determined to get a reply.

"Some," Maggie said.

"What?" Allison said. "Did you eat the burrito? The salad, or the strawberry yogurt?" To me she said: "The food service works very hard to plan the menus so that the students know they can look forward to having three meals every day of food they really like to eat. Pizza, tacos, double cheeseburgers, fries, sometimes even fried chicken. And most of them seem to think it's quite good. The faculty and staff aren't always as happy, but they generally can find something that doesn't gravely offend their taste."

"I had a little of the yogurt," Maggie said. "I didn't like the burrito, and Toby decided he'd be funny and put Thousand Island salad dressing on my salad, which I just hate and he knows it, and that's why he did it. And my milk. But that was all." She paused and brushed at the front of her shirt, as though removing bread crumbs. "I just wasn't hungry, I guess."

Allison pulled her hand away and stood up. Maggie looked up at her fearfully and reached up to take her hand again. "Well, I wasn't," she said, nearly wailing. "I can't help it if I wasn't hungry. Don't go on account I said that."

"Why, I'm not, Maggie," Allison said. "No one's mad at you for anything. I've simply got to stand up. My legs're stiffening up. And besides, I simply can't stay. The longer I stay here with you, the longer it'll be before attorney Kennedy can start asking you the questions that he wants to ask, has to ask, to get the information that he needs, and just get the work done that he came here to do. So I'm going to leave now and let you two get started."

"It won't take us that long," I said. "Fifteen, maybe twenty minutes. Just a few preliminary questions that I need to get out of the way, and then I'll be out of your hair here." That was a flat lie. Twenty minutes'd be nowhere near enough time for me to get through all the stuff I needed to ask her and her sister and brother, but I was already satisfied—not happy, but resigned to it—that the chicken pox germ which had infected Jeffrey had for all practical purposes scuttled any chance I'd had of a productive interview session with his sister. And the fact that I'd approached the first interview with her cold, just dropped out of the sky onto her head (on the stupid assumption that someone would've gotten word to her, what I'd been appointed to do; I must remember to read now and then the sign on my desk that says ASSUME NOTHING), the way I would've a first interview with a mature adult perhaps hardened not only by life but some previous jail time; that'd obviously been counterproductive as well. So I'd inadvertently confirmed what I'd already known for a very long time, and had forthrightly admitted to Royce: when it comes to even using kids as witnesses, much less having them as clients, I'm really not very much good. So all that, piled on top of her habitual passivity, might've contributed something to her obvious jitters too. Perhaps she'd be no more forthcoming talking when she saw me for a second time, when I'd at least be a more familiar figure, with her sibling reinforcements around her, but she certainly wasn't going to be less. As I misjudged the situation at that particular moment, at least.

"And when you've finished your conference," Allison said, "then you can either walk up to where I am, or wave and I'll come back down here to you, and that will be all there is to it." Then she turned and started up the lawn away from us.

My legs were getting stiff too. I took my little Realistic minicassette tape recorder out of my portfolio and then put the case on the ground about four feet away from the kid, so as not to seem to be right in her face, straightened up, and then eased myself down to sit on the case, to avoid getting grass stains on my pants. I made a smooth, level place in the grass and stood the tape recorder there on its end. The kid didn't look at me.

"Maggie," I said, "I know this's going to be painful for you, and all, and I'd much rather not do it, but I'm going to have to ask you some questions about some of things that you saw or heard about happening, around the time of the death of your mother. In the few weeks just before it."

The kid did not reply. She traced those same two fingers of her left hand on the page of the open book, now making a series of figure eights, figure eight after figure eight, over and over, piling infinities on top of infinities, while leaving no trace she'd made them, frowning a little but silent. I said: "Maggie, like I just said, I'm aware this's painful for you, but it's something I do have to do. Just as I'll have to interview Jeffrey and Lucy before I can decide what it is should be done, in this particular case. Okay? Humor me?"

Several more figure eights. The frown deepened. She shook her head, once, and mouthed *no*.

"Maggie," I said, "come on, talk to me. I didn't want to get involved in this, any more than you want me to be involved in it. My old friend Judge Lawler asked me if I'd please do it, as a personal favor to him. Of course I had to say yes, I would, because as Mrs. Bassy told you, he's an old and dear friend of mine. If I asked him to do anything for me, he'd do it at once, if he could. And if he couldn't he'd be just as sad as I would be, that he couldn't manage to help me out.

"Now we both know you and I aren't old friends, of course," I said, "the way that Henry and I are. But I've been learning quite a lot about you, and your brother and sister, and also about your late mother, some of the other people in her life, during the past several weeks. When I've been able to study the records while still keeping up with my regular work. So it's not as though this was actually like what I know it must seem like to you: that I'm just a bolt out of the blue. What you've got to do, and what I hope Jeff and Lucy'll be able to do too, is look at me the way that Judge Lawler looks at me: as an old and good friend you've known for a long time, or who's known you for a long time. We just never happened to meet until now." Remembering the card that Royce Whitlock'd advised me to play: presenting myself—as he the cop could not present himself to her—as her friend and protector; not out to do the Commonwealth's work but out to do her a kindness (the "Henry's friend, friend of yours" variation on the pitch was my own kindly devious idea).

"The job that Henry asked me to do for him isn't anything that'll benefit him personally. He won't get anything out of it for himself, except for the satisfaction he'll be able to take, from knowing he did his job right. The job that I'm supposed to do is make sure you three get everything you should get under the provisions of arrangements that your mother made for you several years ago. Okay? Will you do that much for me? Even a complete stranger, like I am?"

Figure eights, figure eights; the frown holding tight; one more slight shake of the head.

"Come on, Maggie," I said. I was getting somewhat impatient. If she'd been an adult defendant I'd been appointed to defend, I would've been back in my car and a good six or eight miles south down the road on the way back to Boston, looking forward to a Heineken and using the cellular phone to dictate a Motion for Leave to Withdraw as Counsel from her case. And since Ally'd said Jeff was clamped shut and Lucy was closed down, most likely as their lawyer as well. "Gimme a break, willya here? Cut me some slack. I've been doing all the talking here. I drove all the way up here to talk to you, thinking you knew that I'd been appointed, trying to give you a hand,

and you haven't really said a single word to me yet. I don't know you any better, you know, than you know me, and you're making me do all the work. I wouldn't do that to you."

She stopped tracing and turned her head to look at me directly. "I didn't know you were coming," she said, "I didn't ask you to come." It was a soft, modest voice, still piping a little of childhood, without vehemence or malice, or anger or sadness, or the slightest hint of rebuke. I reached forward and turned on the recorder. She saw me to it and surely knew what it was for, but she didn't shut up as I'd been afraid she might; apparently she'd thought it over and (whether out of pity or scorn I didn't know and didn't care) made up her mind that the only way to get rid of me was to talk to me, and so she'd continue to talk.

"I don't know who killed my mother. The last time I saw her she'd been here for the day, Parent Conferences Day, and when we were at lunch I asked her how everything was at home. Because I knew there were some problems, that she and Peter'd been having problems. But I didn't know what they were. She didn't ask me how I'd found out, although I suppose she must've guessed. She just told me, she said oh, he'd gone back to his old tricks again; found himself a new girlfriend while he was racing *Toreador* down in the Caribbean and she'd found out about it and told him he had to either break up with this new hot girlfriend of his or else had to give Mom a divorce. And then he'd come home and they had this terrible fight, and he said he wouldn't give her a divorce, and then he went and checked himself into this hospital. Said what he had was nervous exhaustion, but she said what it was, he'd been drinking too much, and she didn't know what was going to happen. And that was all she said to me about it, that she didn't know what was going to happen, but she did know one thing: that she was going to get a divorce even if he did decide to fight it.

"And then we had to go to the next thing they had on the schedule that day, and we did, and then she had to get going, I guess she had some kind of a date herself that night—she had this way of acting kind of well, you know, *happy*? And *silly*? When she had a new man on the string. And that was the way she was that day. And that was the last time I talked to her, saw her. I never saw her again.

"Lucy was how I'd found out. About Mom and Pete having some problems. She was the one that told me. Lucy'd been home, she'd been back to Enfield. They thought at Mount Holyoke that she had mono, from not getting enough sleep or something. So she'd had some shots, or transfusions or something, gamma globulin, I guess they give you, and then they'd sent her back home to rest. And so she wouldn't be around the other kids, to give mono to them, or maybe get better and then just get it again. They didn't want that to happen. And Lucy called me when she was feeling better and drove down here to see me and Jeff, as soon as she wasn't contagious. I think this was April when she came. Drove down here in her car—she calls her harlot-scarlet, red Mustang; it's a convertible—Peter bought for her brand new when she graduated two years ago. And we went out to have lunch with her. We went to a movie, which I didn't like; *Reality Bites,* I think it was. I'm not really sure though; Jeff liked it, and Lucy said she thought it was okay. Anyway, I thought it was stupid. Then we all came back here and had dinner in the dining hall, and Jeff had a math test the next day so he had to go and study, and me and Lucy went to my room and that was when she told me. That Peter and Mom were having some problems."

"Jeffrey wasn't there," I said, "when Lucy told you that."

"No, like I said, he had a test so he was studying for that."

"And you thought from the way she was acting the last time you saw her, that she perhaps'd found a new man?" I said.

The frown came back. She looked down and rubbed the first knuckle of the index finger of her left hand between her right index finger and thumb. "Yeah," she said, "yeah. Yeah, I did." She looked up at me directly. There was pain in her eyes and she used them to plead. "I wished . . . Mom was real good at that, finding men. Getting men to go with her. Ever since I can remember she was good at doing that. Real good at doing that." She gnawed on that lower lip again. "I used to wish she wouldn't do it. Either wouldn't be so good at it or just, just wouldn't do it."

Right. I was on the brink of the question I'd driven up there to ask, and I didn't dare to ask it. This was no time to get greedy, push the kid so hard so far she'd never open up again. Take the delicate beginnings of the chance she'd taken when she decided to trust me, at least a little, and deposit them in her memory bank, so that by the time I saw Jeffrey and Lucy she would've told them I was a nice guy who could be trusted, and they should talk to me; that would be my dividend. I reached forward to shut off the recorder, but then she started to talk again, and I held my thumb over the button.

"I don't know who he was, this guy she was going to meet," she said, which was of course the answer to the question I'd decided to defer until our next interview. "He could've been someone she knew before. Her old boyfriends'd do that sometimes. They'd come back again, sometimes, be gone a while and then later, they'd show up again, after she'd broken up with them. All of us'd think: 'Well, there goes another one,' and a long time would go by, and then he'd be back again, and she'd be acting silly, like: 'He just can't stay away from me—isn't that just great?' And we had to agree with her: 'Yeah, Ma, we think it's great.' When what we really thought was that yeah, you're just so fucking *cute*. We sure hope when we grow up, we're all just as cute as you. It used to make us *sick*. But like I say, though, I'm not really sure of that—if it was an old boyfriend."

Her voice had gotten stronger. I wasn't sure but thought I saw some actual color in her cheeks. "But I think Jeffrey might be. Jeffrey might know who it was, this guy she was going to see. Jeff was with Mom that day when I wasn't, when she was here that last day and I had a class. Mom might've told him who the guy was. She didn't tell me, but that wouldn't mean anything. She was always acting like that. She'd get Jeff off by himself and then she'd tell him things she'd never tell to us, tell to me and Lucy. And always make him promise that he'd never tell us, either. He didn't like it when she did that, tell him things that he couldn't tell us. I know he used to want to, lots, but he never did.

"She even used to tell us that, like she was bragging to us, her and Jeffy had these *secrets*. No one else knew what they knew. Like we really cared they did—big deal, who she liked the best. But he was it, just the same. Mom's favorite was always Jeffrey. 'My Jeffy,' she would call him. 'Jeffy's got my name, nobody else's. You've got Hugh's, Hugh Cameron's; you've got your father's name. He's the man who fathered you. And Lucy's got her father's, Luke's. That's why she's Lucy Kyle. Because I did marry Lucas, and he was her father, and I almost married Hugh.

"Mom's the only person I know, only one I ever heard of, who was ever 'almost married' to someone she was never married to. I've got lots of friends with parents who've been married lots of times, but I'm the only one I know who ever had a mother who was almost married to the man who was her father. So what does that make me, you think? Am I *her* almost-daughter? Or am I *his* almost-daughter? Or am I no one's daughter, almost, and then, do I almost just exist? or maybe not even that? It's really hard, you know? It's really hard to know."

I wasn't taking any chances. I didn't know what the hell to say, so I didn't push my luck. I settled for what was this time a genuine big grin, and shrugged my inability to help her sort it out.

"That's what I figured," she said, "I don't know the answer either." And I saw more than a glimmer of that smile of hers this time. (Yeah, *finally* starting to get even, I thought. Always feels so goddamned *good*, after a long time, even when it's way too late and doesn't count. Death moots a lot of questions.) She tried something new now, a voice full of giddiness, to ventriloquize her mother's. " 'But when I gave birth to Jeffy, there was no one else around. And when they asked me, the hospital, what his name was going to be, birth certificate and all, well, I just thought and thought and thought: What name was this kid gonna have? What was I gonna do? And it really bothered me. His father wasn't there. *I* did not know where to find him. He was nowhere near around. I did not know what to do. And then *suddenly*, it came to me: *I* was still around, wasn't I? *I* was still around. And right then, I was sure, what it was I had to do. And I said: "Jeffrey"—I had that all ready, a long time; I'd already picked it out—"Jeffrey, Jeffrey Nichols," I said.'

"She always used to tell us that," Maggie said. "I don't know how many times. And then she would always laugh, this little laugh she had? Like she was laughing at herself, but she expected you to praise? And say: 'To this day it's still a wonder that they didn't do just what I said to do, and make out the certificate "Jeffrey Jeffrey Nichols." But they got it right, they didn't, and everything turned out all right. But, and so you can see how it is, now, can't you? Because that's how it really is, how it all turned out like that, that Jeffy's the only one of you that's completely mine, all completely mine.'

"But of course it would've been that way," Maggie said. "Naturally she liked him better. She really thought he'd always be her 'little Jeffy,' the boy who'd never leave her. He'd always belong to her. I don't think it would've happened like that, but now she's made it all come true."

19

Years ago I had a client federally charged with using the mails to defraud. He was easily the least prepossessing man I have ever seen, before or since: short, perhaps five-four; slight, about 135 pounds (that's what he looked like to me; except for the time I had a client who went about 175, accused by a witness who'd told the cops she'd been overpowered and raped by a 245-pound scoundrel, I haven't weighed any of the poor bastards); in his late thirties; had already lost most of his brown hair (what remained was turning gray). He looked like a purebred bookkeeper, and that was what he was; he was employed as an accountant-auditor in the Quincy office of a small Massachusetts insurance company, since swallowed up into bankruptcy during the Carter recession of 1978. He told me they were paying him $10,750. He was the sole support of his mother. Both of them are dead now, have been for several years, she at eighty-one, in 1990, as I recall, he a few months afterward, at sixty-three. They had lived together in Belmont, apparently as inconspicuously as my client had managed to die: pretty much all by himself. In the church on the day of his funeral service there were four whose attendance was not required by preaching and undertaking duties. I didn't know the other three, and they gave no sign of knowing me. If there's no life after death, or if there is but there's no looking back to the one we had before it, my late client didn't know I was there, wasting a morning that I could've spent gainfully employed, and neither did anybody else.

My client's world had been a lonely one, a fact that the sentencing judge, himself a lifelong bachelor, deemed a factor somewhat mitigating his offense. Even the farewell for my trepid private eye, the late, lamented Bad-eye Mulvey, drew a bigger crowd than that. It was still a pitiable few; his childless wife had predeceased him and he had no living relatives; I counted only sixteen other people in the Church of the Most Precious Blood in Hyde Park that day. Six of them I reckoned strays, sitting scattered randomly alone among the pews, regular attendants at 7 A.M. daily Mass welcoming the occasional 10 A.M. funeral as a luxurious opportunity to get some extra sleep, without breaking their consecutive-games skeins of devotion. That left me and nine other people who had come to mourn the death of Bad-eye (when the priest used both his Christian names, bidding Godspeed to "Richard James Mulvey" to the arms of Jesus, I suspect the others were just as nonplussed as I, momentarily wondering if we'd stumbled into a stranger's send-off, instead of the last rites for "Bad-eye"). Eight of them I'd never seen before. The one man I knew by name, Dt. Sgt. Buddy deFranco, had been Bad-eye's last immediate superior on the police force. He could identify three of the other eight: the barber with the one-man shop in Cleary Square who'd cut Bad-eye's hair—the classic inverted-bowl job: boys' regular, short back and sides—for over forty years (pretty near the finish line himself); and two retired cops who'd served with him. Sergeant deFranco told me what I'd already figured out (exactly the sort of thing that most police detectives do best: corroboration of the obvious with the superfluous): most of Bad-eye's former colleagues in PD Boston had gone before him to that great final roll call in the sky. But even Bad-eye, a man who could have blended in with the wallpaper in a painted room—so damned self-effacing he was, as Coop once marveled, "damned-near self-erasing; does he write in invisible ink?"—found my accountant client, Lloyd Prentice, now late and unlamented, "a little pipsqueak wimp." Bad-eye said: "Who'd ever think a Casper Milquetoast like that guy could even dream *up* a darned mean scam like that? Let alone carry it out. Doesn't look like he could kill a flea, much less cheat poor lonely devils, locked up in the can, doing real time for the real crimes they did." The judge, about to sentence Lloyd to one year suspended and five years' probation, softening the punishment as his discretion permitted him to do (and making it very clear to all within earshot that he'd be most displeased if Lloyd's employer took his proven folly as sufficient reason to fire him, which His Honor's discretion probably did not authorize him to do), had called me and the prosecutor to the bench before he imposed it. "This's probably the only mark this Sad Sack'll ever make in his whole life. So I'm gonna go easy on him."

What Lloyd had done was scissor a black-and-white photo out of his high school yearbook. It depicted a comely young bikinied lass in a come-hither pose. He had a couple hundred copies of it made (the amateur psychiatrist in me suspected that Lloyd'd had a sneaker on the young lady in their good old Golden Rule days but'd been afraid of her, and this was his warped, belated way of having his will with her—if in fact he had a will of his own). Under an assumed name, Sylvia M., he'd then proceeded to pretend to *be* her, about twenty years older, of course (in fact as one of his classmates back in the middle seventies when he got started, she would've been well into her forties), writing coyly sexy (friendships he lacked; impure thoughts he had a lot of) letters about how lonely she was—also carefully mentioning in passing how well she'd kept her nice figure—to the pen pal pulp journals for the lovelorn that used to be around in those days, two bits an issue or so. When he got a bite, he'd autograph one of the pictures in carefully dainty handwriting, "With love, Sylvie," and send it to the sucker, along with a steamy letter sprayed with Evening in Paris or some other such inexpensive drugstore aphrodisiac. He used a Quincy post office box number as Sylvia's return address.

I don't know, not having checked, but I suspect those pathetic little pulpers've gone the way of the dinosaurs now. If they weren't fatally obsoleted first by those appallingly explicit personal ads that the so-called respectable newspapers and magazines started to run twenty-five years or so ago, then surely they must've since been run out of existence by the erotic e-mail networks available now. (I know about those because my first new secretary, a lovely child named Carol, forgot to shut off her computer one night, leaving early to go to one of her night classes—at last that's what she said they were: "classes." It took me awhile to figure out how to turn the machine off. Some of the stuff that came up on that screen would've shocked a brothel keeper in Marseilles. The next day I gave Carol two weeks' notice and told her in the interim not to do any more of that stuff on my machine or my time, lest somebody think it was me. She wept and begged for another chance. I refused and she quit on the spot. She sure was a pretty kid, though. If she was really putting out what she'd been promising on that little gray screen, the guys who were writing to her—*if* they were guys—must've been having some fun. I envied the little pricks.)

But I digress, as usual. What Lloyd did, after he'd sent out the hot picture to the poor bastard worse off than he was, usually locked up in some penitentiary—he got a few lumberjacks and some forest rangers, but most of his pigeons were caged up, writing from the slammer—was stroke the guy slowly, having "Sylvia" promise to do all the things to him that Lloyd'd dreamed of having the girl he didn't even dare to say good morning to in high school do to him in the woods behind the school. Or maybe in the middle of the road. The guy, all hot and bothered, would implore Sylvia to come see him in Ohio—or Kansas, wherever he was locked up—since he couldn't visit her. Lloyd would have Sylvia reply forlornly that she had no cash for the journey, or she'd fly at once to his arms. The poor horny bastard'd somehow arrange to get some friend or family member to send a bus fare postal money order to her. Lloyd, God bless him, would stamp his company's endorsement on it, and in his real capacity as the insurance accountant would have no trouble getting it cashed; all kinds of people pay their insurance bills that way all the time. Then he'd take the money home to his mother in their two-bedroom house in Belmont, and she would spend it on dolls.

I didn't believe him at first when he told me that's where the money'd gone. "*All* of it?" I said. "All of it, she spent on dolls? You rooked these guys out of over twelve grand, and that's just the ones that we know about. How many more there're out there, too embarrassed to admit how easy they were, and how much you took them for, we don't even know how to guess. And you sit there and tell me it all went for dolls? All of that dough went *for dolls*, China *dolls*? Not even the kind that pick you up in bars, with their big tits and rough hard-luck stories, so at least for your dough you get blown?"

Nope, that was it. All of it, Mom spent on dolls, plus a good deal more from other sources. Most of her Social Security checks (she and Lloyd's father'd gotten divorced about thirty years before I first learned about Lloyd and his gaga mother; that obsession of hers with the dolls'd been the reason wimpy Lloyd's father'd left) and a chunk of Lloyd's wages besides. She was a collector of dolls, dolls with bisque heads and limbs, some of them life-size, and very expensive they were. The house wasn't very big, but the whole of it was crowded with dolls. Moving through it from room to room was like attending a Mardi Gras masked ball played by immobilized critters of various sizes, from normal down through dwarf to miniature, all of them in fancy dress. Napoleon in full regalia, the cutaway coat, the tricornered hat, the white waistcoat, gilded buttons, sword, boots, and all. Joan of Arc at the stake. Martha Washington. Little Boy Blue. Marilyn Monroe in her *Seven-Year Itch* white halter dress. Babe Ruth in full Yankees uniform, kneeling in the on-deck circle and resting his chin on his right hand on the knob of his bat—Louisville Slugger, of course. Judy Garland, life-size, pigtails and all, dressed up, the red shoes, as Dorothy in *The Wizard of Oz*. It was the goddamnedest inanimate assembly I'd ever seen in my life, and I've sat through addresses by high court justices at annual banquets of the bar association. I'd had no idea there were people who did that, dressed up dolls from the underwear out, often better'n they dressed themselves.

I thought the two of them must be nuts. Then I was invited to guess what the stuff cost, and said of course I didn't know; when they told me, I was *sure* they were both nuts. I almost passed out. I could've bought a Cadillac for the money they'd spent on those dolls—from Teddy I could've bought several. Hundreds and hundreds of dollars, back then, and this was a long time ago. No wonder Lloyd'd turned out to be such a crook. He hadn't had any choice. If Mom was going to have an FDR doll, in a real wooden cane-backed wheelchair, and an Eleanor doll with buck-teeth to go with him, fake little fox pelts looped 'round her neck, long mauve dress and a hat shaped like a pill bottle top, Lloyd's paltry salary just wasn't going to be enough. Any damned fool could see that. He'd had to straighten his shoulders, stand up like a man, and go out and swindle some people. And so that's what he'd gone and done. He was a very good son. Lloyd loved his mother: that's all there was to it. I was tempted to plead the guy nuts. And maybe his mother with him, as well, even though she wasn't charged.

Anyway, that day of the dolls flew across my memory like a soaring bird the first time I met Lucy. She came into my office that Monday afternoon in a dark blue skirted suit, running shoes on her feet—funny shoes for an interview, I thought, but she'd already done that, and changed; she showed me her good shoes from her brief bag—and she was quite simply the most beautiful young woman I'd ever seen in my life.

"Hey," Allison said when I said that to her, "just what was that I just heard? 'The most beautiful young woman' that you've ever seen? Am I going to have trouble with you? Have to order you kept off the campus, you might bother girl students or something?"

I reminded Ally that when my daughter's conception had exempted me from the draft to fight the war in Vietnam, Lucy hadn't been born. She was then minus-ten-plus years old. But now that she was plus-twenty, she had skin the color of the bisque china—or porcelain, whatever it was—of Lloyd's mother's costly dolls. And it was *alive.* She just glowed with life. She was about five-six. She was perfectly proportioned. If she'd gotten her looks from her mother, it was no wonder Sandra Nichols had had no trouble getting men.

She knew what she was. In addition to being beautiful, she was smart. Dangerous combination. I started to explain the theory of the case to her. "I know what it's about, Mister Kennedy," she said. "It's about making Peter give me and Maggie and Jeff all the money he would've had to give to Mom, if he'd divorced her. Because of the contract they had. Their prenuptial agreement."

"Essentially, yes," I said. "What I want to make clear to all of you," I said, "you and Maggie and Jeff, is that this is a very early stage of an experiment, all of which is directed to what is essentially an exploratory effort, to determine whether you three kids can enforce a prenuptial agreement that your mother made, in the expectation that by marrying Peter Wade she'd gain a benefit. That *she* saw as being primarily for herself, because it would guarantee at least your educational futures. And having very little education herself, but obviously valuing it highly, that was what she most wanted in the world."

"Well," Lucy said, "I'd have to think about that. 'Most wanted in the world'? I think what Mom most wanted in the world was some guy hot for her, tonight. Her kids? Yeah, we were important to her, when the fact that we even *existed* crossed her mind—which was usually a couple or three times a day, 'd be my guess. But let's not overdo it. That contract says that if they got divorced, and it was his idea, or something that he did, then Peter'd have to pay for our educations, right?"

"Right," I said.

"Well," she said, "I don't see that as being quite the same thing as saying that was something she made Peter do because she wanted us to get good educations, right? I think her idea was that if he knew he'd have to do that, pay out a lot of money, for our educations, as well as for her, too, that'd make him stop and think before he tried to dump her for another woman, right? And that is what I think. That that agreement was for *her*."

"Yeah," I said. "Well, okay. Maybe it'd be better if we just dealt with the hard facts here then. There's really no question of the validity of the agreement. Or the intention of the parties, especially since Wade had his own lawyer draw it up. If Wade had broken it or caused it to be broken, by some means other than the deadly one he chose, assuming that in fact he was the one who chose it; and if your mother were still here after Wade'd done whatever he'd done instead, that didn't leave her dead, then she'd be fully able to go into court and demand that the agreement be enforced.

"The theory on which I'm recommending to you three that we proceed is that if the prenuptial agreement had called for Wade to give your mother's estate a finite sum, of several million dollars, in the unfortunate event that she died before all of you had completed your formal education—getting him to agree in effect to *insure* the payment of whatever your tuition totals turned out to be—then there'd be no real question but that now he'd have to pay up. Just as The Prudential, or John Hancock, or Lloyds of London would've had to pay, if they'd signed that agreement.

"The problem is that wasn't the agreement that he signed. The deal he made said in effect that he would *do* it, pay all of your tuitions, if the two of them weren't still together by the time you'd finished school, because he'd divorced or left her, but that wasn't what it *said*. It didn't *say* he'd pay up if she'd gotten tired of him, and *she'd* been the one who decided to call it off. And it didn't say he'd pay if she died before you all finished up in school. All it said was what it said, not: what she *thought* it said. There was a loophole in it. That loophole was her death. Contract doesn't mention that.

"She didn't have her own lawyer, to advise her on the thing. Most likely it didn't occur to her that she might predecease Wade, at least not before you got through school. He was considerably older and he was no athlete, however much he sailed. She was in her early thirties, tough as a pound of spikes. Why would it've crossed her mind, she's going to marry him, that he might find a new girlfriend and then have her knocked off? It wouldn't have, of course, and as we know now, it did not.

"So as a result what you and Maggie and Jeff are doing is asking the federal court to put you in your mother's place, and say that because of the way that things turned out, her death, which wasn't mentioned in the paper that Wade signed, amounts to the same thing as the events the paper does describe, if they'd been brought about by him: separation or divorce. And that part of her estate, in which you each have a share, is the large amount of money needed to put all of you through school.

"It's never easy getting courts to enforce agreements that were never specifically made. In the specific terms that would require the action that you want. It's pounded into all of us in law school, time and time again, that the Statute of Frauds requires all contracts, all agreements, involving goods, property, or services, anything, for which the total value is five hundred dollars or more, to be in *writing*. It becomes a second nature: 'I'll do what you want, but I won't do it until you give it to me in writing.'

"The statute doesn't say the contract necessarily has to be signed. It's not that rigorous. If you buy a TV that costs seven hundred dollars, and all you get for paper with it's a cash register receipt, or a credit card receipt, and then you take that TV home and it doesn't work, you can sue the man who sold it if he won't make it good. And a court will listen to you. Because you've got 'a writing' that proves you bought the damned thing from him, and of course you can prove too that it doesn't work. But if you gave that seven hundred to a guy who sold you that thing out of his panel truck, and have no written evidence you bought it, or that you bought it from *him*, you can kiss your dough good-bye, as far's the court's concerned. You haven't got 'a writing.'

"That's the basic principle that makes all the judges nervous, when you go and ask them to declare that the paper that you've got says one thing, means another. The paper says you did indeed buy the TV set. It doesn't say that you'd agreed with the man who sold it to you that if you bought the TV set he'd give you, no extra charge, a seven-piece living room set, kitchen table and six chairs, with a washer-dryer thrown in, too, if the TV didn't work. That's where the going starts to get a little tough, you know?

"Well, what we're trying to do here isn't quite as far-fetched. In fact, it's not far-fetched at all. But that resistance that I mentioned, that ingrained deep resistance that all judges and all lawyers have against interpreting agreements to say something that they don't: that's still an obstacle, what we're up against in this."

I got up, walked around the chair, and sat down in it again. "Our opponent, Arthur Dean, is a highly resourceful lawyer. People underestimate him sometimes. Others hate his guts. He can be a rough-cut gem, and he doesn't always think before he says whatever's going through his head. But that doesn't mean he's stupid, or he doesn't know the law. He's a formidable adversary, and if you make just one mistake, give him one small opening, he'll go through it like a shot and tear your case to shreds. I'm not exaggerating one bit when I say that, either. I've talked to people who got careless up against him, and they said it's not pretty to watch. He can't be embarrassed, shamed into sheepish silence. He has absolutely no pride of person whatsoever. If he has to take a chance on making a public fool of himself, riding a wild hunch that may turn out to be wrong, but'll shower gold on him if his guess is right, he'll take the chance. Do it without thinking twice and devil take the hindmost. So you've got to stay alert at all times. You can never rehabilitate a crucial witness once an Arthur Dean has gotten through destroying him. And neither is there any way to rebuild the superstructure of a case after you've let him into the basement and he's yanked down the main beam.

"So, you never never put a witness on the stand in any case without both you and the witness knowing exactly, in advance, precisely what the witness is going to testify. Every word, and every shading, every emphasis, every nuance of the witness's state of mind, when state of mind's called for. And that, my dear, means preparation, lots and lots of it. We're going to go over, and then over, and then over once again, exactly what I'm going to ask you, and what it is that you'll reply. And then, changing the part I play: then I'll no longer be your lawyer, the guy you know and trust; I'll be the other guy's, now, and I'll be coming after you. Make sure you know what you're going to be in for.

"What I'm going to do now is my very best to break you down. Take you backwards through your story from the end to the beginning, with frequent interruptions to jump around in the middle, and then forward and then backwards, and then forward once again. Out of order, out of sequence, out of rhyme or reason. And going very, very fast. Never letting you catch up, take a deep breath, get a fresh grip on your wits. So that if I'm any good—and as I've told you, Arthur is; Arthur Dean is very good—I'll have your head spinning soon. You won't know up from down." All during this I was doing my best to keep my voice firm but kind and patient, entirely instructional. "You'll be getting desperate.

"And then what I'll do is start being extra nice to you. Partly because the last thing that I want is to have you burst into tears up there on the stand 'cause I've been so mean to you and I'll get blamed for it. No, I don't want that at all.

"And also because now I may not *need* to punish you anymore. The chances are I've done just what I set out to do. Got you nicely softened up, and you'll be so relieved and grateful—at least this's what I hope—that you'll agree with me on almost anything I say, anything that I suggest, if I'll only say it to you in a nice kind, comforting tone of voice, and just stop *yelling* at you, please."

"Mister *Kennedy*," she said, protesting, "I've three teachers who did that, yelled and were sarcastic, one when I was at Strothers and then two more since I got to . . ."

"*No*," I said, the volume still low but hardening the tone, "you have *never* had the treatment that we routinely dish out in the courtroom, when what the witness says is crucial and the money's on the line. Not from any teacher, no matter how nasty he is. And if you think you have, well, you're a plain damned fool. We don't make you feel bad because we just don't like you; because we're having a bad day, or you've misbehaved on us: we do it on purpose; it's one way we do our job. We're trained to do this sort of thing before we even start, and every year that we've been at it since we finished our training, long before you wandered right into our sights, we've gotten even better at it, if we're any good at all. And the fact you can delude yourself, even think or say you've had it, only goes to prove my point: that you not only haven't *had* it done to you; you haven't even *seen* it, seen someone else just get torn down, destroyed in front of strangers. You don't know what it is. You haven't been prepared.

"If you go in there like you are now, we've got a big problem. You'll go on the record, under oath, admitting things that we don't *want* you to admit. Because they aren't true, but people under sudden pressure that they weren't prepared to face sometimes get trapped into doing that, admitting all kinds of things that they really don't want to, that aren't even really so, just to take the pressure off.

"Such as: No, you must admit you're not really sure of *that*; and: You don't remember *this*; and: No, it wasn't quite like *that*; it was the other thing. Besides, anyway, you know, you think he should understand: it was all so *long* ago, and you were just a *little* girl, and, well, maybe you just forget.

"Once that kind of stuff is on the record, Lucy, you know what you'll be worth to me, and to Maggie and Jeff as well? You won't be worth two cents to me. And as for their education, Wade's promise to pay for that, well, it doesn't look so good, now, not too promising at all, not with you out of the lineup testifying for their side, sounding more like you should really be on his. 'Course that may not matter much to you, losing their high-priced educations. After all, as we all know, you've almost finished yours."

Her eyes widened as though I'd slapped her hard across the face. "You son of a *bitch*," she said. "I don't *care* how old you are, how long you've been doing this and how Judge Lawler told us you're the best there is; we're lucky to have you. You're an utter fucking *shit*, say a thing like that to me. Just who the fuck you think are, *Mister Kennedy*, say a thing like that to me." She stood up fast and said, almost gasping: "I'm going to talk to Mag and Jeff, and when I get through with them, after all that we've been through, the three of us together, you'll be fired, you piece of shit. You'll be fired tomorrow morning."

I smiled at her. "And is that how you would've reacted," I said, putting the voice down now once again, soft and kind and patient, purely instructional, "if Mister Dean'd asked you a question that insulted you, or Mag or Jeff? As he's perfectly capable of doing, and well within his rights, to boot: taunt you to his heart's content to try to make you lose control. As in fact he could've, as we both know now, because I just did that very thing, and I'm a friend of yours.

"Now do you begin to see what I mean by preparation?" I said. "Being ready for the kind of viciousness that you'll almost certainly have to face? Suggested in front of all those strangers, who don't know you at all, that you're nothing more than a gold-digging replica of your deceased tart of a mother. A mercenary out to take my poor mentally ill client for every dollar you can. Willing to tell any lie, distort any fact, and deny anything that looks to you as though it might work against your case and that of your blood-sucking siblings. Would you've exploded out of your chair at him, as you just did to me, snarling obscenities? That would've really helped us a lot. I told you he's got no shame; you can't embarrass him. You can't make him lose his temper, either. And if you try to do it, take him down to size, he'll laugh and cut another notch in his gun butt, another case he won by doing nothing more than a pro's job, on an amateur." I let her think a minute. "So, now do you see, perhaps? What you're letting yourself in for?"

She looked down and shook her head. She did not say anything.

"Lucy," I said, leaning forward, "listen to me now. Once you *un*remember something in a court of law, draw a blank on something that in fact you do know very well—because your mind panicked under brutal assault and your will crumpled after that—you cannot *re*remember it afterwards. Come back in another day, and this time get it right. Not successfully, I mean. Not so people will believe you, jurors or judges. You will've sown the seed of doubt. You will've made them wonder, and people who're wondering are uncomfortable, which they do not like. They don't like feeling confused, not knowing what to think. So they get even. They come down against the party who made them do it, made them wonder.

"Few cases are strong enough to recover from that blow, and our case's certainly not among them. Every detail matters to us, every single one. They all have to be right, every one of them in place. You do understand this, don't you? You do want us to win."

She did not raise her eyes. "I'm not sure," she said.

■ ■ ■ **20**

Christ on a crutch," Henry Lawler said to me from his chambers when I called him the next morning, "this I cannot believe. You really mean to tell me that she doesn't want to win? The thing you've got against the guy who almost certainly had her poor trusting mother killed, and she doesn't want to take him good, for everything's he got? Or most of it at least? Is that what you're telling me?"

"Not exactly," I said. "That was my initial reaction, too: that what she'd just said to me made no sense at all. But then after I'd pressed her some, I began to see it might. A weird, skewed sort of sense, to be sure—call it Martian sense. But still understandable, if you looked at it from her point of view."

"You had more patience with the young lady'n I would've had in your place," Henry said grimly. "If you could talk to her long enough to find out what point of view it possibly could be that wouldn't want to win a case like *this* one, you're a prime candidate for sainthood. A case that not only avenges her murdered mother but also makes herself and her sister and her brother reasonably rich, at the murderer's expense, and she doesn't want to *win* it? I would've thrown her out on that cute little ass of hers the minute she so much as *hinted* to me, anything like that. If I'd been the one who put in all the thankless hours you've got in on the thing so far. Jesus, Jerry, I've got to apologize to you. Get down on my knees and beg your kind forgiveness, 'fore you come to your senses and remember who did this to you. Drive on up here and shoot me. Got you into this godawful situation where a court's said that you'd better win a case damned-near impossible to win, and now your leading lady declares she's having second thoughts, and, well, she'd probably rather lose. How I ever make up for what I did when I threw this one in your lap, I will never know."

I laughed at him. "*Sure*," I said, "that'll be the day. Forget it. I do have to say that was about my first reaction, pretty much the way I felt—'How'll I fix Henry?'—before I'd asked her a few more questions. While I was also at the same time giving myself more of a chance to think about what she'd said.

"She hadn't actually said she was sure she didn't want to win, or that she secretly wanted Wade to win the case. What she'd said was that she wasn't sure *she* wanted to win it. Which isn't the same thing at all, not the same thing at all."

"Maybe not *exactly* the same thing," Henry said, "but still close enough for me. I would've kicked her ass out just for saying it, whether she meant it or not. Fired her right there on the spot. It's not fair to your lawyer—not fair to any lawyer and I don't care who he is—to ask a man to win a case you're lukewarm about yourself. Business's hard enough as it is, busting your hump day and night to do the best job you possibly can, and then the guy you're doing it for yawns in your face, burps, and then instead of saying 'excuse me,' tells you he doesn't care enough how it turns out in the end to spend any more of his time helping you to win it for him."

"Yeah, I know," I said, "but just hear me out on this now. First think about this kids's whole life history 'til Wade. Pretty depressing stuff, really. Even her sister, Maggie, four years younger'n Lucy, *she* feels considerable resentment. And at sixteen she's only had two-thirds of the experience that Lucy's had, seeing how their mother behaved. Imagine how Lucy must feel. Bottled-up anger, Henry. This kid's been seething for years. Her mother keeps on dragging home the wrong type of guys, which happen to be the kind that always try to pick up women who serve them their meals in restaurants, it's sort of a hobby with them, and she's the type they succeed with, because she's the kind, never learns. She keeps on thinking they're sincere, and going out in back with them—until then she's gotten so involved she thinks she's got to marry them, or live with them, because she's got her kids. Which Sandra most likely *did* think was the proper thing to do, because *her* mother'd done it—and look how that turned out. Evelyn didn't make it legal before she let a series of low-grade characters move in, after Sandra's tinhorn father took a powder on them. One of those bums was Rudi, the guy who made Sandra so damned nervous he was going to climb into her bed that the only choice she had was giving in or moving out.

"So you could understand why Sandra did it: to her way of thinking that was mostly how you made sure that when you re-mated, your own kids would be okay. But you could also see why Lucy probably hadn't liked that life of hers she had so much of, with her mother, before Peter Wade showed up. Lucy being the child of the first marriage, the one to that locally well known religious stalwart, Lucas Kyle, that prize who faithfully obeys what he seems to believe're the nine commandments God meant to apply to him, she'd had a ringside seat for all her mother's ups and downs. Including their desertion by Lucy's father, which Sandra could not've liked much, but must've devastated the poor kid, at the age of three or four. And then later the Cameron invasion, which got her mother knocked up, and finally her mother's liaison with whoever the masked man it was who brought Jeffrey into the world. Not what you'd call a good example for any mom to set, for any girl-child.

"Especially not for a girl-child as smart as Lucy. After Lucas bolted, but before she was much older, she most likely figured out, if some mean bastard didn't tell her, the explanation for Mom's great popularity with all the men who came into the truck stop. That would not've made our bewildered little girl very proud of her mother, even if she understood that they really needed the big 'tips' Mom earned by what doing she did out there in the back lot in the truck cabs, after she got off her shift.

"Then you had the affiliation with Cameron within less than six months after Kyle'd taken to his heels. The chief impetus for that having been the condition precedent that Sandra'd become pregnant once again. And'd apparently managed to convince Cameron that he was the one who did it. So here's this little kid now; put yourself in her place: no sooner'n her real father lights out for the territories, back from which he seldom gets to see his little girl, than this new guy shows up to take his place, living in the house with Mom and sleeping in the bed with Mom, where *Daddy* used to sleep. Sandra hardly missed a beat. And so here's *another* major disruption for the little girl, right on top the first earthquake, for Lucy to get used to. And if she can't, well, never mind, tough luck for the kid; she can do the best she can.

"But just for the sake of argument here, let's say she does it, gets it all worked out. Because we both know the Lucy of today. We've spent some time with her, so we know that she's got most of her ducks in a row. And even though we don't know how she managed it, we do know that somehow she obviously did. She's got it figured out. Her real daddy's a resounding dud; can't depend on him at all. But Cameron's right there now with them, and he's with them all the *time*, regular as church bells and electric bills. Cameron comes home at night, goes off to work in the morning, pays close to his share of the freight, doesn't whack his girlfriend around, and seems like he not only likes his own kid by his first wife, this'd be Tiffy, and the kid he had with Sandra, this'd be Maggie, now, but he's also good to Lucy. So: 'Things've worked out pretty well,' Lucy starts to think, 'maybe now I can relax.' And Lucy's still only around nine years old. She can let down her guard just a little. Considering the sad shape that they *were* in, not so long ago, things've worked out *very* well. Some more time goes by. Everything stays the same. She starts to feel pretty good. It's all going to work out after all.

"Which is just about the time that Sandra takes a hankering for Brian, and once again a big pail of the good old *stuff* drops right down into Lucy's fan. Cameron gets wind of that—as naturally he would, of course, Sandra being no better at sneaking around'n she was at 'n she had been the rest of her life, putting up a billboard on her ass like that. And Cameron sees it and goes bye-bye, as he naturally would— as you and I would, ourselves. But Lucy didn't see it the way we would. She thought of it as him deserting *her*. He'd done it just as Lucy'd begun to trust him, think of him as 'Dad.' If The Lurch was a wide enough spot on the road in central Massachusetts, Lucy if she'd been of voting age could've claimed it as her residence and registered

Democrat, she'd been left in it so much. This poor kid hadn't even become a teenager yet, and already she'd seen more of life'n George Burns and Gracie saw on the RKO vaudeville circuit, the two of them put together.

"And then it got worse. Our friend Lance Corporal Brian starts coming around every so often, dipping his wick into Sandra every time he got the urge. Although according to what he told Whitlock he was not amused at all when she had *Semper Fi* tattooed on her arse; that was a sacrilege or something; not against him—the marine corps. But that didn't stop him from knocking her up. One more jolt for Lucille.

"So there she was," I said, "barely ten years old and at least the way she saw it, betrayed once again. By her mother. Every single time that this defenseless little kid—and that's another thing that we sometimes forget when we grow up; when we're kids we know that we've got no defense at all if a grown-up hauls off and belts us. We knew then we were helpless, dependent. If the grown-ups hurt us, didn't feed us, keep us warm, we wouldn't be able to do anything about it. We'd get hurt, or we'd starve, or we'd freeze. We forget all that stuff when we've grown up, but when we were small we knew it too well. Lucy couldn't get out of the way if some real thing bore down on her. If she'd had any other place on earth to go, where someone would've taken her in, she would've bolted from her mother in a minute, just like her mother had from Evelyn, when her ma brought Rudi home, and for the very same reason. Sandra didn't trust Evelyn anymore. She didn't trust her 'cause she knew she *couldn't* trust her. Every time that Sandra tried to make—and then keep—things straight and right side up, they'd blown up in her face. And every time the heavy debris's fallen down on Lucy, who by now is starting to get headaches from it. She has not had a happy life."

"Big deal," Henry said. "I'm generally getting pretty sick and tired of that old song and dance. 'I had an unhappy childhood. It's all my parents' fault. And that excuses me from everything I did. Or didn't do, so what're you yelling at me for?' Life's unfair: so what? Everyone knows that. Who gives a good shit, anyway? Nothing we can do about it. On to the next matter."

"That's what I was getting at," I said. "The next matter was Peter Wade. Lucy was fifteen or so, and he was like the *sun* finally coming up in the kid's life. Money ceased to be a problem, which it'd always been, before. Now it was no longer a factor. Any amount that you needed, it was already there. Mom could quit her job and the other duties outside in the back lot after she'd finished work. Lucy went from an okay-but-impersonal regional public high school to a nice friendly private prep school, where the folks looked after her. And all of that happened to her in the blinking of an eye, as it did her sister and her brother. What they were used to seeing on a television set, lifestyles of the rich and famous, they were now living in."

"You're telling me the kid was dazzled," Henry said.

"Of course I am," I said. "It would've dazzled *me*, a transition that extreme, and I'm an old fart just like you. It would've dazzled *you*. The important thing, though, for our present purposes, is not that she was dazzled: it's *why* she was dazzled. This by now was a cynical kid. She'd been around the track more times than Man O' War. She was not easily bamboozled. You had to be real good. Peter Wade was real good. He managed to dazzle her because whenever he said something she was tempted not to believe, he could back it up. And when she tested him on something, back it up he did."

"Okay, Jerry," Henry said, "if you're willing to do this—say that you've got no hard feelings, against me, I mean—I'll be kind enough to say I've got hard feelings against you. For letting me do what I didn't mean to do to you. Which still leaves us with the question: What the hell do you do now?"

"Now I'm going to see Jeffrey," I said. "The nice lady at the school, whose portrait you must make for me, some fine summer day, says he's no longer itchy and is now allowed to mingle with the other inmates in the general population. If I can get out of him what Maggie thinks he knows—Lucy's not so sure, but then she wasn't with her mother the last time she was seen alive; so she didn't see how she was acting that day. Silly, Maggie said, which usually meant she was looking forward to getting laid pretty soon. So for the time being I'm going to go with that, and see what I can get out of Jeffrey. If he says something that proves Maggie's right, then I'll probably have to bring the case. And if he doesn't, then I'm certainly *not* going to bring a case, no matter what Royce Whitlock says."

"Does Royce know this's what you've got in mind?" Henry said.

"No," I said, "he doesn't. He's not part of the case at this stage. It's not his decision to make, so it's not his decision to lobby. When I tell him what I've decided it's come down to, either that the case's going forward or else that I've closed it, he's got to understand that the decision has been made, and that it's staying made. He's got his emotions all tangled up in this. That's an excellent thing in an investigator; for a trial man, until the trial starts, it's just a dangerous bad habit."

■ ■ ■ **21**

This past winter was not as severe as those we had in the two years before it. God put only a little snow on the ground around Boston and left much of its provision further north to the expensive snow-making machinery developed for the ski resort operators. It seemed to me there were many more birds around than there had been other winters, especially more robins. I wondered out loud whether that meant global warming'd confused them out of their normal urge to migrate from the cold.

Allison said they didn't have any such urge, and generally spent their winters close to the places where they spent the summers, flocking in the swamps, preferring those with cedars—"Maybe they're afraid of moths?"—from Ontario to the coast of the Gulf of Mexico. I scoffed and said that couldn't possibly be so: "if they ever tried to do that, most of them'd freeze to death," I said.

"They do," she said.

"They do?" I said. "Come on, be serious."

"I'm *being* serious," she said. "Eighty percent of them die every year. That's normal for songbirds."

"If eighty percent of them die," I said, "how come there're so many of them around?"

"They like to breed," she said. "Same as people do. Same as us: they think it's fun. So even though so many die, you still see a lot of them, because they breed like crazy. Same with the squirrels. When there's lots of mast—chestnuts, butternuts, acorns, and God knows what all—to feed them, you get bumper crops of squirrels. And when the food's in short supply, and the weather's fierce, lots of squirrels starve to death. And then the cycle starts again."

"Then robins're stupid," I said. "Darwin was wrong. They all must be suicidal. The stupid ones survive, and breed. And then they stay, and die."

"They are," she said. "All songbirds're stupid. That accounts for the usual death rate. Good thing for us; if it weren't that high, we'd be up to our earlobes in bird shit. The only reason you think you're seeing more robins this year is because it's been so long since you woke up in the morning in a house outside the city that's got trees and grass and bushes all around it. The robins've been here all along."

Just like the foxes and rabbits, whose tracks I saw in the dustings of snow in the backyard of her house a mile and a half from the school, just over the Tewksbury line; just like the forsythia that encroached the driveway to the garage of the house that Mack and I had bought on Kevin Road in Braintree had been there before we came, and remained after we'd left, scratching someone else's cars—unless the new owners've had more sense than we did and rooted it all out. You see those animals and flowers only if you happen to be present and alert enough to see them when they normally appear; they don't call attention to themselves.

Jeffrey J. Nichols had dark hair, like his eldest sister, Lucy, but he had Maggie's tentative manner. Since he'd been ill, I didn't draw any hasty conclusions from his emaciation. When we met in Allison's office I said I regretted the intrusion on his schedule, knowing that he must have make-up work to do. He said he didn't have that much, and he'd do what he could to help. Allison made available a conference room two doors down the hall, saw to it we were comfortable, and left us on our own. I took my recorder out and put it on the table. "Mind?" I said.

"Should I?" he said.

"Can't think of any reason," I said. "It's just my way of taking notes now. Find that it doesn't miss anything and forgets less of it than I used to when I didn't use it." I turned it on. "Conference with Jeffrey Nichols," I said. "Recorded with his permission. That right, Jeff?"

"Okay by me," the kid said.

"You know what Maggie told me," I said.

"Uh-huh," he said. "Yeah, I do."

"That she thinks maybe your mother told you something she didn't tell Maggie, the last time you saw her alive?"

"Maggie did say that to me, yeah," he said. "That she told you she thought that, about Mom."

"Was she right?" I said.

It took him quite awhile. He squirmed around a bit and resettled his body in the chair, and then he clasped his hands and studied them and thought about the matter some more. The recorder's voice-actuated. It operates only when there's some sound in the room. I let the silence control. Jeffrey cleared his throat. "It's kind of embarrassing," he said. The recorder whirred quietly for that brief instant, and stopped. I waited for him to look up or add to that, but he didn't. He continued to stare at his thumbs.

"I'm not out to embarrass anyone," I said. "My job as the court's defined it is to make sure that you and your sisters get every last penny your mother thought that you'd get. If I can find a way to get that done without going to court, that's the way that I'll choose. If I can't find one, without court, but I think I can find one in court, then I'll tell you, and I'll advise you to do that. If the three of you say you don't want me to do that, that it'd be too much for you to go through it all again, relive when your mother was missing, and then when she was finally found, well, then, I won't do it; I can't. But that's a recommendation I can't offer you until I'm pretty sure I've got all the facts I possibly can. Without you telling me if Maggie was right, and you know who your mother was meeting, the night that she disappeared."

He sat there and looked at me the way Noah must've looked at the flood waters rising around his amphibious zoo, and thinking the same thing that Noah must've thought: "God, I hope you know what you're doing."

He cleared his throat. He said: "She told me Brian'd called her up there, in Enfield, asked her how she was doing. And she was all

232

happy, and silly, you know? And I said to her, you know: 'Hey, Mom, don't do this.' Because I had bad vibes about it. I don't mean it was like I had any kind of idea what was going to happen to her, that she was going to get herself killed, or even like just that something really *bad* was going to happen. But . . . I don't know what it was. I just didn't like it, is all."

"No premonition," I said.

"Right," he said. "Nothing like that at all. But there was still something. I don't know what it was, exactly. Mom was really impulsive. She was always doing things without thinking them all the way through. Just the opposite of what she was always telling us to do. And some of the ideas she had of things that she should do, some of them were really bad. Especially with men. Maybe I just thought she was giving up too fast, on being married to Peter. Peter was good to us. He'd been good to her, too, except until he met this other woman Mom told me he was seeing. Maybe that was it. It wasn't really like she wanted to see Brian again very much; it was more like she just wanted to see someone else, anyone, just as long as it was *somebody else*, and not Peter. You see what I'm saying?"

"Revenge," I said. "Getting even."

"Yeah," he said, "like revenge. It was like there was something, didn't *feel* right, you know? I said that to her. I said: 'Mom, I really don't think you should do this. You know if you start seeing Brian again, Peter's gonna find out. Those guys know each other, remember. And Peter took you away from Brian. You know how Brian is. You know he was mad, when that happened. Maybe he's just calling you now so he can tell Peter after you see him that he's gotten you back, and get on his butt that way.'

"But she said: 'Oh Jeffrey, now, you're just being silly. I'm just meeting the guy for a drink. What harm can there be in that? I'm meeting your dad for a drink. Maybe we want to talk about you.' Yeah, *right*. Like Brian ever gave a good shit about what happened to me. But I didn't say that to her. Would've just made her upset, and it would't've done any good; she would still've gone to meet him, because that's what she wanted to do. And then she said, like she was telling me another one of our little *secrets* she was always telling Maggs and Lucy that she wasn't telling them, like I'm still four years old or something? 'Besides, if Brian does tell Peter that he's seeing me again, maybe that will make Peter stop and think, and dump this broad he's seeing.'

"I didn't say I thought that that'd never happen. Peter would've just said 'Fine,' and kept on doing what he wanted, which was screwing other women. I just said: 'Well, I don't know. I can't really tell you. It just doesn't feel right to me, and that's all—it just doesn't feel right to me.' And then she said I couldn't tell Maggie or Lucy, and then, after that, she didn't say any more. And that was the last time I saw her."

"Brian'd called her at home, up in Enfield?" I said.

"Yeah," Jeffrey said. "He had the number. He knew it. Had it from Peter before Peter knew Mom. From when the green car got restored. That's when he got to know Peter, and then Mom and Peter, Peter met Mom one day when he met Brian, down at the Queen City Diner, to sign work orders on the car. The tires, I think it was. So he'd always had it, the number, all right? Brian'd always had that. The number'd never changed, after Mom and Peter got married. So if Brian wanted to get in touch with her, he knew what number to call. That wasn't anything new."

"But just suppose Peter'd answered," I said. "Wouldn't that've been taking a chance?"

"Peter wasn't there," he said. "Brian knew that. He'd been up to see Peter in Glyndebourne Lodge. He told my mother that's why he called her, 'cause Peter said she was alone, and all lonesome, and maybe Brian could cheer her up. Which you could tell she thought was kind of funny, Peter sending Brian to her, not that she said that. And also that if Peter'd said that to Brian, practically telling him to go see Mom, it wasn't very likely Peter would get jealous if he did. But like I said, Mom didn't make a big habit of thinking things through."

"Anyway," the kid said, "Brian knew Pete wouldn't be there, waiting for her to come home." He frowned. "So no one would see them, they met for a drink, and he told her he had this job up in Lowell here, a car to look over up this way, and so why didn't they meet for a drink."

I turned off the recorder. "Why didn't you tell this to Lieutenant Whitlock?" I said. "Or any one of the other cops with him? Or the judge, even Maggie? Why wait until now, long after she's dead, to admit it and say you knew this?"

"I didn't want to," he said.

"Because she swore to you secrecy?" I said. "Your mother said you shouldn't tell?"

"At first," he said. "At first that was it, when what it looked like was that she'd decided to run away with Brian. I didn't like it very much, but I wasn't going to say something that might make it so Peter would never take her back, if she did come back some day. But then after awhile went by, and they found her and she was dead, then it wasn't that anymore. Then it was more like I didn't want to know it, want to know that she was dead. I didn't want her to go off like she did, that night she went with Brian, and I knew something bad was going to happen if she did it, what she told me she was going to do, and so if she hadn't told me that would mean she hadn't done it, and then maybe she'd come back again, and everything would be all right."

"And then when so much time'd gone by," I said, "that you knew she wouldn't, wasn't ever going to come back, you didn't dare to say you'd known all along who she was meeting. Who she was going to see, because then it would have been your fault, you didn't stop her?" I said.

The kid did not reply. He raised his eyebrows, tilted his head, and then he nodded once. His eyes were full of tears, but he didn't cry while I was there.

■ ■ ■ 22

Royce Whitlock seemed distracted late in the afternoon of his next-to-last day on the job. He was in the shabby paneled cubicle he'd shared with three other cops in the Salem office of the Essex County DA's Office "for about a hundred years. Every day of my life, seems like, since I took off my wet suit and put on my regular pants again, I've been coming in here, and now I'm finally gonna leave, and I'll be damned if I could tell you where the hell anything is." He ran the fingers of his left hand over his scalp, spluttered, and sat down in the wooden swivel chair behind his small white-oak desk. "So, what bad news do you bring?"

I drew a deep breath and took the straight-back wooden chair against the wall sideways in front of Royce's desk. "I just had lunch with Arthur Dean," I said.

"Locke Ober, I presume," Royce said, somewhat resentfully, "since I was not invited."

"Yeah," I said. "My choice, since I was buying."

"And Arthur was so overcome he said he'd plead his client guilty to a charge of murder one, and ask for the death penalty, even though we still haven't got it. And Arthur wants us to see if we can arrange for Peter to be shot while trying to escape, since he's so filled with remorse that's the only way he can atone for what he did."

"Actually, no," I said.

" 'No,' " Royce said. "Well, so much for that idea. What was the result?"

"The result was that I expect after Arthur and his client've had cocktails this afternoon at Glyndebourne, Arthur will bring back to me a written contract, one that *I* prepared, signed, and witnessed, under the terms of which Peter Wade will have agreed to carry out in all respects the terms of his prenuptial agreement with his late wife, Sandra Nichols, including but not limited to all costs of formal education, support, and maintenance thereinbefore provided for her minor children, Lucy, Margaret, and Jeffrey, without any limitation whatsoever on the time they may require to complete said educations, in all respects as though the late Sandra Nichols and the current Peter Wade had been divorced or otherwise parted by decree of a court of competent jurisdiction, pursuant to the terms of the said prenuptial agreement. And Peter Wade, in full settlement of all claims that may be brought against him by the said minor children, from this date until the end of the world, to that end shall forthwith and at once establish a trust fund, Jeremiah F. Kennedy, trustee, and deposit in it a total of three million dollars to the sole use and benefit of said minor children, Lucille Kyle, Margaret Cameron, and Jeffrey Nichols.'

"I figure slightly under a million'll probably cover the education costs. The other two mill's for punitive damages the kids ought to get for the pain and suffering, loss of companionship, guidance and love, that resulted from Peter's decision to have their mother bumped off. Arthur said he thought he'd have a much better chance of selling the agreement to Peter if we just called it all *education*. That seemed reasonable to me—what we're after here is the money. Call it *two over easy with bacon*, makes you feel any better; the check still comes to three million bucks."

"But he's still not admitting it," Royce said. "he's not admitting it. That he had that woman killed."

"Well, he'd be a fool if he did, now, wouldn't he?" I said. "He knows we probably can't prove it, Royce. He knows we can't make Brian talk. Arthur said that to me, when I first laid it out for him. He started laughing at me, said: 'What is this? You joking? Brian Ross come coco? Never happen in this life.' "

" 'Hear me out on this,' this is what I said to Arthur. 'Think about your situation. Your client's situation. I had my secretary prepare this complaint under the Wrongful Death Act. In it we allege that your client retained Brian, for an unknown sum of money, to kill your client's wife. Because he wished to be rid of her—divorce by other, cheaper means.

" 'Obviously your man's not going to stand up on his hind legs in front of God and all the people and admit that's what he did, but claim now that he didn't have all of his marbles. If he does that, the *best* that he can hope for is a lifetime commitment to the Massachu-setts Correctional Institution at Bridgewater, for the Criminally Insane, without even the hope of persuading some harebrained doc-tor some years down the line that he's regained his wits. The sur-roundings and the other celebrants at MCI Bridgewater don't make for quite the same gala ambience as your man has gotten used to, rac-ing sailboats in the Caribbean. He won't like it nearly as well. But he'll have to stay there, forever, won't he? Because if he ever finds a doctor who's dumb enough to believe him when he says he's gotten better, some new evidence may've turned up that'll support a charge of mur-der. No Limitations on murder. And then the *worst* that he can hope for is life without parole in the Big Bad Place. Which makes the Insti-tution look like comfy living quarters. So for now he will do nothing, since that's all that he can do, and sit tight in the booby hatch with a bunch of rich old drunks.

" 'In due course I'll get a trial date, and among my witnesses will be several bank officers producing records, among them Peter Wade's and Brian Ross's. Peter's will show a withdrawal of fifty thousand dol-lars from the Enfield Trust Company, by means of a check he made payable to Glyndebourne Lodge, two weeks before Sandra vanished. Then will appear the treasurer and keeper of the records at Glynde-bourne Lodge. She will deliver records showing that Peter Wade's paid for his stay by several *other* Enfield checks, totaling about eigh-teen thousand dollars, and then testify that the check for fifty grand made payable to the lodge was negotiated through the lodge account purely as an accommodation of Mister Wade, who said that he had large gambling debts to pay and the bookie coming to see him demanded all his settlements in cash. She personally delivered to your client five hundred one-hundred-dollar bills and he gave her a receipt.

" 'Then there'll be some other documents, among them the bill of sale recording Brian Ross's purchase of a new Chevrolet Corvette one week after Sandra disappeared. For which he paid thirty-six thousand dollars, in five different bank money orders, purchased with cash, hundred-dollar bills, from five different banks in southeastern Massachusetts and Rhode Island. I have subpoenas on each of those banks for their video records of those transactions. I'm confident they'll show Brian Ross peeling off the large bills, every single time.

" 'I will then call a retired couple named Ed and Carol Anastasia. They have a ground-floor apartment at One thirty-two Abrams Street in Central Falls, Rhode Island. They are extremely conscious of the comings-in and goings-out of the occupant of the second-floor apartment above theirs, since the tenant before Brian Ross made lots of noise and disturbed their sleep a lot. They like Brian much better, because although they can still hear him, he's much quieter. They will testify that on the night when Sandra Nichols disappeared, Brian Ross did not come home until close to three A.M. A witness from Franco's Club and Lounge in Cumberland, Rhode Island, will testify that the night Sandra disappeared was one of Brian Ross's regular nights off.

" 'You still can't put him on the scene,' Arthur said.

" 'Very true, Arthur,' I said. 'But then I don't think I need to. All I have to do, and suggest to you I will have *done*, is raise an inference, make it likelier than not that Brian Ross was the man who killed Sandra Nichols, in return for fifty K from Peter Wade. And that will put the ball in your court, Arthur, giving you the obligation to prove Peter didn't do that. Think you can pull it off, knowing as you do, he did?'

"Arthur said nothing," I said to Royce. "Arthur said nothing at all.

" 'Then I will call Brian to the stand and put some questions to him relative to whether he had a date with Sandra Nichols the night she disappeared. He'll of course refuse to answer, on the grounds that to do so would be to incriminate himself. I'll ask the judge to hold him in civil contempt and commit him until he answers. *And Judge Henry will see to it that that's done for me*, won't he? Since he's the one, got me onto this matter, in case that thought hasn't yet crossed your mind.' "

"And how did our Arthur take that?" Royce said.

"Quite well, I thought, actually," I said. "He said: 'Yeah, I think he would.'

" 'So that will then leave us with Brian in jail for a spell, getting madder by the minute, and your client immured in Glyndebourne Lodge, where the security's just as good as you want it to be. But now it'll be very good, won't it? Because now Peter Wade will no longer *want* to get out. And when Brian hires a lawyer to get him out of jail, I'll put up just feeble resistance. That'll mean that Brian *gets* out. And what do you think he'll do then, my learned brother, after a few days in stir?'

" 'I take your point,' Arthur said.

" 'Yes,' I said. 'Either he'll come looking for your client with a sizable bill, or else he'll come looking for him with a sizable firearm. Or maybe a sock filled with sand.

" 'So, the issue as I see it is whether Peter Wade prefers to choose between spending the rest of his days in an institution of one kind or another, while keeping all of his money, or part with a large chunk of that money to get what he mostly wanted when he hired Brian Ross to do what he did: his freedom, only now not so cheap.'

" 'Yes,' Arthur said. 'This really is excellent beef. And the wine isn't half bad either.' "

Royce did not look happy. "And I take it you expect to get this agreement," he said.

"Yes, I do," I said.

"So no one will get punished," he said. "No one will get punished for doing this thing. It's almost like they get rewarded." He shook his head. "Somehow that doesn't seem right."

"It isn't right," I said. "That was never my job, to make what was wrong turn out right. My job was the same one that I've always done. It was to represent clients. And that is the job that I've done. I figure near three million bucks."

"I still don't like it," Royce said at last. "The kids get their money, and you get your fee"—in my accounts I specified no sum; Henry later set it at 10 percent, $300,000—"but no one gets punished for this. I still don't like it at all."

"No," I said, "I expect that you don't. You're not getting a fee, or a doctorate out of it, as Lucy probably will. But Peter Wade would disagree, I feel very sure, if you tried to tell him that he wasn't punished for having his wife killed. Every year for the rest of his life he'll get about a quarter of a million less from his family trust fund. It isn't

Cedar Junction, no, but if punishments should fit the crime, this one'll hurt him pretty bad.

"No," I said, "another question: do you think in between all your travels, you could maybe do a few cases for me now and then? I like the way you do things. With what you can find out, and I can make from it, we might pull down a couple of bucks."

"You're a hard man, Kennedy," he said.

"Well," I said, "no one ever called me 'Cuddles.' "

Acknowledgments

My principal source of Jerry Kennedy's information about civil actions for damages in cases alleging wrongful death was the definitive analytical article, "New Wrongful Death Act in Massachusetts Steps Into the Twentieth Century," by Albert P. Zabin and Thomas E. Connelly, published in 58 *Massachusetts Law Quarterly* 345, Winter, 1973–74, and I thank them for their guidance. If Jerry misinterpreted the statute in any way, though, that's my fault and none of theirs.

—G.V.H.